ACTS OF WAR

JAMES YOUNG

This book is a work of fiction. The names, characters, places, and incidents are products of the writer's imagination or have been used fictitiously and are not to be construed as real. Any resemblance to persons, living or dead, actual events, locale or organizations is entirely coincidental.

ACTS OF WAR
COPYRIGHT © 2014 BY JAMES L. YOUNG JR.

All Rights Are Reserved. No part of this book may be used or reproduced in any manner whatsoever without written permission, except in the case of brief quotations embodied in critical articles and reviews.

To Anita,
For "the reasons authors dedicate books to their wives"—the gifts of tolerance, patience, time, and above all, love.

1
CAREFUL WHAT YOU WISH FOR...

Follow me—You have the advantage of necessity, that last and most powerful of weapons.

— ***VETTIUS MESSIUS OF VOLSCIA***

Thames River
0900 Local (0400 Eastern)
23 August 1942

London was burning.

Somehow I doubt that this is quite how anyone expected Adolf Hitler's death to turn out, Adam Haynes thought bitterly as he regarded the burning capital's skyline. The wind, thankfully, was blowing away from where he and his girlfriend stood at the bow of the *Accalon*. Adam had the awful feeling that if it had been blowing toward the 40-foot pleasure yacht, there would have been many, many smells he would have preferred to forget filtering their way.

*Like Guernica, only...*he started to think.

With a roar, a Junkers 52 swept low over the *Accalon*'s deck, its passage so close that the aircraft's slipstream fluttered the white flag hanging from the yacht's antennae mast. An intense, white-hot rage sprung from within him as he watched the canary yellow German transport.

I hope you crash, you bastard, Adam thought, blood rushing into his ears.

"Adam, *my hand!*" A woman's voice broke through his fury.

With a start, Adam realized that he was well on the way to breaking his companion's hand. Although such an act was always unconscionably bad form, it was doubly so when its possessor was the cousin, albeit distant, of England's king.

"God, Clarine, I'm..." Adam started, opening his hand as if suddenly realizing it held a hot brick. His face colored to the roots of his thinning brown hair, making his blue eyes all that more intense. At a shade under six feet, with shoulders broad enough to fit on a man six inches taller, Adam looked very much like a bear wearing an RAF uniform. Unfortunately, when enraged, he had the strength to match.

"That is quite alright," Clarine Windsor replied lightly, doing her best to smile as she worked her hand. A small, wiry woman who stood several inches shorter than Adam in the black flats that came with her Women's Auxiliary Air Force (WAAF) uniform, Clarine was far from weak. Still, her pale face was scrunched up in obvious pain.

Holy shit, I hope I didn't hurt her, Adam thought guiltily. Seeing his worry, Clarine brought up her left hand and brushed back a stray blonde hair, her brown eyes meeting Adam's as she smiled.

"You were just having the same thought I had: wishing you could shoot the bastard," she said simply. "It's understandable, given what has happened these last few days."

Still no reason to try and convert your hand to paste, Adam thought. *You didn't drop the bomb that killed Hitler.*

"Understandable, but most unfortunate," her father, Awarnach Windsor, stated as he joined them at the yacht's bow. "Especially as his escorts would probably blow the *Accalon* out of the water."

Looking up and back toward the vessel's stern, Adam mentally kicked himself for not noticing the eight Me-410s circling roughly four thousand feet above their heads. The gray fighters were hard to see in the haze of smoke roiling off London, but that was no excuse. Smoke had been a fact of life for Fighter Command over the last two weeks, and failing to see an opponent hiding in it was just as fatal as if the assault came from more naturally formed clouds.

"While I am sure you wish you had a *Spitfire* right now," Awarnach observed flatly, "I doubt your efforts would be any more successful than they were previously."

You bastard, Adam thought, fighting to keep his emotions off his face. The tone of Awarnach's voice had far too much "told you so" in it.

"Well father, at least someone was attempting to defend our nation," Clarine observed coolly. "Since many of those who were born to it could not raise themselves from their slumber."

Awarnach turned his baleful gaze from Adam to his daughter.

"Those of us who were 'slumbering', as you put it, merely believed we should have continued to enjoy the peace we had hammered out rather than meddle in affairs on the continent," Awarnach replied. "Instead, that idiot Churchill has now managed to make us forget his idiocy at Gallipoli."

"This is hardly the same as…"

"No?!" Awarnach snapped. He turned and pointed off their port bow, to where London's East End was starting to come into view. "Tell me *that* is not more terrible than some idiotic frontal assault on the Ottomans."

The *"that"* in question was the furious blaze that roared unchecked almost as far as the eye could see. The low rumble of the fire was a constant sound beating upon their senses, but Adam had managed to suppress it by concentrating on the river itself. Now, as if Awarnach had ripped open a shade, the magnitude of Fighter Command's defeat lay before them. It was like looking into a corner of Hell, and Adam was once more glad that the wind was blowing so strongly from their back.

Once you've smelled burning flesh, you have no desire to enjoy that particular sensation again, Adam thought.

"You can't negotiate with the Germans," Adam said lowly, feeling the rage starting to creep back again.

"Oh? Well then, I am certainly glad that you have pointed this out for me, my American friend. Unfortunately, it would appear that your President and Congress feel very, very differently."

"Father..."

"No, please, I would like to hear this fine young man explain to me why we should not negotiate with the Germans when his countrymen cannot be bothered to even help us," Awarnach raged, his own face starting to color to match Adam's.

"It wasn't our President that chose to accept the armistice with Himmler after Bomber Command killed Hitler," Adam snapped.

"Oh? And what would you have had us do? Were we somehow going to invade France by ourselves? Perhaps build a massive bomber fleet like that idiot Portal wanted to and bomb the Reich's cities into rubble? Would that have satisfied your need for bloodlust? There was nothing more that could be done!"

"Yes, well, *perhaps* the people in that," Adam said, gesturing toward the burning city in front of them, "would have preferred you not giving the Germans over a year to perfect their bombing techniques."

"Perhaps, gentlemen," Clarine said crisply, her hand pointing, "we should be more concerned about that patrol boat's intentions."

Adam followed the point and saw the craft she was speaking of. One of the Royal Navy's MTB-class boats, the vessel was moving away from where it had been standing off the docks and turning toward the *Accalon*. As they watched, the craft began accelerating, signal light blinking furiously.

"Conroy, come about!" Awarnach shouted back towards the wheel house. Adam felt the *Accalon*'s engines stop, the helmsman turning her broadside to the oncoming MTB.

Holy shit, Adam thought, translating the other vessel's Morse code. He was about to say something when Awarnach spoke first.

"My God," Awarnach said, his face paling. "Gas?!"

"Obviously you've never read Douhet," Adam observed dryly.

"Who?" Clarine asked.

"The Italian Trenchard," Adam continued smoothly. "He recommended using gas in addition to incendiaries on enemy population centers. Explains the no-confidence vote a little better, I think."

The patrol boat began slowing, its own helmsman swinging the vessel wide so that he could put it alongside the *Accalon*. Three men crowded the bow and, with a start, Adam realized they were wearing full hoods and rubber gloves. Seeing that no one aboard the *Accalon* was in the bulky protective suits, the man standing in the center reached up and pulled the hooded apparatus off of his head.

Well now, small world, isn't it? Adam thought, feeling a smile cross his face as he regarded Lieutenant Commander Reginald Slade, Royal Navy. Tall, almost gaunt, with a face whose left side was thoroughly scarred from the explosion of a German shell, Slade wore his blonde hair closely cropped.

"You seem to be a fair distance from the North Atlantic, Mr. Haynes," Slade shouted as the patrol boat drew smoothly alongside the *Accalon*, his face breaking in a wry grin that reached his eyes. Reaching up, the RN officer scratched the area around his left eyepatch. The motion drew attention to the damaged side of his face, and Adam heard Awarnach inhale sharply.

"Sorry, I have been wanting to do that for hours," Slade said, ignoring the man's gasp.

"Yeah, I can see how that might be the case," Adam replied with a small smile.

"I do hope you folks aren't planning on going any further down the Thames," Slade continued. "By King's decrees the East End is off limits to anyone not on official business."

"I'm trying to find one of my mate's wife, mother, and child. He's in the hospital or else he'd be down here himself," Adam said.

Slade grimaced at Adam's words.

"Where did he say they were living?" the naval officer asked, his tone brusque.

"His mum's apartment is in Poplar," Adam replied, raising an eyebrow at the other man's coldness.

Adam had seen the look that briefly crossed Slade's face enough times to know what was coming next. The man paused for a moment, obviously choosing his words carefully.

"Unless they were extraordinarily lucky, I wouldn't hold out much hope, I'm afraid. The Germans dropped some sort of gas that got all the way through the area, and then followed it up with incendiaries. Without anyone to put out the fires..."

The officer's trailing off said all that needed to be said. In the last couple of days, Adam had heard a word for the phenomenon that some were calling the Second Great London Fire: Firestorm. The East End had become one huge flame pit, and the *Luftwaffe* had returned for three solid days to help things spread.

"Thanks Commander Slade," Adam spoke after a few moments more of quiet. Sighing at the heavy burden that now lay upon him, he looked up again at the smoke-filled sky, hoping to catch a glimpse of the big Ju-52 again.

"Looking for that arse who came tearing through here about ten minutes ago?" Slade asked.

"Yes, actually," Adam replied ruefully.

"I think that was Himmler arriving to negotiate terms with Lord Halifax."

The disgust in Slade's tone at the latter name almost matched the venom reserved for the first.

"Who knew there was a bigger bastard than Hitler in the Nazi Party?" Adam observed grimly.

"Certainly not that bunch of flyboys who killed him," Slade shot back. "Stupid pilots, always mucking things up."

Clarine chuckled behind Adam. Looking at Slade, Adam was unable to tell if the man was serious or not.

"Heard the poor bombardier blew his brains out yesterday," Adam replied. "Not his fault any of this," he continued, gesturing towards the burning city, "happened."

Slade shrugged.

"No, it's not, but that's what happens when you drop your bombs over a capital city. Sometimes you hit things you don't intend to," Slade retorted bitterly.

Spoken like someone who's never had to jettison something in order to make the fuel equation work out, Adam thought. He'd been a pilot since his seventeenth birthday, and non-flyers' superiority complexes never ceased to amaze him.

"Still. Berlin's a big city," Adam allowed. "No way they could've known they'd drop a bomb that would kill ol' Adolf."

Slade uttered a sound that made his disagreement quite clear on that one.

"Yes, and a 500-lb. bomb makes a big mess. No matter, that bastard is dead now, Himmler took over, and our betters were dumb enough to believe that tripe the Germans were spouting about the *Fuhrer*'s loss making them recognize the error of their ways."

"Excuse me, Lieutenant Commander, but as one of those *betters*," Awarnach snapped, "maybe a better explanation was that we did not want to continue losing men such as yourself in a war that we quite clearly were not in position to win."

Slade turned and looked at Awarnach, the contempt in his gaze almost physically palpable.

"So, in order to save *my* life, you buggered the French, spat on the rest of the Continent, pissed off the Americans, and gave Himmler breathing room," Slade retorted, his voice cold as ice. "During which time he hanged Goering, blew some industrialists' heads out at a meeting, and thus apparently motivated them to build a bloody great lot of planes, bombs, gas, and submarines."

Adam watched as Awarnach's face began to color while Slade continued, obviously taking a great relish in venting his spleen.

"Of course, the bloody Krauts then proceeded to kill a whole lot more of my countrymen. Capital work, your Lordship, just capital, please do not go into anything of importance."

Awarnach's mouth worked in shock. Before he could reply, one of the sailors stuck his head out of the patrol boat's bridge.

"Lieutenant Commander, we have been ordered to a new location," the man called.

Slade continued locking his gaze with Awarnach. It was the older man whose stare broke.

"Would hate to keep you, Lieutenant Commander," Awarnach said, his voice strained. "I'll go back to the bridge and con us out of your path."

"Well, guess we will be about it then," Slade replied, watching the man walk stiffly away.

"So what's going to happen to you next?" Adam asked. "If that is Himmler negotiating the peace treaty."

Slade gave a sideways glance to Clarine.

"I do not share my father's views," Clarine muttered quietly. "Indeed, I think he and the rest of the House of Lords were, and remain, a bunch of fools."

"In that case, understand that this war will *not* end here," Slade said lowly. "As Churchill said before the no confidence vote, there is an entire Commonwealth that will sustain the candle attempting to hold the darkness at bay."

"You mean you're going to flee to Australia or somewhere?" Adam asked, genuinely curious.

Slade snorted.

"You'd best do the same," he replied. "Rumor has it that Himmler intends to ask for all foreign fighters to be turned over as part of the peace treaty."

"What?!"

"Well, can't have a bunch of Poles, Danes, Norwegians, and Frenchmen hanging around and possibly doing something subversive, can you? Especially not after they killed Milch while there was allegedly an armistice between Great Britain and Germany," Slade replied grimly.

With a cold feeling in his stomach, Adam could see the government being formed by Lord Halifax agreeing to such madness. Even worse, he knew what the Nazis would likely do with the men.

"I'm flying with a Polish squadron," Adam said quickly, his tone urgent. "How do I get them the hell out of here."

Again Slade gave Clarine a look, then held up his hand before Adam could say something.

"It is not that I mistrust her," Slade said. "However, you of all people know the Nazis as well as I do. Have you heard the stories of how their Gestapo broke several of the Resistance cells in France during the last year?"

Clarine paled, looking almost physically ill.

The thought of being strapped to a metal mattress and electrocuted for hours on end doesn't appeal to most people, Adam thought. *Especially given where those bastards were placing the electrodes.*

"I will go speak with my father," she said simply. "Please hurry—I do not think he would be opposed to making you swim for it."

Taking Adam's hand and squeezing it, Clarine turned and departed.

"Get the whole bloody lot of your men to Portsmouth," Slade said as soon as she was out of earshot. He pulled out a piece of paper and a grease pen from under his rubber top. Scribbling something quickly, he handed it over to Adam.

"You have less than twenty hours," Slade said, meeting Adam's eyes. "After that, you best leave that pretty lass without any idea how to find you and disappear, as I get the distinct feeling that some of my former countrymen will be quite happy to 'help' run down foreign mercenaries."

"Thanks Slade," Adam replied, extending his hand. The Lieutenant Commander took it with both of his.

"No, *thank you*," Slade said, his voice raw with emotion. "You and the others like you tried to save us, even when we have done little to deserve it. Now only you remain."

"I'm sorry we couldn't do more."

"Well, maybe you'll have more opportunity one of these days. Hopefully your President can make people see reason soon, or else it will be too late."

"I think this," Adam said, gesturing towards the burning docks behind Slade, "will help."

"Yes, yes it will. Now get out of here, and see to your men."

With that, Slade drew himself up to attention and saluted. Adam returned the salute, then watched as the man nimbly sprang back to the patrol boat. The small craft backed away under low power, then ponderously turned its bow around. Adam sighed as he heard Clarine's soft footsteps behind him.

"Father is furious," she said softly. "Strangely, I don't give a damn."

"You know that I have to go almost as soon as we get back," Adam said. Turning, he saw Clarine's eyes were moist already.

"Yes, yes I know," she said softly. "And there's no chance father will let me out of his sight until you do so."

Adam could hear the deep tone of bitterness in her voice.

"Life becomes very lonely when you hate your parents," he said chidingly.

"I have half a mind to come with you," Clarine replied fiercely. "That would bloody well serve him right."

"Well, wouldn't be the first scandal an American has caused in this country," he said musingly, rubbing his chin theatrically.

"I am serious, Adam," Clarine retorted.

"I may not even be alive in a fortnight, Clarine," Adam said somberly. "Think about that. Do you really want to throw away your future, inheritance, and family name for some vagabond American mercenary?"

Clarine searched his face.

"Is that really how you think I see you?"

"No, but it's how your father and the rest of your social circle see me. Yes, I come from the right circles and know which fork to start with at dinner, but at the end of the day I am like some exotic animal that is best petted and left alone."

"Adam, *I love you.*"

"And I you," Adam said, fighting the urge to sweep Clarine into his arms. "So much that I will not let you ruin the rest of your life to flee with me."

"What about what I want?" Clarine asked as the *Accalon* came around. "Don't I get to decide the rest of my life, or is that solely the province of my male betters?"

Adam sighed.

Strong women will be the death of me, he thought with a deep sense of melancholy.

"Why don't you tell the truth, Adam?" Clarine continued. "You're scared of what will happen to me if I try to escape with you."

"Yes, the thought of you drowning or freezing to death in the Atlantic does strike me with some trepidation."

Clarine snarled in exasperation.

"Not every event in life ends the worst way possible, Adam!" she breathed lowly through clenched teeth.

Adam turned and looked behind him at the burning London, then back to Clarine.

"Perhaps now is not the time to try and convince me of this. More importantly, Clarine, I have to look after my men."

Clarine opened her mouth to argue, then stopped.

"Then when this boat docks will be the last time we see each other," she replied coolly.

Adam felt as if someone had stomach punched him. He started to reach for Clarine, but she held up her hand to stop him.

"You seem determined to leave Adam," she said. "You are even more determined to make sure I do not leave with you in some misguided attempt to 'save' me. Perhaps it is best then, that I acknowledge you have greater experience in dealing with disastrous circumstances such as these."

The words were delivered with cold precision, and they found their mark with the same brutal finality of a knife thrust.

"I do not want us to end this way, Clarine," Adam bit out, feeling his stomach sinking to his feet.

"If you had stopped after the seventh word of that sentence," Clarine said, her voice quavering, "I might have been inclined to reconsider. Instead, I believe that I am feeling rather nauseous from the smoke and will go below. Have a safe journey, Adam."

With that, Clarine turned and began walking back towards the deckway hatch, moving quickly as she wiped at her face. Adam watched her go, his stomach in knots.

Well, at least it's an improvement from last time I went through this, he thought. Fighting the urge to curse loudly, he slowly rotated back towards the *Accalon*'s bow, and then walked forward to where only the Thames could see his tears.

JAMES YOUNG

RED TWO
NORTH ATLANTIC
1000 LOCAL (0700 EASTERN)
12 SEPTEMBER

Lieutenant (j.g.) Eric Cobb, like many aviators, did not lack for confidence. It took a very confident or very stupid man to step into a single-engined aircraft, then take off from a small postage stamp of a warship on a flight over hundreds of miles of featureless ocean. Some people, to include Eric's father, believed that repeatedly doing this was the height of idiocy. Eric, on the other hand, had developed a liking for the hours of solitude, sunlight, and beautiful ocean vistas that were only visible from several thousand feet of altitude.

Unfortunately for Eric, the 12th day of September in the year of our Lord nineteen forty-two had none of the above.

"Okay asshole, I think we're getting a little bit close to the Kraut fleet's estimated position," Eric muttered, his hands white knuckled on his SBD *Dauntless*'s stick and throttle. The "asshole" in question was VB-4's squadron leader, Lieutenant Commander Abe Cobleigh, and the soup that passed for a sky all around them made following Red One's plane a feat of concentration and skill. The conditions were making Eric's forward canopy fog and he had to fight the urge to take his feet off the rudder pedals and brace himself up to look over the top of the forward glass. At several inches over six feet Eric wouldn't have had to stretch far, but taking one's feet off the rudder in the current conditions was not a recipe for longevity. Even though the radial-engine "Slow But Deadly" was as beloved for its handling characteristics as its ruggedness, Eric had no desire to see how well he could pull out from a stupidity-induced spin.

"What was that, sir?" Radioman 2nd Class Henry Rawles asked from the tail gunner position.

"Nothing Rawles, nothing," Eric called back, keeping his voice level so the young gunner wouldn't think he was perturbed at him.

Not Rawles's fault our squadron leader is a...

Without warning, the *Dauntless* burst out of the cloud bank. Eric had just enough time to register the changing conditions, give a sigh of relief, then start looking around before all hell broke loose. The anti-aircraft barrage that burst around the two single-engine dive bombers was heavy and accurate. With a seeming endless cascade of *crack! crack! crack!*, heavy caliber shells exploded all around Eric's bomber, the blasts throwing it around like backhands from a giant.

Jesus Christ! Eric thought, stomping left on his rudder and pulling back on the stick to get back into the clouds.

"Sir, Lieutenant Commander Cobleigh's been hit!" Rawles shouted.

Before Eric could respond, another shell exploded on the bomber's right side with a deafening roar and flash. Eric felt a sharp sting and burning sensation across the back of his neck as the canopy shattered in a spray of glass, the *Dauntless* heeling over from the explosion. Stunned, Eric instinctively leveled the dive bomber off and found himself back in the cloud bank before he fully recovered his senses.

With full recovery came consciousness of just how screwed he was. First Eric realized that it was only by the grace of God that he hadn't been laid open like a slaughtered animal. His shredded life vest, damaged control stick and throttle, and a very large hole in the cockpit's side were all evidence that several fragments had blasted all around him. Fighting down the urge to vomit, Eric quickly checked both of his wings, noting that the surfaces were thoroughly peppered as he fought to keep the SBD level. Fuel streamed behind the bomber, starting to gradually slow as the self-sealing tanks proved their worth.

Oh we are in trouble now. The two SBDs had been near the limit of their search arc when fired upon. Even with the self-sealing tanks working as advertised, Eric was certain that the damage to the wing tanks had just guaranteed Rawles and he would not be landing back aboard *Ranger*. Swiveling his head, he attempted to find Red One's SBD *Dauntless* dive bomber through the murk.

"Rawles!" Eric called over the intercom.

"Yes, sir?" his gunner responded.

"You see what happened to One?" Eric began, then suddenly remembered Rawles' report. "I mean after he got hit."

"Sir, there was no after Lt. Commander Cobleigh got hit," Rawles replied, his voice breathless. "He just exploded!"

Eric felt the sick feeling return to his stomach. After a moment's temptation to just go ahead and vomit over the side, he fought the puke back down.

"What else did you get a chance to see?" Eric asked.

"It looked like there were at least two battleships, maybe three. Jesus they were close!"

"Okay, you need to get off a position report of those German bastards. Send it in the clear back to *Ranger*, keep repeating it until someone acknowledges, and I will try to figure out if we're going to make it back."

"Aye aye, sir," Rawles replied. A few moments later, Eric heard the Morse code starting to get tapped out. Pulling out his map, he suddenly realized he had no clue which direction he was flying. Looking down at the compass, he felt a sudden sigh of relief when he saw they were heading southwest, away from the Germans and generally towards their own fleet.

"Sir, I've got an acknowledgment from the *Augusta*. She's asking our status," Rawles said.

"Send this in code: Red One destroyed, Two unlikely to return to fleet. Will send crash location," Eric said tersely.

They broke out of the low clouds into an area of open sky, the sun beaming down on the battered *Dauntless*. Eric suddenly felt exposed and began scanning around the horizon. He heard and felt Rawles unlimber his twin .30-caliber machine guns and was glad to see that he wasn't the only one on edge.

Those bastards tried to kill us! he thought, then remembered how close the Germans had come to doing just that.

"Rawles, you all right?"

"I got nicked on my calf, but it's not serious. Are we actually about to crash, sir?" Rawles asked.

"It's about two hundred miles back to the fleet, and we don't have two hundred miles of fuel..."

"Smoke! Smoke to starboard!" Rawles shouted. Eric whipped his head around and saw the smudge that Rawles had sighted low on the horizon.

"Well, you just might have kept us from a day in the raft, Rawles," Eric said happily, grabbing the stick with his left hand. Reaching down the right side of his seat, he opened his binoculars' case and reached in. There was a sharp prick on his gloved finger, and he jerked his hand back. Reaching down more carefully, he realized that while the lid was still present on the case, the container itself was twisted metal.

"Rawles, you still have your binoculars?"

"Roger sir," Rawles came back.

"Let's see what you can see," Eric replied. "Mine are shot to hell."

There was a slight rustling in the backseat as Eric brought the SBD around to begin closing with the smoke. After a few moments, it was clear there was more than one column. About ten minutes later, it was very obvious that the *Dauntless* was closing with an entire group of ships.

"Sir, that looks like the Brits!" Rawles said. "I can't tell very well, but that looks like one of their heavy cruisers and a few destroyers heading away from us."

"Great," Eric muttered. "I get to be shot at by both sides today."

"What was that, sir?"

"Nevermind, just talking to myself. Send this location in code also, then get ready to start signaling with a lamp."

"Approaching aircraft, approaching aircraft, these are Royal Navy vessels," a clear, accented voice crackled into Eric's earpieces. "Do not continue to approach or you will be fired upon."

Eric turned the SBD away, banking to show his silhouette and national insignia. The dive bomber initially complied with the movement, then suddenly staggered and began to roll to the left. Eric fought the maneuver, but found that he was only able to hold the aircraft level with the stick pressed almost completely to the right. Looking out at his ailerons, he saw that both were in the down position.

Great, just great, Eric thought.

"Royal Navy vessel, this is a United States Navy aircraft in need of assistance," Eric said once he had control of his aircraft. "Request permission to ditch close aboard."

There was a pause of a sufficient length that Eric felt his arm starting to shake from the effort of maintaining level flight.

"American aircraft, you may ditch close aboard," came the response.

Eric heard Rawles wrestling around in the rear cockpit.

"Sir, I've got the code books in a sack with a box of ammo. Want me to throw it over the side?"

"Great plan, Rawles," Eric gritted. "Get rid of the guns too, don't want you getting brained when we get out."

A moment later, Eric heard the twin machine guns bang down against the fuselage on their way over the side. Shortly after, there was a similar noise as the code books and ammo followed suit the .30-caliber tail guns. Taking a little pressure off the stick, Eric brought the *Dauntless* around in a gradual left-hand turn to see the large cruiser coasting to a stop. The five destroyers accompanying the vessel circled like protective sheep dogs, smoke drifting up from their stacks.

I hope those tin cans don't find anything. Don't feel like adding "got torpedoed" to my list of bad things that have happened today. His right arm began twitching, warning of impending muscle failure, and he quickly grabbed the stick with his left hand for a couple of moments.

"All right Rawles, I've never done this before so I don't know how much time we have," Eric said, fighting to keep his voice calm. "Stand by to ditch."

As Rawles acknowledged his order, Eric had a chance to give the British cruiser a good look. A twin-stacked, three-turreted ship, the RN vessel was painted in three tones of gray, the pattern seemingly random from above. As the dive bomber circled downward from five thousand feet, Eric realized that the captain had placed the vessel athwart the wind, leaving a relatively calm area on her lee. Eric recognized the maneuver as one occasionally conducted by American cruisers in order to recover their seaplanes.

Glad to see things aren't totally different between our navies. The *Dauntless* shuddered, and Eric noted the engine starting to run slightly rougher. Giving a prayer of thanks that Rawles had sighted the vessels, Eric resolved to put the dive bomber down as quickly as possible. Clenching his teeth, his right arm starting to burn with muscle fatigue again, Eric finished the last turn of his gradual spiral down barely one hundred feet over the water and half a mile from the stopped ship.

Fighting at the edge of a stall, he pulled the nose up slightly to start killing the SBD's forward momentum.

It was an almost perfect ditching. The dive bomber stalled, the wings losing their last bit of lift barely ten feet above the ocean. There was nothing Eric could do to prevent the nose starting to come down, with the result that the landing was not as smooth as he had hoped. The impact slammed him forward, his restraints failing to prevent his head from snapping against the instrument panel. Seeing stars, Eric slumped backward briefly into his seat and took a moment to gather himself. As he ran his tongue over his teeth to make sure they were all there, Eric felt the airplane lurch and start to settle towards starboard. The swirl of water into the bottom of the cockpit told him that he did not have long to get out of the crippled aircraft.

"Sir, you okay?!" Rawles asked, standing on the port wing by the aircraft. Eric turned and looked at him, the movement sluggish. Rawles didn't wait for an answer, reaching in and starting to help Eric unbuckle.

"Get the..." Eric started, fighting hard to get through the mental fog. "Get the life raft."

No sooner had he said that than water began pouring over the edge of his cockpit. The cold North Atlantic did wonders to clear the cobwebs, and he realized with a start that Rawles was already up to his chest in the water. Kicking his feet free of the rudder pedals and disconnecting his radio cord, Eric pulled off his shredded life vest and started to stand up. The movement didn't come off as planned as the *Dauntless* slid out from under him. In moments, he and Rawles were both swimming in the cold Atlantic, their plane a momentary dark shape underneath them before it slid into the depths.

"Guess we could've left the codebooks after all," Rawles muttered. "Damn sir, you look like someone hit your noggin' with a sledgehammer."

Eric kicked his legs to get out of the water while reaching up with his left arm. He winced as he touched the massive goose egg on this forehead.

That explains why I'm a little out of it, Eric thought, pleasantly surprised he was able to form a semi-coherent thought. *Although it would appear going for a swim in cold as hell water helps clear up getting knocked on the head.*

Worryingly, Eric could feel his arm cramps returning as he treaded water.

I'm not sure how long I'll make it without a life vest, he thought worriedly. The sound of a boat moter carrying across the waves was the sweetest sound he had ever heard. Turning, he saw that the cruiser's boat was almost upon them. Eric attempted to start swimming towards the whaleboat and realized with a start that his legs were going numb.

"Just stay there, gentlemen, we will be with you shortly!" a man in the boat's prow shouted.

Minutes later the Royal Navy lieutenant was proven as good as his word, with blankets being dropped over the Americans' shoulders and rum shoved into their hands. Rawles threw his shot back quickly, only starting to shiver once he got it down. Eric, hardly a drinker, took two swallows to get the rum into his stomach and had to fight against retching.

"My name is *Leftenant* Aldrich, medical office for the His Majesty's Ship *Exeter*," the man began as the whaleboat began returning to the cruiser. Eric saw that the man was tall and thin, his navy blue jacket hanging off him like he was a walking clothes hanger.

He must be older than he looks, Eric thought as he took in the man's youthful freckled face and dark red hair. While his voice was deep and firm, Aldrich looked like he hadn't been shaving for more than a week. After a moment's silence, Eric realized the man was awaiting similar information from him.

"Lieutenant junior grade Eric Cobb," Eric said. "This is my gunner, Rawles. Since you guys actually gave us some warning, I'll assume it's not your fleet that gunned us down."

If Aldrich was non-plussed that Eric didn't give him any more information the man did not show it.

"It would appear that you have met our erstwhile adversaries the *Kriegsmarine*," Aldrich replied. "I take it that you, then, are the aircraft who sent the position report in the clear?"

"That would be us," Eric replied. Aldrich smiled.

"Well thank you for not making my wife a widow," Aldrich said. At Eric's look, Aldrich just smiled.

"I am sure Captain Gordon will explain everything to you if he sees fit. Until then, please enjoy our hospitality. *Leftenant* Cobb, you appear to have taken a pretty good knock on the head. I'll need to check you out once we get aboard."

Eric started to nod, then realized that would be very foolish.

"That would probably be a good idea," he began, then belatedly added, "sir."

TEN MINUTES LATER, ERIC STOOD WATCHING ALDRICH'S FINGER AS the young-looking officer moved his hand back and forth. The two men were standing in *Exeter*'s port dressing station, a space that was normally the petty officers' mess. When the heavy cruiser was getting ready to enter combat, the space was set aside for casualty treatment and stabilization before the unfortunate subjects were taken to sick bay below.

"You mentioned something about me saving your wife from becoming a widow?" Eric asked after a moment.

"Yes, I did," Aldrich replied.

"Sir, I can tell the ship is at Condition Two," Eric continued. "Obviously you guys are expecting a fight. I got sort of confused after getting shot up, but weren't the Germans a bit far away for you to be preparing for combat?"

"Very astute observation, *Leftenant*," another voice interjected. Eric saw the two ratings in the room jump to their feet, followed at a more leisurely pace by Rawles. Eric started to turn his head to see what they were looking at.

"I will not be able to tell if you have a concussion if you turn your head, *Leftenant* Cobb," Aldrich said, causing Eric to stop his movement. "Captain Gordon, sir," he said, nodding towards the door.

"*Leftenant* Aldrich," Captain Gordon replied. "I see you've been fishing again."

Aldrich smiled as he finished moving his finger back and forth.

"I think this one is a tad bit large to have thrown back, Captain," Aldrich said, stepping back. "We're done here, *Leftenant*."

Eric turned around, well aware of his sorry appearance in a borrowed pair of Royal Navy overalls. Rawles and he had both gladly handed over their waterlogged clothes in exchange for dry clothing, but now he felt vaguely self-conscious in meeting the *Exeter*'s master. Gordon was a man of slightly above average height, with piercing eyes and gray, thinning hair topping an aristocratic face.

"Well, I must agree," Gordon said, giving Eric a pensive look. "I suppose you play what you Americans call football?"

"I did, sir," Eric replied. "For the Naval Academy."

"Barbaric sport," Gordon said. "Can't see why anyone would enjoy watching roughly twenty men bash each other's brains out over some poor pig's hide."

Eric found himself starting to smile as he contemplated a comeback. Gordon continued without giving him a chance to defend American honor.

"But, that's not what you were talking about to *Leftenant* Aldrich, and time is short. Our mission, when you sighted us, was to gain contact with the German fleet so that we could ascertain its position."

Eric nodded, starting to get a glimmer of understanding.

"Since our own aviators believed that the weather was far too much of a dog's breakfast to fly, the task fell upon the Home Fleet's cruisers, or more correctly, what cruisers broke out of Scapa Flow with His Majesty."

"Broke out of Scapa Flow?" Eric asked, confused.

Gordon and Aldrich shared a look.

"You are aware of the armistice signed a fortnight ago, yes?"

"The one between you guys and the Krauts? Yes, sir, I'm aware."

"There was some fine print agreed to by Lord Halifax's negotiators that did not sit well with the King," Gordon continued simply. "Namely the part about turning over the occupied nations' governments-in-exile and all of their forces that had fought under our command."

"That part was not covered in our briefings," Eric replied.

Of course, we've been at sea ever since it looked like you guys were about to be knocked out of the war, he didn't add. Eric was certain the term "neutral country" would lose all meaning. if the full details of the USN's actions to facilitate Great Britain's war efforts ever came to light.

Which may explain why the Krauts turned two American aircraft into colanders.

"This breakout wasn't exactly long in the planning, *Leftenant*," Gordon replied with a tight smile. "However, this is of no matter. What is important is that the Home Fleet and a few fast liners did manage to break out. What we did not expect was for the Germans to have anticipated our decision and placed submarines in our path."

Eric fought to keep the astonishment off of his face.

The submarines were part of the reason you guys had to surrender! he thought, incredulous.

"The *Queen Mary*, carrying a large contingent of forces, was torpedoed last night," Gordon continued, either not reading Eric's brief change of expression or choosing to ignore it. "She did not sink, but her speed was greatly slowed. This morning, it was decided to offload her passengers and scuttle the vessel."

Eric looked at Aldrich and then Captain Gordon.

"I am coming to the reason behind *Leftenant* Aldrich's comment," Gordon said with a slight smile. "Before the fleet departed Scapa Flow, there were reports that the German fleet was expected to sortie in order to attempt to intercept the Royal Family and compel their return. They were believed to be another two hundred miles east of the position you radioed."

I am beginning to understand now, Eric thought.

"As I noted, our own pilots did not think the conditions were suitable for flying as dawn broke. Which is why this vessel is currently part of a picket line, and as *Leftenant* Aldrich alluded to, would have likely encountered Jerry much as you did—guns first."

Eric could hear the disdain in Gordon's voice and decided to intercede on behalf of his British counterparts.

"Sir, with all due respect, the weather *is* too bad to be flying," he said bitterly. "Our commander volunteered the most experienced pilots in our squadron, and even then he had to persuade Admiral No...our admiral to allow us to fly."

Gordon's small smile broadened.

"Lieutenant Cobb, I am well aware that you are off of the aircraft carrier *Ranger*, specifically from VB-4. I am also aware that your signal was picked up by the cruiser *Augusta* and that your commander, apparently, perished. Finally, I am aware that Rear Admiral Noyes is under strict orders not to engage in direct combat with the *Kriegsmarine* unless they cross the established neutrality line."

This time the surprise was far too great for Eric to maintain any hint of a poker face.

"Guess I could have passed on tossing the codebooks over the side," Rawles said coolly.

"Unfortunately, *Leftenant*, the manner by which I know all this information also means that your fleet realizes we have plucked you out of the Atlantic. That," Gordon continued, his smile disappearing, "places us in a bit of a quandary."

Gordon turned towards Rawles and the two ratings in the room.

"Gentlemen, if you could excuse us?" he asked, the tone of his voice belying the appearance of his question being a request. Eric was glad to see Rawles follow the two men out into the passageway.

"As I was saying, your presence here places us into a bit of a fix. You, *Leftenant*, are an officer of a neutral nation. More importantly a neutral nation with certain elements who would gladly seize upon your death or serious injury in order to support the agenda of keeping your nation from rendering His Majesty's government any aid. I am sure that you are familiar with the term 'impressment' as it applies to our nations' shared histories?"

Eric nodded, starting to see where Gordon was going.

We fought a minor debacle in 1812 over just that issue as I recall, Eric thought somberly.

"So, in order to avoid any discussions of that sort of thing, I have consulted with my superiors. We can hardly just stuff you in a whaleboat and leave you in the middle of the Atlantic. Therefore, I am here to offer you a choice to transfer to the H.M.S. *Punjabi*. This vessel will then be tasked with escorting the liners out of harm's way, and that is probably the safest thing we can provide at the moment."

Well, no, you could actually return me to American forces or put me on a neutral vessel, Eric thought sharply, but decided some things were best left unvoiced.

"What effect will this have on your force?" he asked instead.

Gordon paused for a few moments, and Eric could see the wheels turning in the British captain's head.

"The effects would not be positive," Gordon finally answered. The man then took a deep sigh, with the breaking of his mental dam almost perceptible.

"The division of destroyers with us is one of two that departed Scapa Flow with their actual assigned crews, full complement of torpedoes, and allotted depth charges," *Exeter*'s captain said, his voice clipped. "The size of the German force is unknown, but it is highly unlikely that our advantage is so great that we can afford to lose a destroyer before the action begins. The choice, however, is yours *Leftenant* Cobb."

The silence in the compartment after Gordon's explanation seemed to press in on Eric. At least thirty seconds passed, with Gordon growing perceptibly impatient, before the American replied.

"We were briefed before we departed Newport News that our forces were to make every effort to avoid giving the impression that we were aiding RN forces," he said, and watched Captain Gordon's face start to fall. "However, we were also instructed to respond to hostile acts in kind. Those bastards killed my squadron commander and nearly killed me. While I hesitate to give them another chance to finish the job, I'll be damned if I'll make their lives easier."

Gordon exhaled heavily.

"You do realize that when I transmit this news to Admiral Tovey your own forces are going to overhear it, correct?"

Eric shrugged.

"If I end up in Leavenworth it means no one else will be shooting at me," Eric replied grimly. "Seems to me that the situation is bad enough if I force you to take this ship out of the line, the. After what they did to London, I'm not sure I want them to catch the King or his family."

Eric saw several emotions flit across Gordon's face. The man was about to respond when the ship's loudspeaker crackled. Both men turned to look at the speaker mounted at the front of the compartment.

"Captain to the bridge," a calm, measured voice spoke. "I say again, Captain to the bridge."

"Last chance to back out, *Leftenant*," Captain Gordon said, heading for the companionway hatch.

"We'll stay, sir," Eric said, right before a thought struck him. "However, I do have one request."

"What would that be, *Leftenant*?"

"Do you think that His Majesty could consider asking President Roosevelt to give me a pardon? You know, just in case?"

Gordon stopped dead for a second, confusion on his face. Still looking befuddled, he shrugged.

"I'll be sure to pass along your request," the British officer allowed. "Even though I am unsure as to what you are referring to."

Eric smiled.

"I'm sure His Majesty will have someone who can advise him as to what I mean," Eric replied. Gordon shook his head and opened the hatch. There was a quick exchange of words with Aldrich that Eric couldn't quite hear, then the man was gone. A moment later, Lieutenant Aldrich stepped back through the door.

"What is your hat size, *Leftenant*?" Aldrich asked.

"Seven inches even," Eric said.

"I'll see what we can find in the way of a helmet for you."

Eric felt and heard the *Exeter*'s engines begin to accelerate. Aldrich's face clouded as the loudspeaker crackled again. A few moments later, the sound of a bugle call came over the device followed by the same clipped voice as before calling the crew to "Action Stations".

"Well now, it appears that our German friends have been sighted once more," Aldrich said grimly as he walked towards the speaking tube at the back of the compartment. "Either that or Jerry's bloody U-boats are at it again."

Eric suddenly thought about the implications of either of those events and didn't like what he was coming up with. Rawles and the two British seamen reentered the compartment as Aldrich began calling down to the ship's store for a helmet. Eric gave a wry smile as he saw that Rawles had already been given a helmet. The pie plate-shaped headgear looked slightly different than its American counterpart, but close enough that Eric was sure the gunner wouldn't have looked too out of place aboard *Ranger*.

"I see that our hosts have already seen to your comforts, Rawles," Eric teased his gunner.

"I'd be a lot more comfortable with a pair of guns in my hand aboard a *Dauntless*, sir," Rawles said, his voice tight. Eric could see the man was nervous, and he didn't blame him. He was about to make another comment when Aldrich's voice stopped him in his tracks.

"Right, understood, I will send *Leftenant* Cobb to the bridge with the runner while his gunner remains here," the medical officer said into the tube. "Aldrich out."

"Did I just hear what I think I did?" Eric asked, struggling to keep his tone neutral.

"The captain is afraid that one shell will kill you both," Aldrich replied simply. "That would be bad for a great many reasons."

I hate it when people have a point, Eric thought. *At least, I hate it when said point means I'm about to get a front row seat to people shooting guns at me.*

"Well it's hard to argue with that logic," Eric said, looking up as a man arrived in the hatchway with his helmet and flash gear. "Rawles, try to stay out of the rum."

"Aye aye, sir," Rawles replied, his expression still sour.

"Midshipman Radcliffe, you are in charge until I get back," Aldrich said, then turned to Eric. "Given what I've been told, there's enough time to give you a quick tour of the vessel before I drop you off at the bridge. That is, if you'd like a quick tour."

"Certainly, sir," Eric said. "I did a midsummer cruise on the U.S.S. *Salt Lake City*, so it will be interesting to see how differently your side does things."

U.S.S. Houston
Cavite Naval Base
2020 Local (0820 Eastern)
13 September (12 September)

Whereas most men would have felt butterflies in their stomach prior to meeting their boss, Commander Jacob T. Morton found himself hoping that the rage and bitterness he felt did not show on his lined face. He took a deep, steadying breath as the orderly returned from inside the captain's day cabin.

"Captain Wallace will see you now, sir," the marine said, coming to attention.

"Thank you, corporal," Jacob replied, his accent betraying his Maine roots. With that, he stepped through the hatchway. Stepping forward to three steps before the desk of *Houston*'s master, he saluted.

"Commander Jacob Morton reporting as ordered, sir," Jacob said crisply. Standing well over six feet, with a tall, gangly frame, Jacob forced the short, heavyset man standing behind the desk to slightly crane his head back as he returned the salute of the *Houston*'s newest XO.

"When I heard they called you 'The Stork,' I wondered how someone got a nickname like that," Captain Sean Wallace observed drily, his Texas twang quite evident. "Now I see a slight resemblance to you and a crane. Please, take a seat before I develop a crick in my neck."

Jacob's expression didn't change, his green eyes continuing to hold Wallace's brown ones as he followed orders.

"Why do they call you 'The Stork,' if I may ask?" Wallace continued.

*Why do people always ask if a question is okay **after** it's already been said?* Jacob thought.

"Plebe boxing class, sir," Jacob replied. "One of my opponents stated fighting me was like being attacked by an angry stork. It stuck."

Captain Wallace nodded, running a hand through his thinning brown hair.

"Horrible class, that," Wallace replied. "I think that's probably the worst experience I've ever had in my life. I take it that you did all right?"

"I boxed in the Brigade intramurals," Jacob replied evenly. "I placed second in the light heavyweight class."

Wallace smiled.

"Well, glad to see your aggressiveness won't be a problem," he said with a smile. "Its part of the reason you're here. But before we get started, would you like me to have the mess send up something? There should be sandwiches or something available, I realize you're probably famished after coming all the way out from Pearl."

"No thank you, sir, I actually ate before coming aboard," Jacob said. "I will, with your permission, have some of that water in the corner however."

"By all means," Wallace said, gesturing towards the pitcher and glasses. As Jacob stood, *Houston*'s captain began their discussion.

"I understand that you were somewhat surprised when BuPers cut your orders."

"It's rare that an officer is requested by name, much less by someone he has never met," Jacob replied cautiously. "Serving twice as an XO is lucky, but three times is unheard of."

Wallace grimaced.

"When Captain Rooks got cancer three months ago it was a shock to the entire wardroom," Wallace replied. "Admiral Hart offered every one of the officers the opportunity to transfer to other vessels, and most of the division chiefs were reassigned throughout the fleet or sent back to Pearl. I only requested that Admiral Hart give me the most experienced XO possible, and apparently your name was selected."

Well that explains it, Jacob thought, fighting the urge to curse aloud.

"I understand you had been slated to take a destroyer in about six months," Wallace continued. "I realize that an XO tour, much less one here in the Forgotten Fleet, is hardly an equal trade, but Admiral Hart has assured me that he will personally see to it that your career doesn't suffer."

Jacob was taken aback by Wallace's frankness. Usually mere commanders were not informed of admiral and captain's personnel machinations, much less apologized to for their careers being possibly set back.

"Thank you, sir," he said, feeling a great deal of tension leave his body. Wallace gave a slight smile.

"I think, were I in your position, I would be ready to punch my captain out at the first opportunity. Given that you apparently have some experience with that, I would much prefer to clear the air before we have to work together."

Jacob smiled in return at Wallace's slight joke.

Obviously not one of those men who believes that the captain must appear as a god before all mortals, he thought. As if reading his mind, Wallace continued.

"I'm not a man to stand on protocol between us in private, especially given your seniority. I also won't beat around the bush—I expect you to be my hatchet man. All six departments on this ship are good, but I need you to make them excellent," Wallace said simply. "Especially as I think we'll be in war within a month."

Jacob gave his captain a measured look.

"I'm not saying I disagree, but what is your reasoning, sir?"

"The damn Japs are probably going to take the news out of Europe as a blank check to start 'liberating' some colonies around here, and we need to make sure they don't think the Philippines are also on the foreclosure list."

"I was told before I left Pearl that there's talk of still making the Philippines independent at the end of the year," Jacob replied. "With Great Britain's surrender, is that still going to happen?"

"Apparently that idiot MacArthur thinks that the Philippines can defend themselves with Navy help," Wallace snorted. "So, yes, it will probably happen, but that won't change any of our war plans."

"So Admiral Hart still intends to retreat to the Dutch East Indies if the Japanese attack? That was the last plan I was privy to when I was on CINCPAC staff."

"Yes, we're not staying here to absorb shells for the Army," Wallace replied.

"Instead we're going to die defending some occupied countries' colonies," Jacob replied, his voice more bitter than he intended. Wallace fixed him with a hard look.

"I will forgive that outburst XO since we are alone. But I would caution you that I will have considerably less patience if you display one iota of that opinion in front of any of our junior officers. Do I make myself absolutely clear, commander?"

Jacob reined in his temper, surprised that he had grown so annoyed.

"Very clear, sir," Jacob said calmly. "I apologize."

"It happens that I agree with you," Wallace said with a wave of his hand. "However, neither of us are in charge and the hour grows late. I notice you don't wear a wedding ring, but your personnel jacket indicated that you were married."

"My wife passed away six years ago," Jacob replied evenly. "She had a massive coronary when I was in Norfolk."

Wallace's face clouded for a moment.

"My apologies," Wallace said. "It'd be nice if the damn personnel folks had let me know that before I made an ass of myself."

"For some reason BuPers is incapable of passing that information to any of my duty stations," Jacob replied, his voice with a hard edge. "I go through this every time I have a new assignment. Thankfully to date they have never messed up Jo's file."

"Jo? You have a son?" Captain Wallace asked.

"No, short for Josephine," Jacob said with a broad smile. "My wife started calling her Jo because she swears it was quite obvious to everyone that I had wanted a boy."

"I have three sons myself," Wallace said. "Trust me, in some ways daughters are easier. At least you don't have to worry about them being in harm's way."

"I wish that were absolutely true, sir," Jacob returned, his smile disappearing like morning fog.

HONOLULU, HAWAII

0530 LOCAL (1030 EASTERN)
12 SEPTEMBER

I AM CRAZY. AS IN, "WELCOME TO THE NUTHOUSE, JOSEPHINE, WE ARE so glad to see you" insane, Josephine Marie Morton thought for the fifth time that morning. Fighting back a yawn as she stood on the quay looking out into Honolulu's harbor, she turned to look at her three companions. Two of them loomed far above her own height even in the low heels she wore with her plain brown dress. The other was only a half foot taller than her with the athletic build of a long-distance runner. Giving a sideways glance at the trio, a thought came to her mind that nearly made her giggle.

"You're in somewhat good spirits," the smaller man said quietly. Turning to face him while simultaneously brushing back her shoulder-length brunette hair, Jo finally couldn't hold the light laugh in anymore.

"I'm sorry, Nick, but every time I see you three together I cannot help but wonder how your mother went from big, bigger, biggest to runt," Jo replied.

Nick Elrod Cobb, Lieutenant (j.g.), United States Navy, gave Jo a half smile.

You know, you could really be a lady killer if you tried, Jo thought wistfully. *However, you've made it very clear that you don't want to try with me—but a gal can dream.*

Nick, unlike his three brothers, had dark hair to go with his blue eyes. While none of the Cobbs were hard to look at, the youngest of the four sons had definitely gotten more than his fair share of handsome. Moreover, unlike the two blonde-haired grizzlies behind him, Nick wasn't so big that a woman felt she had to worry about being broken in half.

"I think our father figured he could get just as much manual labor for half the groceries," Nick replied, looking sideways at his two brothers.

"That's a theory..." Samuel Michael Cobb, Captain, United States Marine Corps began.

"...but probably not very valid," David Aaron Cobb, Captain, USMC and Sam's twin, finished.

Nick made a sound of frustration.

"You know, four years away from you two lugs and I'd forgotten just how fu...darn annoying that habit is!"

"You know, Nick, you really can swear around me," Jo said with a chuckle. "I promise, my father has said many, many worse things around the house, to include references to the act of copulation."

"It's not your opinion he's worried about," Sam observed, giving his younger brother a glower.

"No, it would be the fact that we wouldn't want him to ever give the impression that our mother didn't raise us to act like gentlemen around a lady."

Jo shook her head.

"Has anyone ever told you Southerners that the age of chivalry has long since passed?"

"Just because you Yankee women don't know how to demand proper behavior from your men doesn't mean that we have to stop giving it," David replied, looking out towards the harbor. "I do believe that is Patricia's vessel."

"Only half a day late," Nick observed. "Damn merchant..ow!"

Jo was amazed at how quickly Nick turned around, starting to raise his hands to punch one of his brothers then stopping to think better of it.

"Why do I get the feeling I'm witnessing a family story that has played out many, many times over the past twenty-four years?" Jo asked bemusedly.

"Because you're an astute observer of human behavior," Sam said lowly, not taking his eyes off Nick.

"In addition to being highly intelligent," David continued, also watching Nick like a hawk. "Oh, and very pretty."

Jo felt herself starting to blush and was glad for the olive tint of her skin.

Sorry boys, I own a mirror, she thought. While she didn't consider herself *fat* by any means, Jo knew she could stand to lose a few pounds. *Thankfully it seems to go to the right places, though*. Voluptuous was a fair word to describe her even if pretty wasn't.

"Yes, these two think it's funny to both pick on someone," Nick said lowly, his voice making it very clear that there'd be a fight if either brother touched him again.

"Mama raised you better than to curse in front of a lady," Sam replied simply.

The incoming vessel sounded its whistle, interrupting the brothers' discussion. A small liner, the *S.S. Hampton Roads* made a regular trip between Hawaii and the mainland. Usually it returned with mostly military dependents and those seeking to make their fortune working at Pearl Harbor or one of the various Army posts scattered around the islands. Ten minutes after sounding her whistle, the ship's crew was tossing ropes to the men gathered on the dock. Shortly after that, Jo got to see yet another member of the Cobb family.

"Will you look at the hams on that one," a man said a little too loudly to his companion as they walked by. Jo, focusing on the ship, whipped her head around to see that both men were likewise looking at the gangplank as a tall, beautiful brunette began to descend. The woman was wearing a yellow dress and a matching hat, with curly locks trailing all the way down past her shoulders.

I wonder if that's...

"Well that's a sight for sore eyes," the second man replied, "Looks like we're about to get some fresh round eye..."

The man never got to finish his sentence. One second Sam, David, and Nick were standing on opposite sides of her. The next, Nick had seemingly teleported the ten feet to the ogling duo's location. Looking at the two men, Jo could tell that they were soldiers. She couldn't have identified what clued her in about their manner or their walk, but upon a closer look it was blindingly obvious.

"Excuse me, mister," Nick said lightly, "but you wouldn't happen to be about to make a comment about that women in the yellow dress, would you?"

The two men looked at Nick, then looked at each other.

"She your wife or something, pal?" one of them asked belligerently. "Looks a little young to be married."

"As a matter of fact, no," Nick replied. "She's my sister."

The two men looked at one another, then looked at Nick.

"Okay, so even if my buddy and I here were about to say

something, we were having a private conversation. We doubt your sister minds."

Not only soldiers, but stupid ones, Jo thought.

"Yes, but *I* mind, and I know exactly what someone means when they start talking about roundeye," Nick continued. "I would appreciate it if you talked quieter or maybe keep your comments to yourself."

The first man looked somewhat sheepish, but his companion apparently had been having a bad day.

"Well we'd *appreciate* it if you minded your own business," the man sneered. "You'd probably like it a lot more too."

Just like that, I'm standing by myself, Jo thought to herself, as Sam and David both ambled over behind their younger brother.

"You know, we're not quite as sensitive about what we may overhear," Sam said.

"After all, with the wind blowing in our direction, you may not have realized that your comments about our sister were audible to us," David continued.

"But Nick here asked you kindly enough to maybe take your comments elsewhere, and you have refused," Sam resumed, his voice dropping lower.

"So maybe it would help if we told you a bit more forcefully to *go somewhere else*," David finished. Jo felt the hair on the back of her neck rise at David's tone.

Never thought I'd see someone beat to death, she thought nervously. Fortunately the quieter of the two soldiers realized that his friend's mouth was about to put both of them in the hospital if they were lucky, morgue if not.

"Let's go, Matt," the man said. "I don't think that dame's going to give you the time of day if you're in traction."

"Matt" gave all three Cobbs a cold, hard look as he allowed his friend to tug him away. If he was trying for intimidation, he could have saved his breath and energy.

I think he'd have more luck scaring one of the volcanoes around here, Jo thought, fighting the urge to shiver from the adrenaline rushing through her. She was about to say something when she heard a very exasperated, feminine sigh behind her. Turning, Jo saw that the woman in yellow had made a beeline towards the three glowering men, her brow furrowed and mouth in a thin line. Looking at the other woman's features close up, Jo felt a sudden, insane pang of jealousy.

No wonder her brothers are protective of her, Jo thought bitterly. *Probably had plenty of practice.*

"Well, glad to see some things never change," the woman snapped, the ice in her voice freezing the honey of her drawl. "Let me guess? Did someone make an untoward comment about my attire and you three felt the need to defend my honor?"

Jo was in shock at the transformation of all three Cobbs. One moment the trio had been clearly ready to perform carefully choreographed mayhem. The next, Sam, David, and Nick wore almost identically sheepish looks.

Holy shit, I need to take lessons from her, Jo thought.

"I am once again reminded of why I will probably die a spinster," the woman continued, her delivery rapid and tone sharp.

"We figured fleeing Alabama like a wanted fugitive two weeks before your wedding to Beau might have had a bit more to do with that," Nick responded, his face hard. Both of his brothers stepped away from him, the move so quick that it was obviously unconscious. Jo didn't blame them, as if looks could kill Nick would have simply ceased to exist.

Her eyes turned into green death rays, Jo thought, remembering a line from some dime store novel she had read as a teenager.

"The only state I am a 'fugitive' from is matrimony, Nick," the woman observed. "Don't you stand here and judge me when it is *obvious* that you do not find it very palatable yourself—or is the issue more that I jilted your guys' childhood friend?"

Nick sighed exasperatedly at his sister.

"Yes, of course, because I have had so many opportunities to meet women in my line of work. Why, just the other day the *Nautilus* stopped off at this tropical refuge where there were all these doe-eyed maidens..."

"So I suppose we'll just forget all the wonderful young women that mother tried to set you up with? At least Eric was smart enough to finally ask Joyce to marry him."

"Well judging from the current situation, a 'yes' sure doesn't seem to mean…"

Jo stepped between Nick and his sister, the movement causing him to stop mid-sentence. She stuck out her hand, catching the rapidly reddening Patricia by surprise.

"Hello Patricia, my name is Josephine Morton, and I'm a friend of your brothers," Jo said calmly. "As I know Nick here likes to run his trap to excess sometimes, I thought I'd see if you were interested in seeing your room sometime before nightfall."

"My room?" Patricia asked, so shocked that her anger was forgotten. "I'm sorry, there must be some…"

"Mistake? No, not really," Jo continued. "I've known Sam, David, and Nick since they got on the island. Rather than have you live by yourself, or move in with David only to have to move out when he gets hitched to Sadie, your brothers thought it'd be nice if you had a more experienced roommate to show you around."

Patricia released Jo's hand, her expression going from angry to suspicious.

"They did, did they?" she asked, arching an eyebrow. "And what do you get out of this, Miss Morton?"

You mean, other than the chance to see your brothers more often? Jo thought, successfully keeping a smile off of her face.

"I'm living in a four bedroom house by myself," Jo replied. "My father just got sent to join the Asiatic Fleet, and it'd be nice to have someone to help with household chores."

"I have very little independent means," Patricia said. "I was hoping to find a job at the shipyard or someplace else suitable to my skills."

"What skills do you have for the shipyard?" Jo asked, befuddled.

"I worked for an architect for the past four years working on blueprints," Patricia replied. "I understand drafting ships' plans is similar work."

Jo shrugged.

"Got me, but I do know the library is looking for more staff. Seems that one of the girls up and ran off with a *Dauntless* pilot."

"I have never understood why some women are so fascinated with pilots," Patricia replied. "No offense to present company."

Sam and David both gave their little sister a hurt look.

"Yes, it's sort of like having a father in the Navy—I don't get impressed at the sight of men in summer whites, you probably don't find silk scarves anything other than a waste of cloth."

Patricia smiled at Jo's sarcastic tone.

"I think that your offer sounds quite nice, um, Jo," Patricia said. "Especially if you've managed to put up with my brothers this long without going mad."

"So why did we come to meet you at the dock, again?" Sam asked.

"Because you thought some random stranger might ravish me," Patricia replied simply. "Or that I'd fall in with villainous company due to a need for someone to help me with my luggage. Speaking of which, here are my chits."

Sam took the proffered claims forms, scanning them for a moment. Shaking his head, he turned to the other two.

"One would think Mom and Dad would have realized something was afoot when half their belongings disappeared. Nick, you go get the car—no need throwing our backs out."

Patricia sighed.

"If you look closer, oh dim-witted brother of mine, you will see that everything except for two chests of clothing and a container of housewares is due to arrive as a separate shipment. As to how I got everything out of the house, that will just remain my little secret."

"Like how you got the money to pull all of this off?" Nick asked *sotto voce* as he walked off. David and Sam moved off in the other direction, leaving Patricia and Jo standing alone at dockside.

"Have you always been able to get them to listen to you?" Jo asked.

Patricia smiled slightly.

"Only once I stopped being their tomboy shadow," she replied. "I think it's because I look so much like Mom now."

"Well, that and it's readily apparent they love their little sister," Jo observed.

Patricia's smile grew wider.

"Yes, that does help. Being the only girl does have its advantages."

JAMES YOUNG

"Like having your father wrapped around your finger so that he helps you escape Alabama?"

Patricia started, her smile immediately disappearing.

"How did you..?" she started, then stopped.

Jo grinned broadly.

"I'm an only child. I'm also Daddy's little girl. I know there's no way my father would let me marry an idiot or someone who was going to make me unhappy. From the way your brothers talk about your Dad, I think that applies for you also."

Patricia gave Jo an appraising glance.

"I think I understand why my brothers obviously like you," she said slowly.

"Yes, like the little sister they missed, not..." Jo started, then stopped with a blush.

That came out a little bit more bitter than I intended, Jo realized sheepishly.

"Not like you want them to?" Patricia finished for her.

"Well, Sam and Nick, yes," Jo replied, her face still heated. "I love Sadie."

"Ah, yes, the ever elusive Sadie. You know my mother is absolutely furious that David got engaged without her meeting his fiancée?"

"I heard that rumor somewhere," Jo allowed. "Might've been tied in with the Western Union lines melting down a couple weeks ago. I'm sure the telegram folks are going to get really, really familiar with your brothers as soon as your mother knows for sure you've turned up here."

"There are worse reasons to become familiar with the telegraph man," Patricia said, a flicker of worry crossing her face.

"Has there been any more word from Eric? The boys say all they know is that he's on the *Ranger* out in the Atlantic."

"No, none," Patricia replied. "I just hope he's all right."

"He's a Cobb," Jo replied. "Of course he's all right."

H.M.S. EXETER
NORTH ATLANTIC

1330 Local (1030 Eastern)
12 September

Whether or not Eric was all right was likely a matter of opinion. He wasn't flying anymore, as the weather conditions had started to become much worse since he'd left *Ranger*'s deck that morning. The base of the clouds had once again descended, and he estimated that the ceiling was well under ten thousand feet. At sea level, visibility was under ten miles, and an approaching squall promised to make it less than that very soon.

I don't blame the Brit pilots for nixing the thought of flying reconnaissance in this, Eric thought. *Yet for some reason I'd still rather take my chances in that soup than be on this ship right now. She's definitely going into harm's way, and fast.*

The heavy cruiser's deck throbbed beneath his feet, and the smoke pouring from her stack and stiff wind blowing onto her bridge told him that *Exeter* had definitely picked up speed.

"Sir, I've brought *Leftenant* Cobb," Adlich said, causing Captain Gordon to turn around. *Exeter*'s master had obviously been mollified by the worsening conditions, as he gave Eric a wry grin when the American officer stepped up beside him.

Whoa, it's cold out here, Eric thought. As if reading his mind, a petty officer handed him a jacket.

"We remove the windows when we're getting ready to go into action," the man said. "Lesson learned after River Plate."

"Thank you," Eric said. "I guess the windows would be a bit problematic in a fight."

The petty officer gave a wan smile, pointing to a scar down his cheek.

"Glass splinters are a bit sharp, yes."

"Your squadron commander was either a very brave man or a much better pilot than anyone I know," Gordon said solemnly from behind the ship's wheel.

Or alternatively, Commander Cobleigh was an idiot who didn't check with the meteorologist before we took off.

Eric was about to reply when the talker at the rear of the bridge interrupted him.

"Sir, *Hood* should be coming into visual range off of our port bow," the rating reported. "Range fifteen thousand yards."

"Thank you," Gordon replied. The captain then strode to the front of the bridge, stopping at a device that reminded Eric of the sightseeing binoculars atop the Empire State Building. Bending slightly, Gordon wiped down the eyepieces, then swiveled the binoculars to look through them.

"Officer of the deck," Gordon said after a moment.

"Yes, sir?" a Royal Navy lieutenant answered from Eric's right. Roughly Eric's height, the broad-shouldered man looked like he could probably snap a good-sized tree in half with his bare hands.

"Confirm with gunnery that the director's tracking *Hood*'s bearing to be three one zero, estimated range fourteen thousand, seven hundred fifty yards."

"Aye aye, sir," the officer replied. Eric heard the RN officer repeating the information as Gordon stepped back from the sight and turned to look at him.

"Well, if you want to see how the other half lives, *Leftenant* Cobb, feel free to have a look."

Eric hoped he didn't look as eager as he felt walking forward towards the bridge windows. Bending a little further to look through the sight, he pressed his face up against the eyepieces. Swinging the glasses, he found himself looking at the H.M.S. *Hood*, flagship of the Royal Navy. With her square bridge, four turrets, and rakish lines, the battlecruiser was a large, beautiful vessel that displaced over four times the *Exeter*'s tonnage. Black smoke poured from her stack, and her massive bow wave told Eric that she was moving at good speed.

"You can change the magnification with the switch under your right hand," Gordon said, startling Eric slightly. He followed the British master's advice, continuing until he could see the entire approaching British force as it closed. Destroyers were roughly one thousand yards in front of and to either side of the *Hood*. Behind her at one-thousand-yard intervals were two large vessels, either battleships or battlecruisers, with another one starting to exit the mist like some sort of great beast stirring from its cave. After a moment, Eric recognized the distinctive silhouette as that of a *Nelson*-class battleship.

"That is the *King George V*, *Prince of Wales*, and *Nelson* behind her. *Warspite* should be next."

Eric nodded at Gordon's statement, continuing to watch as the final battleship made its appearance. A moment later, Gordon starting to give orders to the helmsman. *Exeter*'s bow began to swing around to port, causing Eric to step back from the sight with a puzzled expression.

"We'll be passing between the destroyer screen and the *Hood* to take our place in line," Gordon said. Eric turned back to the device, continuing to study the British battleline. A few moments later, there was the crackle of the loudspeaker.

"All hands, this is the captain speaking," Gordon began. "Shortly we will be passing by the *Hood*. All available hands are to turn out topside to give three cheers for His Majesty. That is all."

Eric stepped back from the sight, his face clearly radiating his shock. Gordon smiled as he came back up towards the front of the bridge with the officer of the deck.

"The *King* is going into battle?" he asked incredulously. "Isn't that a bit..."

"Dangerous?" Gordon finished for him. "Yes, but much like your situation, circumstances precluded His Majesty's transfer to another vessel."

"What? That doesn't make any..."

"His Majesty was apparently aboard the *Hood* receiving a briefing from the First Sea Lord when the *Queen Mary* was torpedoed," Gordon said, his voice cold. "We were not expecting the German surface units to be as close as they were, and it was considered imprudent to stop the *Hood* with at least two confirmed submarines close about. Is that sufficient explanation to you, or would you like to continue questioning our tactics?"

Eric could tell he was straining his host's civility, but the enormity of what was at risk made him feel he had to say something.

"I'm no expert at surface tactics..."

"That much is obvious," Gordon snapped.

"...but the *Hood* is a battlecruiser," Eric finished in a rush. "While I didn't get a great look at the Germans before they shot up me and my commander, Rawles saw at least two battleships."

"Your concern is noted, *Leftenant* Cobb, but I think that you will see the *Hood* is a bit hardier than a dive bomber."

Okay, I'm just going to shut up now, Eric said. *I may have slept through a lot of history, but I seem to recall the last time British battlecruisers met German heavy guns it didn't go so well. A quote about there being problems with your "bloody ships" or something similar comes to mind.* The Battle of Jutland hadn't been that long ago, as evidenced by the *Warspite* still being a front-line unit. Eric sincerely hoped Gordon's confidence was well-placed.

"Sir, we are almost on the *Hood*," the officer of the deck interrupted. Eric turned and realized that the lead destroyer was indeed almost abreast the *Exeter*, with the *Hood* now a looming presence just beyond.

"The *Hood*, after her refit, is the most powerful warship in the world," Gordon continued, his voice a little less frigid. "The *Bismark* and *Tirpitz* have only recently gone through refit, while the *Scharnhorst* and *Gneisenau* have not been in the open ocean for almost six months. There should not be any major danger."

If you're looking around the room and you can't find the mark, guess what? ***You're*** *the mark*. Eric's father's words, an admonishment to always be suspicious of any situation that seemed too good to be true, came back to him with a cold feeling in his stomach.

The Germans would ***not*** *be out here unless they had a plan*, Eric continued thinking. *Somehow I think that, much like the Royal Air Force, the Royal Navy is about to receive a rude shock.*

"All right lads, three cheers for His Majesty," The loudspeaker crackled. "Hip...hip..."

As the *Exeter*'s crew yelled at the top of their lungs, Eric studied the *Hood* in passing. The two vessels were close enough that he could see a party of men in white uniforms standing on the battlecruiser's bridge and the extraordinarily large flag streaming from the *Hood*'s yardarm. Picking up a pair of binoculars resting on a shelf near the bridge's front lip, he focused on the pennant.

"That's the Royal Standard," Gordon said after the last cheer rang out. The device consisted of four squares, two red with the other pair gold and blue, respectively. The two red were identical, forming the top left and bottom right portions of the flag. Looking closely, Eric could see elongated gold lions or griffins within the squares. The gold square had what looked like a standing red lion within a crimson square, while the blue had some sort of harp.

"What do the symbols mean, sir?" Eric asked. Gordon shook his head.

"*Leftenant*, I could probably remember if I thought hard enough about it, but I do not think that is very important right now."

Eric nodded, placing the binoculars back down as the *Exeter* continued to travel down the battleline. After *Warspite*, there were two more British heavy cruisers. At Gordon's command, the *Exeter* finished her turn, taking her place behind the other two CAs. Satisfied with his vessel's stationing, Gordon began dealing with the myriad tasks that a warship's captain was expected to perform before battle. Eric observed these with a sense of detachment, noting that the bridge crew operated like they had been there dozens of times. Mentally, he compared the men to those he had observed aboard the American heavy cruiser *Salt Lake City*.

Things are so similar, yet so different. You can tell these men have been at war for over three years, Eric thought, feeling strangely comforted by the obvious experience in front of him. The feeling was fleeting, however, as the talker at the rear of the bridge broke the routine.

"Sir, *Hood* reports multiple contacts, bearing oh three oh relative, range thirty thousand yards," the talker at the rear of the bridge said. It was if his words touched off a current of electricity around the entire compartment, as each man seemed to stiffen at his post.

"Well, glad to see that she's got better eyes than we do," Gordon muttered under his breath. "Pass the word to all stations."

Eric saw motion out of the corner of his eye and turned to see the *Exeter*'s two forward turrets training out and elevating.

"Flag is directing a change in course to one seven zero true," the talker continued. "Vessels will turn in sequence. Destroyers are to form up for torpedo attack to our stern."

Gordon nodded in acknowledgment, and Eric could see the man was obviously in pensive thought. After their earlier exchange, Eric had no desire to attempt to discern what he was thinking. Judging from the look on the man's face, it was probably nothing good. Looking to port, Eric could see the British destroyers starting to steam past for their rendezvous astern of *Exeter*, a scene that was repeated a moment later on the starboard side.

Is it my imagination, or is it getting a little bit easier to see again? Eric thought. *If so, is that a good or a bad thing?*

"Enemy force is turning with us," the talker said quietly.

*Now **that** is definitely a bad thing.*

Eric had a very passing familiarity with radar, as he had been the target dummy for *Ranger*'s fighter squadron to practice aerial intercepts. It was obvious, given the visibility, that the *Hood* hadn't sighted the enemy with the naked eye. Unless the Germans had a team of gypsies on their vessels, it appeared that they also had the ability to detect ships despite the murk.

Explains how they were able to shoot down Commander Cobleigh, Eric thought, feeling sick to his stomach. *My God, they probably knew we were there long before we came out of the cloudbank but wanted to make positive identification.*

The visibility was definitely starting to get better, at least at sea level. With only the distance of the British line to judge by, Eric guesstimated that visibility to the horizon was somewhere around twenty thousand yards.

Well within maximum range of everyone's guns, he thought. *I hope someone on this side knows what size force we're facing, as I doubt the Germans are idiots.*

"Sir, the *Hood* reports she is..."

With a roar and spout of black smoke from her side, the British flagship made the talker's report superfluous. The rest of the British battleline rapidly followed suit, the combined smoke from their guns floating backward like roiling, black thunderheads.

I can't see what in the hell they're shooting at, Eric thought, searching the horizon as he felt his stomach clench.

IN TRUTH, *HOOD* AND HER COUNTERPARTS HAD ONLY A GENERAL idea of what they were engaging. Indeed, if the commander of the opposing force, Vice Admiral Erich Bey, had actually followed his orders to simply compel the Home Fleet to sail a relatively straight course while avoiding contact, there would have been no targets for them to engage. Instead, Bey had decided to close with the last known position of the Home Fleet in hopes of picking off the vessel or vessels the *Kriegsmarine*'s U-boats had allegedly crippled that morning. Regardless of his reasoning, Bey's aggressive nature had inadvertently led to his superiors' worst nightmare—the hastily organized Franco-German force being brought into contact with the far more experienced Royal Navy.

Admiral Bey, to his credit, played the hand he had dealt himself. Moments after *Hood*'s initial salvo landed short of his flagship, the KMS *Bismarck*, the German admiral began barking orders. The first was for the radar-equipped vessels in his fleet to return fire. The second was for the entire column to change course in order to sharpen the rate of closure and allow the Vichy French vessels, limited to visual acquisition, to also engage. The final directive was for a position report to be repeatedly sent without any encryption so that nearby U-boats could immediately set course in an attempt to pick off any stragglers.

"WELL, LOOKS LIKE THE OTHER SIDE IS GAME," CAPTAIN GORDON drily observed as multiple waterspouts appeared amongst the British battleships. A moment later the distant sound of the explosions reached Eric's ears.

"Looks like they're over-concentrating on the front of the line though," Eric observed.

Gordon turned to look at the American pilot.

"Would you prefer they spread their fire more evenly so we can have a taste, *Leftenant*?"

"No sir, not with the shells that are being slung out there."

Gordon brought his binoculars back up.

"Still can't see the enemy yet, but that's why the boffins were aboard during our refit," Gordon said. The man turned to his talker, jaw clenched.

"Tell Guns they may fire when we have visual contact or the enemy reaches nineteen thousand yards, whichever comes first," Gordon said, his voice clipped. "Inform bridge of the eventual target's bearing so we may get a look."

"Aye aye, Captain."

Gordon turned back towards Eric and opened his mouth when he was interrupted by the sound of ripping canvas followed by the *smack!* of four shells landing between *Exeter* and the next British cruiser in front of her. A moment later, a bell began ringing at the rear of *Exeter*'s bridge. Eric was about to ask what the device signified when the heavy cruiser's forward turrets roared, the blast hitting him like a physical blow. The look of shock was obviously quite apparent, as Gordon gave Eric an apologetic smile.

"Sorry, guess I should have..."

Exeter's captain was again interrupted, except this time by two bright flashes aboard the cruiser forward of her the British battleline. The other vessel was visibly staggered by the blows, with a fire immediately starting astern.

"Looks like *Suffolk* has worse luck than we do," Gordon observed grimly. The British heavy cruiser's turrets replied back towards the enemy, but it was obvious, even to Eric, that their companion vessel was badly hit.

"Guns reports target is at bearing two nine zero, range twenty thousand yards..."

The bell ringing cut the rating off, as it was followed immediately by the *Exeter* unleashing a full broadside. Gordon had already begun to swing his sight around to the reported bearing, and bent to see what his guns were up to. Eric, looking past the captain, saw *Suffolk* receive another hit, this one causing debris to fly up from the vicinity of her bridge. He suddenly felt his mouth go dry.

Someone has the range, he thought grimly.

"Bloody good show Guns!" Gordon shouted into the voice tube near his sight. "Give that bastard another…"

The firing gong rang again, *Exeter*'s gunnery officer apparently already ahead of Gordon. Eric braced himself, the roar of the naval rifles starting to cause a slight ringing in his ears. He turned to look towards the horizon, following the direction of *Exeter*'s guns.

"These will help," the officer of the deck said from beside him, handing him a pair of binoculars.

"Thank you," Eric said, turning towards the officer only to see the man go pale.

"Oh bloody hell! Look at the *Hood*!"

Eric turned and looked down the British line, noting as he turned that the *Suffolk* was heeling to *Exeter*'s starboard with flames shooting from her amidships and rear turret. Ignoring the heavily damaged heavy cruiser, he brought up his binoculars as he looked towards the front of the British line. In an instant, he could see why the officer of the deck had made his exclamation. The battlecruiser's guns appeared frozen in place, and oil was visibly gushing from her amidships. As Eric watched, another salvo splashed around her, with a sudden flare and billow of smoke from her stern indicating something serious had been hit.

"Captain, the *Hood* is signaling a power failure!" the officer of the deck shouted. Eric turned to see the man had acquired another set of eyeglasses and was also studying the flagship.

Gordon nodded, stepping back from his captain's sight and brought his own set of binoculars up to study the battlecruiser. Eric quickly handed his over before the OOD could react.

"It would appear that our Teutonic friends can shoot a bit better than we expected," Gordon said grimly.

ADMIRAL BEY WOULD HAVE AGREED WITH GORDON'S ASSESSMENT had he heard it, as he too was pleasantly surprised at how well his scratch fleet was performing. Unfortunately for the Germans, however, the British could shoot almost as well, their guns seemed to be doing far more damage, and they had much better fire distribution. The only

British capital ships with major damage were the *Hood*, set ablaze and rendered powerless by the *Tirpitz* and *Jean Bart*, and *Nelson* due to hits from the *Bismarck* and *Strasbourg*. Among the cruisers, only the *Suffolk* had been hit, being thoroughly mauled by the KMS *Hipper* and *Lutzow*. In exchange, only the *Jean Bart, Gneisenau,* and *Bismarck* remained relatively unscathed among his battleline. Of the rest of his vessels, the French battlecruiser *Strasbourg* had been thoroughly holed by the H.M.S. *Warspite*'s accurate shooting, *Tirpitz* was noticeably down by the bows, and *Scharnhorst* had received at least two hits from *Prince of Wales* in the first ten minutes of the fight.

Bey's escorts, consisting of the pocket battleship *Lutzow* and a force of German and Vichy French cruisers, had arranged themselves in an *ad hoc* screen to starboard. The fact that they outnumbered their British counterparts had not spared them from damage, albeit not as heavy as that suffered by the Franco-German battleline. Moreover, while *Exeter*'s shooting had set the lead vessel, the French heavy cruiser *Colbert*, ablaze and slowed her, this was more than offset by the battering the *Suffolk* had received from the *Lutzow, Hipper*, and *Seydlitz*. As that vessel fell backward in the British formation, the remaining cruisers split their fire between the *Exeter, Norfolk*, and the destroyers beginning their attack approach.

Word of the British DDs' approach caused Bey some consternation. While it could be argued that his force was evenly matched with the British battleline, the approaching destroyers could swiftly change this equation if they got into torpedo range. Deciding that discretion was the better part of valor, Bey ordered all vessels to make smoke and disengage. It was just after the force began their simultaneous turn that disaster struck.

The KMS *Scharnhorst*, like the *Hood*, had begun life as a battlecruiser. While both she and her sister had been upgraded during the Armistice Period with 15-inch turrets, the *Kriegsmarine* had made the conscious decision not to upgrade her armor. The folly of this choice became readily apparent as the *Prince of Wales*' twentieth salvo placed a pair of 14-inch shells through her amidships belt. While neither shell fully detonated, their passage severed the steering controls between the light battleship's bridge and rudder.

The *Scharnhorst*'s helmsman barely had time to inform the captain of this before the second half of *PoW*'s staggered salvo arrived, clearing the battleship's bridge with one shell and and hitting *Scharnhorst* on the armored "turtle deck" right above her engineering spaces with a second. To many bystanders' horror, a visible gout of steam spewed from the vessel's side as all 38,000 tons of her staggered like a stunned bull. Only the fact that her 15-inch guns fired a ragged broadside back at the British line indicated that the vessel still had power, but it was obvious to all that she had been severely hurt.

One of those observers was the captain of the KMS *Gneisenau*, *Scharnhorst*'s sister ship and the next battleship in line. Confronted with the heavily wounded *Scharnhorst* drifting back towards him, the man ordered the helm brought back hard to starboard. In one of the horrible vagaries of warfare, the *Gneisenau* simultaneously masked her sister ship from the *Prince of Wales'* fire and corrected the aim of her own assailant, the H.M.S. *Nelson*. No one would ever know how many 16-inch shells hit of the five that had been fired at the *Gneisenau*, as the only one that mattered was the one that found the German battleship's forward magazine. With a massive roar, bright flash, and volcanic outpouring of flame, the *Gneisenau*'s bow disappeared. *Scharnhorst* and *Jean Bart*'s horrified crews were subjected to the spectacle of the *Gneisenau*'s stern whipping upwards, propellers still turning. The structures only glistened for a moment, as the battleship's momentum carried her aft end into the roiling black cloud serving as a tombstone for a 40,000-ton man-of-war and the 1,700 men who manned her.

"Holy shit! Holy shit!" Eric exclaimed, his expletives lost in the general pandemonium that was *Exeter*'s bridge.

"Get yourselves together!" Gordon roared, waving his hands. As if to emphasize his point, there was the sound of ripping canvas, and a moment later, the *Exeter* found herself surrounded by large waterspouts.

"Port ten degrees!" Gordon barked, the bridge crew quickly returning to their tasks.

"Sir, *Nelson* is signaling that she is heaving to!"

"What in the bloody hell is the matter with her?!" Gordon muttered, a moment before *Exeter*'s guns roared again.

"Guns reports we are engaging and being engaged by a pocket battleship. He believes it is the..." the talker reported.

Once again there was the sound of ripping canvas, this time far louder. Eric instinctively ducked just before the *Exeter* shuddered simultaneously with the loud *bang!* just above their heads. Dimly, he saw something fall out of the corner of his eye even as there was a sound like several wasps all around him. Coming back to his feet, Eric smelled the strong aroma of explosives for the second time that day, except this time there was a man screaming like a shot rabbit to accompany it.

"Damage report!" Gordon shouted. "Someone shut that man up!"

Feeling something wet on his face, Eric reached up to touch it and came away with blood. He frantically reached up to feel if he had a wound, and only came away with more blood. Looking around in horror, he suddenly realized that the blood was not his, but that of a British rating who was now missing half of his head, neck, and upper chest. Eric barely had time to register this before a litter crew came bursting into the bridge. The four men headed to the aft portion of the structure, obviously there for the man who had been screaming before a gag had been shoved in his mouth. Eric followed the litter team's path, then immediately wished he hadn't as his stomach lurched. The casualty's abdomen was laid open, and Eric saw the red and grey of intestine on the deck before turning back forward.

Oh God, he thought, then had another as he thought about the injured man's likely destination. *I hope Rawles is okay.*

"Hard a starboard!" Gordon barked. Eric braced himself as the *Exeter* heeled over, the vessel chasing the previous salvo as her guns roared back at the German pocket battleship. He noticed that the guns were starting to bear even further aft as the cruiser maneuvered to keep up with the remainder of the British battleline. Looking to starboard, Eric saw the battleship *Nelson* drifting past them on her starboard side. The vessel's forward-mounted triple turrets, still elevated to port, fired off a full salvo once *Exeter* was past, but it was clear that the battleship had suffered severe damage.

"Sir, we took one glancing hit to the bridge roof," the OOD reported, pointing at the hit that had sprayed splinters into the structure. Eric was amazed at the man's calm. "We took another hit aft, but it detonated in the galley."

"*King George V* signals commence torpedo attack with destroyers," the talker interrupted. "All ships with tubes to attack enemy cripples."

Six waterspouts impacted approximately three hundred yards to port, and Eric found himself questioning the wisdom of staying aboard the heavy cruiser after all.

"Well, looks like this ship will continue her tradition of picking on women bigger than her," Gordon observed drily. "Flank speed, port thirty degrees. Get me the torpedo flat."

Eric looked once again at the hole in the bridge roof.

A step either way and I'd probably be dead, he thought wildly. *Or worse, if that shell had it full on we'd all be gone.* Shaking his head, he turned to look off to port as the throb of *Exeter*'s engines began to increase.

"You ever participate in a torpedo attack during your summer cruise, Mr. Cobb?" Gordon asked after barking several orders to the helm.

"No sir," Eric croaked, then swallowed to get a clearer voice. "Our cruisers don't have torpedoes. I'm familiar with how to do one theoretically..."

Exeter's guns banged out another salvo, even as the German pocket battleship's return fire landed where she would have been had the cruiser continued straight.

"Well, looks like you're about to get to apply some of that theoretical knowledge," Gordon said, bringing his binoculars up. The man scanned the opposing line.

"The three big battleships are turning away under cover of smoke along with the majority of the cruisers. That Frog battlecruiser looks about done for, and that pocket battleship and heavy cruiser will soon have more than enough to deal with when the destroyers catch up," Gordon said, pointing as he talked. *Exeter*'s master turned to give his orders.

"Tell Lieutenant Commander Gannon his target is the pocket battleship! Guns are to…"

The crescendo of incoming shells drowned Gordon out, this time ending with the *Exeter* leaping out of the water and shuddering as she was hit. Once again the bridge wing was alive with fragments, and for the second time Eric felt a splash of wetness across his side. Looking down, he saw his entire left side was covered in blood and flesh. For a moment he believed it was his, until he blissfully realized that he felt no pain.

"Damage report!" Gordon shouted again. "Litter party!"

"Sir, I believe I am hit," the OOD gasped. Eric turned to see the man's arm missing from just below the elbow, blood spraying from the severed stump.

"Corpsman!" Gordon shouted angrily, stepping towards the lieutenant. The captain never made, it, as the OOD toppled face forward, revealing jagged wounds in his back where splinters had blasted into his body.

"Helmsman! Zig zag pattern!" Gordon barked. "Someone get me a damage report! Midshipman Green, inform damage control that we need another talker and an OOD here!"

"Aye aye, Captain!"

"*Leftenant* Cobb!"

"Yes sir?" Eric asked, shaking himself out of stupor.

"It might be prudent for you to go to the conning tower," Gordon said.

"Sir, I'd prefer to be here than in some metal box," Eric said. "With the shells that bastard's tossing it won't make a lick of difference anyway."

"Too true," Gordon said. "Looks like the heavy cruisers and that pocket battleship are covering the bastards' retreat."

Gordon's supposition was only partially correct. In truth, the pocket battleship *Lutzow* had received damage from the *Exeter* and *Norfolk* that had somewhat reduced her maximum speed. This had prevented her from fleeing with the rest of the screen, their retirement encouraged by a few salvoes from the *Nelson*. Realizing that she could not escape the closing British destroyers, *Lutzow*'s captain had decided to turn and engage the smaller vessels in hopes of allowing *Scharnhorst* to open the distance between herself and the British. Unfortunately, *Lutzow* had failed to inform the heavy cruiser KMS *Hipper*, trailing in her wake, of her desire to self-sacrifice while ignoring Admiral Bey's signal to retire. Thus the latter vessel, her radio aerial knocked out by an over salvo from the *Nelson*'s secondary batteries, found herself committed to engaging the rapidly closing British destroyers along with the larger, crippled *Lutzow*.

The British destroyers, formed into two divisions under the experienced Commodore Philip Vian, first overtook the damaged French battlecruiser *Strasbourg*. Adrift, afire, and listing heavily to port, the *Strasbourg* wallowed helplessly as the British destroyers closed like hyenas on a paralyzed wildebeest. Just as Vian was beginning to order his group into their battle dispositions, flooding finally compromised the battlecruiser's stability. With a rumble and the scream of tortured metal, the *Strasbourg* rotated onto her starboard beam and slipped beneath the surface.

That left the crippled *Scharnhorst*, the *Lutzow*, and the hapless *Hipper*. Still receiving desultory fire from *Nelson* and *Warspite*, the trio of German vessels initially concentrated their fire on the charging *Exeter* and *Norfolk*. After five minutes of this, all three German captains realized Vian's approaching destroyers were a far greater threat. The *Lutzow* and *Hipper* turned to lay smoke across the retreating *Scharnhorst*'s stern, the maneuver also allowing both vessels to fire full broadsides at their smaller assailants. The *Hipper* had just gotten off her second salvo when she received a pair of 8-inch shells from the *Norfolk*. The first glanced off the heavy cruiser's armor belt and fell harmlessly into the sea. The second, however, impacted the main director, blowing the gunnery officer and most of the cruiser's gunnery department into disparate parts that splashed into the sea or onto the deck below. For two crucial minutes, the *Hipper*'s main battery remained silent even as her secondaries began to take the approaching British destroyers under fire.

• • •

THE RESPITE FROM *LUTZOW*'S FIRE HAD ARRIVED JUST IN TIME FOR *Exeter*, as the pocket battleship had been consistently finding the range. Staggering to his feet after another exercise in throwing himself flat, Eric looked forward to see just where the heavy cruiser had been hit this time. His gaze fell upon the devastation that had been *Exeter*'s "B" turret, where a cloud of acrid yellow was smoke pouring back from the structure's opened roof to pass around the heavy cruiser's bridge. Damage control crews were rushing forward to spray hoses upon the burning guns, even as water began to crash over the cruiser's lowering bow.

"Very well then, flood the magazine!" Gordon was shouting into the speaking tube. "Tell the *Norfolk* we shall follow her in as best we can."

Looking to starboard, Eric could see the aforementioned heavy cruiser starting to surge ahead of *Exeter*, smoke pouring from her triple stacks and her forward turrets firing another salvo towards the *Hipper*.

"We are only making twenty-three knots, sir," the helmsman reported.

"Damage control reports heavy flooding in the bow," the talker stated. "Lieutenant Ramses states we must slow our speed or we may lose another bulkhead."

Gordon's face set in a grim line.

"Torpedoes reports a solution on the pocket battleship," the talker reported after pausing or a moment.

"Range?!" Gordon barked.

"Ten thousand yards and closing."

"Tell me when we're at four thousand..."

The seas around the *Exeter* suddenly leaped upwards, the waterspouts clearing her mainmast.

"Enemy battleship is taking us under fire!"

Looking over at *Norfolk*, Eric saw an identical series of waterspouts appear several hundred yards ahead of their companion.

"Two enemy battleships engaging, range twenty-two thousand yards."

"Where's our battleline?" Gordon asked bitterly. "Report the news to the *King George V*."

Another couple of minutes passed, the *Exeter* continuing to close with the turning *Lutzow*. Four more shells exploded around the *Exeter*.

"The *Nelson* is disengaging due to opening range," the talker replied. "The remaining ships are closing our position to take the enemy battleship under fire."

Again there was the sound of an incoming freight train, and the *Exeter* was straddled once more, splinters ringing off the opposite side of the bridge.

"Corpsman!" a lookout shouted from the crow's nest.

Okay, someone stop this ride, I want to get off, Eric thought, bile rising in his throat.

"Commodore Vian reports he is closing."

"Right then, continue to attack!" Gordon shouted. Eric winced, convinced he was going to die.

UNBEKNOWNST TO ERIC, THE *BISMARCK* AND *TIRPITZ* HAD ONLY returned to persuade the British battleline to not pursue the *Scharnhorst*. Finding the two British heavy cruisers attacking, Bey had decided some 15-inch fire was necessary to discourage their torpedo run as well. In the worsening seas the German battleships' gunnery left much to be desired, but still managed to force the *Exeter* and *Norfolk* to both intensify their zig zags.

Unfortunately for the Germans, the decision to concentrate on the heavy cruisers meant that Commodore Vian's destroyers had an almost undisturbed attack run. Vian, realizing that he would not be able to bypass the aggressively counterattacking *Hipper*, split his force into two parts. The lead division, led by himself in *Somali*, continued after the crippled *Scharnhorst*. The second, led by the destroyer *Echo*, he directed to attack the *Hipper* in hopes that the heavy cruiser would turn away.

The German heavy cruiser reacted as Vian had expected, switching all of her fire to the approaching *Echo* group. For their part, the British ships dodged as they closed, the *Echo*'s commander making the decision to close the range so that the destroyers could launch their torpedoes with a higher speed setting. Seeing the German cruiser starting to turn, *Echo*'s commander signaled for his own vessel, *Eclipse*, and *Encounter* to attempt to attack from her port side, while the *Faulknor* and *Electra* were to move up to attack from starboard.

Discerning the British destroyerman's plan, *Hipper*'s captain immediately laid on his maximum speed while continuing his turn towards port. Ignoring those vessels attempting to move in on her starboard side, the German vessel turned her guns wholly on the trio of British destroyers that was now at barely seven thousand yards. With a combined closing speed of almost seventy knots, there was less than a minute before the British destroyers were at their preferred range. In this time, *Hipper* managed to get off two salvoes with her main guns and several rounds from her secondary guns. Her efforts were rewarded, the *Echo* being hit and stopped by two 8-inch and four secondary shell hits before she could fire her torpedoes. That still left the *Eclipse* and *Encounter*, both which fired their torpedoes at 4,000 yards before starting to turn away. The latter vessel had just concluded putting her eighth torpedo into the water when the *Hipper*'s secondaries switched to her as a target, knocking out the destroyer's forward guns.

Pursuing the *Hipper* as the German cruiser continued to turn to port, the *Faulknor* and *Electra* initially had a far longer run than their compatriots. However, as the German cruiser came about to comb the *Echo* group's torpedoes, the opportunity arose for the two more nimble vessels to cut across her turn. Hitting the heavy cruiser with several 4.7-inch shells even as they zigzagged through the *Lutzow*'s supporting fire, the two destroyers unleashed their sixteen torpedoes from the *Hipper*'s port bow. Belatedly, the German captain realized that he had placed himself in a horrible position, as he could not turn to avoid the second group of torpedoes without presenting a perfect target to the first.

It was the *Eclipse* which administered the first blow. Coming in at a fine angle, one of the destroyer's torpedoes exploded just below the *Hipper*'s port bow. The heavy cruiser's hull whipsawed from the impact, the explosion peeling twenty feet of her skin back to act as a massive brake. The shock traveled down the vessel's length, throwing circuit breakers out of their mounts in her generator room and rendering the

Hipper powerless. Looking to starboard, the vessel's bridge crew could only helplessly watch as the British torpedoes approached from that side. In a fluke of fate, the braking effect from *Eclipse*'s hit caused the heavy cruiser to lose so much headway the majority of the tin fish missed. The pair that impacted, however, could not have been better placed. With two roaring waterspouts in close succession, the *Hipper*'s engineering spaces were opened to the sea. Disemboweled, the cruiser continued to slow even as she rolled to starboard. Realizing instantly her wounds were fatal, the *Hipper*'s captain gave the order to abandon ship. The order came far too late for most of the crew, as the 12,000-ton man-o-war capsized and slid under the Atlantic in a matter of minutes.

"WELL, THE DESTROYERS JUST PUT PAID TO THAT HEAVY CRUISER! Let's see if we can get a kill of our own!" Gordon said, watching the drama unfolding roughly twelve thousand yards to his west. Another salvo of 15-inch shells landed to *Exeter*'s starboard, this broadside somewhat more ragged due to the heavy cruiser's zig zagging advance.
"Battleships are returning to aid us."
"About bloody time!" Gordon snapped.

WHEN THE *WARSPITE*'S FIRST SALVO LANDED JUST AFT OF *JEAN BART*, Admiral Bey had more than enough. Signaling rapidly, he ordered the *Scharnhorst* and *Lutzow* to cover the remainder of the force's retreat. Firing a few desultory broadsides, the Franco-German force reentered the mists.

ERIC WATCHED THROUGH HIS BINOCULARS AS *LUTZOW* GAMELY attempted to follow Bey's orders, slowly coming about so she could continue to engage the destroyers closing with *Scharnhorst*. Barely making fifteen knots, the pocket battleship was listing slightly to port and down by the bows. Just as *Lutzow* finished her turn, several shells landed close astern of the German vessel.

"*King George V* is engaging the pocket battleship."

"Good. Maybe she can slow that witch down so we can catch her."

"*Warspite* and *Prince of Wales* are switching to the closest battleship."

Gordon nodded his ascent, continuing to watch as *Lutzow* attempted to begin a zig zag pattern.

"Destroyers are running the gauntlet," Gordon observed drily, pointing to where the *Lutzow* was engaging the five destroyers passing barely eight thousand yards in front of her. Eric nodded grimly, then brought his attention back to *Lutzow* just in time to see the *King George V*'s next salvo arrive. Two of the British 14-inch shells slashed into the pocket battleship's stern, while a third impacted on the vessel's aft turret with devastating effect. Eric was glad that *Exeter* was still far enough away that he could not identify the contents of the debris that flew upwards from the gunhouse in the gout of smoke and flame, as the young American was sure some of the dark spots were bodies.

"Looks like you got your wish, sir," Eric observed as the *Lutzow* began to continue a lazy circle to port. There was a sharp crack as the *Exeter*'s secondary batteries began to engage the pocket battleship, leading to a disgusted look from Gordon.

"Tell Guns we may need that ammunition later," he snapped. "I'm not sure those guns will do any damage, plus she's almost finished."

I was wondering what good 4-inch guns would do to a pocket battleship, Eric thought. *Especially when* **Norfolk** *is pounding away with her main battery and a battleship has her under fire.*

"*King George V* is inquiring if we can finish her with torpedoes?"

Gordon looked at the pocket battleship, now coming to a stop with fires clearly spreading.

"Report that yes, we will close and finish her with torpedoes, she may assist in bringing that battleship to bay," *Exeter*'s master stated.

"*Norfolk* is firing torpedoes," the talker reported.

Eric brought up his binoculars, focusing on the clearly crippled *Lutzow*. As he watched, one of the German's secondary turrets fired a defiant shot at *Norfolk*. Scanning the vessel from bow to stern, Eric wondered if the gun was the sole thing left operational, as the pocket battleship's upper decks were a complete shambles. Looking closely at the *Lutzow*'s forward turret, he could see two jagged holes in its rear where *Norfolk*'s broadsides had impacted. The bridge was similarly damaged, with wisps of smoke pouring from the shattered windows, and the German vessel's entire amidships was ablaze. The vessel's list appeared to have lessened, but she was clearly much lower in the water.

"Should be any time now," Gordon said, briefly looking at his watch. "Tell guns to belay my last, we're not wasting any more fish on her than necessary."

Eric turned back to watching the *Lutzow*, observing as *Norfolk* hit the vessel with another point blank salvo an instant before her torpedoes arrived. Given that the *Lutzow* was a stationary target, Eric was surprised to see *Norfolk*'s torpedo spread produce only a pair of hits. It was still enough, as with an audible groan the *Lutzow*'s already battered hull split just aft of her destroyed turret. Five minutes later, as *Exeter* drew within five hundred yards and Eric could see German sailors jumping into the sea, the *Lutzow* gave a final shuddering metallic rattle then slipped stern first into the depths.

"Stand by to rescue survivors," Gordon said, dropping his binoculars. "How are the destroyers doing with that battleship?"

THE ANSWER TO GORDON'S QUESTION COULD BE SUMMED UP WITH two words: very well. The *Scharnhorst* had briefly managed to work up to sixteen knots, and had *Lutzow*'s fire been somewhat more accurate, may have managed to escape the pursuing destroyers. However, as with the *Hipper*, Vian's destroyers split into two groups even as *Scharnhorst*'s secondaries increased their fire. Another pair of hits from *Prince of Wales* slowed the German light battleship even further, and at that point the handful of tin cans set upon her like a school of sharks on a lamed blue whale.

Like that large creature, however, even a crippled the *Scharnhorst* still had means to defend herself. As the *Punjabi* closed in from starboard, the battleship's Caesar turret scored with a single 15-inch shell. The effects were devastating, the destroyer being converted from man-of-war to charnel house forward of her bridge. Amazingly,

Punjabi's powerplant was undamaged by the blast, and the destroyer was able to continue closing the distance between herself and the larger German vessel. The timely arrival of a salvo from *Warspite* sufficiently distracted the *Scharnhorst*'s gunnery officer, preventing him from getting the range again until after both groups of destroyers were close enough to launch torpedoes.

Severely damaged, *Scharnhorst* still attempted to ruin the destroyers' fire control problem at the last moment. To Commodore Vian's intense frustration, the battleship's captain timed his maneuver perfectly, evading twelve British torpedoes simply by good seamanship. Had *Scharnhorst* had her full maneuvering ability, she may have then been able to pull off the maneuver *Hipper* had attempted by reversing course. Whereas geometry and numbers had failed the German heavy cruiser, simple physics served to put the waterlogged battleship in front of three torpedoes. Even then, her luck remained as the first hit, far forward, was a dud. Then, proving Fate was indeed fickle, two fish from the damaged *Punjabi* ran deep and hit the vessel just below her armored belt. Finishing the damage done by *Prince of Wales'* hits earlier, the torpedoes knocked out the German capital ship's remaining power and opened even more of her hull to the sea. Realizing she was doomed, her captain ordered the crew to set scuttling charges and abandon ship.

"KING GEORGE V IS INQUIRING IF ANY VESSELS HAVE TORPEDOES remaining."

Gordon gave the talker a questioning look.

"I thought Commodore Vian just reported that the enemy battleship appears to be sinking?" Gordon said, his voice weary. "No matter, inform *King George V* that we have all of our fish remaining."

Wonder what in the hell that is about? Eric thought. Looking down, he realized his hands were starting to shake. Taking a deep breath, he attempted to calm himself.

Well, this has been a rather...interesting day. I just wish someone would have told me I'd get shot down, see my squadron leader killed, and participate in a major sea battle when I got up at 0300 this morning.

"*Leftenant* Cobb, are you all right?" Gordon asked, concerned.

Eric choked back the urge to laugh at the question.

"I'm fine sir, just a little cold," he said, lying through his teeth. The talker saved him from further inquisition.

"*King George V* is ordering us to come about and close with her. She is also ordering Commodore Vian to rescue survivors from *Punjabi* then scuttle her if she is unable to get under way. *Norfolk* is being ordered to stand by to assist *Nelson*."

"What about the Germans?" Gordon asked.

"Flag has ordered that all other recovery operations are to cease."

There was dead silence on *Exeter*'s bridge.

"Very well then, guess the Germans will have to come back for their own. Let's go see what *King George V* has for us," Gordon said.

Eric was struck by just how far the running fight had ranged as the *Exeter* reversed course. From the first salvo to the current position, the vessels had covered at least thirty miles. The *King George V* was a distant dot to the south, with her sister ship and *Warspite* further behind.

No one is going to find any of those survivors, Eric thought. *Especially with this weather starting to get worse*. He could smell imminent rain on the wind, and even with *Exeter*'s considerable size he could feel the ocean's movement starting to change.

"I hope this isn't about to become too bad of a blow," Gordon observed, looking worriedly out at the lowering sky. "Not with the flooding we have forward."

"If you don't mind, sir, I'd like to avoid going swimming again today," Eric quipped.

"Wouldn't be a swim lad. If we catch a big wave wrong, she would plow right under," Gordon replied grimly. "What has got *King George V* in such a tussy? She's coming at us full speed."

Eric looked up and saw that the battleship was indeed closing as rapidly as possible. As she hove into visual range several minutes later, the *King George V*'s signaling searchlight began flashing rapidly.

. . .

DO YOU READ THIS MESSAGE? DO YOU READ THIS MESSAGE?

"Acknowledge," Gordon said. A few moments later Eric could hear the heavy cruiser's signal crew employing the bridge lamp to respond to the *King George V*.

YOU WILL PROCEED TO *HOOD*. ONCE ALL SURVIVORS ARE OFFBOARD, YOU ARE TO SCUTTLE.

"What in the bloody hell is that idiot talking about?" Gordon exploded. He did not have time to send a counter message, as the *King George V* continued after a short pause.

YOU HAVE TWENTY-FIVE MINUTES TO REJOIN. FORCE WILL PROCEED WITHOUT YOU IF NOT COMPLETE. TOVEY SENDS GOD SAVE THE QUEEN

"God save the...*oh my God*!" Gordon said.

Eric looked at the *Exeter*'s captain with some concern as the man staggered backward, his face looking as if he had been personally stricken.

"Ask," Gordon began, the word nearly coming out as a sob before he regained his composure. "Ask if I may inform the ship's company of our task?"

Three minutes later, the *King George V* replied.

AFFIRMATIVE. EXPEDITE. HER MAJESTY'S SAFETY IS THIS COMMAND'S PRIMARY GOAL.

. . .

"Acknowledge. Hand me the loudspeaker," Gordon said, his voice incredibly weary. Eric could see tears welling in the man's eyes.

This is not good, Eric thought. *This is not good at all.* Although he was far from an expert on British government, he dimly remembered seeing a newsreel when *Ranger* had been in port where the Royal Family had been discussed. He felt his stomach starting to drop as he began to process what the *King George V* had just stated.

"All hands, this is the captain speaking," Gordon began. "This vessel is proceeding to stand by the *Hood* to rescue survivors. It appears that His Majesty has been killed."

Holy shit, Eric thought. *Isn't Princess...no,* **Queen** *Elizabeth barely sixteen?*

Eric looked around the bridge as the captain broke the news to the *Exeter*'s crew. The reactions ranged from shock to, surprisingly, rage. As *Exeter*'s master finished, the young American had the feeling he was seeing the start of something very, very ugly for the Germans.

I would hate to be someone who got dragged out of the water today, he thought. *That is, if* **any** *Germans get saved.* Eric's father had fought as a Marine at Belleau Wood. In the weeks before Eric had left for the academy, his father had made sure that his son understood just what might be required of him in the Republic's service. One of the stories had involved what had befallen an unfortunate German machine gun crew when the men tried to surrender after killing several members of the elder Cobb's platoon. Realizing the parallels to his current situation given the news he had just heard, Eric fought the urge to scowl.

Looks like you don't need a rope for a lynch mob, Eric thought as he reflected on the "necessity" of leaving the German and French sailors to drown. He was suddenly shaken out of his reverie by the sound of singing coming from below the bridge.

"*Happy and glorious...long to reign over us...*"

The men on the bridge began taking up the song, their tone somber and remorseful.

"*GOD SAAAAVEEE THE QUEEEEENN!!*"

. . .

ALMOST A HALF HOUR LATER, THE *EXETER* SAT ONE THOUSAND YARDS off of the *Hood*'s starboard side, the heavy cruiser's torpedo tubes trained on her larger consort. The *Hood*'s wounds were obvious, her bridge and conning tower a horribly twisted flower of shattered steel. Flames licked from the vessel's X turret, and it appeared that the structure had taken a heavy shell to its roof. Further casting a pall on the scene was the dense black smoke pouring from the *Hood*'s burning bunkerage, a dull glow at the base of the cloud indicating an out of control fire. The battlecruiser's stern looked almost awash, her bow almost coming out of the water with each swell, and as Eric watched there was an explosion of ready ammunition near her anti-aircraft guns.

Might be a waste of good torpedoes at this point, Eric thought. He realized he was starting to pass into mental shock from all the carnage he had seen that day.

"I'm the last man, sir," a dazed-looking commander with round features, black hair, and green eyes was saying to Captain Gordon. "At least, the last man we can get to."

"I understand, Commander Keir," Gordon said quietly. "I regret we do not have the time to try and free the men trapped in her engineering spaces."

"If we could have only had another hour, we might have saved her," Keir said, his voice breaking. It was obvious the man had been through hell, his uniform blackened by soot and other stains that Eric didn't care to look into too closely.

It's never a good day when you become commander of a vessel simply because no one else was left. From what he understood, Keir had started the day as chief of *Hood*'s Navigation Division. That had been before the vessel took at least three 15-inch shells to the bridge area, as well as two more that had wiped out her gunnery directory and the secondary bridge.

Captain Gordon was right—she was a very powerful warship. Unfortunately that tends to make you a target.

"Commander, you are *certain* that..." Gordon started, then collected himself. "You are *certain* His Majesty is dead."

"Yes sir," Keir said. "His Majesty was in the conning tower with Admiral Pound when it was hit. The Royal Surgeon positively identified His Majesty's body in the aid station before that was hit in turn. We cannot get to the aid station due to the spreading fire."

"Understood. His Majesty would not have wanted any of you to risk his life for his body," Gordon said.

"I just..." Keir started, then stopped, overcome with emotion.

"It is not your fault lad," Gordon said. "Her Majesty will understand."

Gordon turned and looked at the *Exeter*'s clock.

"Very well, we are out of time. Stand by to fire torpedoes."

"Torpedoes report they are ready."

"Sir, you may want to tell your torpedo officer to have his weapons set to run deep," Keir said. "She's drawing..."

There was a large explosion aboard *Hood* as the flames reached a secondary turret's ready ammunition. Eric saw a fiery object arc slowly across, descending towards the *Exeter* as hundreds of helpless eyes watched it. The flaming debris' lazy parabola terminated barely fifty yards off of *Exeter*'s side with a large, audible splash.

"I think we do not have time for that discussion," Gordon said grimly. "Fire torpedoes!"

The three weapons from *Exeter*'s starboard tubes sprang from their launchers into the water. Set as a narrow spread, the three tracks seemed to take forever to impact from Eric's perspective. *Exeter*'s torpedo officer, observing *Hood*'s state, had taken into account the battlecruiser's lower draught without having to be told. Indeed, he had almost set the weapons for too deep a run, but was saved by the flooding that had occurred in the previous few minutes. In addition to breaking the battlecruiser's keel, the triple blow opened the entire aft third of her port side to the ocean. With the audible sound of twisting metal, *Hood* started to roll onto her beam ends. She never completed the evolution before slipping beneath the waves.

JAMES YOUNG

2
AFTERMATH

We should never despair, our Situation before has been unpromising and has changed for the better; so I trust, it will again. If new difficulties arise, we must only put forth New Exertions and proportion our efforts to the exigency of the times.

— **GEORGE WASHINGTON**

Cape Town, South Africa
0700 Local (0100 Eastern)
26 September

"Well now I know things have gone to Hell," a familiar voice said from just behind Adam. "There are bloody Americans here, and Lord knows they always portend something very, very bad."

Adam whipped around from his breakfast so quickly he nearly fell out of his chair. Stumbling to his feet, he made sure the speaker was whom he thought it was, taking in the man's tall, lanky frame and sandy brown hair before wrapping him in a giant bearhug.

"Braddon Overgaard, how in the hell are you doing?!" he asked.

"Pull up a chair. I was just finishing breakfast, courtesy of His...*Her* Majesty's government."

"Yes, it is a bit difficult to change that, isn't it? Although, if certain individuals get their way you may be reverting back to what you started to say," Overgaard replied.

Adam stopped, fork halfway to his mouth.

"What? I sort of thought that line of succession thing was pretty set," the American said.

Overgaard had a seat at the table across from Adam.

"You can tell that you have been stuck aboard some tub for the past two weeks," Overgaard said.

"Hell, we hadn't even heard about the Battle of the Regicide until we were a couple hours out from harbor yesterday," Adam said. "What the hell else has happened?"

"The Duke of Windsor has returned to London."

Adam recognized the title but was not immediately able to recall why that was important. Seeing his perplexed look, Overgaard saved him the trouble.

"The Duke of Windsor is also known as King Edward," the South African officer said quietly.

Adam raised an eyebrow.

"I must confess I do not completely understand the Royal Family despite spending the last nine months in its employ," Adam said carefully. "Didn't he abdicate the throne because he had a similar problem to King David?"

Overgaard gave a thin smile.

"While I am sure Ms. Simpson would be flattered by the comparison to Bathsheba, that wasn't exactly what happened," Overgaard replied.

"Close enough," Adam replied around a mouthful of eggs. "Basically the man got the chop, as you guys put it, for taking up with another man's wife."

A couple of South African men at the table to their left turned and gave Adam a glance that was hardly favorable. Feigning obliviousness, Adam continued.

"I mean, I seem to recall there being an Act that basically said he wasn't the King of England anymore, correct?"

Overgaard nodded.

"Yes, but in light of recent events the Halifax government is attempting to reverse the Abdication Act and restore King Edward to the throne," Overgaard said.

Adam shook his head in amazement.

"Is that legal?" he asked.

"Well therein lies the rub," Overgaard said bitterly. "When the current sovereign is in another country that sort of prevents many people from raising a fuss."

"You know, I thought things couldn't get much worse a couple weeks ago," Adam said grimly. "Now I realize that I suffered from a large dose of ignorance."

"Well, Her Majesty is only sixteen," Overgaard continued. "There is a push from Prime Minister King for all the Commonwealth nations to recognize Her Majesty as the current sovereign with Churchill as head of a reformed Commonwealth government. But..." Overgaard said, then stopped suddenly and shrugged as if to say he had no idea what would happen. Their conversation was interrupted by the waitress, a rather plain-looking brunette, interrupting to ask Overgaard if there was anything he'd like to eat.

"So how did you get back here?" Adam asked after the woman had left Overgaard water and gone to make him his eggs benedict.

"Caught a liner back," Overgaard said simply. "The Germans accorded us non-belligerent status."

"What?!"

"Prime Minister Halifax, for all his faults, negotiated a decent treaty. Between you and me, if you've read that bastard Hitler's book you'd realize that France and England were a sideshow to the Nazis," Overgaard said, taking a sip of his water. "Hitler only attacked us to clear his backside before he went east. Hell, he didn't even technically attack us—just went after Poland."

Adam made a face at that one.

"Sorry mate, but as much as I know you love those Polish blokes you flew with, it's not like either us or the French really kept their promises to them," Overgaard said. "I mean, between the Germans and that bloody bastard Stalin, I'm not so sure the men who got away should not just consider themselves lucky and call it a day. Realistically, there is probably nothing worth going back for, and even if the rest of your countrymen decide to grace this war with their presence, it is highly unlikely anyone will be prying Poland from the Germans and Soviets anytime soon."

"Would you leave someone like Himmler or Stalin in charge of your home?" Adam asked incredulously.

"There comes a point when you have to accept reality," Overgaard said. "My grandfather fought against the English during the Boer War. His commando swore they would fight until the death. Well, you notice the Boers aren't in charge and my grandfather is still out on my family farm."

"The English never compared to anything the Nazis or Soviets have done," Adam snapped.

"Really? Remind me again where the term concentration camp comes from?" Overgaard replied easily.

Adam felt his face warm.

"The English *never* did what the Nazis have just done," he seethed. "They didn't even do something as horrible as Guernica."

"But would they have if they'd had the capability?" Overgaard asked simply.

Adam opened his mouth to protest, then stopped.

He has a point. Unfortunately... Adam mentally conceded as the waitress returned with Overgaard's order.

"Now the difference is the English would not have gassed or burned about forty thousand people *today*," Overgaard continued after taking a bite of his eggs. "Well, at least they would not have until a couple of weeks ago. Which is part of the reason Himmler and Halifax were able to come to an agreement, albeit one that is probably going to make you Yanks a bit upset."

"I haven't even seen a newspaper talking about this treaty yet," Adam said. "So please, do tell."

"That's because Prime Minister Smuts is studiously avoiding starting any discussion of it in Parliament," Overgaard replied quietly.

"You are probably not aware, but my government was split on whether or not we should enter the war. There are those among us who do not necessarily disagree with the Nazis' philosophy regarding a master race."

Adam put his fork down, suddenly feeling sick to his stomach.

"Thankfully the number of those who absolutely feel that way is relatively small, but I think that was part of the reason Himmler allowed for the immediate release of all Commonwealth forces," Overgaard said. "The man does not want to give Her Majesty's government any assistance by upsetting Australia, New Zealand, Canada, or South Africa."

"What about any forces from the Occupied countries he could lay his hands on?" Adam asked bitterly. "I suppose they were shot out of hand?"

"Strangely enough, no. Himmler offered them a choice—they could basically serve in the Nazi armed forces for three years or be imprisoned for six," Overgaard replied.

"What?!" Adam exclaimed.

"You'd be surprised how many takers the Germans had," Overgaard continued. "Not many Poles, of course...but there were a fair number of so called 'Free French' who seemed to be a whole lot less willing to spend the next six years in a German prison camp rather than three years someplace else."

"Can't blame them, really," Adam sighed. "His Highness and Halifax persuading Churchill to call for a truce sort of screwed the French. Add on shooting up their fleet back in 1940 and I would start to wonder just how good of allies the British were."

"There's only so much that one nation by herself can do. It's not like you Americans were giving any indications of coming into the war anytime soon."

"Too many people still think we did enough last time," Adam replied. "In their mind, we don't need dead Americans cleaning up Europe's mess again."

"If your country waits much longer, they will be facing all of bloody Europe," Overgaard said resignedly. "Or at least a large European coalition led by Germany. But I'm obviously preaching to the choir."

"Yes, and this particular singer is thinking it might be a good idea to keep moving along," Adam said.

"Well you're about nine months too late for China," Overgaard observed. "At least, not unless you want to be shooting up Warlord A so that Warlord B can take over his territory then proclaim his fealty for the Nationalists."

"Yes, well, no one saw the Japanese leaving. I wasn't following that close enough to know what in the hell happened there," Adam observed. "One minute it looks like we're getting ready to go to war with them last December, Churchill sends four more battleships to Singapore, and next thing you know they go and attack the Russians."

"In retrospect I think they would like to have that decision back," Overgaard observed wryly.

"Getting an entire army annihilated will do that," Adam observed. "What did the Russians say they were going to call Manchuria, Manchukuo, or whatever it was?"

"I don't remember," Overgaard said. "I just remember that one minute they were on the offensive against the Russians, then four months later that Soviet general's accepting their surrender in South Manchuria."

"Zhukov was his name," Adam said. "Looks like he studied *blitzkrieg* at the same school the Germans did."

"I don't care if he learned it from Mars himself, he sure used it to kick the Japanese right out of China. My father told me just the other day that there was some rumor their entire cabinet committed suicide over the loss of face," Overgaard replied, putting a fork of eggs in his mouth.

"Well, I lost track of the situation about the same time you did, and for the same reasons," Adam replied, his voice haunted. "Something about the *Luftwaffe* trying to kill us."

Overgaard nodded grimly as he chewed on his eggs.

"So where do you think you'll go then?" the South African asked after swallowing.

"According to the consulate here the isolationists are talking about stripping all of us of our citizenships," Adam replied. "There's even some poor bastard who the Germans shot down over the Atlantic that they're trying to have banned from ever reentering the country."

*H.M.S. **PRINCE OF WALES***
HALIFAX HARBOR, CANADA
1000 LOCAL (0900 EASTERN)
26 SEPTEMBER

SO THIS IS HOW AN ANT FEELS IN A ROOM FULL OF ELEPHANTS, ERIC HAD time to think to himself as he walked into the admiral's day room of the H.M.S. *Prince of Wales*. Scanning the room, he saw more gold braid and stars than he had ever witnessed in his life in one place. That the civilian dignitaries present made the aforementioned constellation seem rather dim by comparison was more than enough to make a junior officer pray for invisibility.

"Speaking of *Leftenant* Cobb, here he is right now," Vice Admiral John Tovey, commander of Home Fleet, stated.

Oh look, the ant is now expected to play the trombone for everyone, Eric thought as all eyes turned towards him. There were five individuals in the large compartment besides Vice Admiral Tovey. Eric immediately recognized Secretary of the Navy Frank Knox and Admiral Ernest J. King from the pictures that *Ranger*'s captain had required every one of his officers to memorize prior to coming aboard. The other four star standing with them, on the other hand, Eric had no clue about. The tall, dark-haired man regarded Eric with a neutral expression, as if he was weighing and measuring the aviator. The other civilian in a dark blue suit similar to the one worn by Secretary Knox was standing beside the mystery full admiral. Lastly, sitting in a chair next to the four standing Americans was none other than Winston Churchill, the man puffing contentedly on one of his trademark cigars with one hand, the other clenching a tumbler of some amber liquid.

Okay, now I'm really starting to worry, Eric thought as he came to attention.

"Lieutenant Cobb reporting as ordered, sir," he said to Secretary Knox as the highest ranking man in the room. In actuality, it had been

Tovey that had requested his presence from the officer's barracks ashore one hour previously. Eric had been rather surprised at the summons, as the American ambassador to Canada had conveyed, in no uncertain, terms that neither Rawles nor he was to set foot aboard another British vessel until further notice. As that particular missive had been delivered in the presence of Captain Gordon before *Exeter* had even pulled up to the dock to unload her wounded, Eric had a feeling Admiral Tovey was well aware of it.

Knox gave Admiral King and the mystery four star a bemused look, then turned back to Eric.

"At ease lieutenant, you're not here for a court-martial," Knox said easily. "We just want to hear what happened to you in your own words."

What the hell? Didn't anyone get my after action review? Eric thought to himself. His surprise must have showed because the unknown admiral spoke up.

"Son, we know you already prepared a report for Lieutenant Colonel Gypsum," the man said, referring to the American military attaché to Canada. "However it's important that Secretaries Knox and Hull hear your story for themselves."

"What Admiral Kimmel is actually saying, in polite terms, is that he bloody thinks we altered your report!" Winston Churchill thundered.

Okay, there's a little tension here, Eric thought. Tovey stood stonefaced as Churchill took a puff of his cigar, daring any of the Americans present to deny his accusation.

"*Mr.* Churchill is correct," King responded, bitterness in his voice. "There are those in Congress and elsewhere in the United States government who have come to wonder just how coincidental it would be that you and your squadron leader just happened to blunder into the German fleet at a time when the British had been forced to dispatch cruisers to make contact with it."

"Permission to speak freely, sir?" Eric asked quietly.

"Go ahead, Lieutenant Cobb," King snapped, glaring steadily at Churchill.

"The reason why we just *happened* to be there is Commander

ACTS OF WAR

Cobleigh convinced Rear Admiral Noyes that the best *Dauntless* pilots could establish a search even in that weather."

King snorted, his nostrils flaring.

"Yes—and of the twelve of you who launched, only six recovered successfully," King snapped.

Eric fought to keep his face expressionless.

*Some of those men are, or maybe **were**, my friends*, he thought grimly.

"Lieutenant Cobb, why don't you tell us what happened?" Kimmel broke in. Admiral King pivoted as if he was about to snap a response when a stern look from Secretary Knox stopped him in his tracks. "Come on over here to the plot if that will help."

"We started the day at 0300..." Eric began. He spent the next thirty minutes recounting his role in the Battle of Regicide, or as the British fleet was calling it, the Battle of the Remnants. As he talked, Eric realized just how lucky both Rawles and he had been to have survived. By the time he had stopped, he realized that his hands were slightly shaking while he stood at parade rest.

"How long until the *Exeter* is back in action?" Admiral Kimmel asked thoughtfully. "From what Lieutenant Cobb described, she sounds almost a total wreck."

"Six months," Admiral Tovey replied. "She'll be sailing for Sydney within the fortnight."

"What? You don't have any facilities closer?" Secretary Knox asked, shock clear in his voice.

Churchill and Tovey shared a pained look. After a moment, the former Prime Minister spoke.

"There is some discussion among the Commonwealth nations as to whether they will agree to be bound by the Treaty of Kent," he said solemnly.

"It appears that the former king returning to claim the throne threw a monkey wrench in your plan to continue to fight if England fell," Admiral King observed.

Eric could tell from the shocked looks on every other American's face that he was not the only one horrified by King's bluntness.

"Another 'monkey wrench' was our belief that a certain nation's assistance would go beyond fine words and promises," Churchill said after a moment's pause.

"What Admiral King meant," Secretary Hull said, his tone making it quite clear that nothing good would come from King contradicting his next words, "is that it does not seem as if the possibility of England's fall was discussed among the Commonwealth during the truce period."

"Of course not," Churchill sneered. "No one wanted to consider the fact that the Germans might resume hostilities. Hell, I had a hard enough time persuading Parliament to continue producing the items already authorized. No one wanted to believe that bastard Himmler was just playing for time to strengthen the *Luftwaffe*."

"Having your agents attempt to kill Heydrich in Prague and a Free Frenchman blow up Alfred Rosenberg might have had something to do with the Nazis resuming the war," Admiral King observed, gaining him a rancorous look from Hull and Knox alike. Eric watched Churchill's face start to redden as the Prime Minster opened his mouth to speak only to be cut off by Tovey.

"Perhaps you would be more interested in the present situation than a discussion of the past, Admiral King?" Home Fleet's commander asked, his voice colder than the gusts blowing through Halifax Harbor.

"Actually, gentlemen, We would be very interested in hearing about the present situation as well," a calm woman's voice observed from the hatchway behind Eric. He turned to a slender, short brunette in a black mourning dress. Out of the corner of his eye Eric saw Churchill and Tovey both whirl away from the map, then come immediately to attention.

"Your Majesty, we were not expecting you for another three hours," Churchill said evenly as the woman strode into the compartment followed by two very large men in the bright red tunics and bearskin caps of the British Army's Guard Regiments. Eric was somewhat shocked to see that both men carried Thompson submachine guns. Judging from Admiral Tovey's face going pale, he was not the only one. While both men ensured their weapons were not pointed at anybody in particular, Eric could feel the tension rise in the room.

I'm guessing, given that she's currently the Queen, just had her father assassinated by the Germans, and has no issue, these men would kill everyone in the room if they thought it necessary, Eric thought. *I don't blame them one bit.*

"My...*Our* apologies, Lord Churchill," Queen Elizabeth replied, her voice genuine. "The meeting with the new Air Minister took far less time than expected. Admiral Tovey, for your information Captain Leach was given direction from me not to interrupt your meeting. We are the ones off schedule, not you gentlemen."

"Your Majesty, all of us appreciate that you made time in your busy schedule for us," Secretary Hull began. "It is a difficult time for both our nations." Behind him, Eric saw Secretary Knox give Admiral King a look that could have blistered paint.

I'm not sure I want to be in the same room with men who can silence a full admiral just with a look, Eric thought quietly. *I'm reasonably certain that Secretary Knox will relieve him on the spot if there is another outburst.*

"Thank you, Secretary Hull," Her Majesty replied. "My father considered the United States to be our strongest friend even if not strictly an ally."

Pointed comment there, Eric thought, seeing Admiral King starting to color somewhat.

"There are those in our nation, even now, who do not realize that the Nazis intend to conquer the entire world," Hull replied.

"Well, let us discuss how we will stop them from doing that, shall we?" Queen Elizabeth stated firmly.

"Your Majesty, I want to be perfectly clear—I do not have the power to negotiate a treaty and, to be frank, President Roosevelt does not anywhere close to the votes in Congress for a declaration of war."

Queen Elizabeth II regarded Secretary Hull with a gaze that radiated determination.

"I am certain that, sooner or later, Nazi Germany will provide you with no other choice than to go to war. At that time, the Commonwealth will stand with you even if England proper does not."

"That is part of the reason we are here, Your Majesty," Secretary Knox interjected smoothly. "There has been no public information regarding just what is involved in the Treaty of Kent. All we have in

Washington is rumor, and some of them are so wild as to hardly be believable."

"You may find that some of the agreements Lord Halifax and my uncle have made are as terrible as you imagined," Queen Elizabeth remarked.

Is it just me, or does it seem like the teenager in the room is dealing better with the world turned upside down than all the men? Eric thought, stunned at the Queen's composure. *I'd be a wreck if Dad died, nevermind was **killed**.*

"Naturally I am sure the United States' primary concern is the disposition of our fleet units," Queen Elizabeth continued. "I believe your isolationists have been roaring with full throat about President Roosevelt's folly in lending us aid when the 'bulwark of the Atlantic remained even if England did not,' correct?"

Eric had to struggle not to wince at the cold politeness in Queen Elizabeth's tone. Looking over at Secretaries Hull and Knox he could see that the young sovereign's words had stricken home.

"President Roosevelt intends to lend whatever aid he can..." Secretary Hull began.

"Yes, of course," Queen Elizabeth snapped, her reserve slipping for the first time. "That is precisely what he told Lord Churchill aboard this very vessel in August of last year."

Eric, looking at Admiral King's face, realized the man was turning an unpleasant shade of red.

"Strange then, is it not, how my nation lies prostrate and *my father slain* yet your 'political exigencies' still seem to prevent action," the Queen finished.

I didn't think that shade was possible on a person, Eric thought. *Admiral King is almost purple.*

"Admiral King, why don't we go get some fresh air?" Secretary Knox said. King whipped around and was about to respond, then belatedly realized suddenly realized that his superior was not actually making a request.

*When the Secretary of the Navy asks you to step outside, you **step** outside.*

With a slight neck bow to the Queen, Secretary Knox gestured for Admiral King to lead the way out of the compartment. Eric noted that

Admiral King pointedly did not render any honors to the Queen on his way out of the hatch.

"Perhaps it would be best if *Leftenant* Cobb and the other two gentlemen left as well," Admiral Tovey stated.

"Those two gentlemen have been given direct orders to go with Her Majesty everywhere she goes," Churchill snapped. "While I trust we have nothing to worry about from anyone in this room, it would be best if we not set the precedent now."

"*Leftenant* Cobb may stay," Her Majesty said, favoring Eric with a small smile. "Given his luck so far, this will probably be yet another thing he can tell his grandchildren about."

Assuming I survive the next six months, nevermind long enough to marry Joyce, Eric thought. *That is, if she got my letter. Hell, I don't even know if* **Mom** *knows I'm still alive. I think I'm going to end up missing Patricia's wedding next month at this rate.*

"Please proceed Admiral Tovey," Queen Elizabeth continued.

"Your Majesty, Secretary Hull, at this moment the Commonwealth controls the majority of our ships. The only exceptions are four battleships, two carriers, a dozen cruisers, and twenty destroyers," Admiral Tovey said.

"What do you mean by 'control'? There are hardly that many ships here in Halifax," Admiral Kimmel asked.

Tovey and Churchill shared a look, then the latter answered.

"By 'control,' we mean ships that are not currently answering the orders of the Halifax Government or pledging allegiance to the Duke of Windsor."

Queen Elizabeth's nostrils flared at the last.

"My uncle renounced all of his titles the minute he set foot in London to usurp my throne and authority," she snapped.

"Your Majesty..." Churchill began.

"Lord Churchill, that topic is not open for discussion," Queen Elizabeth continued, even more forcefully

Eric saw several emotions flitter across Churchill's face, but there was no mistaking the steel in Queen Elizabeth's voice.

I would not want to cross this woman, he thought.

"Your Majesty, I for one would like to know what he should be called then," Secretary Hull said quietly. "If you allow our newspapers to come up with a name, they may choose something which gives the Halifax government the very legitimacy you seek to deny them."

Queen Elizabeth turned her gaze from Churchill to Secretary Hull.

"The Commonwealth government will refer to my uncle as The Usurper," Elizabeth said coolly. A look of surprise briefly flitted across Churchill's face so quickly that Eric was fairly certain no one else noticed it due to their focus on the Queen.

"Back to your original statement, Admiral Tovey—how did these vessels end up outside of your control?" Admiral Kimmel asked.

"*Anson*, *Howe*, and *Lion* are just completed," Tovey responded, his tone somber. "The remaining vessels either are not Home Fleet, were recently damaged, or were en route to Great Britain and could not divert due to their fuel state."

"Why didn't the crews scuttle their vessels?" Kimmel asked, his voice disgusted.

"Because the Germans threatened to resume hostilities if there were any more incidents," Churchill snapped. "To be more specific, that bastard Himmler threatened to rip up the Treaty of Kent and lay scourge to every city within Southern England."

"So what will be the vessels' ultimate disposition?" Hull asked, his voice conveying that he was already resigned to what the answer would be.

"The Germans expect to face you sooner or later and intend to use the vessels until their three new battleships are complete. *Anson* and *Howe* have apparently already been dispatched to Wilhelmshaven along with several of the destroyers. *Lion* will be sent within thirty days. It is expected that they will take six months to be in German service."

"So you're saying the Germans just got three modern battleships gift wrapped and dropped off at their door?" Kimmel asked, his tone one of disbelief.

"Are you familiar with the effect of nerve gas on unprotected civilians, Admiral Kimmel?" Queen Elizabeth asked quietly. "I can place you in touch with several officers who can tell you exactly just how agonizing a death it appears to be."

"No one is suggesting that your government should have called Mr. Himmler's bluff," Secretary Hull said smoothly, giving Admiral Kimmel a hard look. "Admiral Kimmel is understandably upset, as this will affect our own strategic calculus."

"We understand your concerns, Secretary Hull," Queen Elizabeth said. "However, given your upcoming construction we do not see cause for quite that level of alarm."

"Do not understand the reason for that level of alarm?" Admiral Kimmel asked unbelievingly, his Kentucky drawl getting more pronounced due to his anger. "How about those are three modern battleships that we will now have to account for in order to maintain open supply lines to Iceland? Or that we will have to destroy in order to return you to your throne?"

"Again, *Anson* and *Howe* will take at least six months to be worked up with German crews, *Lion* even longer." Admiral Tovey snapped. "I doubt that they will be anywhere near as experienced as your own."

"You're making the assumption they will have *German* crews," Kimmel said seethingly. "Our intelligence indicates that the Halifax government has not necessarily ruled out supplying 'volunteers' in exchange for concessions."

"That is a ploy to ensure that we continue grain shipments from Canada," Churchill observed, nostrils flaring slightly.

There was a moment when Kimmel and Hull both looked at him in shock.

"From your response you make it appear that you are thinking about continuing to do so," Hull said after a moment, his voice heavy.

"We will not starve our subjects," Queen Elizabeth said flatly.

"Perhaps you do not understand the gravity..." Secretary Hull started to say.

"I will *not* be lectured like I am some ignorant child, Secretary Hull," Queen Elizabeth snapped, her icy demeanor finally cracking. "You have the *audacity* to tell any one of us that we do not *understand* the *gravity* of the situation? Tell me, Mr. Secretary, when was the last time your home was bombed? Your capital burned? Your father *murdered?*"

Hull bit back a response, taking a deep breath.

JAMES YOUNG

I know a thing or two about willful women, Eric thought. *I'm pretty sure all of you underestimate this woman at your peril.*

"The American people will find it hard to understand how on one hand you can consider your uncle a...*usurper* yet you continue to supply grain to the people who follow him. There will be those who wonder if you are prepared to do what is necessary to regain your throne."

*If looks could kill...*Eric thought as Queen Elizabeth stared venomously at Secretary Hull for a brief moment before regaining her composure.

"Our government has done what is necessary throughout this conflict, Secretary Hull. We do not think the same can be said of yours," the monarch replied, her tone almost making Eric shiver from the intensity it contained.

The proverbial pin drop would have echoed like thunder in the compartment.

"Perhaps, Your Majesty, a break is in order," Churchill suggested after a moment, his voice neutral.

"That sounds like a wonderful idea, Lord Churchill," Queen Elizabeth replied, her lips pursed.

"Gentlemen, let us return in fifteen minutes," Churchill said briskly, looking at the clock on the far bulkhead.

"I will have a steward bring some coffee for our guests," Admiral Tovey said, heading for the watertight door.

"Lieutenant Cobb, we should probably get you ashore," Admiral Kimmel spoke from behind Eric. "A detachment should already be at your guest quarters collecting your gunner, and they should have transportation for you to return to the *South Dakota*."

I recognize an order wrapped in a suggestion when I hear it, Eric thought. *Not that I mind—an ant does not need to be standing around when elephants are dancing.*

"Yes sir," Eric replied, turning for the hatch.

"*Leftenant* Cobb," Queen Elizabeth called after him, causing Eric to stop dead in his tracks.

"Yes Ma'a...Your Majesty?" Eric said, tripping over himself.

"Thank you," Queen Elizabeth said simply.

"You are welcome, Your Majesty," Eric said, giving a slight neck bow. He stopped to wait for Admiral Kimmel to go out the hatchway, but the senior officer gestured for him to lead the way. Five minutes later, Eric found himself standing with Secretary Knox along with Admirals Kimmel and King next to the *Prince of Wales*'s gangway. The fleet's service launch approached the battleship, bobbing in the choppy harbor water from the stiff wind.

"Lieutenant Cobb, I think it goes without saying you are to not to speak about anything you saw or heard today," Admiral Kimmel said quietly.

"Yes sir," Eric replied.

"Especially anything having to do with your senior's behavior," Secretary Hull snapped, staring directly at Admiral King.

"I will not be lectured by some teenaged skirt with delusions of grandeur," Admiral King snapped as he took a heavy draw on his cigarette. Eric watched Secretary Knox's face start to color as he looked to make sure no one was in ear shot.

"The British lost," King continued. "They left the Germans a pretty sizeable portion of their fleet and we don't have the necessary power to go smash up Scapa Flow like they did the frogs when France fell. So pardon me if I don't get all wrapped up in protocol when I'm thinking about all the American boys who are about to die because some overwrought girl wants to avenge her daddy."

King looked out over the side as he flicked away his cigarette, and suddenly Eric could have swore the admiral aged five years right before his eyes.

"I've got six girls of my own, and I don't think anyone's going to ask several thousand boys like Lieutenant Cobb here to die if I end up on the wrong end of some German shell."

"Your personal opinions aside, I need to know if you can control yourself, Admiral King," Secretary Knox seethed.

"Gentlemen, I'm not sure now is the time..." Kimmel attempted to interject soothingly, only to be cut off by King.

"Mr. Secretary, if you think I'm incapable of fighting this war perhaps you need to go ahead and send me back to the General Board," Admiral King said lowly. "Especially if that job requires treating the people in there as equal allies who are bringing as much to the table as they're taking off of it. I took an oath to uphold and defend the Constitution, not cater to the Queen of England."

Secretary Knox took a visibly deep breath.

"We will discuss this further when we return to Washington," he said, his voice heavy with emotion. "For now, I think Lieutenant Cobb has a boat to catch."

Eric came to attention at the top of the gangway, saluting his seniors.

"Good luck, Lieutenant Cobb," Secretary Knox replied, returning Eric's salute.

"Thank you, sir," Eric replied, then started making his way down to the launch.

I have a feeling I just saw something that's not going to end well, he thought as he stepped into the small boat. The coxswain let him sit down, then began the small launch's journey back towards shore.

Ewa Air Station, Hawaii
1800 Local (0000 Eastern)
30 September (1 October 1)

"So I hear the new admiral's a real nutcracker," Sam said as he worked the ratchet in his hand.

"Is this why you stay late, Sam?" his brother asked disgustedly. "So you can gossip while you're helping to service a freakin' engine?"

There was a muted guffaw as one of VMF-14's enlisted mechanics struggled not to laugh. Master Sergeant Schwarz, VMF-14's chief mechanic, looked up from the other side of the engine to fix the offender with a baleful glare. While Sam and David had been strenuous in their declarations that they were just there as handymen and observers, Schwarz was not about to let one of his young Marines abuse their hospitality. Sam had developed the distinct impression that the tall, wiry gray-haired master sergeant sometimes enforced discipline with a bit more than his sharp tongue and gaze that would make a gorgon proud. While he hadn't brought the topic up with David in the three months the twins had been with the squadron, he doubted his brother had seen anything that would contradict that impression.

He reminds me of ol' Deputy Guston who used to oversee the chain gang back home, Sam thought grimly. *Nice man, polite to his peers and betters, but hell on wheels to those under him.*

"No, I stay late so I learn how my airplane works," Sam replied to David. "I'm just trying to make conversation."

"Well, whether the man's a nutcracker or not, he's already got Colonel Benson hopping," David said lowly, referring to Marine Aircraft Group Twenty-one's commander. "It's not like the man was a bump on the log in the first place."

Sam double checked his handiwork then went on to the radial engine's next cylinder head. Examining it closely, he raised an eyebrow and gestured for Master Sergeant Schwarz to take a look.

"This looked cracked to you, Master Sergeant?" he asked, reaching up to angle the shop light so the enlisted man could have a look. Schwarz leaned in close, squinting, then cursed.

"Yes, sir, it does. Guess we know why this aircraft was such a dog yesterday," Schwarz said, his annoyance clear.

"Better to find the fault now rather than end up going for a swim later," Sam replied.

"Attention on deck!" someone shouted, causing a rustling inside the hangar bay. Sam released the light as he stepped out from behind the engine to face the door, David close behind. Seeing the visitor, he felt the blood drain from his face as he snapped to attention.

Okay, Mom always used to say if you speak the devil's name he shall appear, but this is absolutely ridiculous, Sam thought.

Striding into the hangar was a man who looked, to quote one of their squadronmates, "older than Moses." Tall and broad shouldered, with an erect gait that made his stature seem even larger, Admiral Hank William Jensen was the newly minted Commander in Chief Pacific Fleet (CINCPACFLT), having been assigned when Admiral Kimmel had been tapped for CINCATLFLT. The senior officer's wizened features and wispy hair made him look a full decade older than his sixty years, but looking into his dark brown, almost black eyes was enough to show that age had not affected the man's mental abilities one bit. His dark, bushy eyebrows showed what color the few wisps of combed over white hair on his head had once been.

Standing beside Jensen was a rear admiral that Sam immediately recognized.

Holy shit, that bastard Bowles really does look just like his old man, Sam thought, thinking of one of his squadron mates.

Vice Admiral Jacob Bowles Sr. was a man that looked like an older Clark Gable, but with green eyes and a full head of brown hair. As he stepped away from the *Wildcat*, Sam noted the submariner's dolphins on the right side of the man's uniform shortly before Admiral Jensen started to speak. Three more men, two captains and a full commander, accompanied the admiral.

"Who is the senior man here?" Jensen thundered.

There was a moment's pause as all of the enlisted men looked at Sam and David, who in turn looked at each other.

"Sir, I am," David said, stepping around Sam to stand beside him. "Captain David Cobb, VMF-14."

"Why are you out of uniform, captain?" Jensen snapped, showing no sign of surprise at being presented with twin Marines.

"Begging the Admiral's pardon, Marine regulations clearly stipulate that when conducting services personnel are allowed to wear coveralls as their duty uniform," Sam replied evenly.

"That regulation only applies to enlisted personnel!" Admiral Bowles snapped. "Do not correct Admiral Jensen ever again."

I see being an asshole is a family trait, Sam thought quietly.

"Yes , sir," Sam replied. "Then, begging the admiral's pardon, the regulation in question is not rank specific."

Sam heard David's sharp intake of breath and watched as Bowles face started to color. Before the admiral could unleash a tirade, the hangar door opened again.

"Captains Cobb, two ea..." Major Max Bowden started to bellow, then stopped as soon as he realized that the squadron had company. A short, stocky man with thinning blonde hair and blue eyes, Bowden had so far proven to be quite capable as a squadron leader. He was also the third commander VMF-14 had had since Vice Admiral Bowles had arrived in Hawaii.

Someone is trying to do his damndest to get their son a squadron commander slot early, Sam thought bitterly.

"Good evening Admiral Jensen!" he said loudly, immediately recognizing CINPACFLT. The reason for his extra volume was apparent a moment later as Colonel Benson walked in followed by a man in civilian clothes.

"Good evening, sir," Benson said solemnly, coming to attention as he removed his cover. "Welcome to Ewa Air Station. I would have prepared a tour if I had known you were coming."

He looks tired, Sam thought as he looked at the group commander. An older man with a shock of gray hair and blue eyes, Benson had been a Marine aviator long enough to have seen action in several of the Banana Wars throughout the Caribbean. At just a shade under six foot normally, Benson seemed to be bowing under the weight of command that had descended upon his narrow shoulders.

"That's quite all right, Colonel," Admiral Jensen said. "Captain Cobb was just informing me of the finer points of Marine regulations."

There was a moment when both Benson and Bowden gave the Cobb brothers looks which clearly signified they doubted the junior officers' sanity. Before either man could speak, the chaplain politely cleared his throat.

"Admiral Jensen, I hate to interrupt, but I have some urgent news for both Captains Cobb."

"And you are?" Bowles thundered.

"Rear Admiral Bowles, I am Chaplain McHenry," the man replied evenly. "Specifically, I am *your* staff chaplain. We met six weeks ago when you took over as Chief of Staff. I understand if you do not recognize me—while I saw your son at church last week, I had not seen you recently. It is a large congregation, of course."

Whoa. Talk about soft answer turneth away wrath, Sam thought, watching as Bowles' mouth worked a couple of times in shock. McHenry turned away from the man and backed to Admiral Jensen.

"I apologize Admiral, but I am covering for MAG-21's chaplain," McHenry continued. "I just received a telegram that I need to deliver to Captain Cobb. Both of them."

*Oh no...*Sam thought.

JAMES YOUNG

"I think that the message..." Bowles began.

"Go ahead, chaplain," Admiral Jensen said, cutting his chief of staff off. "As a matter of fact, why don't you step outside with the two captains for a moment?"

"If you gentlemen will follow me?" McHenry said.

Feeling numb, Sam began following the chaplain out the door. There was never a good reason for a chaplain to come deliver a message.

"Who is it?" David asked as soon as they were standing outside the hangar.

"Your brother Eric is fine," McHenry replied quickly. "However, he was shot down by the Germans on September 12."

"*What?!*" Sam and David asked simultaneously. McHenry held up his hands.

"Easy, easy, let me finish then I will answer what questions I can," McHenry said. He quickly told both Cobb twins what their brother had been up to for just a little more than a fortnight.

"That's all the information I, or for that matter, anyone else here in Hawaii has," McHenry finished. "I'm sure there is additional information, but the communiqué mentioned your brother hasn't been fully debriefed and that the other information was classified."

"Holy shit," Sam breathed, then caught himself. "Sorry chaplain."

"Captain Cobb, I think if I just found out my brother had been in Canada for a fortnight after nearly getting killed by the Germans I'd probably be using some blue language as well."

"Has anyone informed our brother, Nick?" David asked.

"Rabbi Howe, the Submarine Force chaplain, was hoping to make arrangements after I informed him of the telegram. I received the news courtesy of a friend of mine who is on Admiral King's staff," McHenry replied. "He indicated that the Navy had only informed your mother your brother was 'missing' yesterday."

"Oh Jesus," David breathed. "Mom is going to be *pissed* at Eric."

"In your brother's defense, I suspect that he was either ordered not to contact your family or that someone held his mail," McHenry replied evenly. "The poor young man is already more famous than he is probably going to like."

"What do you mean, Chaplain?"

McHenry looked at both men.

"Neither one of you read the newspapers, do you?"

Sam and David both looked sheepish.

"No Chaplain," Sam replied.

"The Germans are rather incensed and are demanding Lieutenant Cobb's incarceration upon his return to the United States," McHenry replied evenly. "Secretary Hull has pointed out that the German Navy did open fire on a neutral aircraft so they are hardly the wronged party."

"You know, he always had a knack for finding trouble," Sam muttered.

"This is a bit different than stealing peaches from Widow Fitzsimmons," David drawled. Turning to look at his brother, Sam could see that David was obviously more upset than he was.

"Well he's safe now, and he's headed home," Sam replied evenly. "I'm pretty sure he'll have one hell of a story to tell Mom."

SINGAPORE
1700 LOCAL (0500 EASTERN)
4 OCTOBER

I almost feel sorry for the man, REAR ADMIRAL TAMON Yamaguchi thought as he stoically regarded the fuming Englishman in front of him. Of average height, with close set, almost catlike features and a stocky build, Yamaguchi had once been likened to a gregarious catamount by one of his Princeton classmates. Like that predator, he remained almost perfectly still except for his almond eyes that tracked the tall, lanky, and clearly agitated British officer in front of him. Almost casually, he dropped his hand to the officer's sword on his left hip. He could see his superior, Vice Admiral Chuichi Nagumo, similarly tensing in front of him.

There are only three of them in this room, Yamaguchi thought. *I would not think they were so foolish as to cause an incident, but I know what path I would take in this situation.*

"I will tell you what is *reasonable*, Admiral Ciliax," Lieutenant General Arthur Percival hissed through his two protruding front teeth. "*Reasonable* is that I be advised that your nation had no intention of taking possession of this colony, but rather intended to turn it over to this bunch of barb...*gentlemen. Reasonable...*"

"I demand that you would not speak of the Reich's allies as if they are not standing here, General," Admiral Otto Ciliax thundered, both his hands on Percival's desk. "We are not, in any way, *negotiating* terms. The Treaty of Kent is clear, and the fact that you or your staff remain here is merely a formality and courtesy."

Percival glowered at his German opposite number, his face reddening around his clipped moustache.

"I have three divisions of troops under my command..." the Englishman began, only to be cut off again by Ciliax.

"Field Marshal Kesselring has over three *thousand* aircraft poised like a dagger at England," Ciliax said coldly, his accent growing thicker with emotion even as he casually waved. "How many women and children are you willing to kill with your pride?"

Percival opened his mouth then shut it again. Taking a deep, shuddering breath the man turned and looked at Vice Admiral Nagumo, then back at Ciliax.

"Then I will be damned if me or my staff will stay here to help some *Jap*," Percival spat. "For men who talk of the white race's superiority you seem to be awfully willing to do the slant eyes' dirty work."

Yamaguchi felt a rush of blood to his face even as he tried to keep his features impassive.

"Perhaps now would be a good time to tell you that Vice Admiral Nagumo will be the *Kriegsmarine*'s outside representative for inspecting the Royal Navy's indemnity payments for the loss of the *Scharnhorst*, *Gneisenau*, and damage to the *Bismarck* and *Tirpitz*?"

Percival's eyes narrowed.

"What the devil are you talking about?" he snapped.

"I am sure you will find out soon enough," Ciliax replied icily. "I believe you were taking your leave?"

Yamaguchi was as perplexed as General Percival. Even as he

watched the British officer and his staff storm out of Singapore's command post, he found his mind alive with questions.

What outside representative? How is Nagumo-san going to inspect warships in Europe? Yamaguchi thought, confused.

"Gentlemen, I am sorry that you had to deal with...that," Ciliax said stiffly.

"His attitude is typical," Vice Admiral Nagumo replied, his English somewhat slow and stilting. "All of the West has long considered us inferior."

Ciliax gave a thin grimace at that.

"Despite that idiot's claims, the Fuhrer does not share that view," Ciliax replied, as a gradually building hum could be heard. "Indeed... who is flying those aircraft?"

The headquarters windows were vibrating with the roar of piston engines by the time that Ciliax finished his question.

"Admiral Yamamoto thought it best if we prepared some additional persuasion," Yamaguchi replied, his face still blank other than a slight narrowing of the eyes. "Just in case General Percival misunderstood our relative positions."

TEN THOUSAND FEET OVER REAR ADMIRAL YAMAGUCHI'S HEAD, Sub-Lieutenant Isoro Honda gave his *Zero* some gentle right rudder to follow the maneuvers of Lieutenant Commander Shigeru Itaya, *Akagi*'s fighter squadron commander. Looking back at the two other aircraft in his *chutai*, the IJN's typical three-plane formation, Isoro allowed himself to feel a small degree of pride. Their configuration was perfect, Warrant Officers Watanabe and Yoshida moving as if they were extensions of his own aircraft. The nimble, responsive *Zero*es were weaving four thousand feet over the assembled strike aircraft of the *Kido Butai*, the Imperial Japanese Navy's strike force of six heavy carriers.

I only hope the British are stupid enough to start a fight, Isoro thought with grim satisfaction. *It will be nice to face worthy opponents again after three years of killing Chinese.* The Chinese had been like schoolchildren armed with rocks set upon by a horde of samurai, and the eight kills he had scored felt almost shameful given the *Zero*'s superiority.

Not that the Russians were much better, Isoro thought bitterly. *Perhaps if the Army had actually managed to slow the Russians down then we might have gotten to test our mettle against them some more. Or maybe if we had been given a chance to fight those foreign mercenaries down in the south...*

Shaking himself out of his reverie, Isoro sighed as he continued to scan the skies around his aircraft. Several wingmen had often made fun of him for his tendency to always move his body in the cockpit, nicknaming him "Sea Snake" due to the undulations of his long, gangly frame. His nickname had taken on a decidedly different connotation when he started being the first to spot, then kill hostile aircraft. He turned back forward just in time to see a red and green flare arcing out from the lead torpedo bomber below.

No trade for us today, Isoro thought, shaking his head in disappointment. *It would appear that the British are going to accept the Germans giving us Singapore after all.* There had been rumors in the ready room that the Germans had not only ceded Japan Singapore but Malaya as well. If so, it was a gesture of goodwill that had Isoro reconsidering his view of Japan's alliances.

"*Akagi* fighters will land ashore," his headphones crackled with Lieutenant Commander Itaya's voice. "All others will return to carriers."

Well, well, looks like Lieutenant Commander Itaya wants to be the first to see Japan's latest colony, Isoro thought. *Hopefully the women will be friendlier than the Chinese were...or at least the Army dogs won't have time to make them hate us.*

U.S.S. **HOUSTON**
MANILA BAY
1434 LOCAL TIME (0134 EASTERN)
6 OCTOBER

JACOB LOOKED THOUGHTFULLY AT THE CHART SPREAD OUT ON THE table before him, then back across at the captain of the U.S.S. *Houston*.

"So, Admiral Hart has decided that we are going to ally with the Dutch and attempt to keep the Japanese from the East Indies?" Jacob asked incredulously.

"Yes, XO," Captain Wallace replied. "I take it you do not approve."

"The damn Japs have Singapore," Jacob said, incredulous. "That's like trying to close off a flooded compartment when the overhead's been blown away.

Captain Wallace regarded him calmly for several seconds, then replied.

"How much oil is there in the Philippines?"

"None, sir," Jacob replied, instantly seeing the light.

"Exactly. Just as there is none in Japan, which is why it is widely believed the East Indies is one of her primary objectives if war breaks out. I don't see the Germans trying to maintain convoys from Iraq during open hostilities, do you?"

I still can't believe we're just letting the Krauts sail tankers right by us, Jacob thought. *What's the good of having a navy if we're afraid to use it?*

"But that's not what our war plan states we are to do," Jacob replied. Captain Wallace smiled benignly.

"War Plan Orange is somewhat vague on what we're supposed to do, actually," Captain Wallace replied evenly. "Other than die bravely, and if I'm going to do that I want it to be for some other reason than General MacArthur's pride."

"I'm not sure I follow, Captain," Jacob replied.

"The fate of the Philippines is directly linked to that Army bastard's reputation, his 'place in history' as he's always telling Admiral Hart," Captain Wallace said, the disgust veritably dripping off his words. The man paused to take a drink from the coffee mug at his left elbow.

"Should the Philippines fall, General MacArthur would be disgraced. Especially since he has been spending so much to train the Filipinos over the last year."

Captain Wallace jabbed his finger at Lingayen Gulf.

"MacArthur sees our fleet as something to hurl against the Japanese transports to disrupt them when they land here," Wallace sneered. "He doesn't comprehend that the Japs will probably bring up battleships to blow this vessel out of the water."

Jacob nodded at that statement.

Trying to explain to an Army officer that 8-inch guns aren't all that heavy is like trying to explain to a toddler that the bath water isn't all that hot, he thought bitterly. *It's all a matter of scale and experience.*

"The Commonwealth commander, Admiral Phillips, just spent the last two days guaranteeing Admiral Hart that Her Majesty's Navy will fight for the Dutch East Indies," Captain Wallace continued.

"Be nice if he'd had some of that fighting spirit for Singapore or Malaya then," Jacob observed, doing his best to keep his voice matter-of-fact. Captain Wallace's glare told him that he'd succeeded only enough not to be immediately relieved.

"Rumor has it that admiral the Krauts sent out here basically told the Brits they'd gas London again if they tried to put up a fight. Given that Percival still answered to King Edward, he really didn't have a choice. Phillips, on the other hand, answers to the rightful Queen."

Jacob nearly laughed at that, but stopped himself.

Rightful *Queen?! He says that as if she's* ***ours***, he thought as Captain Wallace continued.

"Admiral Phillips, per previous agreement with the Dutch, will set out from Sydney for Java if hostilities appear imminent. There he, and we, will combine with the Dutch East Indies fleet and deny the oil fields to the Japanese."

"Sir, that's suicide with the little bastards owning Singapore," Jacob replied in disbelief. "Hell, they can row small craft from there to Sumatra, never mind bring any fleet units they station in the harbor! How will we fight under enemy air cover?"

"We won't," Captain Wallace snapped. "With the amount of air power the Dutch and Commonwealth will have concentrated in the Dutch East Indies, intelligence estimates that the Dutch and Brits have the Japanese air force outnumbered two to one. Factor in their advantage in quality, and it's probably going to be a rout. Air superiority is a two-way street."

Looking at the charts in front of him, Jacob found himself slightly mollified.

Yet the Japanese aren't stupid, he thought. *I have to imagine some little yellow son-of-a-bitch is staring at his own charts right now.*

"You seem unconvinced, Commander," Captain Wallace observed.

"Sir, I can't help but think that the Japanese have to have figured this out as well," Jacob said slowly. "They picked a fight with the Russians and got their heads, hands, and feet handed to them before they slunk back to Tokyo to lick their wounds. A thorough beating tends to make a man introspective."

"Commander, there's a natural order of things," Captain Wallace replied. "A bunch of people who were in the Dark Ages less than eighty years ago aren't going to beat us, the Brits, and the Dutch. That's why they backed down back in '41, and if they don't remember what's good for them we'll give them a beating that will make the Russian fight seem like a love tap."

"What about the Philippines?" Jacob asked.

"If the Japanese don't take the East Indies, they can hold this place until Judgment Day—they won't be getting any oil through to their Home Islands, German or otherwise. Six months to a year of that and we'll be able to sail right into Tokyo Bay."

Captain Wallace stepped back from the map.

"But enough talk of fighting in the Dutch Indies," the man said, looking at the clock. "What's our status?"

"Well, when it comes to a fight, I think we're as ready as we can be," Jacob stated firmly. He pulled out a small notebook in which he had written notes to himself.

"All departments completed their last checks early yesterday, and we finished taking on ammunition about an hour ago," he said. "I still think our damage control is shaky, but it's getting better and I've drilled as much as possible without asking for the *Boise* to shoot us with a live shell."

"I don't think having his cruisers shoot one another is what Admiral Hart intended when he stated we needed to conduct realistic training," Captain Wallace replied sardonically. "Admiral Hart is conducting a captain's call at his quarters in about an hour and a half. Set a skeleton watch and get the men some liberty—I get the feeling we're about to start training with our new allies."

"Aye aye, sir," Jacob replied.

"Oh, and Commander—not a word of our discussion to any other officers," Wallace warned. "We don't need talk getting around about what our plans are. General MacArthur has many connections. I don't want some fat, dumb, and happy senator in Washington deciding this vessel is expendable after all, just as long as precious Dougie doesn't get hurt."

"Understood, Captain," Jacob acknowledged.

"Until then, I'm going to my cabin to get cleaned up." With that, Captain Wallace turned from the chart table and headed for the hatch leading from his day cabin to his quarters. After he left, Jacob took another look at the map.

It's going to be one hell of a fight if it comes to that, he thought. *It's almost as if everyone is just waiting for a reason to go to war.*

3

CATALYSTS AND DIABOLISM

Changes in military systems come about only through the pressure of public opinion or disaster in war.

— **BRIGADIER GENERAL BILLY MITCHELL**

MOBILE, ALABAMA
1000 LOCAL (1100 EASTERN)
1 NOVEMBER 1942

"MAYBE IF WE just pretend the calendar's not there, your leave won't be almost over," Joyce Cotner said quietly, her breath moving the hair on Eric's chest. The couple were laying in her bed, a large king size with mahogany posts, dark red drapes, and a similarly colored bedskirt that hid the box spring underneath.

Eric chuckled as he looked down at the petite blonde, stroking her back.

"I've still got two weeks. That is, if I don't decide to go over the hill," he replied.

"Why Mr. Cobb, whatever would make you want to do that?" Joyce asked sarcastically as she ran her hand down his stomach. He gasped as she gently gripped him underneath the sheets.

"I don't know, Miss Cotner," he replied evenly. "Maybe getting to lay with you like this more often than just when your parents conspicuously decide to go to the Gulf Coast for vacation?"

"Well if you'll recall, they were planning on hosting a certain married couple along with them," Joyce said, her voice getting a bit of an edge.

So is it generally a bad idea to have your manhood in your fiancée's hand when she's thinking about strangling your sister? Eric thought with a slight edge of dismay.

"Penny for your thoughts?" Joyce asked, looking at him with her blue eyes.

"Just hoping that you remember it's not my sister's neck you're holding," Eric said worriedly. Joyce's mouth dropped in shock, then she started laughing.

"I love you, Eric Cobb," she said as she lay her head back down on his chest. "And I wouldn't be doing *this*," she replied, giving him a few strokes, "with your sister's neck."

"I would hope not," he snorted, his hips moving involuntarily to meet her touch. "But how about we stop talking about relatives..." he started, then stopped as Joyce slid her lower body over onto his.

"Good plan," she replied lightly, then slid herself onto him. "Or stop talking period."

"Okay, I think you're trying to kill me," he said later as they both sat down for lunch.

"Eric, you've known me almost my entire life: Would *that* really be how I tried to kill you?" Joyce asked sarcastically as she spread some salad dressing on homemade bread. Eric felt a slight smile cross his face.

"The fact it would be so unexpected would more than make up for the unpleasantness I had to suffer," Eric retorted, then whipped his head out of the way as Joyce flung some salad dressing at him.

Even in that white sundress she throws better than some men I know, he thought. *Must be the only daughter thing.*

"It'd be hard to explain to mom how I got salad dressing on this shirt," he replied, checking to make sure no errant dressing had ended up on his collar or shoulder. "It will definitely show up with this blue."

"Gee, maybe you should have thought about that before you were such a smarty pants."

"I think my exertions may be causing me to have a delirious stretch," Eric replied. "Being ridden like a stallion does that to a man."

Joyce blushed deeply under her tan.

"You know, some women firmly believe in waiting until they're married to do what we just did," Joyce said archly. "Do not convert me to that way of thinking by your complaints."

"I don't think you'd be able to resist my dashing good looks that long," Eric said. "Besides, I've said many times we should just go to the Justice of the Peace..."

Joyce gave him a look that would have combusted a gorgon.

"Right, Buck Rogers, because you've got a space ship for us to escape both of our mothers parked out in your barn. Or were you planning on sailing to Berlin for our honeymoon so someone could collect on that alleged bounty on your head?" Joyce continued, then switched to a mock German accent. "Ja, Herr Cobb, vee will make your death quick and painless."

Eric searched Joyce's face to see if she was joking, then realized that there was more than a little edge in her voice.

"It's just...I want to start the rest of our life together *now*, not on our mothers' schedules."

"Then why don't you take Secretary Knox up on his offer to let you out of your commitment then?" Joyce asked hopefully. "Father could probably find you a job at one of the steel mills, or you could go back to school to be a lawyer..."

"Yes, I could," Eric replied. "But what kind of man would I be to cheat my country like that?"

"A sane one?" Joyce replied incredulously. "You can't tell me or anyone else what happened, but father says if the Germans ever catch you, they will *shoot you*."

"Your brother just volunteered for flight training!" Eric snapped back, then instantly regretted it Joyce's face went pale with rage.

"Yes, and do you think just *maybe* he's finding a spectacular way to commit suicide thanks to a certain person *fleeing to Hawaii?*" Joyce screamed. "Which you seem to just want to ignore every time it comes up!"

Why does she keep mentioning that? Eric thought as he took a deep breath.

"I will *not* have you screeching at me, Joyce," Eric said slowly. "That's not acceptable."

Joyce opened her mouth, then stopped as she saw the look on Eric's face.

"Well, I see that having things your own way remains a Cobb family trait," she observed icily. "What if I think screeching at you is perfectly, as you say, *acceptable?*"

"Then I would wonder if the woman I loved was driven away by my sister hurting her brother or me disappearing for two weeks," Eric said flatly.

Joyce's face fell, her eyes starting to well with tears.

"Get out," she sobbed.

"You can't just…"

"I said, *get out!*" Joyce said, pushing back from the table. Turning from him, she stalked back towards her bedroom, her shoulders shaking with sobs as she went. A few moments later Eric heard the door slam from upstairs.

Well that could have gone better, he thought to himself. After cleaning up the kitchen, he followed Joyce's orders.

Twenty dusty minutes later found him standing in front of the Cobb family's home. A gleaming white two-story, the house was at the end of a long double lane of cedar and maple trees. A squirrel ran up one of the latter and chattered at him from one of the lower branches. Eric favored the animal with a glare.

"You know, I can shoot *you*," he said hotly. "I'll even wear you like a hat as a warning to the others."

"Your mother would never forgive you," his father said from behind him, causing Eric to jump and the elder Cobb to start laughing.

"So what has you so distracted your old man was able to sneak up on you like a ghost while you were threatening your mother's squirrels with haberdashery?" Samuel Cobb asked. The Cobb family patriarch looked like a slightly older and heavier version of his eldest sons, from the bear-like physique to the mischievous blue eyes. While a pair of wire-rimmed glasses and worry lines made telling the three men apart quite easy up close, they were easily confused from a distance.

"Nothing," Eric replied uneasily, unable to meet his father's eyes as he fibbed.

Samuel shrugged.

"Well I hope you're better at cleaning up than you are at lying, because unless my nose deceives me Joyce was really happy to see you."

Eric looked at his father, feeling a warm blush rise to his cheeks.

"What? The eyesight goes as you get older so something has to make up for it," Samuel replied, holding his hands up in innocence. "Now you'd better hope your mother isn't outside because the wind's blowing from behind us, and if there's one smell a woman can detect from five miles away it's another woman's perfume."

Eric sniffed himself.

"Does it really smell that strong?!" he asked, horrified.

Samuel looked at his son and shook his head.

"Actually, no, I can't smell a thing—but you sure do look guilty now."

"Dad!" Eric replied, aghast.

"You must be a joy to play cards with, son," Samuel said, shaking his head.

"There's a reason I stopped playing with Nick, Sam, and David," Eric replied heatedly.

"So why the long face? I know it's not because Joyce is pregnant...yet."

"You know, you're enjoying us all being grown up a little too much," Eric said, shaking his head.

"Well I thought once I got your sister out of the house..." Samuel said wistfully.

Eric felt his face scowl before he caught himself.

"Ah. I take it the lovely Miss Cotner is a bit upset with Toots?"

"You could say that," Eric replied quietly.

"Tell me, son, do you really think Beau would have been able to handle Toots?" Samuel asked.

"What?"

"Seriously. Beau's a good man, may possibly even be a great one—but I think he wanted to marry Toots more out of a sense of that's what his mother told him to do than actually loving your sister. She ran circles around him in more ways than one," Samuel observed.

Eric looked askance at his father.

"I thought you liked Beau, Dad?" Eric said, shocked.

"I think of Beau like another son, Eric, you know that," Samuel replied with a heavy voice. "I now Toots hurt him desperately, and I worry about him going off to flight school with that pain."

"But?"

"Your sister is a strong woman just like her mother," Samuel continued. "Your mother's a handful and despite twenty-eight years I've never been under any illusions as to which one of us was smarter, law degree or no."

The depth of emotion in Samuel's voice made Eric smile, which in turn made Samuel get a sheepish look on his face.

"So, father, what do you think of Joyce and I?" Eric asked with raised eyebrow. Samuel's smile only dimmed a slight amount.

"That you guys love each other enough that you shouldn't have to rush into marriage because there's a baby on the way?"

"Oh no, that's never happened in this family before," Eric observed.

"Yes, and your grandfather never forgave me until he died. You want to give Theodore and Elma more reasons to hate us?"

"You're avoiding answering the larger question, Dad."

Samuel took off his glasses and pulled out a handkerchief to wipe them down.

Uh oh, Eric thought. *I may not have a poker face, but Dad has a couple of hellacious tells.*

"There is no question that you love Joyce with the fury of a thousand suns," Samuel said slowly. "I do believe that she *thinks* she loves you that same way, but I'm not sure she does."

Eric felt as if he had just been punched in his chest.

"Well Dad, don't hold back," he said quietly.

"Believe me, son, that *is* holding back," Samuel replied. "You pushed, son. I raised you kids well enough o know you shouldn't push unless you're prepared to face the truth."

"She asked me to take Secretary Knox up on his offer," Eric replied hotly. "I think that says something, doesn't it?"

Samuel turned and regarded his son with a pained look.

"That she truly doesn't know you at all," Samuel replied. "That she's certainly fond of you, more fond of you than a brother, but not that she loves you."

"How could you say that?" Eric snapped.

"Experience, son, experience," Samuel replied.

The front door to the house slammed open.

"Eric Thaddeus Cobb, is there a *reason* you left your fiancée looking at her lunch while you sit here gabbing with your father?" Alma Cobb shouted from the front porch, a jar of olives in her hands. Standing on the front porch in a blue gingham dress with matching flats, the Cobb family matriarch had her brunette hair up in a bun behind her head. Tall, with an aristocratic face and piercing blue eyes, Alma still looked almost exactly the same as she had on her wedding day.

"I guess that I must have misunderstood what she sent me over here for," Eric called to his mother.

"Oh no, that doesn't sound suspicious at all son," Samuel muttered.

"How hard is it to understand *olives*?" Alma asked sardonically.

"You know, Alma, you could act like you're still overjoyed to see your son," Samuel observed. "I mean, it's not like he's just had a near death experience or anything."

Alma turned to look at her husband, and Eric suddenly found himself glad that he was not in direct line of sight.

"Gee, maybe someone should not have talked him into being an aviator rather than a normal sailor or a marine?"

"What, so he could be sitting on some godforsaken island waiting for the Japs to show up or going swimming in the Atlantic?"

"Funny, I thought he ended up in the Atlantic anyway?" Alma observed archly. "Then he was so busy hobnobbing with royalty he couldn't be bothered to send a telegram."

"More like they wouldn't *let me*," Eric breathed.

"You know, I can *see* you sassing me, young man, even if I can't necessarily *hear* it." Alma continued. "Now are you going to get these olives or do I have to take them to the Cotner's to have lunch with Joyce myself?"

Eric shook his head as he fought not to smile. Walking up to the porch, he took the jar from his mother, sweeping her into a hug.

"Love you, Mom," he said in her ear.

"Love you too, son," Alma replied tenderly. "You guys should come here for dinner, but only after you wash up. You smell like a bordello."

Rose of Amsterdam
Tjilatjap, Dutch East Indies (DEI)
1100 Local (2300 Eastern)
4 November (3 November)

"Excuse me, sir, I'm looking for a Mr. Adam Haynes. Do you know where I might find him?" a man asked in heavily accented English.

That accent sounds suspiciously German, Adam thought without turning around. *Guess I should have stayed up in Surabaya with Petr and the boys*. Much to his surprise, five of his Poles had decided to accompany him to China from South Africa. Adam was fairly certain that the American Volunteer Group wouldn't mind some additional veterans even if their English wasn't the greatest.

"Do I need to be worried?" Adam asked lowly of the black-haired woman sharing the table with him. A short, slightly overweight woman whose caramel skin and blue eyes bespoke of mixed heritage, Marta and he had met the day before in the local market. Now she looked at him with a raised eyebrow, watching the bartender and the stranger interact behind him.

"How should I know?" she responded in her lilting voice. "Are you a wanted man?"

"Let's just say that depends on whom you ask," Adam replied.

"Well if memory serves, that man works at the local constabulary office," Marta replied. "But I don't get down here all that often, and I certainly don't tend to get involved with the *politie*."

Adam gave her a slight smile.

"Well I generally don't either, but thanks for making me a little more comfortable," he said, standing up. The stranger saw the movement out of the corner of his eye and turned towards Adam, raising his hand in greeting. The balding man's tan jacket, black shirt, and slacks plus his demeanor reminded Adam more of a pastor than a police officer.

"I assume you are Mr. Haynes, yes?" the man asked in barely understandable English. "Mr. Worcasaw told Wing Commander Collins we could probably find you somewhere down here."

"Okay, you found me," Adam replied. "Mind telling me who you are?"

"Oh, sorry...I am, how you English say...um...oh yes, *Officer* Stille with the Tjilatjap Constabulary. Mr. Worcasaw told me to tell you, first of all, that the 'sun always shines in Krakow'."

Adam had to fight not to laugh at Stille's pronunciation and diction.

"Okay, I'm somewhat mystified as to what could be so important that a policeman would come and find me, but I'm sure it must be critical given Worcasaw gave you a code. What is the message?"

"That you need to return to Surabaya as soon as possible," Stille said. "I do not know why, I just know that my chief normally does not usually use me as an errand boy."

Shit, Adam thought.

"Okay, when is the next train to Batavia?"

"In twenty minutes," Stille said.

Adam sighed.

"Could you give me a couple of minutes to meet you outside?"

"Certainly," Stille replied.

Adam went back to his table, giving Marta an apologetic smile.

"I'm not sure if I am a wanted man, but I must be a stupid one to leave a beautiful woman for parts unknown," Adam said sorrowfully. "I've had a good three days."

"So have I, Adam," Marta replied. She pulled a piece of paper from her purse and quickly scribbled down some information.

"If you are ever in Surabaya, please look me up. I work at the governor's office in the mailroom if you're unable to ring me here."

Adam nodded, placing the paper in his pocket. Marta stood up and wrapped him in an embrace. After a moment's surprise, Adam embraced her back.

Okay, apparently I was much more charming than I thought over the last couple of days, he thought to himself as he inhaled her perfume.

"Now off with you," she said with a smile, kissing him on the cheek. With a last wave, Adam turned to join Stille outside.

Perhaps I should have stayed in Tjilatjap, Adam thought to himself four hours later. He and the five Poles were sitting on thatch chairs along a grass runway, cold drinks in hand as they watched ground crews swarming over a group of *Spitfire* fighters. The elliptical-winged, elegant aircraft were painted in the dark green tropical colors of the Dutch East Indies Air Force.

"Did I just hear you right, Wing Leader Collins? You're wanting us to fly *Spitfires* and commit an act of war against Imperial Japan?" Adam asked slowly.

If Adam had been standing, the wing commander would have been a couple of inches shorter than he was, with a runner's build. The Australian ran a hand nervously through his parted blonde hair.

"I'm not sure I would have put it quite like that, Mr. Haynes," Collins replied.

"No, because then we'd all justifiably look at you and wonder why the Australian government is asking a bunch of Poles and one American to do this when, correct me if I'm wrong, your pilots flew those planes in."

Collins pressed his lips together.

"Due to the Ottawa Compact, all Commonwealth forces are restricted from…"

"Wait, the Ottawa what?" Adam asked. His question got him a bewildered look from Collins before there was a flash of cognition.

"Of course you wouldn't know. Apparently your Secretary of State and Prime Minister King forced Her Majesty to agree not to engage in any offensive operations against the Axis powers," Collins explained, obviously agitated. "Therefore, none of my men can fly north of Java."

"That doesn't explain why the Dutch can't fly them, given that they're all nice and painted now."

"He was not here," Petr Worcasaw reminded the Australian officer. Tall, with a shock of dark hair and brown, almost black eyes, Petr looked positively emaciated. Thankfully, the look was just his normal one as opposed to a sign he had caught some tropical disease.

"Well, let me catch you up to speed, Mr. Haynes," Collins said after a moment. "The reason why 'the Dutch can't fly them' is that they're not qualified. Oh, and that slight matter of having several of their best pilots killed yesterday."

"*What?*" Adam asked.

"It was an ambush," Petr said. "The Japanese come over every morning at 0800, then every afternoon at 1400. Yesterday the Dutch tried to catch the morning flight with their *Hurricanes*. It ended poorly."

"I thought the Japanese flew pieces of crap?!" Adam observed. "That was the rumor."

Petr shrugged.

"Apparently the Japanese 'crap' should scare plumbers everywhere," Petr observed grimly. "The Dutch took off with twelve fighters, came back with four. Another three crash landed elsewhere."

Adam whistled.

"Given that disaster we did not think it was a good idea to send pilots up again in aircraft they had just received," Wing Commander Collins observed drily.

"Instead you're going to have six men who haven't touched a *Spitfire* in literally months do so?" Adam snapped.

"Mr. Haynes, you are a double ace who, if rumors are to be

believed, was currently heading to China to seek further employment flying P-40s against warlords," Collins responded. "Perhaps I missed something, but when have you ever flown the *Tomahawk*? Because I know none of your companions have."

"Funny, I missed the part where His Majesty was still paying me," Adam observed drily.

"*Her* Majesty," Collins corrected, his voice stiff.

"Either way, I believe last time I flew *Spitfires* was for a certain government that proved willing to turn me over to its former enemies," Adam observed.

"No Americans were turned over to the Nazis..." Collins started to say.

"No, just some more of those stupid Poles," Petr interrupted darkly. "But I guess we should be used to Englishmen abandoning us by now."

Collins pursed his lips again, giving Petr a disapproving glare.

You know, I think Petr just might hurt you, Adam thought with a slight grin that broadened as the Australian looked away.

"Your hosts may not look kindly on your refusal to help," Collins said with an edge to his voice.

"If our 'hosts' want our help, they can pay for it. Otherwise I'll be happy to inform the U.S. consulate that we're being detained for refusal to partake in a military act. I'm sure *that* will go over swimmingly."

Collins looked positively apoplectic.

"Are you that much of a mercenary, Mr. Haynes?" he asked.

Adam laughed outright at him.

"How many Fascists have *you* killed, Wing Commander?" he asked pointedly, noting the lack of decorations on Collins' uniform.

"Excuse me?" Collins asked.

"I'm just thinking that for someone who is questioning my ethics, you seem to be rather bereft of combat experience yourself," Adam observed conversationally.

"You bastard!" Collins shouted, taking a step towards him. The man didn't get to complete the maneuver before Petr was already out of his chair and stepping between the Australian and Adam, the Pole's face split by an ear-to-ear grin. Adam didn't even move, instead noting that a couple of the ground crew had stopped working on the *Spitfires* and were watching the festivities.

"Now Wing Commander, there's no need to get yourself grievously injured," Adam continued, his tone condescending. "It'd be a shame to sit out an entire war only to have some crazy Polack break your jaw in five places."

Collins went pale with anger but wisely didn't take another step towards Adam.

"Her Majesty's government is willing to offer you one hundred pounds..."

Adam guffawed.

"...apiece. The Dutch government will offer you three hundred gulden as well."

Well now that's more like it, Adam thought.

"How much per kill?" Petr asked speculatively.

Collins looked at him, then back at Adam.

"I am sure we can come to some arrangement," the Australian gritted through clenched teeth.

"Those *Spitfires* don't look like the Mark Vs we flew," Adam replied. "We'll take them for a test flight, then come back and see what you come up with as far as payment goes."

A LITTLE OVER SIXTEEN HOURS LATER, ADAM WAS GLAD THAT HE HAD insisted on the test flight. Even after a taking a second hop to familiarize themselves and a good night's sleep, he still felt only slightly better about his ability to fight in the new *Spitfire*.

The kite may look similar but it sure as hell doesn't handle like a Mark V, Adam thought as he led the Poles north from Sumatra. Thirty thousand feet below him, the blue-green waters of the Strait of Malacca glistened from the early morning sun. He took a deep breath and looked at his watch.

I really hope the Aussies weren't wrong about the general vector and timing the last flight took, Adam thought. *I'd hate to be short fuel because some newbie radar boffin messed up his intercept data.* It had been somewhat of a surprise to find out that the Australians had placed three of the radar sets along Sumatra's north coast in the past two weeks.

It's almost like they really do plan on helping the Dutch hold this place if the Japanese come south, Adam thought. *Folks in their government must be sweating buckets.*

The glint of sunlight off glass below and to his port side stopped his thoughts. A moment later, the reflection became a single aircraft heading south on an opposite heading just at the edge of his vision.

Well at least these guys are as punctual as the Germans, Adam thought. He gave the *Spitfire* left rudder to swing wide of the reconnaissance aircraft, pulling back on the stick to give himself more height.

Now let's just hope the Japanese are much, much less observant...and don't have radar, he thought. *Of course, if all you're expecting is Hurricanes, you're probably not looking up at this point.*

Continuing north, Adam continued to search the sky ahead. Five minutes after the reconnaissance aircraft had passed, a swarm of dots followed along the same general path appeared to his port side below him.

Well, well, well, sometimes it's nice when your opponent is predictable, Adam thought. *Looks like the guests of honor are falling into the trap, but let's just keep flying to make sure there are not any party crashers coming up from behind.*

Five minutes later, Adam was sufficiently satisfied there were no additional Japanese fighters behind the eighteen or so they'd sighted. Waggling his wings, he brought the *Sptifire* around in a gentle turn so as not to cause any vapor trails from his wing, then advanced his throttle. With a gentle shudder and black smoke from its nose, the *Spitfire* leapt ahead.

Even though the Dutch do only have Hurricanes, if I'm that Japanese commander then I'd still expect them at altitude. Easy does it, Adam thought, looking at his altimeter.

A few minutes later, Adam was glad to see that the new *Spitfire* appeared to have a significant speed advantage over the Japanese fighters. As he closed, the American could see the single-engined craft were painted dark olive green and arranged in groups of three flying in a V of Vs.

Odds could be better, but it looks like we're calling the tune here, Adam thought, his pulse increasing. *Hope everyone remembers the plan and doesn't get buck fever, we **cannot** stay here.* Making one last check of his guns, he pushed the spade control panel forward and shoved his throttle to war emergency power.

Choosing the rearmost V, he aimed for the leader as he came down from the sun. The aircraft swelled in his sight as he skidded to add slight deflection, watching as he could pick out more and more detail. Just as Adam was pressing his trigger, the Japanese pilot apparently saw Death plunging at him from above. Smoke was pouring from the fighter's exhaust and its wings starting to come up in a snap roll when the twin cannons and machine guns in the *Spitfire*'s wings began shaking the gunsight. Before Adam had a chance to register any hits, the Japanese aircraft exploded, debris flying towards him and causing him to flinch upwards.

Dammit, he thought, then quickly reacted by bringing his nose around to line up an aircraft in the lead trio as he hurtled over the Japanese formation. Smoke poured from the enemy fighter's radial engine as the pilot added throttle and started to reef his aircraft around. Unfortunately for the Japanese airman, his maneuver put the dark green fighter directly in front of Adam's second quick burst, his cannon and heavy machine guns slicing the aircraft's port wing from its fuselage. The shattered plane started to spin crazily as Adam hurtled past while bringing his nose up as he headed south. He glanced briefly to make sure Flight Officer Kantor, his wingman, was still with him then continued to haul ass away from the bedlam behind him.

Well that went better than expected, Adam thought, fighting the temptation to turn back around and have another go at the chaos he had left behind him. Then a thought occurred.

I wonder if that reconnaissance plane is still in front of us? he thought with a slight smile. He continued to scan the horizon as he ran like a thief from a bank robbery, adrenaline making his hand jittery on the stick. A couple of minutes later, his persistence was rewarded, as he sighted the reconnaissance aircraft for the second time that day, headed on a reciprocal course to his starboard front. Turning, he glanced back to see empty sky.

Well this ought to be interesting, he thought, skidding to bring his nose around in a pursuit curve. The reconnaissance aircraft saw him and put its nose down, trying to add speed. Despite the pilot's best efforts, Adam was quickly able to close within range, the twin engines swelling in his reticle. The aircraft's tail gunner opened fire on him, the tracers arcing back behind the *Spitfire* just as Adam squeezed his own trigger. White flashes all along the fuselage, exploding glass, and sudden cessation of return fire told Adam he had hit the tail gunner, while white smoke that quickly became black from the port engine told him that the reconnaissance aircraft had been severely damaged. Adam pulled up to avoid running into the back of the aircraft, turning to look behind his wingman...where he saw a single olive green aircraft closing rapidly from behind.

"Break Kantor! Break!" Adam shouted in Polish as he brought his own nose around. Flight Officer Kantor didn't question his order, whipping his own *Spitfire* into a tight turn just as the closing Japanese opened fire. Adam's sense of relief turned to horror as the olive green fighter managed to cut inside of the *Spitfire*'s turn, gaining enough lead to open fire again even as Adam was closing from the Japanese pilot's port side. Firing a snapshot, Adam saw his burst knock pieces off his target's tail just before the two fighters crossed paths.

He just fucking outturned a **Spit**, Adam thought with a moment's panic, pulling up into a loop. Looking through the top of his canopy, he watched the enemy fighter continuing to turn after the now diving Kantor. Rolling through the loop into an Immelman, Adam followed the two other aircraft down.

Dammit, dammit, dammit, Adam thought, angry at himself for getting greedy. Slipping side to side, he checked his rearview mirror to make sure there were no other enemy fighters behind him, then poured on the coal. The enemy pilot never realized that Adam had a speed advantage, presenting an easy target as he focused on trying to catch Kantor. Lining up the reticle, Adam fired and this time was rewarded with a brilliant streamer of fire that engulfed the enemy fighter's fuselage. Before Adam's horrified eyes the Japanese fighter's canopy came hurtling back, followed a moment later by a burning comet with writhing limbs.

Ignoring the falling fighter, Adam rejoined with Kantor. Turning, he looked the other *Spitfire* over, noting several bullet holes just behind the cockpit and down the fuselage.

"You all right Two?" he asked in French.

"Yes, yes," the shaken Pole answered. "But next time, I think we let the extra kill go."

Adam laughed in relief.

"Follow me, I think we've done enough for today," Adam said. Even as they winged back towards Java, he kept a sharp lookout behind them, expecting more Japanese to make an appearance.

Well we can outrun and outdive them, but I'll be damned if I try to outturn one of those bastards if we do this again, he thought as his hands shook on the controls as he came down from the rush of adrenaline and fear, and he took several deep breaths to calm himself. Unbidden, the image of the burning Japanese pilot came back to his mind, and he found his mouth suddenly thick with saliva as he had the urge to vomit. He swallowed forcefully, hating his reaction.

Then again, the point where burning another man alive becomes blasé might be the point where I need to eat a bullet, he mused to himself. It wasn't the first time he had set a man afire, and he had the sinking suspicion it was not going to be the last.

Batavia was upon him before he knew it. As Adam passed over the airfield while Kantor landed, he noticed a group of twenty or so people gathered at the front of the four *Spitfire*s that had already landed.

I'm always worried when there's a welcoming committee. Turning into his own final approach and lowering his landing gear, he wondered who the gathered people were. Shrugging, he plopped down in a perfect landing and then taxied over to the end of the line of *Spitfires*.

You know, it might be a good idea to start staggering these aircraft, Adam thought as he opened the *Spitfire*'s canopy and was hit by Batavia's tropical heat. He quickly shrugged out of his flight jacket, just as a flashbulb burst at the edge of his vision. As if that had been a starting gun, he was suddenly beset by a horde of questions shouted at him in Dutch. Adam stepped out on the wing, then took off his Mae West, oxygen mask, and flight helmet. Placing the items on his seat, he shrugged out of his flight tunic and immediately felt cooler as the cacophony died down around him.

"Mr. Haynes! Mr. Adam Haynes!" someone shouted. Adam snapped around, recognizing the speaker's Midwest twang. He saw that the individual calling to him was a slightly rotund, brown-haired man in a tan suit. Two of the local constabulary were making a hole for the man as he got closer to the *Spitfire*. Stepping to the ground, he turned to face the man as the latter was furiously mopping at his face.

"Adam Haynes, you are a hard man to find," the stranger said.

"I'm sorry, have we met before?" Adam asked, casually crossing his arms so that his right hand was closer to his still holstered revolver. The Dutch policeman standing to the man's right noticed the movement and tensed.

"My name is Harold Parks, and I'm with Standard Oil," the man continued, extending his hand. Moving his hand away from his holster, Adam extended his own hand as the hubbub around the two of them died down.

"Is there someplace private we can talk?" Parks asked, looking at the reporters pressing all around them.

"Clear the way!" someone shouted, then repeated their statement again in what Adam could only assume was Dutch. The two policemen, hearing the voice, immediately started gesturing for the gathered press to get out of the way. Adam recognized Wing Commander Collins walking behind four more Dutch police, but did not recognize the man walking beside him in the uniform of a Dutch East Indies officer.

"Well Mr. Haynes, glad to see that you made it back in one piece," Wing Commander Collins said stiffly.

Why does your tone make me doubt your sincerity? Adam thought.

"That makes two of us," Adam replied wryly as the Poles joined him.

Collins gave him a slight smile, his face softening. He turned to the officer beside him.

"This is Wing Commander Wevers of the Dutch East Indies Air Force," Collins continued.

Commander Wevers shot out his hand, and Adam took it. The

Dutchman shook vigorously then, giving a sound of joy, dragged the American in for an immense bear hug.

"Thank you! Thank you!" the man said in heavily accented English as he let Adam go, then turned to the gathered group. "Thank you all for...how you say...*avenging* my men."

Ah, that explains it, Adam thought, slightly bemused.

"Our pleasure," Petr returned. Adam could see the Pole was almost overcome with emotion himself.

Kindred spirits, these men, Adam thought. *Which is unsurprising given that their home countries are still occupied.*

"Mr. Haynes, I really do need to give you my information as soon as possible," Parks said, getting a strange look from Collins.

"Wing Commander Wevers, is there someplace we can go in private?" Adam asked. Getting a puzzled look, Adam was about to ask Collins for help when Parks rapidly translated. Nodding emphatically, Wevers began barking at the gathered reporters and the police, gesturing towards a cluster of buildings at the north end of the airfield. There was a low murmuring among the crowd but the press throng began to grudgingly move away from the group of pilots.

"I'll be along in a moment, Wing Commander," Adam said, gesturing for Parks to follow him. Once they were out of earshot, Adam turned to find his companion reaching inside of his suit jacket to pull out an envelope.

"I have a message from your father," Parks said flatly.

*Oh you can go fuck...*Adam thought, his expression turning into an ugly scowl.

"Please Mr. Haynes, I think you need to read this," Parks pressed. "It's urgent, and he's had a hell of a time finding you."

"Funny thing about that," Adam snapped. "I seem to recall last time he saw me he considered me a disgrace and that I could consider myself disinherited for being a 'paid assassin'."

Parks handed the message over without saying anything further. Adam snatched the envelope from his hands then put it in his pants pocket. Parks shook his head.

"I was given clear instructions to make sure you *read* the message," Parks said sharply.

Adam shook his head in disgust as he took the envelope back out of his pocket.

"Well can't have one of father's minions go back without..." Adam started, recognizing the handwriting as that of his father's personal assistant, Cassandra.

Oh my god...

"When was this letter written?!" he snapped.

"It was given to me two days ago. I understand it first arrived in England in mid-August."

"Fat lot of good it would have done me there," Adam muttered, then said louder, "I assume you have a way for us to get out of here?"

"Yes," Parks replied. "I have an itinerary, but only if you can leave in the next three hours. Otherwise you will have to wait until tomorrow morning."

"Give me a few moments to make my goodbyes," Adam said, his voice thick as the enormity of the letter's contents began to register.

"Understood. I'll get my driver to come around to the flight line," Parks said.

Adam headed back to the clump of officers, fighting the burning in his eyes. Seeing the look on his face, the Poles took a couple of steps towards him.

"Adam, what is wrong?" Kantor asked in heavily accented English.

"My mother..." Adam began, his voice cracking. "My mother has cancer. She may already be dead. I am sorry, my friends, but I must leave you."

ACTS OF WAR

Sea of Japan
1000 Local (2000 Eastern)
7 November (6 November) 1942

With a muttered curse, Isoro shoved the throttle forward, waited for the engine to respond with a spew of black exhaust smoke, then pulled back gently on his stick while applying left rudder pedal. The round nose of his *Shiden* fighter skidded back online with the carrier

JAMES YOUNG

Akagi's gently pitching deck, and he felt the fighter begin to lift slowly back from just above the waves. Sweat beading all over his face, Isoro watched as the carrier's landing lights indicated that the *Shiden* was back on the correct path for touching down on the carrier's deck.

I am glad we do not use an officer for this as the Americans do, Isoro thought grimly. *I would be so ashamed that another pilot saw how I am handling this aircraft.* Even as an experienced pilot, Isoro had found the *Shiden* to be a handful during familiarization flights the previous week. Biting his tongue in concentration, Isoro tried to avoid thinking about the two men whom had died because their skills had been found wanting.

Almost there...almost there...now! Isoro thought, feeling the fighter thump down hard and immediately pulling his throttle backward. A moment later he was jerked forward as the arresting hook stopped his forward movement. Exhaling in relief, he allowed himself a moment of giddiness before shutting down the engine. As the prop finished whirring, the *Akagi*'s deck crew sprinted out to shove the fighter forward. Isoro unbuckled, jumped out of the cockpit, and then almost ran towards the *Akagi*'s island while the deck crew manhandled the *Shiden* forward.

"Honda!" Commander Mitsuo Fuchida shouted, causing Isoro to whip his head around. He saw the older man standing with Lieutenant Commander Itaya and a couple of other officers.

Nothing good comes from being called over, he thought, steeling himself as he made his face impassive.

"What do you think?" Fuchida asked amicably, gesturing towards the *Shiden*.

*It is a farm girl to the **Zero**'s geisha...* Isoro thought internally.

"It is much faster and it rolls quicker," Isoro said tentatively.

"Oh come on, we are not your sister asking how her kimono looks," Itaya sneered derisively. "What is your honest opinion?"

Isoro turned and looked as the next *Shiden* made its approach. He could tell the pilot was struggling with the controls, the fighter getting further and further out of the best glide path. Finally, with what he imagined was probably a scream of frustration in the cockpit, the pilot applied throttle and brought the fighter around to attempt another pass.

"It is hard to learn," Isoro said simply. "I enjoy the additional power and the way it rolls, but I miss flicking my wrist and changing directions like a bird."

Fuchida nodded, smiling slightly.

"I can understand that," the senior officer replied. "Still, if Captain Genda's reports from Germany are to be believed, the *Zero* is close to being eclipsed by both the British and German fighters which battled over Britain last summer."

"Which means those American bastards will probably have something almost as good by the time we fight them," Itaya said grimly. His response drew a sharp look from Fuchida, to which the *Akagi* fighter commander shrugged.

"The man is not an idiot, Fuchida-san," Itaya continued with a shrug. "It is easy to see that the Germans will be fighting the Americans before a year is out. When that happens, the oil flow stops and we are right back to late 1941 when we attacked the Communists."

We all know how well that went, Isoro thought.

The roar of the next *Shiden* landing ended the conversation before Itaya could reveal more. The pilot hit the deck heavily, but still managed to catch the last arrester wire on the *Akagi*'s deck. Itaya shook his head in disgust.

"We are going to break these fighters before we even get a chance to use them," the man muttered.

"Everyone is having a difficult time with their new aircraft," Fuchida said stiffly. "We will do what we must for the Empire."

"Of course," Itaya said. "I just do not look forward to the next few weeks."

IJNS MUSASHI
1030 LOCAL (2030 EASTERN)

FIFTY MILES TO THE *AKAGI*'S SOUTHWEST, REAR ADMIRAL Yamaguchi found himself echoing Itaya's sentiment. The *Musashi*'s flag plot was relatively empty, the cavernous space currently holding less than two dozen men gathered around a large scale map of the Pacific. The air passing through the vessel's open portholes carried the normal sounds of a man of war at sea, from the sound of petty officers bawling out an unfortunate sailor to the low, steady rumble as the massive warship cruised at the head of the battleline stretched out behind her.

"With the support of the aircraft from Singapore, I do not think that I need the carriers," Vice Admiral Nobutake Kondo was stating. The stocky man with a broad, open face continued in a firmer tone as he gestured towards the Dutch East Indies. "I would rather have more escorts for the transports than have destroyers and cruisers tied to the *Hiyo*, *Junyo*, and *Ryujo*."

Across the table, a bald man in gleaming whites that contrasted with the other officers' dark blue uniforms placed both hands on the table and pressed himself to his feet. The maneuver drew all eyes briefly to the missing index and middle fingers on his left hand, shortly before the taller, older man spoke.

"Yamaguchi-san, can the *Kido Butai* fit the additional planes on their carriers?" Admiral Isoroku Yamamoto asked simply.

This is why I wish Vice Admiral Nagumo had not been chosen to do the inspection, Yamaguchi thought to himself.

"It will drastically lengthen the time it takes to launch and recover strike waves, sir," Yamaguchi replied evenly. "We will hit harder, but only at the cost of having a second wave that has completely lost surprise. Losses will be heavy given the shore based fighters."

Yamamoto regarded the map.

"What if we no longer planned to strike the Americans in Pearl Harbor?" Yamamoto asked, his eyes meeting Yamaguchi's.

There was a sharp intake of breath from one of the other conference participants. Yamaguchi kept his own face impassive even as he felt a current of shock course through him.

For Yamamoto to argue that we will no longer attempt surprise means that a great deal has changed in the talks with the Germans, Yamaguchi thought to himself. *I wonder what they have offered us in concessions to so change our war plan. No matter, I am a sword for the Emperor.*

"According to our consulate Admiral Jensen, the new American commander, has begun rotating capital vessels on a three, rather than six, day schedule. He has also directed all vessels will be prepared to steam within four hours notice," Yamamoto replied, his voice solemn. "For this reason, I believe it unlikely that we will catch most of the American fleet in harbor."

"It would be preferable to let the Americans come towards us in that case," Vice Admiral Kondo said stiffly. "We would be able to attrit them as they steamed towards the Marshalls."

Kondo-san is always one for caution, Yamaguchi thought.

"Rear Admiral Yamaguchi, do you think you can find the Americans at sea?" Yamamoto asked.

"Yes, sir, I can," Yamaguchi replied, his tone puzzled. "However, I would think Vice Admiral Nagumo..."

"Vice Admiral Nagumo will be remaining in Germany for the near future," Yamamoto replied, his tone pleasant despite having cut Yamaguchi off. "You are now in command of the *Kido Butai*, Vice Admiral Yamaguchi."

Yamaguchi felt a sense of shock as Vice Admiral Ugaki, Yamamoto's Chief of Staff, stood with an ornate box in his hand. Opening it, the Chief of Staff revealed a Vice Admiral's epaulettes as the gathered men began applauding.

"Sir, I am honored," Yamaguchi said, feeling his chest tighten as the shock wore off.

"You have earned it, Yamaguchi-san," Admiral Yamamoto replied formally. "I am sorry that our current exigencies have prevented us from having a formal ceremony. Nagumo-san indicated that you have always sought to conduct operations in the most aggressive manner with your division. When I asked him who should undertake this task if he were unavailable, you were his first choice."

Today is just full of surprises, Tamon thought to himself, feeling numb even as Kondo and Ugaki began to replace his epaulettes. Looking across the compartment, he saw that not everyone was as enthusiastic as the Combined Fleet's senior officers. Indeed, Rear Admiral Ryunosuke Kusaka, the *Kido Butai*'s chief of staff, looked as if he had just had a full lemon shoved into his mouth.

I may need to think about staff changes, Yamaguchi thought grimly.

Kusaka has always been far too cautious, and I am sure he has some belief that this job should be his. He had no more time to consider things as the compartment's occupants came one by one to congratulate the Imperial Japanese Navy's newest Vice Admiral.

"Now, let us continue," Admiral Yamamoto said once everyone had shaken Yamaguchi's hand.

"With the six carriers reinforced by *Hiyo* and *Junyo*'s air groups, I will likely sink three battleships if I face them at sea..." Yamaguchi began.

"That is a very optimistic estimate," Kondo interrupted him. "This will be much different than attacking these same vessels in harbor!"

"I will launch over three hundred aircraft," Yamaguchi replied simply. "Since I no longer have to worry about attempting to destroy battleships with level attacks, all of my torpedo bombers will be available to attack."

"Yes, and they will likely cause grave *damage*. But to sink three battleships?" Kondo replied. Yamaguchi was about to respond when Admiral Yamamoto cleared his throat.

"Captain Sugiura, now would be as good a time as any to give your briefing," Admiral Yamamoto said, gesturing towards a tall, slender officer standing in the back of the room. Yamaguchi had never met the man, but was familiar with his work as one of the IJN's foremost torpedo experts. The officer bowed slightly towards Admiral Yamamoto, clearly nervous.

"Honored superiors," Sugiura began, his voice trembling "superior," "I was sent to Germany along with Vice Admiral Nagumo. As per the Treaty of Kent, the Royal Navy was forced to share technical data with the *Kriegsmarine*. One of the projects that the British was working on was a new explosive substance for their torpedoes which was far superior to anything either the Germans or our mission had seen."

There was the noise of chairs moving along the deck as most of the Japanese officers shifted. The IJN, as a force that expected to be outnumbered in any war it fought, had long believed itself the foremost experts in all aspects of torpedo warfare.

"The British called this experimental warhead material TORPEX in all of their documents," Sugiura continued. "Our navy has determined to call it *Sandaburo*, and it is roughly one and a half times as powerful as the compound we currently use."

"How soon can we begin producing this material?" Vice Admiral Kondo asked. "Can you fit it to our destroyer and cruiser torpedoes?"

"The explosive is complicated," Admiral Yamamoto answered for the junior officer. "In our initial experiments, we have discovered that if the production is not conducted with the proper materials the results are not favorable."

That explains why there have been several torpedo bomber crashes as of late, Yamaguchi thought to himself. *There had been rumors of possible sabotage or shoddy production.*

"The Ordnance Bureau, at Admiral Yamamoto's direction, have focused our production on aerial warheads until we were confident in our ability to produce safe weapons," Sugiura continued. "The loss of a torpedo bomber, while unfortunate, is nothing compared with damage to a cruiser or destroyer."

"How many warheads?" Yamaguchi asked.

"We expect to have three hundred and fifty aerial torpedo warheads available by March," Sugiura replied.

A collective gasp rippled across the compartment.

"Even with the new warheads, things will be extremely difficult for my operation," Yamaguchi stated. "Have the Germans given us a date they intend to attack?"

"March 26th," Yamamoto replied.

So we have a date for war, Yamaguchi thought. His stomach clenched like an angry man's fist as he turned to the map.

"The *Kido Butai* will be ready by then," Yamaguchi said tersely. "We will do our part to preserve the Empire."

Pearl Harbor
0600 Local (1100 Eastern)
9 November

Captain William Greenman, USN had a major problem. Tall, with narrow features, and aristocratic bearing, slightly graying brown hair, and dark brown eyes, the new Pacific Fleet G-2 had the sinking suspicion that his predecessor had been handed a blessing in disguise.

Whether Captain Layton was fired or simply reassigned, Fortune certainly gave him a golden ticket, Greenman thought, feeling acid starting to rise in his throat.

"What do you mean, the Japanese changed their code, Lieutenant Commander Crewe?" Greenman asked archly, looking at the lieutenant commander standing in front of him. The short, overweight officer gave him an unimpressed look that bordered on belligerency, and Greenman fought the urge to scream at the man.

I may have to see about getting Commander Rochefort back here, no matter what our new chief of staff's opinion of him was, Greenman thought angrily. *His replacement is an idiot.*

"Around 0100 hours there was a transmission that read 'a tiger slinks silently through the grass.' It was repeated three times, then next thing we know, we're looking at gibberish," Crewe said with a shrug. "There were a couple of out stations that asked for a repeat of the signal, but they were ignored."

Admiral Jensen is going to hit the fucking roof when I tell him this, Greenman thought, suddenly feeling as if his collar was two sizes too small. One of the reasons that Layton and Rochefort had been transferred was CINCPACFLT felt the two men were far too confident in their abilities. The lesson Greenman had taken from that experience was to add some shadow of doubt in his statements, but still rely on the information coming from the broken Japanese codes.

"Do we still have the ability to tell what operators are signaling?" Greenman asked. "I mean, if we have the same signal techniques, that's at least something."

"Still trying to determine that, sir," Crewe replied, running a hand through his thinning brown hair.

"I suggest you try *harder*, Lieutenant Commander," Greenman snapped. "Admiral Jensen has requested a briefing at 0900 on what the Japanese are up to now that they have Singapore and Burma."

Crewe looked as if he wanted to say something, then thought better of it.

I need to get in touch with ONI, Greenman thought. *Maybe the boys in*

Washington have some idea on what in the hell the Japanese are doing, as I certainly don't. The captain glanced up at the clock.

"This is going to be an utter disaster," Greenman muttered to himself.

FIVE AND A HALF HOURS LATER, THERE WAS CONCRETE PROOF THAT Greenman at least understood his own navy's chain of command even if his window into the IJN's had just become opaque.

"Sir, we don't know why the Japanese changed their..." he began again, before once more being cut off by Admiral Jensen slamming his hand on the desk.

"It is readily apparent, *Captain*, that you would not know where your feet were if they weren't attached," CINCPACFLT said. The man's volume had barely raised above normal, but there was no doubt as to the intense anger the four-star admiral was feeling.

"Perhaps we should have General Short's intelligence officer come and brief us," Vice Admiral Bowles observed airily. "Even if it's wrong, it will be nice to have someone actually give us information and stand by it."

I have spent the last hour and a half giving you information, Greenman thought. *The fact you are more concerned with stabbing your son's squadron commanders in the back than reading the packets I give you...*

"Sir, I only give you the information I can verify," Greenman replied, a little heat coming into his voice. "It is a fact that the Japanese have moved three battleships and two light carriers south to Singapore. It is a fact that their air groups have begun flying shuttle missions between Formosa to Singapore and Vichy French bases in Indochina."

"So what does all that mean, Captain? A bunch of slant eyes burning fuel doesn't tell me anything about what the threats *here* may be," Jensen barked.

"Sir, it tells me that the Japanese are practicing reinforcing Singapore in preparation to seize the East Indies," Greenman stated, fighting to keep his voice calm. "They know President Roosevelt will reenact sanctions if they formally occupy Indochina again, so they are making sure pilots know the way from Taiwan to their new bases."

"So are you telling me that the Japanese are not going to try and strike here?" Admiral Jensen asked.

"Sir, with all due respect, I don't think *we* could sail all the way across the Pacific in one go and successfully strike a fleet at sea," Greenman replied evenly. "There is no reason to believe that the Japanese are able to do so."

"Layton and Rochefort believed that this 'First Air Fleet' was formed for just that reason," Vice Admiral Bowles retorted. "Are you saying that they were wrong?"

"Sir, everyone looks at data differently," Greenman said. "Captain Layton..."

"That was a yes or no question, Captain," Bowles interrupted.

"Yes, sir," Greenman bit out sharply. "I think that the First Air Fleet has been formed for strictly administrative purposes. Given what we know of the IJN's structure and customs, the placement of a junior admiral such as Yamaguchi in charge of it would be indicative of it being a minor command."

"Nagumo was in command of it before Yamaguchi, according to your packets," Bowles challenged.

Well maybe he did read what we put out, Greenman thought.

"Sir, Vice Admiral Nagumo was sent to Germany," he replied evenly. "I don't think admirals in good esteem are sent several thousand miles away from any available fleet."

Admiral Jensen's eyes narrowed at that, and Greenman remembered the man had been assigned to Great Lakes Training Command before his ascension to CINCPACFLT.

"Sir, the men are getting tired of our alert schedule," Vice Admiral Bowles noted. "I've also got Secretary Knox asking very pointed questions about our fuel and parts expenses."

"So in your opinion, Captain Greenman, are the Japanese going to attack soon?" Admiral Jensen asked directly.

"Sir, I don't think the Japanese will be attacking in the next sixty days," Greenman replied.

"Based on what?!" Bowles asked derisively. "Your crystal ball?!"

"No sir, based on the *calendar*," Greenman snapped back. "Japan is not going to go to war with us without Germany, and the Krauts aren't going to attack the Russians in November."

Admiral Jensen held up his hand before Bowles could respond.

"Vice Admiral Bowles, we will reduce our readiness for the next month," Jensen said. "Furthermore, we will send Pye's division and escorts back to the West Coast for refit, effective next week."

Greenman was sure the burning sensation he felt as Jensen's gaze swiveled back to him was all in his head.

"You had better be correct, Captain Greenman," Jensen said ominously. "A lot of men are going to die if you are not."

4
GIVING THANKS

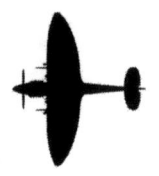

The American people will not relish the idea of any American citizen growing rich and fat in an emergency of blood and slaughter and human suffering.

— **PRESIDENT FRANKLIN D. ROOSEVELT**

HONOLULU, HAWAII
1400 LOCAL (1900 EASTERN)
25 NOVEMBER 1942

"You should have seen the look on his face," Sam said, laughing as he leaned back from the table. "Bastard never saw it coming!"

My brothers are nuts, Patricia thought to herself as she regarded the dining room table. *They've barely been here for fifteen minutes and Sam's already acting like he knows everyone.*

"Glad I was able to find those eaves," she heard Jo state behind her in the kitchen. Usually able to sit four, Jo had produced two eaves that allowed the furniture to seat eight place settings. The three Cobb brothers sat on one side of the table, with Sam nearest the head, David next to him, an empty place for Sadie next, then Nick nearest the foot.

All three siblings were in their dress uniforms, something that had surprised Patricia when the trio had appeared on her doorstep.

Who knew that CINCPACFLT had the power to tell people what to wear while on liberty? she thought. *Guess that's the downside of living on what's basically an outpost.*

"Sam, language!" David said, even as his own face was split in a wide grin. Sam shook his head, then scrunched his face up as if he was going to cry.

"'B-b-but my Daddy just got out here and everything!'" he mock whined, changing his usual drawl to mimic Bowles flat Northeastern accent. "'Don't you know I'm the *Chief of Staff's son?*'"

The guests on the other side of the table were all relatively unknown to Patricia. To the left of the table head sat a Navy lieutenant (j.g.) that appeared far too old to hold that rank. Patricia had heard her brothers talking about "mustangs" before, but had never actually met one before Peter Byrnes. Next to him, a Navy commander that Jo apparently knew from her father's time in Newport News was also smiling at Sam's impression.

Jo kept calling him Uncle K, Patricia thought.

"Sorry Commander Hertling," David said, giving Sam a look that basically screamed for his twin to be quiet.

"I think you can call me Keith while we're here," the tall, broad shouldered man said, his blue eyes twinkling. "I'm not a fan of Vice Admiral Bowles, and glad to see the scuttlebutt about his son getting a surprise reassignment to Pensacola was true."

"Patricia, can you grab these potatoes?" Nancy Hertling asked, causing Patricia to jump. Like her husband, Nancy was tall with salt and pepper hair. There the resemblance ended, as Mrs. Hertling's build was willowy to her husband's athletic.

"Certainly Nancy," Patricia replied, grabbing a pair of oven mitts from the hooks on the wall. She had to shake her head at the kitchen's navy blue with pewter trim color scheme.

Those colors just might drive me crazy, Patricia thought. *Makes the place seem claustrophobic.*

"Is Sam sewing discord again?" Jo asked. "I think he's still annoyed that you couldn't make your mother's famous corn pudding."

"That takes too much time and groceries," Patricia said as she grabbed the bowl of potatoes.

"I've never even heard of corn pudding before today," Nancy observed with a shake of her head.

"We fellow 'Yankees' apparently don't know what we're missing," Jo observed, her tone clearly indicating she'd be completely okay going to her grave without checking that particular box.

"You truly don't," Patricia said teasingly as she headed back out into the dining room. She was careful to hold the potatoes away from her body so as to avoid getting any flour on her dark green dress, the movement as natural to her as breathing after years helping her mother.

"From what my friend in the G-1 tells me, Vice Admiral Bowles was just as surprised as his son was," Commander Hertling was saying. "It appears that Admiral Jensen felt his Chief of Staff was too, shall we say, *distracted* by his son being here."

"Well when VMF-21 gets three squadron commanders because those men *dared* to correct your precious baby boy..." Sam began.

"What?!" Nick said, incredulously.

"Yeah, it was..." David started to say, before being interrupted by a knock on the door just as Patricia sat the covered bowl of potatoes down.

"I'll get it," she said, waving David back to his seat.

"It's probably Sadie," David protested.

"I don't care if it's Santa Claus, you know better," Patricia replied with a smile. "Don't want my new sister-in-law thinking I was raised without manners."

Oh mother is going to be powerfully angry when she finds out you guys eloped, Patricia thought. *I may have just moved down her priority of wrath by at least a couple slots.*

Opening the door, Patricia found herself facing a brown haired woman who was only a couple inches shorter than her. Dressed in a dark blue dress that matched her eyes and with her light brown hair falling off her shoulders in curls, Joanna Sadie Cobb (nee Leonard) looked like she had just come from a salon rather than riding herd on a bunch of fifth graders.

"Hello Patricia," the woman said in her soft contralto. "May I come in?"

"Of course!" Patricia said, embracing the other woman in a hug as she stepped through the foyer. "We are always open for family."

Sadie chuckled quietly at that as she hugged Patricia back.

"It still takes some getting used to realizing I just inherited a sister," Sadie replied lowly, her Minnesota accent making the words sound strange to Patricia's ears.

"Us only daughters have to stick together," Patricia quipped as she released her sister-in-law. "Let me get your purse, you timed it almost perfectly."

"Well Mr. Archibald had some last minute remarks for us teachers over the holiday," Sadie said. "All of which can be summed up in 'don't be stupid.'"

"Oh?" Patricia asked, raising an eyebrow.

"He's an old-fashioned principal," Sadie replied with a shrug after handing her coat over. "I'm lucky I'm even still employed, as he seems to be the type who thinks married women should be at home, not working."

"How old is he again?" Patricia asked as they walked from the foyer into the dining room.

"Pushing seventy, although you wouldn't know it from the way he rides herd on the kids," Sadie replied. There was the scraping of chairs as the men came to their feet, David stepping forward to embrace her with a kiss.

"Glad you made it, Sadie," Jo said, walking in with a plate full of sliced ham and pineapples. Nancy was right behind her with a big dish full of stuffing, and Patricia noted the creamed spinach had already made its way from the kitchen.

"Sorry I'm late, Jo..." Sadie began.

"Oh stop apologizing," Jo said mirthfully. "It's your husband and his brother's fault for volunteering to be the duty officers tomorrow."

Sadie stopped dead and turned to look at David.

"Volunteered?!" she asked in shock.

"The two duty officers that were assigned both have newborns,"

Sam said quickly. "One of them didn't know it, but his parents were going to surprise him today."

Sadie looked at both twins.

"Sam, someday we are going to have to get you married so you stop doing nice things for *other people's families*," Sadie said evenly.

"Or alternatively his brother could let him ride off a cliff by himself just this once," Peter observed lowly, drawing a heated look from David.

"I seem to recall a certain pilot cadet that benefited from David and I being joined at the hip," Sam replied, drawing a pained look from Byrnes and a puzzled look from Nancy.

"I should probably do the introductions for Sadie's sake," Jo said lightly. "Sadie, this is Commander Keith Hertling, or 'Uncle K.' He was in my father's destroyer squadron when we were all at Newport News. Beside him is his wife, Nancy, who basically raised me as a teenager."

"Hello Sadie," Nancy said. "Josephine, sorry to interrupt, but we should probably serve the food before it gets cold."

Jo looked nonplussed for a moment at having forgotten that the dishes were already on the table.

"Whoops! Yes, everyone sit down. Uncle K, will you say grace?" Jo said sheepishly.

"Certainly," Commander Hertling replied.

As she took her seat, Jo felt herself mildly embarrassed.

I should have put Uncle K at the head of the table, she thought. *But I didn't want all of the Cobbs to feel like they were back in the mess.*

"Amen," she said, then raised her head to look down the table, a feeling of lightness in her chest.

They say this is a holiday for family, she thought. *I guess family's what you make of it.*

"You seem pleased with yourself," Nancy observed as the food started getting passed around.

"Oh, just feeling truly thankful," Jo said, causing a chuckle around the table. "A lot of happenstance had to take place to get everyone at this table."

"Well happenstance is one word for it," Nick said teasingly as he looked at Patricia. As Sam turned to say something, the younger Cobb continued smoothly, "But whatever you choose, I'm glad to have Toots here with us. It's almost like Mom put herself in a time machine."

"You know, Dad warned her about letting you read H.G. Wells," Patricia replied, drawing a chuckle from Peter and her brothers.

"I can only imagine what it was like for your parents having all of you in the house," Sadie observed. "When I met David I found it hard to believe that he had a twin, much less four siblings."

"Just think, you haven't even met all of them yet," Peter said. "Eric's the sane one at least."

"How did you meet Eric?" Jo asked, intrigued.

"He was doing basic flight training just as these lugs were finishing getting me through advanced," Peter replied as he finished preparing his plate. "From what I understand, he's a gifted pilot."

"Apparently fairly lucky as well," Commander Hertling observed. Jo saw Nancy's arm move slightly.

Pretty sure she just pinched him under the table, Jo thought.

"So speaking of how everyone met," Nancy said airily, "Just how did you meet your husband, Sadie?"

"Well my school invites a group of officers in to talk to the kids every couple of weeks," Sadie said. "David was chosen to talk to my class, and the rest is history."

Oh no, there's much more to the story than that...but we'll let it pass, Jo thought, giving the newest Mrs. Cobb a conspiratorial look. *The phrase "whirlwind romance" definitely applies here, but when two people click...they click*. Looking at Sam, she felt a moment's sadness.

Then again, when the powder train doesn't ignite, she thought wistfully.

"I just hope Mom forgives her sometime before this century ends," Sam observed, giving his sister-in-law a smile.

"Is your mother not a forgiving woman?" Nancy asked.

"Mom is very forgiving..." Sam began.

"...once she gets her pound of flesh." David finished. He reached over and squeezed his wife. "I think we'll live, and it's been worth it so far."

Sadie blushed slightly, and Jo had to fight to keep her face passive at that one.

Yes, I imagine being newlyweds with no responsibilities and your own house would make that worth it, Jo thought. *Especially if we look up and there's a little Cobb in July or August.*

"Well maybe she will actually respond to your letters," Patricia observed.

"Oh, she responded to your letters," Nick said. "She just didn't respond to *you*."

"Nick!" Sam and David said simultaneously, as Patricia looked at her brother in surprise.

"What do you mean, she responded?" Patricia asked.

"Nothing," Nick said, looking as if he was suddenly quite aware that both his brothers were within easy arm's reach. "Family business, it can wait until after dinner."

"For someone who is in the 'silent service' you sure do talk a lot," Sam stated pointedly.

"Which submarine are you on?" Commander Hertling asked pleasantly.

Thank you, Uncle K! Jo thought internally.

"Sir..." Nick began.

"Stop that at the table," Jo chided with a smile.

"Sorry, Keith," Nick started again. "I'm on the *Nautilus*."

"Ah, Lieutenant Commander Freeman goes to our church," Nancy observed. "Have you met Agnes and the girls?"

"Yes, ma'am, I mean, Nancy I have," Nick said. "Lieutenant Commander Freeman makes it a point to rotate the wardroom through his house on Sunday evenings. Good way to meet some of the other sub commanders as well."

"Those girls are angels," Nancy observed wistfully.

The fates are cruel for never letting you have children, Jo thought sadly. *You would have made a great mother.*

"Smart as whips too," Nick observed. "Going to be a handful when Sadie gets to teach them."

Sadie smirked.

"Being a handful and a fifth grader go together like peanut butter and jelly. How many girls are you talking about?"

"There are five of them," Nick replied. "No brothers, so it seems like the oldest one has become a tomboy. She apparently gave one of the neighbor kids a black eye for making her younger sister cry."

"Sometimes a young man needs a good right cross," Patricia observed quietly, causing all three of her brothers to smirk.

"Or a shove out a tree house," Sam and David said in unison.

Cobb Residence
Mobile, Alabama
1700 Local (1800 Eastern)
26 November

"I don't think Beau was ever the same after your sister shoved him out of that thing," Samuel Cobb said, causing Eric to jump. The younger Cobb had been regarding the old, broken down tree house that sat in the notch of a massive elm tree in the Cobbs' backyard.

"Well anyone with a lick of sense could have told him it was a bad idea to tell Patricia she wasn't allowed in the tree house anymore because she was getting boobs," Eric observed after a moment. "Sorry to leave so suddenly, I had to get out of the house to catch some air."

"Yes, your mother was quite put out until I told her, in no uncertain terms, you weren't being rude, and she'd remember why if she thought about it," Samuel said evenly. "It took me ten years after getting back from France to be able to stand the smell of pork chops cooking."

Eric looked at his father in shock.

"But Mom cooked them every Sunday as far back as I can remember," Eric said when he regained his composure.

"Yes she sure did," Samuel replied. "Said she told me not to go off to that fool war, and she was going to be damned before she went the rest of her life without a pork chop because I was too stubborn to listen."

Holy shit, Eric thought. *No wonder Grandma Cobb said Mom had the disposition of a cottonmouth when suitably crossed. Sure that was when Grandma had had a couple drinks too many and Mom pushed her, but still...*

"You never forget what a man burning smells like," Samuel said quietly. "Your mother didn't understand that then, and maybe watching you rush out of the house like you'd just seen Old Scratch come in the front door will make her understand."

"I just didn't want her to think it was because Beau came in wearing his uniform with his new flame," Eric said.

"That was her first thought, yes," Samuel allowed. "Which is why I was so forceful in making sure she understood it had nothing to do with that. Your mother is still wrapping her mind around what happened to you, son. I still don't know all the details—but I recognized that look on your face."

"I never knew it would be like that, Dad," Eric said in a rush, the words surprising even him. "I always thought it would be clean, antiseptic."

"Well of course you did," Samuel said. "That is why I told all of you boys to plan on flying, because I'd had enough time in mud, blood, and filth for three generations."

"I still see Lieutenant Commander's Cobleigh's plane blowing up in my sleep," Eric said. "The British sailors cut to shreds or burning."

"I won't tell you it ever stops," Samuel said. "I will tell you that eventually it doesn't happen as often. The first year, I had to sleep on the couch because I almost strangled your mother."

If dad is going for the record of "most times I can shock my son in one night," he's well on his way, Eric thought, aghast.

"I tell you these things because they are matters people who haven't seen the elephant don't understand," Samuel said. "You need to be aware of them, and you need to make sure Joyce is aware of them."

"I...I never knew, Dad," Eric said.

"There were days I thought your Uncle Nicholas was the lucky one," Samuel said, his voice breaking slightly. "If I hadn't had you kids and your mother, I don't know what I might have done."

There was the sound of footfalls behind them before Samuel could continue. Both Cobbs turned around in the dusk gloom.

"Hello Beau," Samuel said.

Beauregard Jackson Cotner was almost as tall as Eric, but of an athletic build that recalled a racing animal or sleek jungle cat. His blue eyes were so light to be almost dull, and his hair was so blonde to be almost white. With sharp features standing out from his heart shaped face, Beau was the kind of man who would always be considered attractive but not strikingly handsome. An impartial observer, however, would have noted that his Army uniform, complete with second lieutenant bars and flight wings certainly helped matters.

That is a man who found a good tailor, Eric thought.

"Hey Mr. Cobb," Beau drawled, his accent belying his parents' Mississippi origins. "Just came out to see if Eric was okay."

Samuel smiled in return, then clasped his son on the shoulder.

"Funny, I did the same thing," Samuel said. "If both of us stay out here, dinner's going to be a little frosty for everyone involved."

With that, Samuel clasped his son on the shoulder and gave him a reassuring squeeze before walking back towards the house with a nod to Beau.

"Beau, I'm sorry," Eric began.

Beau looked at him in bemusement.

"You ran out of there like you'd seen a water moccasin, Eric," Beau replied sardonically. "While Deborah is many things, snakelike is not one of them."

"No, that she is not, from what little bit I saw before my stomach told me it was time to leave," Eric said, grinning. "Although I didn't think blondes were your thing."

Beau shrugged.

"Hadn't had much luck with brunettes lately," he replied evenly.

Eric winced inwardly.

"I'm sor..." he started.

"Will you stop apologizing for stuff you did not do, Eric?" Beau asked, exasperated. "Everyone in your family acts like your sister stabbed me in my sleep or something."

Eric was taken aback by the vehemence of Beau's words.

"I think we all feel somewhat responsible," Eric said.

"Or alternatively that's what your mom wants you all to feel," Beau said with a smirk. "In reality, I think we all should have seen it coming from a mile away."

It's just a night for people to say all sorts of unexpected shit to me, Eric thought.

"Oh don't look like you bit down on a lemon when you were expecting a peach," Beau continued, the smirk becoming a full smile. "Toots was...*is* a mule-headed woman. Wait, that's not fair to her or mules. She's a very *strong* woman."

"Do they teach you some of that Far Eastern mumbo jumbo at Army flight training or something?" Eric asked. "Because you seem to be way too calm about this."

"On the first day of flight instruction, we had a crash," Beau said simply. "Instructor was showing the cadet how to do loops, and the top wing of that Stearman came right off. No idea how, no idea why, but at eight hundred feet there's not a lot someone can do other than make their peace with God."

Eric pressed his lips in a flat line at the statement's grim truth.

Sometimes the check for that farm you bought clears quicker than you expect, he thought grimly.

"Sort of brought it home for some folks that we are doing some serious shit, pardon my French," Beau said. "So that's when I had to ask myself if I was just running away from this situation when I went and joined up, or if this is truly what I wanted to do."

Eric nodded towards the wings on Beau's chest.

"Well seems like you have your answer," he said with a smile.

"Yes, but part of getting to this point was sorting out what happened with your sister," Beau said. "In retrospect, when she asked me to learn chess and I refuse, that should have been my clue."

"The girl loves her chess," Eric said.

"Your sister's a full blown woman, Eric," Beau said, causing Eric to turn and give him a glance. The Army officer held up his hands defensively before continuing. "No, I don't mean in that sense, although I think it'd be pretty rich of you to go getting self righteous."

Eric felt color start to come to his face as Beau went on.

"I mean it in that she has her own wants, desires, interests, and way she views things," Beau stated. "I mean, how many women can carry a conversation about Buck Rogers or talk about some Tolstoy guy? Not many, and I came to realize that she needed a man who could keep up with her. I'm many things, but I am *not* that man."

"She still didn't need to leave you that way," Eric said.

"No, she didn't," Beau replied. "Then again, last time I checked she didn't have enough money in her bank account to make it out to Hawaii on her own."

"No, no she didn't," Eric allowed. "I think Mom is still quite perturbed with Dad on that front."

"Your father has sworn up and down he wasn't the one who gave her the funds," Beau said with a smile.

"No, he probably didn't directly," Eric replied. "But he's a shrewd businessman and a lawyer to boot. If someone else put the money in her account in exchange for a future favor, Dad's still telling the truth, isn't he?"

Beau gave Eric a conspiratorial smile.

"You sound as if you know what happened," Beau replied.

"No, but I know Mom was muttering about how he could apparently make accounts balance better than Al Capone," Eric said with a shrug. "Of course, there are lots of other suspects who could have been involved, and Grandpa Cobb did bequeath all of us children some money for when we become adults."

"Joyce says you're going to use yours to pay for law school starting in January," Beau said. "So I take it that the extra thirty days Secretary Knox gave you 'to just think about it' are pretty much additional vacation time?"

"I think I've done enough," Eric said solemnly.

"Yes, and I'm told you are quite adamant about having been sworn to secrecy about it," Beau replied teasingly. "Despite there being some articles in the Saturday Daily Post and Life about when and where you were shot down."

"Hopefully you'll never find out just how accurate German flak is," Eric replied. "I don't think my squadron leader ever knew what hit him."

The comment turned the mood awkward for a moment.

"Well odds are I won't be seeing any Germans," Beau said. "No unless President Roosevelt can raise Atlantis between now and January when the Republicans and American Firsters make doing so illegal."

Eric gave Beau a questioning look.

"I'm flying medium bombers," Beau said. "I'll be riding a Baltimore Whore."

"*What?*" Eric said at Beau's deadpan delivery.

"The Martin Marauder," Beau said laughingly. "Martin's main plant is in Baltimore, so they call the plane the Baltimore Whore because of its wing."

"This is me having no idea what you're talking about," Eric said.

"It's got a high wing on the fuselage that looks like it's not supported by any struts," Beau explained simply. "Fast as hell though, even if it's a bit tricky to fly."

"Must be nice," Eric said, then caught himself. "I don't know why I care, it's not like SBDs are my aircraft anymore."

"Well you could always change your mind again," Beau said with a smile.

"No thank you. The Queen is a nice young lady..." he began, then shut his mouth.

Beau looked at him speculatively.

"So, met the Queen have we? Does my sister need to worry?" Beau asked.

"You need to keep that to yourself," Eric snapped. "Seriously."

Beau made a show of zippering his lips.

"Sealed, my friend. Sealed."

"If you boys are done being antisocial, dinner's ready!" Alma called sharply from the back porch. "Hurry up so we can eat before the President's Fireside Chat!"

"Also known as 'Franklin Explains Why He Got His Hide Tanned,'" Beau said with a grin.

"You are aware he's your boss now, right?" Eric observed with a matching smile.

"Yes, but probably not in another two years at this rate," Beau replied as they reached the back porch. "I can understand losing the House, but the Senate too? Goodbye New Deal."

"I think now is a good time to remind both of you of the house rules," Alma said, giving the two young men matching glares.

"Yes Mom, we know, no politics until after dinner," Eric said. Moving quickly, he wrapped his Mom in a hug, causing her to sputter on whatever she was about to say.

"Love you, Mom," he said lowly. "Sorry about running out on you."

Alma wrapped her arms around him in return.

"I'm not going without pork chops for you either, young man," she sighed, gripping him tightly.

"So I've been told," Eric replied. He felt Alma stiffen slightly as Beau continued inside.

"You must think me a horrible person," Alma said evenly after a moment.

"No, just human," Eric replied simply. "Come on, we have dinner to eat."

ALMOST TWO HOURS LATER, WITH THE DISHES CLEARED OFF AND peach cobbler consumed, Eric sat down heavily in the Cobb family's living room. Tan walls and a finished floor gave the room a very earthy appearance, and four easy chairs and two recliners all finished in brown contributed to the atmosphere. A pair of glass tables and matching glass end tables near the recliners were the only things that were not dirt or tan colored in the room, and the three lamps provided just enough light to see faces without being blinding.

It's like a small den or rabbit warren, Eric thought, just before a gust of cool air came in through the screened windows. *Minus the airflow, of course.*

"Here's everyone's ashtrays," Samuel said, handing out the circular pottery pieces.

You know Mom and Dad love you when they let you smoke in their house, Eric thought wryly.

"Thank you, Samuel," Theodore Cotner said, taking a receptacle to share with Beau. The elder Cotner was clearly responsible for his son's looks, minus a large pug nose that made his appearance average at best.

JAMES YOUNG

The man wore a gray sporting jacket that concealed his slight paunch, but his fleshy features and balding, graying dark blonde hair.

"Thank you, Samuel, for condoning our imposition once again," the room's only female occupant, Anna Deakyne said with a smile.

Well after almost twenty years the "Duchess" is finally losing her accent, Eric thought with a smile of his own. Anna Deakyne, nee Borislava, was the widow of the late Commander Winston Deakyne, USN, retired. While Eric remained somewhat unclear as to just how Anna had ended up in Alabama, he did know that Commander Deakyne and his wife had met when the former was assigned to a destroyer in the Black Sea. Rumors of her being White Russian royalty had led to her nickname, while her continued ownership of two textile mills explained why the men in the room treated her as an equal.

"Never an imposition, Duchess," Samuel replied to the short, slender blonde woman.

If Mom and her weren't such good friends or if Dad wasn't so madly in love after all these years I'd wonder about those two, Eric thought for the umpteenth time. His father had helped Anna navigate the intricacies of probate court, as well as fend off unscrupulous competitors attempts to steal her plants right out from under her. In the process, the widow Deakyne had adopted all of the Cobb children, to the point where all of them had learned conversational Ukrainian and Russian.

Not sure Mom was pleased about us all being able to talk without her understanding us, but that's water under the bridge.

"I wish they'd get past these commercials and get to the President," Theodore said impatiently.

"Probably some production problems in the studio," Eric said, listening to the radio's pop, whistles, and crackles. "Sounds like when a carrier has a problem with its antenna."

Beau nodded knowingly, but Eric could see that his comment had confused everyone else. He was about to explain when the familiar voice of Franklin Delano Roosevelt came through the speakers.

"Finally!" Eric heard his mother exclaim from the kitchen.

"My fellow Americans, thank you for allowing me into your home this evening," President Roosevelt began. "This has been a momentous year, and there is a great deal our nation has to thank the Almighty for."

"Yes, like us not being at war," Theodore muttered as he puffed on his pipe.

"Unlike other places in the world, the United States continues to hold elections," Roosevelt continued. "The American people spoke on November 3rd, and I respect your decisions. However, I come to you tonight in response to the intemperate statements made by those you have elected, and to illustrate why they are wrong."

Oh boy, Beau sure misunderstood how this was going to go, Eric thought. *Things are about to get interesting.*

"Senator Taft of Ohio has accused my administration of wanting to involve this nation in European affairs, and has declared that he will ensure that your sons will not be called upon to die to, and I quote, 'return some princess to her father's throne,'" President Roosevelt went on, his tone indignant. "He is joined by gentlemen such as Mr. Lindbergh, who in his recent speeches has repeated his un-American claim that I am a tool of 'Jewish interests' and 'a British puppet.' Finally, the Saturday Evening Post claims that I fancy myself an incipient Caesar, who offers this fine Republic nothing but war and entanglements in the interest of gaining power."

The president paused for a moment, as if giving his audience a chance to digest his words. Looking around the room, Eric could see skepticism on Theodore's face, a speculative look on Beau's, and an inscrutable look on the Duchess' face.

"What Senator Taft does not know, or refuses to acknowledge, is that thoughts of raising our ramparts and trusting in our oceans to defend us are a dream that the United States can no longer afford," Roosevelt said, his tone firm. "As they have shown by their vicious actions against London, Warsaw, and Rotterdam, Nazi Germany has no compunctions about using the forces of terror against innocent women and children to suit their needs."

"We will ignore what the British did," Theodore snapped, drawing a look from Samuel.

"...that the airplane negates our traditional defenses. As surely as our own scientists and engineers are working on ways to bridge the

Atlantic should the need arise, the Germans are designing aircraft to bring the same horror to New York, Philadelphia, and Boston that they delivered to London."

Eric had only been to New York once in his life when Samuel had taken Sam, David, and he on a train ride to the great city for Fleet Week. It was hard for him to imagine it burning as the newsreels had shown London.

Then again, that's probably what many Englishmen thought before it happened, he mused.

"Indeed, shortly before I spoke these words, I was informed that the Germans have entered into a lease that gives them basing rights to the Azores, a group of Portuguese islands in the center of the Atlantic," Roosevelt said evenly. Eric, in the midst of drinking water, aspirated as the shock hit him.

"You okay son?" Samuel asked as the President continued on to explain why a German base in the Azores was a dagger pointed directly at America.

"Yes, I'm fine," Eric croaked. "Just kind of shocking to hear someplace I've flown near."

"...will allow Himmler's submarines to prowl our coasts, his aircraft to darken our skies, and his vessels to choke off our trade with other countries. This, my friends, is what allowing Germany time to develop their position in safety will do for us," Roosevelt finished. There was another gap and the faint sound of rustling papers.

"Of course, all of this is known to an aviation expert such as Charles Lindbergh," President Roosevelt said. "I am saddened that such a great man has stooped to such a foul level as to talk about religion, and will give that line of argument no more concern than any of you listening should."

Yikes! Eric thought at the clear tone of admonishment in President Roosevelt's voice.

"However, the terrible lie of claiming that I am a tool of British interests must be addressed," President Roosevelt continued. "It is particularly galling coming from a man who still maintains a *Luftwaffe* medal despite that force's continued atrocities."

I didn't know Lindbergh had a German medal! Eric thought. Looking across the room, he saw a similar look of shock on Beau's face...but indifference on that of his father's and Theodore's. *Guess it must be something that happened when I was too young to care.*

"For those who question the differences between German and English nature, I will simply tell the story of four of our fliers from the carrier *Ranger*," Roosevelt said.

Eric felt his stomach start to drop as every eye in the room turned to him.

"Flying as part of our Neutrality Patrol, two of our bombers were engaged without warning or provocation by the German fleet. The lead bomber, flown by Lieutenant Commander Abe Cobleigh of Springfield, Illinois, was immediately destroyed by the German barrage."

Whereas his stomach had been dropping before, it now began to resemble an Empire State Building elevator whose cables had been cut. Suddenly Eric's collar was far too tight, and he felt sweat beading on his forehead as the President's voice took him back to that day.

"Lieutenant Commander Cobleigh and his gunner left behind two widows and five children who will never grow up with their fathers," President Roosevelt continued. "The second bomber, flown by Lieutenant junior grade Eric Cobb, was gravely damaged, with both Cobb and his gunner wounded."

There was the sound of breaking dishes and a thud from the kitchen.

Oh shit, Eric thought, as Anna sprang to her feet, waving the men to stay seated.

"I think Alma can use some assistance," the Duchess said, her accent thicker as it always grew in times of stress. Eric could see that the woman was pale as a sheet.

Wait, she didn't know what happened, he thought with a sudden rush. *No one else did, either.*

"...at great risk to themselves plucked this crew from the sea. They then proceeded to take strenuous measures to keep them safe throughout the sea battle that saw the *Kriegsmarine* murder the King of England."

Eric couldn't help the nervous guffaw that came out of his mouth at that statement, the sound causing the other men in the room to jump. Taking a deep breath, he calmed himself as they continued to listen.

"...difference could not be more stark. As long as I am President, the United States' interests will always align with the nations that aid others rather than attacking them, that provides succor to those in need, and safeguards those who are vulnerable," Roosevelt said, his cadence steady. "In that same way, we will always oppose those who attack great men such as Lieutenant Commander Cobleigh and Lieutenant Cobb, have the audacity to demand that we turn over our servicemen to them, and are aggressive against our interests."

Anna poked her head back through the entryway.

"Eric, Joyce fainted," she said, her voice flat. "Alma and Elma request that you walk her home."

Eric began to raise, but Samuel held up his hand.

"I think Joyce can wait a few minutes," the Cobb patriarch said, his tone quite clear that he wasn't suggesting as his eyes fixed his son's. Anna, her face expressionless, nodded, and to Eric's shock, pulled the door to the living room shut behind her.

"...expressed her gratitude regarding Lieutenant (j.g.) Cobb to me personally. She stated that she hoped that our nation 'had many more men that were willing to fight back the tide of Fascism.' I responded to Her Majesty that America loves freedom and dignity, and this nation will have no problem finding young men like Lieutenant Cobb, as long as this nation's leaders do not fail them," Roosevelt began, his voice rising. "It is up to you, my fellow Americans, whether or not those leaders hear your true desire to stop Fascism now rather than having our children do it in their time. I pray to God that this does not come to pass, and I ask you to join me in beseeching the Almighty for intervention in these dark times. Good night to you all."

Eric was shocked at how quickly his father moved to turn off the radio. Turning, Samuel fixed his son with a firm glance.

"You cannot leave the Navy now, you realize that, right?" Samuel asked solemnly.

"Samuel Cobb, I think it is best that we let our child decide what he is going to do," Alma said quietly from the doorway. "His future wife should probably have a say in that as well."

Eric felt as if the room was closing in on him. Setting his water down with shaking hands, he pushed to his feet.

"A walk with Joyce *alone* sounds like a very good plan right now," Eric said, heat in his words. Without waiting for further comment, he squeezed past his mother and found his Joyce waiting for him by the front door, her mother holding her steady. As Eric approached, Elma released her daughter and stepped back.

"Good evening, Mrs. Cotner," Eric said quietly as he took Joyce's arm. "I think Joyce and I need to go talk for a little bit."

"Of course, Eric," Elma said with a small smile. Eric held the front door open for the ashen Joyce, then passed through himself without looking back. The cool evening air hit him with a bit of a shock.

Temperature sure dropped during dinner, he thought, shrugging out of his suit jacket to drape it over Joyce in her grey and black print gingham dress. Joyce hardly reacted as he did so, her eyes seemingly fixed on something distant only she could see. The two of them walked for about ten minutes in silence until she finally spoke.

"How could you keep secrets from me, Eric?" she asked quietly.

"I was sworn to secrecy by Secretary Knox himself, Joyce," Eric replied flatly.

"Well that makes it all better," Joyce snapped, her voice waspish. "Why here I thought I was the woman you were going to spend the rest of your life with."

"I took an oath," Eric retorted. "You know, that whole raise my right hand and promise to obey the orders of those appointed over me thing?"

"Well glad to see you take your oaths so seriously," Joyce spat.

"For a woman who is expecting me to make several vows to her..."

Joyce whirled towards him before he could finish.

"Go to Hell, Eric Cobb," she sobbed, hitting him hard in the chest. "You go straight to..."

The rest of her statement was lost in the sound of her sob as Eric wrapped his arms around her. Crying and shaking uncontrollably, Joyce initially tried to shove him away, then dropped her arms helplessly to her side and leaned into his chest.

"I don't want you to go," she said, her chest heaving in between words. "I don't want you to die."

"I could die back here, Joyce," Eric said, then realized he had messed up.

"So you have decided to go back?" she asked, sniffling.

"I don't know," Eric replied wearily. "I just want the world to stop spinning so I can get off."

"I don't think that's possible for you anymore, Eric," Joyce said softly. "The President seems bound and determined to force a fight."

"I can't say that I blame him," Eric replied. "I can only imagine the Germans with bases that are just a short stretch from New York City."

"Has it ever crossed anyone's mind just to let the Germans mind their own business?" Joyce asked plaintively. "We're not European, we don't *have* to fight them."

Eric sighed.

"No, we don't *have* to," Eric said wearily. "But I think the President is right in that if my generation doesn't, any sons we may have will."

Joyce looked up at him, her eyes sad.

"If you live that long," she said. Taking a deep breath, Joyce stepped out of his embrace and shrugged out of his jacket. Looking at her face, Eric knew what was about to happen.

"Eric, I can't do this," Joyce said. "Your father's right, you now have no choice about what you want to do. I do, and I choose not to be sitting there waiting every day whether or not I will ever see you again."

With that, Joyce slipped the engagement ring off her finger and extended her hand. As he looked at the diamond, Eric felt a strange emptiness.

"Keep it," he said.

"What?" Joyce asked.

"Keep it," Eric stated again, his voice empty. "Let it be a reminder of just how steep the price was for your perfect house, safe husband, and kids who are still free." With that, Eric turned to walk away.

"I'm sorry, Eric," Joyce called after him, her voice almost a sob.

For a moment, Eric considered turning around. But only for a moment.

IJNS *AKAGI*
1510 LOCAL (0110 EASTERN)
7 DECEMBER

THE SLAUGHTERHOUSE SMELL WAFTING FROM THE FLIGHT DECK MADE Isoro's mouth water and the contents of his stomach shift in a most unpleasant manner. Listening to Lieutenant Commander Itaya go over what had gone right and wrong during their missions that day was somewhat distracting, but Isoro had to admit fatigue was severely limiting his ability to focus.

Idiots, Isoro thought unkindly as he looked to where the carrier's flight deck was being quickly covered with sand. *It takes a true moron to run into a still whirling propeller.*

Without warning, one of the warrant officers from the squadron's first *chutai* suddenly doubled over and spewed onto the deck. The young man's vomit had scarcely hit the wooden deck before Lieutenant Fujimoto, *Akagi*'s newest fighter leader, brought his hand down in a chop across the man's neck. The unfortunate warrant collapsed in a limp heap, his face ending up in the fluid from his stomach. Muttering a curse, Fujimoto kicked the man over onto his side, then turned and bowed apologetically to Lieutenant Commander Itaya.

"I am sorry for my man's disgraceful actions, squadron commander," he said, his tone terse. Itaya nodded, then continued as if nothing had happened.

"I will suggest to Commander Fuchida that we do not tie the *Shiden*'s to the strike group," Itaya stated. "Today showed that we will land with far too little fuel if we do so, and because we are heavier than the *Zero*es it takes far more time to move us into place for the next strike."

*While I am growing to like the **Shiden**, I do miss the fact we could fly forever in the **Zeroes***, Isoro thought. *It is going to be a long swim if our plan does not work.*

"Lieutenant Honda, what are your thoughts?" Itaya asked, startling Isoro.

"Sir, I have concerns about the American Army fighters," Isoro said. "If the enemy stays close to shore, we may have to fight our way to their fleet or back out."

Itaya smiled.

"Not worried about the Grummans after flying against them last week?" the *Akagi*'s squadron leader asked.

Isoro grinned. The *Akagi*'s air group had been given the opportunity to fly against several captured Royal Navy *Martlet*s, as the British had called the Grumman *Wildcat*s, just two days before.

"It cannot climb and it is underpowered," Isoro replied. "I am not saying I do not fear them, but we will be able to dictate the range at which we fight them."

Itaya nodded.

"Do not be too confident," the squadron leader cautioned. "The Germans tested several to destruction in front of Captain Genda. He said it is a very rugged aircraft, and that the machine guns will probably rip through anyone dumb enough to blunder in front of one."

Well that seems like a pretty good reason not to do something so foolish, Isoro thought. He felt the *Akagi* shift under his feet, the bow coming around.

"Hmm. It appears we are not going to try a fourth launch after all," Itaya noted, looking back at the flag bridge. "We will continue this discussion in the ready room."

"How many more men would you like to see killed, Captain Genda?!" Rear Admiral Kusaka sneered. "I am sure Captain Aoki can replace some of his deck hands with the galley staff."

Vice Admiral Yamaguchi continued to look out the windows of *Akagi*'s flag bridge as Kusaka and Fuchida sparred. Grasping his hands behind him, he watched as two other pilots dragged the semi-conscious warrant officer towards the carrier's island. Behind the trio, a handful of deck hands were already moving forward with mops and buckets to clean up the large spot of blood from the two dead plane handlers.

"We must launch four strikes! If we send only two, we will allow the Americans to mass their combat air patrol and interceptors against them! Our losses will be far heavier than..." Captain Genda began, his voice full of heat.

"You *dare* to speak to me that way, Captain?!" Kusaka barked, cutting the junior officer off.

Enough of that, Yamaguchi thought.

"Rear Admiral Kusaka, it would likely irk Admiral Yamamoto greatly if I were to have to ask him for Captain Genda's brevet promotion," Yamaguchi said simply, not turning around. "Captain Genda, you will speak to Rear Admiral Kusaka with more respect no matter how fervently you disagree with him. I need you to both work together, not fight like a pair of starving tigers."

As he heard both men come to attention and begin voicing their contrition, Yamaguchi turned around.

"Captain Genda, Rear Admiral Kusaka is right," Yamaguchi continued. "We cannot launch four strikes in a single day, no matter how hard we push the deck crews now. They have gotten noticeably faster, but as we just witnessed there is a point where they become clumsy."

Captain Genda nodded, his face impassive. Yamaguchi saw the beginnings of a smirk cross Kusaka's face.

"Rear Admiral Kusaka, you are requiring us to hold back too large of a combat air patrol," Yamaguchi said. "You are more cautious than a schoolgirl's father."

Well that wiped the smile off his face, Yamaguchi thought.

"We will not use any of the *Shiden* for combat air patrol," Yamaguchi directed. "We will also launch the first strike only one hour after the search planes depart."

Genda and Kusaka's faces both paled.

"Sir, what if the search planes do not find the American fleet?" Kusaka sputtered.

"The declaration of war will arrive, at most, five hours before dawn

Hawaiian time," Yamaguchi said. "Tell me, with cold boilers, how long would it take to get our entire fleet out of Kobe or Yokosuka? "

"Our last estimate was four hours," Kusaka answered.

"That estimate assumed steam was up, all ships were manned, and preparatory orders had been given," Yamaguchi replied. "Pearl Harbor has a single narrow channel, and I doubt that the Americans always have their ships fully manned. I do not think we will catch them in harbor, but if we launch in darkness we will catch them as they are still forming into their fleet formation."

"What if they have carriers at sea, sir?" Captain Genda asked.

"The *Tone* is being equipped with a Type 11 radio detection set," Rear Admiral Kusaka interjected. "This, plus the set on *Shokaku* should give us plenty of warning of an inbound raid."

"There are still land-based aircraft to be concerned with," Genda replied. "I do not want us to shoot all our arrows at unworthy targets while an enemy task group strikes us in the back."

"We will do a search in all directions with the other vessel's aircraft," Yamaguchi said, his tone indicating the finality of the discussion. "There is a reason I asked for our escort to be reinforced with the *Mikuma* and *Mogami*. Even so, the Americans have only four carriers in their entire Pacific Fleet. The consulate in Victoria has reported that the *Enterprise* and *Victorious* have begun joint training to integrate the latter into the Pacific Fleet. That leaves three carriers to our six."

He is still unconvinced, Yamaguchi thought as he looked at Kusaka's face. Before he could open his mouth, the group was interrupted by Commander Fuchida entering the flag bridge.

"Ah, Fuchida-san, good to see you," Captain Genda said, relief evident in his voice.

"Sir," Fuchida said, coming to attention and saluting. Yamaguchi returned the salute, then gestured for the steward who had followed him in to bring them some tea.

"Commander Fuchida, how many strikes do you think we can accomplish?" Vice Admiral Yamaguchi asked.

"Two, sir," Fuchida replied without hesitation. "Three if we discover another target of opportunity."

The junior officer's response surprised Vice Admiral Yamaguchi.

"Explain," Yamaguchi stated stiffly.

"Sir, there will be damaged aircraft and wounded pilots," Fuchida said flatly. "We have now flown mock strikes for two weeks, with the target ships noting when they first detect us and the defending fighters limited to reacting based solely on that information. Not once have we been able to fight our way to the target without facing heavy interception, and the ships have always been able to man their anti-aircraft batteries."

Yamaguchi pressed his lips together, noting that Kusaka was much better at concealing his satisfaction.

"The other problem will be ordnance," Fuchida continued. "Even storing as many of the new torpedoes as we can, we barely have enough for two waves. If there is a third strike, we would have difficulty destroying anything larger than a cruiser. I am not sure the risk would be worth it."

At least the man is honest in his assessment, Yamaguchi thought disappointedly.

"Very well," the *Kido Butai*'s commander said out loud. "Plan for two waves, forty-five minutes apart. The first wave will launch forty-five minutes after the reconnaissance aircraft to give them time to radio in the enemy's position. If we only come away with a handful of cruisers for our trouble, I will take responsibility. "

Ascalon Estate
Upstate New York
0900 Local
8 December 1942

"Here you go, Adam," the tall, powerful looking man in the Packard truck's driver's seat stated solemnly. With a high forehead and close-cropped black hair, Don Blakeslee looked every inch the squadron commander he had been in the RAF.

Adam looked out the truck's windshield into the gathering gloom on the western horizon. Judging from the high drifts to either side of the road, the approaching clouds would simply add more to an already abundant snowfall.

Lake effect snow at its finest, Adam thought.

"You sure you're okay to keep driving?" Adam asked. "You've already put in eight hours and that sky does not look good to the west."

"That storm's at least two hours away from dropping serious snow," Blakeslee replied, his blue eyes matching his smile. "Plus if I'm gone, it's harder for your father to kick you back out."

Adam gave a grim smile.

Without mother to stop him, I don't think the angel Gabriel could dissuade the man from doing so, Adam thought. *But that's not your problem.*

"I'm sorry for your loss," Blakeslee said.

"Not your fault the fucking Feds were arresting us," Adam said heatedly. "I think J. Edgar Hoover better pray I never meet him face to face. He just might find out just what one of his 'lawless mercenaries' can do."

"I'm told that the Army's looking for anyone with combat experience," Blakeslee said. "That light colonel I told you about said if you go down to Dayton Field with your log book, they can see about getting you commissioned based on how much you've flown. I imagine they'd make you a colonel!"

"Look who's talking," Adam grunted as he lifted out his two pieces of luggage. "Eight Germans for sure, another couple you probably sent home with dead crew."

"Yeah, and look all the good it did us," Blakeslee replied, his voice haunted.

"Well at least we've got a country again," Adam stated emphatically. "Get out of here, and I'll be in touch."

"Definitely," Blakeslee replied. "If they give me a squadron, I'm serious—I'll make you a flight commander."

"I'll think about it," Adam said. "Might have to sit this next one out. I keep seeming to pick the losing side."

Blakeslee shook his head.

"You can no more sit this next one out than I can sprout wings and fly," he replied. With that he dropped the truck into gear, then started pulling away. Adam watched the blue truck pull back onto the New York state road a half-mile away, its engine rumbling away into the distance.

Well, glad President Roosevelt finally gave all of us a collective pardon, Adam thought. *Was getting awfully sick of sitting in Canada.*

Grabbing his luggage, Adam began the quarter mile walk up the gravel driveway to the gates of Ascalon. Named for St. George's lance, the estate had originally been purchased by his great grandfather during the Gilded Age. While Jeremiah Haynes had not been a robber baron, he'd dabbled in enough of their operations to become reasonably rich in his own right.

"You will never find us in the history books, but our fingerprints are always there," Adam thought, hearing his grandfather Jonathan's voice in his head. He set his shoulders as he approached Ascalon's main gate, seeing two figures in the gate house. The one that stepped out into the cold was a truly massive man, closer to seven feet than six, with a barrel chest and build that was better suited for a lumberjack than a gate man. Recognizing Adam, the man took his hand from inside his great coat.

"Well at least my father has not indicated I should be shot on sight, Mr. Keefe," Adam said.

"No laddy, I suppose not," Rioghnan Keefe, Ascalon's security manager, said in his faint brogue. Second generation Irish, Keefe's red hair had finally started to go to gray, and his blue eyes had crow's feet that indicated his advancing years. Still, even if he were armed, Adam was reasonably certain Keefe could kill him where he stood without even a second's hesitation.

He actually looks relieved to see me, Adam thought, somewhat surprised. Keefe was not an expressive man, but Adam could swear he could see the start of a smile on the older man's face.

"If you'll leave your bags here, I'll have someone from the house staff get to them," Keefe said. "Your father's expecting you in the main house…"

"Of course," Adam said tiredly.

"But I think that there's going to be a problem with the gatehouse phone after we call one of the household staff," Keefe said, showing no emotion at being interrupted. "Can't leave only one man here, so I guess the news will have to go back with your bags."

Adam looked at Keefe in shock.

My father is not exactly the type of man you cross like that, Adam thought. *Not at all.*

"You can go talk to your Mum before you talk to him," Keefe said, a hint of sadness in his voice. "She tried to hold on as long as she could."

Adam clenched his teeth, fighting back the tears that wanted to fall from his eyes.

"Thank you," he rasped.

"You're welcome," Keefe replied, his voice also slightly choked. "Now get on before someone sees you."

The estate's gate whirred open on its electric motors. With a nod to Keefe, Adam passed through the opening for the first time in almost two years.

A BRISK FIFTEEN MINUTE WALK IN THE INCREASING WIND BROUGHT him to the Haynes family cemetery. Set on a small rise about a half mile behind the main house and bordered by a waist high stone wall, the plots had been gouged from a dense copse of cedars. The massive trees made the gloomier day even more so as Adam finished walking up to the newest plot. Decorated by a square, granite headstone upon which two angels stood grasping hands, the slightly mounded turf and muddy ground around the stone were the only indication a service had occurred the week prior. Mora Haynes had apparently had a large turnout, the circle of disrupted dirt going at least forty deep.

That's what happens when you spend the majority of your life helping others, Adam thought with a mournful smile.

"Hi Mom," Adam said, fighting back a sob. "Sorry I could not make it back in time."

The wind echoing through the graveyard was the only response Adam received. Sighing, he stepped forward and placed his hand on the granite headstone. As if the tactile touch was some trigger, his tears burst through his reserve. For five minutes Adam sobbed uncontrollably, his shoulders shaking as the last four months' worth of emotion poured from him.

It was only when he heard footfalls coming up the path behind him that he forced himself to stop and draw erect. Extracting a handkerchief from his pocket, he blew his nose and gathered himself. Making his face impassive, he started to turn around.

"I will need a ride to the train..." he started, then stopped in shock.

When Adam had left, Seth Haynes had still possessed a full head of thick, brown hair and had looked ten years younger than his fifty-five years. Although the man before him still stood erect, Adam's father's severely lined face, thinning gray hair, and dull blue eyes made it look as if he'd aged in dog years.

"You look like you've seen a ghost, Son," Seth said quietly. "Or just an old man who has lost the love of his life."

"Thank you for sending someone to find me," Adam said flatly. "If that bastard Hoover..."

"I know why you didn't make it, Son," Seth replied. For a brief moment, Adam saw anger in the other man's gaze before it was once again subsumed by abject grief. "How long are you staying?"

"I can leave as soon as you want me to," Adam said. He was shocked to see his father recoil from him as if he'd suggested conducting a séance.

"I am sorry, son," Seth said after a moment. It was Adam's turn to be startled as his father continued, his voice shaking. "I am sorry for the things I said when you returned from Spain, and for what I told you before you left for England. Please, please forgive me."

Who are you, and what the Hell have you done with my father?

"Your mother made me promise that we would stop what she called 'our senseless fighting,'" Seth said after a moment, seeing that Adam was speechless with shock.

"And poof, just like that, I'm no longer your vagabond, ne'er do well son?" Adam asked, trying to keep his tone level but failing miserably.

"I don't expect you to forgive me 'just like that,'" Seth said, his voice sad. "But in the time your mother and I had before she died, I came to realize it was fear that drove me to say horrible things to you."

"I doubt you have ever suffered true fear a day in your life, Father,"

Adam said bitterly. "You've suffered the fear that you'll lose status, or be embarrassed, but name one time you've actually feared death."

"When you were six months old with the measles," Seth snapped, then caught himself. "You are my son and the only heir to this fortune that generations have strove to build, Adam. Your grandfather and his father did not expend their sweat and blood just to have it pass to some unscrupulous men who married your cousins."

Adam rolled his eyes.

Yes, because the possibility that said men may actually be decent people in their own right rather than the money grubbing scoundrels you always made them out to be never crossed your mind, Adam thought.

"Again we start with the familial obligations," Adam snarled. "When the damn Nazis are knocking at the door you'll still be reminding me I'm your only son and heir."

"I did not come out here to revisit our numerous arguments before you left for England, Adam," Seth said wearily. "There are men I have known since before you were born who were massacred by Himmler's goons, died in London, or who Halifax's government turned over. The Nazis are abominations which must be stopped by any means necessary."

Adam looked at his father, his eyes narrowing.

"Don't give me that suspicious look," Seth replied. "You got your mule headedness from your mother, not me."

Adam saw the flitter of pain that passed over his father's face even as the two men smiled at the old family joke.

Mom did have a way of persuading us through sheer fatigue, he thought. Again he felt grief trying to force its way back to the forefront.

"I miss your mother desperately," Seth sighed, his own voice choked with near tears. "As stubborn as she was, it should be no surprise to you that she also made me swear to use whatever connections I could to get you an officer's billet."

Adam could not have been more shocked if his father had started speaking flawless Chinese.

"W-wait, what?" Adam asked.

"Even when your mother was dying, she thought of others," Seth said. "You know that your uncles all served during World War I. What you do not know is that a week after the *Lusitania* sank, your grandfather called all the children into the parlor and informed them he was certain war was coming."

Seth paused and looked towards the east.

"He then proceeded to inform all four of your uncles that he expected them to do the proper and correct thing when the time came, and told your aunts that he expected any current or future children who desired their hand to do the same," Seth continued, his voice shaking. "It was to your mother's eternal shame that I did not volunteer when the time came."

So now I understand, Adam thought. *That's why Grandfather Jefferson bequeathed my mother's share of his property and land to me directly.*

"You were thirty, Father," Adam replied, his voice incredulous. "What did Grandfather Jefferson expect you to do?"

"Go and defend those who could not defend themselves," Seth replied sadly. "Fight for the Republic at the very least. He never said anything directly, but I could sense his disgust every time we took you to visit."

Also explains why he bought me the books he did as I grew older, Adam thought. *Most kids do not get Thucydides for their fifteenth birthday.*

"I think some part of your mother never forgave me for putting her in that position," Seth continued. "I think that was part of the reason she was so proud of you for choosing to take your pilot's license and go to Spain."

Adam stiffened, thinking of the things Seth had said when he'd left.

Mom wanted us to bury the hatchet... he reminded himself.

"I have taken the liberty of contacting some of my friends in the Navy Department. It appears they were already aware of you," Seth said, his tone sardonic. "Your recent exploits have only increased their interest."

"When we were in Canada, I was already talking with some of the pilots from the Eagle Squadrons," Adam replied. "Chap named Don Blakeslee offered me a flight command."

"Let's talk about this inside," Seth said, as a strong gust of wind presaged the storm's beginnings.

Adam took one last long look at his mother's grave, then turned to follow his father down the path towards the house.

I hope I make you proud, Mother, he thought.

Four days later, Adam was looking up at the brick façade of the Marine Corps headquarters at the corner of 8th and I Streets. Dressed in a plain black suit with blue shirt, Adam was surprised to find his mouth slightly dry. A slight chill that had nothing to do with the damp dawn air passed through Adam, and he adjusted his red and white striped tie.

"Sir, can I help you?" an NCO called from the building's front steps.

"Yes Sergeant," Adam said, somewhat surprised to see a slight smirk cross the man's face. "I'm here to see a Major Pendergraft."

"Who may I tell him is calling, sir?" the NCO asked, his voice level.

Well here is where the rubber meets the road, Adam thought.

"Squadron Leader Adam Haynes, formerly of the Royal Air Force," Adam replied. To the NCO's credit, he had no reaction before picking up the nearby phone.

Just what am I getting myself into? Adam pondered. *I figured there'd be at least a skeptical look or some questioning. Not sure I'm professional enough for this group.*

After a brief conversation, the NCO put down the phone.

"Sir, Major Pendergraft will be right down," the NCO replied.

"Thank you, sergeant," Adam said, fighting hard not to show his nervousness.

True to the sergeant's word, Major Pendergraft walked through the barracks' front doors a couple of minutes later. Tanned and athletic, with brown hair graying at the temples, Pendergraft stood well over six feet in height in his service uniform. His green eyes looked Adam up and down as he placed his cover on his head, gaze expressionless. The Marine officer returned the guard NCO's salute, then joined Adam on the sidewalk.

"Let's go for a walk, Major Haynes," Pendergraft said, causing the NCO and Adam to both do a double take.

"I think there's been some mistake," Adam said.

"You've killed, at least if what your dossier says is true, about seventy to a hundred Germans, Italians, and Japs," Pendergraft said as he began stepping down the sidewalk. "The only mistake would be if I forgot to have you sign your orders and take the oath after we get some breakfast.

"How soon can you report to Quantico, Major?" Pendergraft said. "I understand that your mother recently passed and that you haven't been home for almost two years."

"I can report tomorrow if that is when you need me," Adam said simply.

"How about one week?" Pendergraft replied. "After you in-process, go through some training, and qualify on the *Wildcat*, the plan is to send you to either Cherry Point or Pensacola depending on availability."

"Major it seems as if the Corps is one hell of a rush," Adam replied.

"You of all people should know there's a war on," Pendergraft said with a slight smile as the duo reached the officer's mess.

"Not yet," Adam challenged back.

"Only a formality, Major Haynes," Pendergraft said. "The Krauts and Japs are coming for us, and anyone who thinks differently is either in Congress or hasn't been paying attention."

5
TRANSITIONS

We must remember that one man is much the same as another, and that he is best who is trained in the severest school.

— **THUCYDIDES**

U.S.S. NAUTILUS
200 MILES NORTHEAST OF OAHU
0430 LOCAL (0930 EASTERN)
23 MARCH 1943

"SIR, just who did we piss off?" Nick Cobb shouted, struggling to be heard over the intensifying wind and crash of waves over the bow and bridge of the U.S.S. *Nautilus*. The submarine's master, Lieutenant Commander Jason Freeman, shook his head at the younger officer's comment as a stream of water sloughed off the platform the two men shared with three lookouts. Only slightly taller but much thicker than Nick, Freeman looked like a drowning, sandy blonde terrier in his rain gear.

"Don't ask me questions like that, Lieutenant Cobb," Jason shouted back. "I keep wondering if you were caught with some admiral's daughter!"

Before Nick could reply, another wave hit the entire bridge crew full on. For a moment Nick felt his footing slip, and had a horrible moment where he wondered if he was going to slip off the conning tower and inot the sea. Even as his feet scrambled for purchase, he felt the bridge's wire railings securely under his armpits.

"Sir, if it would make this rain stop, I'd be happy to wire a proposal back to Pearl Harbor," Nick replied. Freeman flashed a grin at that. The senior officer waited until the next wave passed before replying.

"I don't think that would work, Lieutenant Cobb," Freeman laughed.

Nick smiled back, shaking his head as he looked out over the desolate seascape. *Nautilus* was Freeman's second command, and he ran a very unconventional ship compared to some of his peers. One of the lieutenant commander's principles was that officers got paid enough to suffer, while sailors did not. Even in the egalitarian world of submariners, such a view was almost sacrilege.

While I could do without being soaked to the bone, he has a point, Nick thought. *Although this storm is starting to get bad enough, I'm wondering if we'll be able to stay up here*. According to the rest of her wardroom, the *Nautilus* handled better than most other submarines in rough weather due to her larger displacement and length. Given the vessel's current motion, meant Nick considered that statement akin to someone remarking a plough horse was far prettier than some surrounding mules.

Nick felt the bottom drop out of his stomach, the sandwich and coffee he had consumed just before coming onto watch doing flip-flops. He peered out into the darkness to try and distract himself, but looking at the sea's churning surface only made things worse.

Dear lord, please don't let me get sick, he thought to himself as the *Nautilus*'s bow dropped into another trough. Despite over three years in submarines, Nick's sea legs were suspect. This storm was the roughest things had ever been for him, and it didn't look like his stomach was going to live up to the challenge.

Why doesn't Commander Freeman dive the damn boat already?! Nick thought helplessly.

"Try to think about something else, Mr. Cobb," Freeman said lowly, where only Nick could hear. "It'll pass, trust me. If this weather doesn't clear up in about an hour, I think I'll take her down."

An hour? A fucking hour? Nick thought, desperation starting to fill his mind as he scrambled for something to talk about.

"Sir, what do you think our chances are of going to war in the next week?" Nick asked.

Nautilus's captain looked at him briefly, and then looked back out into the storm. Looking behind them, Nick could see one of the lookouts suddenly paying rapt attention to the conversation of the two officers on the board. He realized why the other officer was considering his words carefully.

Whatever the Old Man says will be all over the boat less than thirty minutes after this watch is over, Nick thought, watching as the seas drained from over the forward deck gun.

"Mr. Cobb, as you know, we left Pearl Harbor two days ago with a full load of fuel, and for the first time since I've been in command of this boat, a full load of torpedoes," Freeman started. Nick noted he spoke normally, well aware of the lookouts listening. "Shortly before we left, I received sealed orders directly from Vice Admiral Bowles."

Wait a second, Bowles shouldn't have handed him those orders! Nick thought. *That son of a bitch is pissing all over Rear Admiral Graham's shoes again.* Bowles, as a former submariner, regularly overstepped his bounds with regards to the chain of command. Rear Admiral Daniel Graham, as the commander of the Pacific Fleet's subs, should have been the one to give Lieutenant Commander Freeman any orders or directives.

Admiral Jensen is letting his personal hound run all over the place, Nick thought. *That man has had way too much time on his hands since ol' Junior got sent back to the mainland. Sam and David are right, that guy's an asshole.*

"I intended to publish those orders at the end of this watch, but I will give you a preview of what they said," Freeman continued. "Long and short of it, if we find a Japanese warship within three hundred miles of Pearl Harbor, we are to, I quote, 'act under the discretion of the commanding officer' and immediately engage said vessel."

Nick found himself holding his breath.

Sweet Jesus, Admiral Jensen just declared war on the Empire of Japan, Nick thought, his seasickness completely forgotten. *I knew things were bad, but when they sent that battleship division back to the West Coast over the holidays I thought things were calming down.*

"Why didn't these orders come from Admiral Jensen?" Nick asked, raising an eyebrow. "It would seem like the commander-in-chief himself would want to sign something that important."

"Mr. Cobb, it is not the place of a junior officer to question why and who his orders come from," Freeman replied firmly. "However, if you think about it, the answer will come to you, as unimportant to this discussion as it is."

Nick nodded, knowing that he had overstepped his bounds. To him, it should not matter if the orders came from Santa Claus—he was to obey them.

"Concurrent with these orders, in a separate order that will take effect in about an hour and a half, the Pacific Fleet will be put on two hours' sailing notice. All shore leaves will be cancelled, and all crews will have to remain on their ships until further notice. Those orders *are* by the hand of Admiral Jensen himself."

Suddenly, it hit Nick like a thunderbolt, with a visible pause in his actions.

*The reason Admiral Jensen didn't sign **our** orders is should we fire the opening shots of war, he can say he knew nothing about it,* Nick thought. He looked over to see Lt. Commander Freeman giving him a slight smirk.

While it won't be much of a defense to say "I was following orders," Nick thought, *it will still make it so the worst thing that would possibly happen to Admiral Jensen in that case is a relief and cashiering from the service. More likely, Bowles would make a sufficient sacrificial lamb to mollify Congress.*

"Sir, what are your intended actions should we encounter enemy warships?" Nick asked, his mouth suddenly dry. *Because odds are they'll try to burn the rest of us with you, orders or not.*

Lt. Commander Freeman looked at the young lieutenant, searching Nick's face in the much lighter dawn.

Old Man's seeing if I'm asking because I'm concerned for my career (I'm not) or my well being (of course!), Nick thought as he looked back at his commander, his face expressionless.

"I take it you played killer poker during your Academy days, Lieutenant Cobb?" Jason asked, as spray drenched both of them.

"I held my own, sir," Nick replied. "Especially when handed a pair of deuces with my month's paycheck in the pot."

"How many times did you lose in that situation?" Freeman asked, his voice indicating he was genuinely curious.

"Sir, I didn't lose. I found that bluffing one's way through risks usually works," Nick replied evenly.

"Well, let's hope that we don't get called on our bluff," Jason said, looking out into the ocean. "It looks like it's actually clearing up a little bit," he said, the sky starting to lighten. Nick noted the subject change and decided to let his question drop.

Not that I disagree with taking such a measure, he thought to himself. *It's not like we've invited the Japanese Fleet in for a Naval Review. Like a stranger being in your house at two in the morning, they likely won't be stopping by for tea and biscuits.*

Startled, Nick realized that either his stomach's crisis had passed or Lt. Commander Freeman's observation about the weather was correct. Picking up his binoculars, Nick tried to see if he could catch the horizon.

"So what's this I hear about half of your family being in Hawaii now?" Freeman asked, startling him.

"Well depending on where the *Hornet* is headed, all of us kids will be here shortly, sir," Nick replied. "My brother Eric was reassigned after taking two months' leave." Out of the corner of his eye, he saw one of the lookouts turn to his compatriot in disgust.

"Is the rumor out them giving him a Navy Cross off the books true?" Freeman asked.

"Sir, I have no idea on that one," Nick replied. "I just know my mother is sore at him for coming back over the hill when he should be in law school."

"Mothers tend to be that way," Freeman observed.

"Mom more than most," Nick observed. "Cobbs don't seem to have a problem going to war. It's the coming back that we are 50-50 on."

Freeman winced.

"I can see why she might be a bit concerned," the senior officer said.

"At least with my brother on this side of the world the Germans can't get at him," Nick stated with disgust. "I can't believe they put a price on his head."

"I think with a few million Russians sitting across their border they aren't going to be too worried about one American naval officer," Freeman observed.

"It seems like the world's gone mad, sir," Nick stated, shaking his head. "Something's about to pop, and I don't think it's the cork on a champagne bottle."

"The President had the right of it," Freeman replied grimly. "I'd rather have a war in my lifetime than my daughters'."

Your wife might not feel that way if she has to raise them all on her own, Nick thought.

"Speaking of children and marriage, Agnes does wonder when you are going to finally bow to the proper way of things and find yourself a wife," Freeman observed.

Which is why I volunteered for duty the last couple of times it was my turn to come over for dinner, Nick thought.

"Just haven't met the right woman yet, sir," Nick said sheepishly. "Judging from my siblings' example, even that does not necessarily get the job done."

"Well, Agnes does have a younger sister," Freeman said speculatively. "She's seventeen and needs a pen pal."

Holy shit, sir, that's a little young for me don't you think? Nick thought, keeping his face impassive. After a moment Freeman broke out in a smile.

"You really do have a good poker face, Cobb," Freeman said, laughing. "Agnes' sister is actually twenty-two and teaches English to Mexican kids in California."

Nick shook his head and brought his binoculars back up to scan the horizon again.

"I'll drop her a line if you'd like, sir," Nick said. "I think it will be a while before we get a chance to meet one another though. Rumor has it there's about to be a war on. Plus my sister seems determined to set me up with every single woman she meets at work."

"I have this vision of your sister being as relentless as an escort whose convoy we just attacked," Freeman said.

Unbidden, a mental image of his sister as the figurehead on the bow of a destroyer charging with a bone in its teeth came to Nick's mind. He guffawed out loud, drawing a strange look from all of the lookouts.

"Sorry sir, but even I'm not crazy enough to be on record as comparing my sister to a man of war," Nick replied.

"Smart man," Freeman said.

PENSACOLA NAVAL AIR STATION
1100 EASTERN (0600 HAWAIIAN TIME)

THE ROOM WAS SO QUIET THAT ADAM could actually hear the clock ticking above and behind him on the wall. Both hands on the lectern, he took a moment to survey the gathered young pilots before him. VMF-21, as a fighter squadron, had four more pilots than it did planes, meaning that the classroom was quite packed with twenty testosterone-laden neophytes.

Green as grass, every last one of them, Adam thought, his blue eyes scanning over each face as he looked around the room's white walls. *Well, let's get the introductions over with.*

"Gentlemen, I am your new commander, Major Adam Haynes," Adam began. "I've been informed that the better connected among you have already made some discreet inquiries as to who the Hell I am."

Adam stopped and stared directly at the two individuals he was speaking of. Both young captains suddenly realized that they had obviously overestimated their contacts' discretion.

"To ensure everyone who doesn't have an admiral father or uncle is as informed, let me state up front that I did not exist as a Marine prior to this previous December," Adam stated bluntly.

Well that got everyone's attention, Adam noted.

"Some of you may think that this little fact is a travesty or somehow makes me unqualified to lead this squadron," Adam continued, his voice almost a growl. "Indeed, some of you were foolish enough to say this aloud and in public."

There was a rustle as several officers shifted uncomfortably.

"Let me state this once, and only once, gentlemen," Adam said, his tone icy. "Your opinion on my pedigree is of no concern. What *is* of importance is that you went outside of the chain-of-command. That bullshit stops effective immediately, and the next man who does it better pray to God or sacrifice a virgin, because I'll make you wish your mother had joined a convent."

All twenty men in front of him stiffened, with a couple even starting to glare at him in defiance. He met the eyes of one and held the gaze until the junior officer flinched away.

Bowles, Adam thought. *Going to have to break that man, I see. I get the feeling he'll give me a chance sooner rather than later.*

"Unless there's something missing from your personnel jackets, I'm the only man in this room whom has actually put a burst of fire into an enemy aircraft and got to watch the poor bastard burn all the way to the ground," Adam snarled. "So sorry if you think four years sitting in some finishing school on the Severn means you get to look down on me, but I care even less than the Krauts we will be fighting do about where you went to school."

Looking over the group, Adam saw that he had gotten most of the group's attention.

"Since very few of you gentlemen have ever seen death, outside of some elderly relative lying all pretty in a coffin, I assure you that when some *experten* jumps you it will be neither a quaint nor noble demise," Adam continued, his eyes swinging until he locked gazes with Bowles again.

"There won't be many open casket funerals, provided your remains are even found. You will die screaming for your mothers, choking to death on your own blood, or looking down at the mess between your legs that used to be your balls because you weren't paying fucking attention," Adam said. "Or because some stupid bastard *who thinks having an admiral daddy* means he doesn't have to earn squadron command forgets to clear your tail."

Adam might as well have slapped Captain Bowles with a gauntlet. The junior officers nostrils flared even as he struggled to keep his face passive.

Good, I seem to have gotten their attention, Adam thought. *Let's see how many of them might be worth saving.* Adam stepped from behind the podium, looking at his watch as the second hand finished its journey.

"I have 1120 hours," Adam stated. "The squadron flight roster has been posted in the ready room with the fifteen of you flying with me today checked off. At 1150, you will be at the flight line with your gear, preflight complete, and ready to take off. Group, attention!"

The majority of the men sprang up as one. Adam noted the four or five, taking their cue from Bowles, who were a tad bit slower.

Well, well, well, looks like the rumors about ol' Bowles being a bit presumptuous about lucking into a squadron were true, Adam thought. He let the gathered group stay locked at attention for a few moments.

"Gentlemen, if you're here to fly and fight, you'll be on time to the flight line," Adam reiterated. "If you're too damn yellow or too damn stupid to want to fight in the war that's coming, you'll be late—and I'll stop wasting my time on you. Dismissed!"

Without a second look, the young men began heading for the exits. There were slight murmurs and pensive glances as they moved through the two doors. The door swung closed only briefly before it was pushed open by an arm clad in Royal Air Force blue. Adam's eyes narrowed until the arm's owner stepped all the way into the room, then suddenly brightened as the newcomer spoke.

"A stirring speech, if I do say myself, Squadron Leader Haynes," Connor O'Rourke said in his Irish brogue. "Now once the gentlemen finish cleaning their underwear, I'm sure they'll be quite ready to follow you into battle."

"You rat bastard!" Adam cried, rushing forward to embrace his old comrade.

"Easy mate, the skin grafts still stretch crazy if you catch them wrong," Connor said, throwing his arms around his friend. Adam stepped back after the first hug, looking over his friend's face.

"Amazing what they can do with plastic surgery these days," Connor said grimly. "Or I guess I should truthfully say at least I don't make small children scream the minute they see me."

Adam wanted to disagree with his friend, but didn't have it in his heart to tell an obvious lie. Connor had been an incredibly dashing man the last time the two men had seen each other. What had been ruggedly handsome face with piercing blue eyes and reddish brown hair had been forever altered by the 20-mm shell that had ignited the *Spitfire*'s fuel tank.

"A face made for radio, eh?" Connor said, smiling. From his moustache up, the man's face looked only slightly blemished. From there down, however, it looked as if someone had melted him with hot wax, then tried to force the pieces together.

"How bad was it?" Adam asked.

"Doctors said I was lucky to live," Connor replied brightly. "Don't know about all that. Be nice to see Margaret, Mum and Sarah, maybe get away from all this."

I at least hope it was quick for them, Adam said. *Especially Sarah. No one deserves to die burning to death, nevermind as a newborn.*

"I'm so sorry," Adam said, his voice catching. "I went..."

"I know," Connor said. "Commander Slade came to visit our rehab center in Toronto, try to cheer us chaps up. Thank you for that."

Adam simply nodded, not trusting himself to speak.

"I see that the Commonwealth has finally decided to give you rank commensurate with your flying abilities," Adam said, changing the subject.

"Well, we always said no one over Squadron Leader could fly a glider, nevermind a *Spit*," Connor observed. "Here's to hoping we were exaggerating a little bit."

The Irishman looked Adam over.

"I find it hard to believe that the Colonial Marines are in dire enough straits that they are allowing such disreputable characters as you to take command of squadrons," Connor responded dryly, his Irish brogue adding a slight lilt to the words. Adam started to punch him in the arm, then caught himself.

Adam shrugged.

"Seems killing Germans for fun and profit has secondary benefits," Adam observed. "Although I had to sit in Canada for a few weeks because of it. Didn't get a chance to talk to my mother again."

Connor nodded sympathetically. The roar of engines passing overhead caused Adam to look at his watch.

"We need to walk towards the flight line," he said. Connor nodded, letting Adam lead him out of the classroom, then the building itself. The two men strode quickly, saluting passing Marine and Navy officers as they walked.

"Good thing your President sprung you all," Connor observed after a few minutes. "These blokes all look so young."

"That's because they are," Adam said grimly. "There was some consternation about me even being given a squadron because of my age."

"What?" Connor asked incredulously. "If Douglas Bader, God rest his soul, was given a second chance with artificial legs, certainly your age shouldn't disqualify you."

"Yes, well, thankfully it was made clear to some folks who wanted to put me in a training unit that I wasn't made a Marine to teach pilots which switches to turn on."

"Besides, given some of the blokes we flew for, it's been proven you can teach a monkey to do acrobatics," Connor spat. "It takes a *real man* to keep his head out in a dog fight."

"You sound like Sailor," Adam said.

"You know he's here with me along with Stanford Tuck, right?"

"What?! I thought South Africa voted to sit the rest of this one out?! How is Sailor here?" Adam replied, amazed.

"South Africa did," Connor replied. "One Wing Commander Malan, not so much. He's basically a man without a country now."

"I know that feeling. I rented a house off post, you guys need to come visit," Adam said. "How long are you guys going to be here?"

"Don't know," Connor said. "We were supposed to give a lecture to some of your squadron leaders along with a couple of your blokes just back from China. But now the Training Command is talking about us training some Fleet Air Arm chaps on the new *Seafire*. Be nice if I knew how to fly one myself, of course, but that's supposed to be getting fixed here in the next couple of days."

"Interesting," Adam thought, his mind awake to some possibilities.

"Speaking of your house, do you have an extra room?" Connor asked. "I was told I needed to be on my best behavior if I stayed at the hotel our representative set us up with. I'd rather actually go out and live a little."

What he really means is that he doesn't want to disturb anyone with his screaming, Adam thought. *Some of us know a thing or two about nightmares.*

"Sounds good to me," Adam replied. "I was thinking I'd have to play Russian Roulette with roommates here soon."

A small white lie, but he doesn't need to know that, Adam thought.

"Knowing your luck, you'd end up with some buxom blonde with loose morals," Connor said with a grin.

A shadow of pain flitted over Adam's face.

"I haven't exactly had the best luck with women as of late," Adam said. "But if you'll excuse me, I've got to try and save the lives of some very inexperienced young men."

"Funny, I feel in the mood for a scrap," Connor said, a twinkle in his eye. "I figure since I could beat your arse if we were both in *Spitfires*, embarrassing you in that junk heap you call a fighter plane should be fairly easy."

Adam bared his teeth in a slight smile.

"In a few days, I'll be happy to take you up on that offer," Adam said. "First, however, I've got to see what I'm working with. If these idiots can't keep simple formation, I'm not going to take my chances with them in a dogfight given what happened to my predecessor."

"Terrible thing that," Connor observed. "From what I am told, they could hear his wingman screaming the whole way down."

Adam shrugged.

"Well, it happens. Let's say another week at least, and I suggest you bring Sailor or someone to cover your tail…I'll be gunning for you."

Connor snorted as they reached the VMF-21 squadron area.

"With that bunch of fresh meat you have there, a wingman will hardly be necessary for me. I'll be at the Officer's Club when you get done," Connor said.

AT PRECISELY 1150, ADAM STOOD IN FRONT OF HIS LIGHT GRAY *Wildcat* in full flight gear. A monoplane fighter with a short, stubby frame, the *Wildcat* was the standard fighter of the Navy and Marine Corps. With its very narrow undercarriage holding up its tubby frame, the *Wildcat* looked like an ugly duck. In the case of VMF-21, the group flew the most recent model, the F4F-4. This meant the fighter's mid-fuselage mounted wing carried six machine guns instead of the earlier model's four, plus had numerous improvements such as cockpit armor and folding wings.

Four guns or six, it's still a dog, Adam thought bitterly. *About as good as a Hurricane, and that thing has been meat on the table since 1941. Twenty knots too slow, can't climb worth a damn, and it looks like your buddy's sister that your taking to the prom just so she won't feel bad.*

Clearing those thoughts from his mind, Adam turned from looking at his fighter to staring at the three captains who stood in front of him. They were the most senior members of the squadron present, with Captains Bowles, Kennedy, and West having decided that punctuality was a principle of little importance.

I have half a mind to replace Bowles and his friends with the spare pilots, but that would probably start a shit storm I'm not quite ready to unleash, Adam thought grimly.

"Gentlemen, I judge by the fact that you are standing here that my instructions were clear?" Adam stated. "Since it is apparent that the previous flight, correction, division leaders do not speak English as their first language, they will have to be put in a position where they can learn simple concepts, such as telling time."

"Sir, I think Captain Bowles had to go to the mess hall to grab lunch," Captain Keith Seidel said, his Southern drawl somewhat tremulous. The stocky, black-haired officer looked rather nervous, as if he was about to get drawn into a fight he wanted no part of.

"Interesting," Adam said. "Tell me, Captain Seidel, did you grab lunch?" Adam asked.

"No sir," Seidel replied, his brown eyes briefly narrowing as he thought about Adam's query.

"Captain Walters, how about you?" Adam said, turning to the tall, rangy brown haired officer standing to Seidel's right.

"No sir," Walters replied easily.

"I'm guessing Captain Kennedy's wife made his lunch for him," Adam said, causing Kennedy to briefly look astonished.

At least the poor bastard before me had a good personnel book even if his luck was shit, Adam thought. *Lots of interesting facts in there.*

"So, as I was saying, Captain Walters will take Green Division, Seidel will take Blue, Kennedy will take yellow," Adam said evenly. "Captain Seidel, your second section will be led by Lieutenant Mathias, while Captain Kennedy's second section leader will be Lieutenant Terrell."

Seidel and Kennedy glanced down the flight line to where the two first lieutenants were waiting by their fighters, then back at Adam.

"There is Captain Bowles," Captain Walters said, his voice full of relief. Adam turned and fixed the man with a baleful glare.

"Are you a hound dog, Captain Walters?" Adam asked quietly.

"Uh, no sir?" Walters stated.

"Good, because that will be the last time you point and yip like an excited retriever," Adam snapped. "I believe you have your orders, so I do not understand why you are still standing here."

All three men came to attention at that, saluting. Adam returned the salute, then turned to head towards his own fighter.

"Sir, is there something I should know about?" Master Sergeant Seaver, VMF-21's senior crew chief, asked. "It appears that some officers are heading for the wrong fighters."

Adam smiled, and it was a look that would have scared most men.

"Nothing that you probably won't hear the explanation for in a moment if you listen close," Adam replied as Seaver began helping him strap in. Seaver's lined, tanned face split into a smile at that comment.

"Always happy to get free entertainment, sir," Seaver replied, running a hand through his gray hair.

"Major Haynes!" Bowles shouted, moving down the tarmac towards

JAMES YOUNG

Adam's fighter. Adam saw several heads snap around in their own cockpits at the obviously agitated officer's tone.

Oh good, witnesses, Adam thought, pointedly ignoring the man as he reached the *Wildcat*'s starboard wingtip.

"Major Haynes!" Bowles barked as Seavers hopped off the fighter's port wing.

"I am quite certain, Captain Bowles," Adam said, his voice dripping menace, "that you are merely projecting your voice in fear that my engine might soon drown you out and most assuredly *not* speaking to me in an insubordinate tone."

Bowles opened his mouth, almost assuredly to tell Adam just what he thought about his *projection* when Captain West saved his friend.

"Sir, there appears to have been a misunderstanding," West said, his voice dripping forced politeness. Fair haired and blue eyed, West looked a slightly overweight boxer, complete with a crooked nose.

"Interesting," Adam replied. "Given that there are apparently twelve other officers who comprehended me quite clearly, perhaps the issue isn't understanding but condescension?"

The sound of several engines turning over almost made Adam smile.

Looks like Master Sergeant Seavers is goading the angry bucks, Adam thought.

"Sir! The wing commander clearly stated in his policy that seniority..." Bowles started to shout. Checking to make sure the propeller on his fighter was clear, Adam signaled to Seavers that he was about to start up the *Wildcat*'s Pratt & Whitney engine.

"I suggest you gentlemen get to your planes," Adam called. "Unless you're planning on flapping your wings to get to altitude."

With that, Adam pressed the ignition switch. With a puff of black smoke and sound of its shotgun shell starter, the radial engine began to turn over. Out of the corner of his eye, Adam saw Bowles start to take a step towards his fighter before West grabbed him. Shoving off his companion's grasp, Bowles turned and stalked back towards his own mount.

Probably doesn't realize I'm not really too concerned about his Daddy,

Adam thought. *When my own father calls the Commandant and Chief of Naval Operations by their first names, pretty sure I hold trump.*

FORTY MINUTES LATER, ADAM WAS WONDERING IF HE SHOULDN'T have taken Blakeslee up on his offer.

Sweet mercy, the near collision in Green Division on takeoff was just the start of our troubles, Adam thought, stamping on his rudder. *While that could be chalked up to the new division leader, the fact that* **no one can fly outside of formation** *means the late Major Pressler was a little too concerned with appearances.*

"Okay dammit, what part of 'get upsun of those bombers before you bounce them' was unclear, Blue One?!" Adam barked over the radio net. The flight of Army *Marauders* conducting a training mission had seemed the perfect opportunity for some impromptu training. Adam was suddenly glad that the olive green planes weren't sporting black crosses and carrying live ammo.

Oh, these boys would be amazing as an aerobatics demonstration team, Adam thought, feeling almost helpless with anger, *but I'd sooner go into combat with a pack of nuns than these idiots. At least then God would be on my side, for He's surely forsaken me now.*

"Okay dammit, let's head for the barn," Adam said, glancing at his watch. "We're going to stop wasting the Corps' fuel. All pilots will meet me in the classroom thirty minutes after landing. Bring paper and pencil for notes. Division leaders acknowledge."

As the radio replies came in, Adam shook his head.

Well, I guess I asked for this, he thought. *But I'm definitely starting to think about that Dutch bounty money again.*

PEARL HARBOR, HAWAII
0600 LOCAL (1100 EASTERN)

PATRICIA LOOKED AT HERSELF IN THE MIRROR AND WAS NOT HAPPY with what she saw.

Need to lay off the sweets, she thought uncharitably, the green sundress just a tad bit too tight across her hips and breasts for her to feel comfortable wearing it. *One would think walking three miles to work every day would have helped with that, but apparently not. Who knew being a librarian was hell on the figure? Especially with how much work it is...*

"Stop looking in that mirror and being hard on yourself, you look fine," Jo chuckled from the bathroom doorway. "Or are you worried that the good Lieutenant Byrnes is coming by to walk us home again today?"

Patricia looked at her roommate with a raised eyebrow.

"I don't think Peter comes for my company," she replied archly. "Even if some of us are too oblivious to realize that."

Jo rolled her eyes at her, causing Patricia to flush slightly in annoyance.

You could try a acting a little less like you're the valedictorian of the school of hard knocks, Patricia thought unfavorably. *Yes your mother died right in front of you and your Dad's stuck in the Philippines, but life's hard all over.*

Jo gave Patricia a slight smirk,

"You're thinking I need to get over myself again," Jo observed.

Patricia felt an altogether different coloring occurring on her face.

"Your brother is great at poker," Jo continued. "You, on the other hand, really, *really* suck at keeping things off your face."

"Jo, I didn't mean..." Patricia started to say, before the other woman waved her off.

"You're right, I need to stop throwing a damn pity party for myself," Jo replied. "The problem isn't that I don't realize Peter has a thing for me, by the way. It's that I'm not sure I have a thing for him, and think you two would make a much better match."

"Oh? Just why is that?" Patricia asked.

"Gee, I don't know, the fact that try as he might he keeps looking at your rear end whenever you walk in front of him?" Jo answered with a smile.

Damn you, Patricia thought, feeling the blush getting deeper.

"On a serious note, you both like to read like fiends," Jo said. "I used to think I liked to read a little bit, but you've already devoured half the library."

"Don't exaggerate, Jo," Patricia sighed.

"Fine, just the mythology section," Jo said with a small laugh.

"You know, that's not a good thing to remind me of," Patricia replied. "Men are put off by that. No one wants a smart girl. I'm going to die a spinster."

Jo looked her up and down, then shook her head.

"I doubt that," the shorter woman observed drily.

"Fine, I'm going to end up with some man who's going to try and change me as soon as we get married," Patricia replied.

"Keep thinking that and you just might prove me wrong on the spinster part," Jo said after a moment's consideration.

"Well at least I'd have a say in that," Patricia observed. "While not as bad as my mother, my brothers do seem to keep trying to set me up with people."

Jo looked at her as if she'd grown a second head.

"Right. You mean the same brothers who promise a painful end to any man who even looks at your funny in their presence? Those brothers?"

"That's only Sam and David," Patricia scoffed. "They're harmless."

"Of course, completely harmless," Jo sneered. "Why, just the other day I seem to recall your older brother nearly beating a man to death for looking at you too long while you were getting off a ship."

Patricia absent-mindedly fiddled with the center button of her dress, afraid that it was going to gape open at an inopportune time.

Definitely have to lay off the sweets, Patricia thought. *I can't afford to buy a new dress right now.*

"You know, if you tug on that damn thing one more time, you're going to cause it to do the thing you're worried about," Jo observed laughingly.

"I'm glad you find this amusing, Jo," Patricia said, her Southern drawl starting to thicken as it always did when she was embarrassed or flustered.

"Well, you just look like someone who's getting ready to go meet the love of her life, not just spend the day at work," Jo said, stepping back out of the bathroom to grab her brush. "Maybe you like Peter more than you realize."

Patricia took a deep breath to get control of herself. *Jo, you're a great friend, but there are days.*

"I mean, sure, when the 'brother of the day' stops by with one of his shipmates or squadron members, there may be sparks," Jo called from the bedroom, referring to the fact that Nick, Sam, and David seemed to always stop in with a different shipmate on days that Peter didn't walk her home. "But I don't think one button out of place will change his mind on whether or not you are beautiful."

Jo entered the bathroom as she finished her sentence, taking a quick glance at herself in the mirror. Quickly brushing her hair, an evil thought crept into her mind.

"Not that he won't have mussing up your hair on his mind in the first place," she said with an evil grin.

Patricia gave Jo a dirty look.

"Just because you grew up among sailors and their somewhat more earthy habits doesn't mean you know all of them that well, Jo. Some of my brothers' comrades are the utmost gentlemen," Patricia replied.

Jo gave a sharp, braying laugh at that comment.

"You know, thank God you ended up with me as your housemate," Jo said. "It's going to be tough, but I just might manage to keep you a virgin until your wedding night."

Oh you little... Patricia thought, fighting the urge to box Jo's ears.

"I'm just saying you need to take a look around, Patricia, and realize that there aren't that many single, available *white* women here," Jo continued. "In some ways it's a blessing, but in just as many it's a curse."

Patricia started to speak, but was cut off by Jo continuing.

"Now, while I'm sure your brothers have screened many of their more amorous shipmates away from you, it never hurts to be just a bit cynical. Not to mention, anyone you hitch up with just might find themselves suffering from a slight case of *death* in the near future."

I have had about enough of you, Patricia said, giving Jo a glare to indicate she'd crossed the line. Jo at least had the decency to look sheepish in return.

"While I do not have the luxury of, nor need the looming presence of the 'meanest bastard in the navy,' Jo, I am not an idiot," Patricia snarled. "Please, do not lecture to me as if I am a child," Patricia said severely.

Seeing she'd truly struck a nerve, Jo winced inwardly.

Okay, I see someone else has been talking to you about my Dad's time at BuPers, Jo thought. *For the record, he really didn't send that lieutenant to the Philippines because he checked me out when I was fifteen.*

"I just don't want to see you get hurt," Jo said, stepping back from her friend.

"I have a bit more experience with men than you apparently think. Now, I believe if we do not hurry, we will be late for work," Pat said coolly, stepping past her friend.

One of us has probably barely kissed a man, while the other one of us is a commander's daughter, Jo thought. *A commander's daughter who was a rather rebellious teenager that made a few mistakes in attempts to hurt her father. I'd dare say poor Lieutenant Foster probably didn't think my virginity was worth being assigned to a gunboat in Shanghai*, Jo thought wryly. It had been a wonderful six-month love affair, and she didn't really regret it, but it had ended badly for all involved.

I wonder why I have not heard from Dad for two weeks? Jo thought.

U.S.S. Houston
0015 Local (1115 Eastern)
25 March (24 March)

The harsh light of the igniting flare was an unpleasant shock to Jacob's eyes.

Jesus Christ that's bright! he thought, blinking to clear the white dots now hovering in his vision. Out of the corner of his eye, he could see Battle Two's helmsman and look outs shielding their eyes from the glare. He dimly heard the sound of aircraft engines as he squinted into the darkness around the heavy cruiser.

Didn't even hear the bastards! Jacob thought angrily. His musings were interrupted as the *Houston*'s crew sprang into action.

"Hard to starboard, aye! All ahead full!" the talker, Seaman Third Class Teague, relayed the bridge's command from the rear of the compartment. In the brightness from the still falling flare, Jacob could clearly see Teague's freckled features set in a shocked expression. Of average height, the talker stood with his powered by sound handset clutched in one hand, the other gripping a nearby stanchion to remain steady as the cruiser lurched in acceleration.

So much for traveling at a slower speed so we didn't leave a wake, Jacob thought angrily.

Battle Two was a structure located just forward of the cruiser's hangar in which all of the functions performed by the bridge were duplicated. In case the main bridge was destroyed or lost the ability to relay steering commands to the rudder, it was the job of Battle Two's occupants to continue maneuvering the ship. In addition, Jacob was able to monitor the *Houston*'s damage control information, thus freeing the captain to fight the ship.

"How in the Hell did those Aussie bastards find us?" someone muttered as the American heavy cruiser heeled over into her turn.

Good question, Jacob mused. *Maybe those airedales had a reason to be cocky when they arranged for this night flight. Their radar must be better than anything our boys have.*

"Aircraft, port bow!" Teague said anxiously, drawing a stern look from Chief Petty Officer Roberts, Battle Two's NCOIC. Jacob waved in acknowledgment, and was about to say something when there was the roar of aircraft engines passing from *starboard*. Everyone in Battle Two reflexively ducked as there was a brief sensation of a shadow passing overhead.

Is this how the mouse feels before the talons hit? Jacob thought.

"Holy shit!" Teague said, frightened.

"Belay that talk!" Roberts barked. The older, slightly heavyweight NCOIC's skin was pallid even for being illuminated by the descending magnesium, and Jacob had the feeling the man did not feel as confident as he was letting on.

If that had been a Jap torpedo plane we'd have a hole in the side of the ship right about now, Jacob thought bitterly. A few moments later, the aircraft initially sighted from port passed over the ship, and again Jacob marveled at how quiet the airplanes were.

"What did they call those birds, sir? Beauties or something like that?" Lieutenant Robert Locher, Battle Two's Officer of the Deck (OOD), asked.

"*Beaufighters*," Jacob said grimly. "Should probably call them owls after that performance."

Mercifully, Battle Two became dark again as the magnesium flares went out upon falling into the ocean. Stepping outside of the compartment, Jacob attempted to look astern of the *Houston* and realized his night vision was completely shot. Closing his eyes for a long ten count, he reopened them to find he could once more make out the light cruiser *Boise* astern and destroyers *Ford* and *Whipple* to the two cruisers port side.

"Sir, Captain Wallace requests your presence on the bridge," Lieutenant Locher called from the entry hatch behind him.

"Understood Lieutenant Locher," Jacob said. "You have the station until I return."

"Aye aye, sir," Locher replied.

A LITTLE UNDER FIVE MINUTES LATER, JACOB WAS STANDING ALONE with Captain Wallace on the bridge's starboard wing. Having sent the lookouts inside, Wallace turned to look at his XO.

"I just received our new orders," Wallace said solemnly. "We are to return to the Philippines at once."

"Sir, I take it Admiral Hart lost his argument with General MacArthur?" Jacob asked drily. Surprising no one, General MacArthur had gotten wind of Admiral Hart's plan to retreat to the Dutch East Indies with all of his surface ships. The former had immediately contacted General Marshall, his ostensible superior in Washington, and raised political cain.

Considering the Philippines allegedly became independent as of the 1st of this month, I'm not seeing where Admiral Hart was violating orders, Jacob thought. *Apparently Secretary Knox or, more likely, President Roosevelt felt differently.*

"It would appear that way," Captain Wallace said grimly. "Or more correctly, I believe Admiral Hart decided he wasn't going to get relieved over this just yet."

Jacob kept his face expressionless in the gloom.

So the plan remains the same, we're just waiting until war breaks out, Jacob mused. *At least we'll start having regular mail service again.*

"Those Aussies were an unpleasant surprise," Captain Wallace said, changing the subject.

"Sir, if they can do that when people are shooting back, unpleasant surprise is not going to begin to cover it," Jacob observed. "We didn't even see the flare plane, and at least one of the bombers would have caught us by total surprise."

"We're supposed to return to Sydney for one of those *radar* sets ourselves in a couple of months," Wallace observed, his tone showing his inexperience with the new technological word. "If the *New Mexico* and *Idaho* are released from the Atlantic for duty here, we may be able to go all the way back to Pearl."

Or alternatively, if pigs fly we could have bacon season, Jacob thought sardonically. *No one besides the Brits are sending battleships out here. Especially with Congress wrangling over paying for anymore new ones.*

"I hope we get someone who knows how to use it as well as those Australians apparently do," Jacob observed. "That is a game changer."

"That squadron leader said they've been training with it for five months," Wallace replied. "I'm not sure how much use it would be if someone just got their hands on it."

"I'd love to try that out, I know that much," Jacob replied.

"Hopefully the other side doesn't have anything like it," Wallace stated grimly. "Although who knows what our German friends gave them."

"The Commonwealth radio said there's been a couple of incidents in eastern Poland," Jacob said. "I guess they'll be fighting over there sooner rather than later."

"Which probably means we'll be fighting here," *Houston*'s master said. "With the whole weight of the Jap fleet barreling down at us."

NORTH PACIFIC
1845 LOCAL (2145 EASTERN)
25 MARCH

It is a gorgeous day, Isoro Honda thought, giving his *Shiden* a slight left rudder to line up behind the twin columns of carriers. *Nothing at all like the last three. Not that I am complaining—we could not have asked for better weather during our approach.*

The entire *Kido Butai* was steaming into the westerly wind, and Isoro thought briefly of how striking the fleet was. The six carriers were steaming in two columns of three, the sun turning their wooden decks a fiery orange as it reflected off them. The flattops were surrounded by the battleships *Hiei* and *Kirishima* roughly equal with the middle of the columns, and the heavy cruisers *Tone*, *Chikuma*, and *Mogami* steaming forward of them in a semi-circle. Beyond the heavy ships, two light cruisers and ten destroyers made up the rest of the escort. Even as Isoro watched, two of the latter broke inward to take up their position as plane guards, ready to pluck any member of the twelve strong CAP out of the sea.

How horrible would it be to suffer a mishap today? Isoro mused. *To go through all these months of training only to be killed by some mechanical error or accident. Or even worse, be saved and not be able to take part in the strike tomorrow?* Shaking his head, Isoro turned away from the fleet beautifully outlined against the red orb of the setting sun and looked over his *chutai*. He felt a warm sense of pride as the two other *Shiden* in perfect formation.

We have come so far since we first started flying these fighters. I look forward to meeting the Americans tomorrow, Isoro thought. Gently, he moved astern of *Akagi*, noting that the carrier's funnel smoke was moving straight behind her like black yarn trailing behind a running child.

Thank goodness, no cross wind, he thought. *The weather gods continue to smile upon us, and tomorrow we shall make history.*

. . .

IT IS GOING TO BE A RESTLESS NIGHT, VICE ADMIRAL YAMAGUCHI thought, looking at the map board in front of him. The flag plot was quiet, almost funereal as his staff went about their business and left him to his thoughts.

I am forgetting something, Yamaguchi thought. *I just know that I am.*

"I wish we had struck back in '41, sir," Rear Admiral Kusaka said, moving up beside him.

"A few more hours of warning is more than balanced by the new aircraft," Yamaguchi replied with a sigh. "I doubt we would have succeeded as well as we had wished two years ago, plus the British would have been much more of a problem."

Kusaka grunted at that, bringing a smirk to Yamaguchi's face.

Yet they say that I am far too aggressive, the *Kido Butai*'s commander thought.

"Sir, we have recovered all fighters," the *Akagi*'s XO informed him.

"Thank you, Commander," Yamaguchi said, dismissing the man. The commander had barely left the hatchway before another officer was stepping through. Captain Tomeo Kaku had been captain of the *Hiryu*, Yamaguchi's former flagship. The man had come out of command the previous January, and Yamaguchi had immediately offered him a post as his intelligence officer.

I did not realize how much he and Kusaka would fight, Yamaguchi thought, looking as his chief of staff's brow furrowed.

"We have the final code report from the Honolulu consulate," Kaku said. "The *Maryland* and *Colorado* returned from the West Coast last night. This brings the American strength to nine battleships."

Arizona, Pennsylvania, Tennessee, California, Colorado, Maryland, West Virginia, Nevada, and Oklahoma, Yamaguchi thought. *I was hoping that they would lose at least one more to the Atlantic, but it is not to be.*

"The carriers?" Yamaguchi asked.

"*Lexington* has returned from Wake Island, *Enterprise* has been confirmed off Victoria Island with the British *Victorious*, *Saratoga* has just left dry dock, but the consulate does not know where *Yorktown* is," Kaku said. "*Hornet* has transited the Panama Canal but was allegedly en route to San Diego according to intelligence."

Yamaguchi took a deep breath then released it.

Four enemy carriers and I do not know where two of them are, he thought.

"Very well, we will remain with our plan for minimal CAP," Yamaguchi said, feeling as if he was shoving all of his chips into a colossal craps bet. "Inform the *Tone* that her reconnaissance will focus on finding the carriers between the first and second waves. We can outrun the battleships, but I cannot outrun the American aircraft."

U.S.S. HORNET
650 MILES EAST OF HAWAII
1930 LOCAL (0030 EASTERN)

ERIC STOOD ON THE FRONT OF THE *HORNET*'S FLIGHT DECK IN HIS service khakis and stared into the sunset. The *Hornet* was heading west at a steady twenty knots, the breeze refreshing in his face. Behind him, the deck was a quiet place, the last of Air Group Eight having just been struck below.

I love this time of day, Eric thought. *It's so peaceful.* The United States Navy usually didn't conduct night operations, although scuttlebutt had it that the *Enterprise* and *Victorious* were starting to conduct experiments off of Bremerton. That thought made Eric shudder.

Dive bombing is dangerous enough as is, Eric thought. *I sure as hell don't want to try **that** at night.*

"Stare long enough into that sun you're going to go blind, Lieutenant Cobb," a deep, gravelly voice said from behind him. Eric turned to see Lieutenant Commander Palmer Couch, the commander of VB-8, walking up the wood deck behind him. Shorter than Eric, Couch still retained the sinewy build of the collegiate wrestler he had once been. His black hair had started to get some pepper in it, but with very few lines around his green eyes and a youthful looking face, Couch could have easily passed for being Eric's contemporary rather than a man who'd held his commission since 1925.

"Just like to remind myself there's more to the world than gray bulkheads, sir," Eric replied.

"Yeah, I can understand that," Couch replied, standing in the breeze. The two men stood in silence for a few minutes until the senior officer spoke.

"I'm not one to give advice on what an officer does with his personal time," Couch said. "But you could spend more time with your squadron mates. It's been noticed that you tend to hold yourself apart from your peers."

"Sorry sir," Eric said evenly. "It's been a bit of a rough few months."

"I think everyone on board realizes that's the case, Lieutenant Cobb," Couch replied, then held up his hand as Eric was about to respond. "No one is thinking you're holding yourself up as somehow better than everyone else, just so we're clear. It's that you've been aboard for four weeks and most folks don't know anything beyond what they've seen in the papers or heard on the radio."

I never wanted to be a celebrity, Eric thought bitterly. *That hasn't helped me want to talk to other people.*

"Sir, being honest, I fully expected to be in my second month of law school with a new wife at this point," Eric said bitterly. "I was not aware it's colored my actions as much as it apparently has, but that has taken some time to get used to."

Couch raised an eyebrow in surprise.

"You sure you wanted to be a lawyer? You seem to take to dive bombing very well," Couch replied.

Fat lot of good skill did Lieutenant Commander Cobleigh, Eric thought grimly.

"I think the refresher course helped with that," Eric said, referring to the three weeks he'd spent getting recertified on the *Dauntless*. "I'm still surprised that Admiral Kimmel has been rotating so many pilots through the school."

Couch nodded knowingly, having gone through the school just before taking over VB-8 five months before.

"The torpecker pilots can talk about being the Sunday Punch all they want," Couch said, referring to VT-8, *Hornet*'s torpedo squadron. "Everyone knows you have to land jabs to make the punch count, and even with those new turkeys of theirs they're going to have trouble hitting anything we don't cripple."

Eric smiled beside himself. There was a friendly rivalry between the dive bomber and torpedo pilots, with the latter often pointing you sank ships quicker by letting water in than blowing air out.

"Sir, I'm pretty sure if we start laying thousand pounders on something, the torpedoes might just be speeding up the process," Eric observed. Couch looked at him speculatively.

"We just might at that," Couch replied. "So how is your fiancée taking the abrupt career change?"

Eric closed his eyes.

"My *former* fiancée decided she'd rather find someone who did something nice and safe," Eric said. "Judging from my mother's last letter, that hasn't gone so well given how we parted."

"How you parted?" Couch asked.

"Let's just say that Mobile has a very small social circle," Eric replied wearily. "In case you've never heard, Russians are a vengeful people."

"I'm not sure I follow, Lieutenant Cobb?" Couch said, his face puzzled.

"Well sir, let me explain about the Duchess," Eric replied with a smile.

6
PREAMBLE

Wise men learn by other's mistakes, fools by their own.

— **HENRY GEORGE BOHN**

Pensacola NAS
0545 Eastern
26 March 1943

THE PHONE WAS RINGING at an ungodly hour, and it made Adam's head reverberate like a church bell that had been struck by a clapper.

Note to self—never drink with a man who has been through skin grafts, Adam thought. *To think I'd believed I'd stopped early enough to avoid a hangover.*

"This had better be someone telling me the Germans are off the coast," Adam muttered. Taking a deep breath, he picked up the phone.

"Major Haynes," he said, surprised at how clear he managed to sound.

"Major Haynes, this is Major Anthony," the voice on the other end began.

Oh shit, Adam thought. Anthony was the adjutant of Marine

Aircraft Wing Two (MAW-2), and if he was on the phone it would appear as if Bowles had already gone whining to the Air Group commander.

"Good morning Major Anthony," Adam responded with obviously faux pleasantry. "I'm guessing that you're not calling to tell me world peace has broken out."

"Colonel Gatling has ordered that you report to his office no later than 0645." Anthony paused, then said in a lower tone, "I'd bring a good reason why you relieved all three of your division leaders without his permission."

"Understood. I will be in his office in less than one hour," Adam said resignedly.

Why am I no longer surprised at some people's anal retentiveness? Adam thought.

"Thank you. Sorry to wake you up so early," Anthony replied, then hung up.

He sounded genuinely apologetic, Adam thought. *Must be an adjutant trait to be able to lie so easily.* Hanging up the phone, Adam sat up in bed to find Connor standing in the doorway. The scarred officer wore a tattered RAF issue smoker's robe, a mug of coffee in his hand.

"How did you guess I'd need that?" Adam asked grimly.

"What? Bloody idiots are the same in every service," Connor said, handing him a cup of coffee.

"I'm just amazed that you've been up long enough to make a pot of coffee," Adam replied.

"Well, it's not like you and your squadron gave me much of a workout yesterday," Connor replied, a grim smile on his face.

Adam just sighed.

*That will teach me to try and match up flights of **Wildcats** versus **Seafires***, Adam thought grimly. He'd foolishly rang Connor prior to VMF-21's second, and last, sortie for the day. In what Adam had thought was a fortuitous occurrence, Connor, Sailor, Stanford, and some guy named Brown had all been open to mixing it up in some mock dogfights.

In addition to nearly killing themselves, my Marines nearly killed them, Adam thought with a resigned sigh. *I thought that bastard Major Hendry* had been unfortunate before. *Now I think he deserved **exactly** what happened to him, and it's too bad his wingman's prop probably killed him instantly.*

"You're thinking ill thoughts about the dead again, aren't you?" Connor said with a smile as the two of them moved to the kitchen.

"I prefer truthful," Adam replied, his tone annoyed. "I hope that stupid bastard is roasting in Hell, because odds are he's going to get several of his pilots sent there if we have to go to war tomorrow."

The cuckoo clock in the front foyer sounded.

I guess I better go in there and get my ass chewing," Adam noted.

"Is it going to change anything you do?" Connor asked.

"After yesterday I was going to try Bowles and his friends out back in their old jobs anyway," Adam replied. "But now? That little son-of-a-bitch might have just bought himself another two weeks as a wingman."

THIRTY-FIVE MINUTES LATER, HE FOUND HIMSELF ENTERING MAJOR Anthony's office.

Sometimes arriving early helps to seize the initiative, Adam thought with an inner smile as the adjutant looked up in surprise. *Even if the senior officer was intending to make you wait anyway, now whatever schedule he had in place is slightly disjointed.*

Recollecting himself, Major Anthony smiled a mischievous smile, as if he knew something Adam didn't. Before Adam could say anything, the adjutant sprung to his feet and opened the door to Colonel Gatling's office. Looking past Major Anthony, Adam felt his temper starting to flare as he saw who else was sitting in the seat directly in front of Gatling's desk.

Well, well, well Captain Bowles, decided to take your case directly to the man, did you? I don't think you have any idea how much you're going to regret that later, Adam thought fiercely as the younger officer gave him a smug grin. *Oh no, you have not **got a clue**.*

"Sir, Major Haynes is present," Anthony said. Gatling was also surprised to see Adam. Looking him dead in the eye then pointedly looking away, he turned to Anthony.

"Have the Major wait until I am done hearing testimony from the good captain here," Gatling stated pompously. Anthony nodded, then closed the door. Looking at his face, Adam could see that he was not impressed by the way that his boss was acting.

"Colonel Gatling is trying to ride our fair-haired boy to that first star, is he?" Adam asked levelly, instantly wishing he hadn't let those be the first words from his mouth. Anthony's face immediately became impassive, every inch the professional officer.

"Captain Bowles is simply taking advantage of every officer's right to use the chain-of-command," the adjutant stated quietly. After a moment's pause, he stated, "The fact that his father is an admiral should not have any bearing on this case." *It is unfortunate it does*, hung in the air unsaid.

"Apparently boy wonder did not learn anything from being hustled out of Hawaii," Adam said lowly. "What exactly is he trying to state I did wrong?" Adam asked, raising an eyebrow.

"Violation of a direct order, conduct unbecoming an officer, and reckless endangerment of your men," Anthony replied, keeping his voice low so that he could not be heard in the office. "Hopefully, Gatling's just going to take you down a peg. Unfortunately, I think he's actually angry enough to think about relieving you."

Adam smiled and pulled out a sheet of paper, causing Anthony's eyes to narrow.

You've probably thought I've lost my mind, Adam thought with smile. *No one should be happy going before the old man. Too bad for him that I've got a hole card.*

"Major Haynes, report!" Colonel Gatling shouted from in the office before Adam could respond to his junior officer. Adam felt Anthony look at him in surprise.

Oh, I know how insulting asking me to report in front of a subordinate is, Adam thought, clearing his expression. *Bowles is going to wish he was never born later today. He'd actually better pray that we never go to combat, as at this point I might gun him down myself.*

"Enter!" Gatling roared. Adam reached for the door knob and pushed forward, entering and stopping exactly three steps forward of Gatling's desk. He brought his hand up and snapped a salute.

"Major Haynes reporting as ordered," Adam stated, holding his salute. Gatling remained standing behind his desk, looking over Adam's uniform for any excuse to tear into him. Finally, he returned the salute.

"Explain to me why you should not be relieved, Major Haynes," Gatling said snidely. "I mean, I guess you must believe that being a worthless mercenary and son of some rich bastard gives you the right to do whatever the hell you want."

*Oh hell no, you will **not** talk to me like that*, Adam seethed.

"Sir, with all due respect, if you call my father a bastard again I will injure you," Adam said lowly and menacingly. He heard Bowles sharp intake of breath behind him, then the sound of the captain's tittering laughter.

"Sir, I will be happy to testify against Major Haynes at his general court martial for threatening a superior officer," Bowles said snidely.

"Shut up until spoken to, pilot!" Haynes barked. Bowles, looking every bit like the petulant child, turned to him and laughed in his face.

"That is enough, Captain," Gatling snapped. Bowles turned and locked eyes with the colonel. Adam looked on with interest, waiting to see who would break first.

"There can be more than one court martial, Captain," Gatling said, his voice full of ice. "I suggest that you remember your father is an ocean away, and I can have you sharing a brig cell with Major Haynes before either of you have an opportunity to make a single phone call."

Bowles snapped back to attention, realizing that he had pressed his luck too far.

"As for you, Major, do not ever threaten me again," Gatling snapped. "You have two hours to return and receive your orders from Major Anthony and comply with your transfer. Do I make myself clear?"

"No, sir, you do not. I would advise that the colonel read the letter I have here prior to relieving me," Adam said, holding up the piece of paper.

"Personally, unless that's from the Commandant himself, I don't care what it says," Gatling said, waving his hand away.

"Yes, sir," Adam said.

I gave you your chance, you pompous ass, Adam thought grimly.

"Dismissed," Gatling said, waving Adam away. "Captain Bowles, report to your squadron and inform them that you are now acting commander."

"Yes, sir," Bowles said. Adam executed a sharp about face and exited the office, followed by Bowles. As soon as the door click shut behind the junior officer, Adam whirled on him, his face inches from Bowles'.

"I hope that you gained some small delight from that, Captain," Adam seethed lowly. "Because I assure you that you have made a mistake beyond your imagination."

Bowles' face worked as the younger man tried to keep from laughing in Adam's face.

"Sir, this isn't England, and quite frankly I think it's about time someone broke that fact to you," the captain smirked. "I hope you enjoy your next assignment, I'm sure it will be somewhere far from any fighting squadron. Speaking of which, I need to go train *my* men."

With the last, Bowles pushed past Adam.

All good things come to those who wait, Adam thought, stopping himself from punching the man dead in his face.

"I should have your orders ready for you by eight thirty," Anthony said from behind his desk. "As soon as I get the old man to tell me where you're going."

"Actually, I'll save you some ink. Let me use your phone." Anthony looked at him with puzzlement, than handed Adam the receiver.

"Yes, operator, put me through to Major General Geiger's office. Please tell him it is Major Haynes calling. Thank you," he said. Anthony's face snapped up in surprise and shock. Adam favored him with a grin.

"The man said unless the letter was from the Commandant himself," Adam noted to Anthony, then stopped as he heard a gruff, familiar male voice identify himself as the head of Marine Corps Aviation.

"Good morning, sir, this is Major Haynes," Adam began, then stopped. "Yes sir, precisely as you predicted. Yes sir, he's in his office right now. Yes, sir, Major Anthony is here."

With that, Adam turned to the adjutant.

"Major General Geiger for you," Adam said simply.

"Sir, Major Anthony," Anthony said. Adam watched the man's face drain of color as he listened to Major General Geiger. After a couple more acknowledgments, the adjutant hung up the phone. A few moments later, the phone rang on the other side of the office door. Anthony looked up in awe at Adam.

"Most of my kills don't see it coming," Adam said simply. "Now if you'll excuse me, I think I have some discipline to administer. When Lieutenant Colonel King gets in, do please tell him that I hope to make an office call this afternoon after our first flight."

With that, Adam turned and left. As he hit the door, he started whistling.

This is going to be a good day, he thought. *The first one I've had in a long time.*

Ten minutes later, Adam strode into the squadron administrative area. He was utterly unsurprised to find the place empty other than the duty corporal and two runners. Before any of the trio could call the squadron to attention, Adam waved them to silence and indicated they were to sit back down. Looking down the Quonset building, he saw that the light was on in his office.

"Who is here?" he asked simply.

"Captain Bowles, sir," the corporal replied, sweat starting to bead on his forehead. Looking the skinny man up and down, Adam had to wonder if he was truly old enough to be a Marine, much less an NCO.

Guess some people just look younger than their years, Adam thought.

"Corporal Banks, you will go outside and stand guard with your runners," Adam said. "You will not let anyone enter the squadron area until such time as I tell you differently. Is that understood?"

"Y-y-yes, sir," Banks said after a moment.

"Let me guess: You heard from Captain Bowles that I'm no longer the squadron commander?" Adam asked with a smile.

"Yes, sir," Banks replied.

"Well, he was misinformed," Adam snarled with a smile.

"Amendment to my last order—if an ambulance shows up, you may want to let them pass. That is all."

"Yes, sir," Banks replied. Gesturing for his runners to follow, he immediately moved outside the door.

Adam could hear the sound of drawers opening and closing, and the sound of broken glass as if someone had been careless with something. Taking a long, shuddering breath, he threw open the door to his office.

"Somewhat presumptuous, aren't we, Captain Bowles?" Adam asked, catching the junior officer in the act of tossing the second of his two picture frames into a crate.

"Jesus Christ, you just don't leave, do you?" Bowles asked snidely. "I think Colonel..."

It was the last words the captain got out of his mouth. Springing like a tiger, Adam cleared the desk and tackled the younger man into the wall behind him. Bowles breath exploded with an oof, the exhalation preventing him from screaming when Adam's knee came shortly and violently up into his groin. As the man doubled over and retched, Adam swung both his clenched hands down into his kidneys. Crumpling to the ground, the sound Bowles made as he tried to scream past a mouthful of vomit was strangely pleasing. While the junior officer was trying to figure out how to breathe again, Adam kicked him hard in the stomach twice.

"You're right, this isn't England," Adam observed as the younger man curled up into a fetal position, sobbing. Adam kicked him again in the abdomen, and was rewarded by the smell of urine wafting up as the blow caused Bowles to wet himself.

"You see, if this was England, I would finish beating you into the hospital," Adam continued conversationally. "Watched a squadron commander do that very thing to a belligerent Flight Lieutenant during the fifth week. Things were a little grim then."

"You...you cannot do this to me," Bowles gasped.

"Oh, I think you're confused," Adam said. As Bowles looked at him and started to say something, Adam swept his foot forward and kicked the man dead in the face. The crunch of bone and sharp squeal of agony told Adam he'd most likely broken the man's nose.

Maybe a reminder every time you go to shave will be good for you, Adam thought uncharitably.

"You see, funny thing about being a, what was it?" Adam said, adopting a thoughtful pose. "Oh, that's right, a *mercenary*, is that I'm a little rough around the edges, Bowles. So, if you bring this matter up to Lieutenant Colonel King, I'll swear you threw the first punch. I doubt, given that Colonel Gatling is probably cleaning out his desk right now, that the new air wing commander is going to ask many questions."

Bowles looked up at Adam in shock, pain, and fear as what the squadron commander said sunk in.

"That's right, you stupid fuck, I can call in favors just like you can," Adam snarled. "Except I'm not going to play your game. This will be the *last* time we have a discussion like this, or so help me I won't try to have you transferred, I'll *kill you.*"

Bowles looked up at Adam as if he was staring at Satan himself. Adam didn't give him time to mentally recover.

"So, you decide if you want to die," Adam gritted through his teeth. "But whatever you are going to make, you're going to get the fuck out of my office and go clean yourself up *now.*"

Bowles staggered to his feet as the phone rang. Adam disdainfully turned his back on the man as he picked up the phone.

"Fighting Twenty-One, Major Haynes, sir," Adam said.

"Major Haynes, not sure if giving you thanks is exactly appropriate in this situation," Lieutenant Colonel King said. "Either way, Major Anthony has told me you wish to have an office call in a couple of hours to discuss your command. I'll do you better than that—when are you taking off?"

Hearing the scuffling of feet, Adam turned to see Bowles leaving the office.

"Sir, I think that a 1000 take off time was the original plan," Adam replied.

"Very good," Lieutenant Colonel King replied. "I'll be there with Captain Michaels as my wingman. I understand you have some friends across post who you like to fly with?"

"Yes sir, I do," Adam replied. "They were going to meet us out over the water at 1030."

"Well then, I've always wanted to see those new Commonwealth fighters in flight. King out."

Looks like what Major General Geiger said about Lieutenant Colonel King taking this job a bit more seriously was dead on, Adam thought as the other officer hung up the phone. *Thank God.*

U.S.S. HOUSTON
SULU SEA
2130 LOCAL (0830 EASTERN)
27 MARCH (26 MARCH)

"GENTLEMEN, YOU MAY CONSIDER THIS A WAR BRIEFING. NONE OF the information discussed herein is to leave this room, nor is it for the general consumption of the crew until such time as we find ourselves at war. Do I make myself clear?" Captain Wallace stated, his face somber.

The officers gathered in the wardroom gave an affirmative, sitting gathered around a map of the Dutch East Indies spread across the main dining table.

Hell of a Saturday night party, Jacob thought to himself. Most of the officers, especially the younger ensigns and lieutenant (j.g.)s, looked excited and expectant, as if they were getting ready to partake in a football game.

At least I'm glad to see I guessed right on what Vice Admiral Hart intended to do as soon as the balloon went up, Jacob thought grimly. *Houston*, in company with the cruisers *Marblehead* and *Boise*, had sortied from her berth at Cavite just after sundown to minimize the number of Japanese or U.S. Army eyes that could see her departure. After joining with their destroyer screen, the cruisers had initially headed north, then swung back south. Two hours after leaving Manila, they made a rendezvous with two Commonwealth cruisers, the *Exeter* and *Perth*, and continued their journey towards Java.

Glad to have the liaison officers aboard, Jacob thought, looking at the man in a Royal Australian Navy uniform standing at the table's head. Commander Thomason, the *Perth*'s executive officer, had brought three bottles of rum for "medicinal purposes" when he'd come over to the *Houston*.

"Thank you, Captain Wallace," the Australian said, his accent less pronounced than some of his countrymen's. Tall and gangly, Damien Thomason's gaunt frame and face made Jacob seem positively gluttonous. Despite being clearly tailored, the Australian's uniform hung off his shoulders like a sack as he brought up his map pointer with a wan smile.

"Gentlemen, over the next half hour, I will explain the situation in the Pacific as Vice Admiral Phillips' staff sees it. Please hold all questions and comments to the end."

With that, Thomason took a long pull from the glass of water at his left hand, then brought the pointer to the tip of the Malay peninsula.

"As you all know, this is the former colony of Singapore, turned over to our yellow friends when Jerry realized that Berlin is very far away from Asia. As near as we can tell, none of the base's facilities were rendered unserviceable." The look of disgust and anger on Thomason's face had an almost physical aura as he relayed that bit of intelligence.

Even several months on, I still can't believe that shit, Jacob thought disgustedly. *At least the Commonwealth officers seem just as angry.*

"The Japanese, overjoyed at having a wonderful naval base handed to them," Thomason continued wryly, "have moved several elements of their fleet into the harbor. As of last week, there were two battleships, six cruisers, and at least two dozen destroyers."

Thomason turned to look at the gathered group as he let the size of that force sink in.

"I say last week because as of the twentieth, all of our operatives went silent," Thomason continued grimly.

Which means they're all guests of the Japanese, who now know everything that you think you know, Jacob thought. *I hope most of them died quick, as the boys down from the Shanghai gunships say the Japanese have interesting ways of making people talk.*

"We expect the Japanese to strike within forty-eight hours," Thomason said. "Their initial objective will be to make initial landings on the east coast of Sumatra, hopping across from Singapore. Once there, under the cover of their own air power, they will make the jump to Java, then down the East Indies towards Australia."

"Why wouldn't they land on Sumatra and Borneo simultaneously?" Lieutenant Adam Connor, Engineering officer, asked.

Thomason gave Connor the same look that a schoolmaster might give a child who had asked a particularly stupid question. Immediately, Jacob felt his hackles starting to rise.

We're not part of a navy that got its boss killed, Commander, Jacob seethed.

"Hold all questions until the end," Captain Wallace snapped. "Sorry for the interruption, please continue."

"To meet the Japanese ships, Vice Admiral Phillips is bringing the *Revenge* and *Ramilles*, with air cover from the *Hermes* and *Furious*, north from Sydney to the East Indies," Thomason said.

*With us, that makes a total of two carriers, three battleships, the **Repulse**, and ten cruisers*, Jacob thought. *The Japanese must have something else up their sleeve other than the group in Singapore.*

"Submarines have reported that the Japanese Main Body is coming south from Formosa and the Home Islands," Thomason said as if he had read Jacob's mind. "To answer the young lieutenant's question, we doubt without these reinforcements the Japanese have the ability to make simultaneous attacks across the East Indies. There is also that little matter of what forces they intend to use to attack the Philippines."

There was a collective intake of breath at that statement. Jacob knew several officers shared his detestation with Admiral Hart's decision to leave the Philippines to their fate.

"With the work we have done establishing communications," Thomason said, "we believe that our combined force should be able to inflict unacceptable casualties on the Japanese. Now I will be happy to take questions."

"How certain is your intelligence on their amphibious capabilities?" Jacob asked conversationally. To his surprise, Thomason bristled at the question.

"I think both Her Majesty's Navy and yours would be very hard pressed to cover multiple amphibious operations," the Australian snapped. "Surely you don't think the Japanese are better at amphibious operations than we are?"

Hate to admit it, but the asshole might have a point, Jacob thought. He was about to respond when the compartment's hatch suddenly swung open.

"Excuse me, sir, but there is a priority message from Cavite in the encoding room," an ensign, whose name temporarily escaped Jacob, stated in a rush. "We are double checking our coding, but I thought you would want to see it immediately."

Captain Wallace gave the young officer a baleful gaze as he stood.

"I trust that this will be worth interrupting a briefing, Ensign Moorstein," Wallace said archly. He turned to look at Jacob, and *Houston*'s XO realized his commander was also angry with him.

*I guess the Old Man is **not** happy with the way I questioned our guest*, Jacob thought, realizing that he was in for a serious ass-chewing later.

"Commander Morton, I trust that I can leave you to supervise the proceedings?" Wallace asked, his tone indicating his displeasure even more than his look.

"Aye aye, sir," Jacob returned, coming to attention when he did so. With a start, he realized the Captain was apparently of the opinion that Jacob had violated one of the Wallace's golden rules: *You may disagree with a peer in private, but **never** in public and in front of subordinate officers.*

All of the officers stood until the captain left, then turned to look at Jacob.

"Please, Commander Thomason, continue," Jacob said, his tone indicating that the matter was past on his end. The look Thomason gave him indicated that he would not be so forgiving, something that Jacob mentally kicked himself for.

"Our plan, as the Japanese come down from Singapore, is to contest their landings on Sumatra. The waters here are quite restricted, so this will be mainly cruiser and destroyer work. We do not expect them to commit their heavy units into these waters as that will put them at undue risk." Thomason paused, as if expecting Jacob to interject.

Seems like a valid assumption to me, Jacob thought. *Bringing a battleship to a fight in those waters seems like a good way to end up with her at the bottom of the sea thanks to lucky torpedoes.*

"The Dutch have mined most of the beaches off of Sumatra, which will give us extra time to meet the Japanese amphibious group," Thomason continued. "Dutch and Commonwealth fighter units have moved forward to Palembang to provide aerial cover for our operations. They will be supported by Australian fighter squadrons, some of whom I believe you've already become acquainted with."

Jacob's eyes narrowed at that statement as a mournful chuckle made its way around the room.

"No one can argue that you guys aren't committed," Jacob said.

"Her Majesty's forces have been committed since 1939," Thomason noted caustically, causing a sharp intake of breath around the table.

Yes, well, hopefully your luck will begin to change, Jacob thought as he locked eyes with Thomason.

"Has Vice Admiral Phillips' staff identified what forces will be used to counter the landing?"

"Upon identification of the Japanese beaches, the Dutch have stated they will commit their light cruisers and destroyers in a night raid," Thomason replied, his tone somewhat softer. "ACDA Command has decided that two heavy cruisers will provide distant cover for this raid if the enemy landing force is heavier than we expect. If the raid is successful, it will hopefully draw the Japanese heavy units in earlier than they intended, and we can fight them in the Java Sea."

Jacob was about to open his mouth to ask a question when the hatch opened. Captain Wallace passed through the hatch, his face grim. As soon as he closed the door, General Quarters began to ring throughout the ship.

"Gentlemen, as of 2100, Vice Admiral Hart has ordered this vessel and all Asiatic Fleet units to adopt war footing," Captain Wallace said solemnly. "The Navy Department issued ordered that all American vessels are to engage any unidentified vessel or aircraft they encounter and to expect attack from the same. Commander Thomason, I am afraid we cannot put you back aboard the *Perth*. The rest of you have posts you need to report to, immediately."

JAMES YOUNG

Captain Wallace could not have stunned the gathered group of men more if he had come back and stated that Martians had just sunk the *Perth*. After a moment of disbelief, the men all stood and burst for the hatchway past their captain, headed for their stations. In moments, the room was empty save for Wallace, Thomason, and Jacob.

"Allow me to be the first to say for the Commonwealth that we are glad to have you gentlemen as formal allies," Thomason said, coming to attention and saluting. "I am sure the Nazis and Japanese are going to regret this day."

"Let us hope so," Captain Wallace said. Until such time as we are able to put you back aboard *Perth*, I am sure that Commander Morton will be happy to show you his hospitality."

Jacob was slightly startled, but then realized that Captain Wallace was giving him a chance to redress his earlier sins. Looking at Thomason, he extended his hand.

"I hope that this is the start of a long and fruitful alliance," Jacob said calmly. Thomason gripped his hand, nodding.

"Commander Morton, I trust that you will be able to find Commander Thomason a set of anti-flash gear?" Wallace asked.

"Aye aye, sir," Jacob returned. "Commander, if you would follow me," Jacob stated, heading for the wardroom's exit.

As the two officers left, Captain Wallace turned and looked at the "medicinal" rum that Thomason had brought over with him. Like his executive officer, he was a non-drinker, a rarity in and of itself among Navy officers. He had not touched the stuff for over fifteen years, ever since his wife had threatened to leave him after a particularly rowdy night among the bars.

"Sir, is it okay for me to clean up?" a soft, young voice came from behind him. It was Mess Attendant 2nd Class Harold Biggs, the only black member of the crew. Hailing from Chicago, Biggs had joined the *Houston* in late 1939 and had been with the vessel ever since.

Wallace looked at the expansive wardroom, with its fine china service and piano in the corner. The elegant wood furniture, adornments, and plush carpeting made the vessel feel more like an upscale hotel than a man of war. For a brief moment, Wallace's mind turned back to the last night with his wife before he had left San Diego.

Janice is probably still asleep right now, he thought, looking at his watch. *It's not even daylight back in California.*

Turning to look at the young mess attendant, Wallace took a deep breath.

"Biggs, do you drink?" Wallace asked.

"Yes, sir, I do," Biggs replied evenly. Wallace knew that the man was very, very smart, even had a degree in biology or something like that.

A man with a degree, and he's here cleaning up some mess that my officers left, Wallace thought. *Tomorrow, he could be dying, and me along with him, yet he basically has to worship the ground I walk on: one, because I am master of this vessel, and two, because of the color of my skin.* Wallace mentally shook his head. *Well, dammit, I **am** master of this vessel, and this young man is going to have a spot of rum before I ask him to die for me.*

"Well, then let's have a shot of rum and toast to an end to this madness," Wallace said.

"WOULD YOU CARE FOR A PIECE OF ADVICE?" THOMASON ASKED Jacob as the two of them made their way aft towards the *Houston*'s stern. Unsurprisingly given their similar builds, the Commonwealth officer had fit into Jacob's spare anti-flash uniform. Now, as the two of them moved about checking all of the stations and making sure the ship was ready for combat, Jacob wondered what the Commonwealth officer was up to.

"Certainly, if you're willing to share," Jacob replied.

"You may want to begin stripping this vessel as soon as we reach Surabaya," Thomason stated diplomatically. "As in, everything that is not metal or directly related to her primary function should be immediately removed and placed into storage."

Jacob turned and looked at his opposite number, opened his mouth, then shut it.

I never would have thought of that, but I guess two years of combat in the

Mediterranean teaches you some things, Jacob thought. Dimly, he remembered reading that the *Perth* had fought three of her Italian opposite numbers to a standstill, crippling one enemy light cruiser and taking serious damage in return.

In other words, if Thomason is giving me advice on how to keep things from getting out of hand when we get hit, I should be listening, Jacob thought.

"Thank you," Jacob said, his tone sincere. "I'll tell Captain Wallace of your suggestion when we reach port."

Thomason looked at him for a moment, and Jacob had the uncomfortable feeling that the man was wondering why he needed the captain's approval.

I start taking an axe to the wardroom, the captain will skin me alive, Jacob thought. *It's his ship.*

"Good, then let us continue," Thomason said. "I've never been on one of your cruisers, and I have to say I'm slightly jealous of the construction. Do all of your bulkheads use armor plate?"

PEARL HARBOR
0330 LOCAL (0830 EASTERN)

TWO THINGS SIMULTANEOUSLY AWOKE JO FROM A DEEP, PEACEFUL sleep. The first thing was the sound of the air raid siren located outside her bedroom window breaking into its raucous song. The second, following shortly behind the first, was the sound of Patricia opening Jo's bedroom door, her eyes so wide the whites were showing.

"What in the Hell is going on here?" she muttered, swinging her legs out from underneath the covers.

"I don't know," Patricia replied, her face drawn of all color. "I was coming to ask you and hoping you'd tell me it was all a drill."

Jo looked at her and fought down the urge to laugh. It always amazed her that despite the fact that Patricia had four brothers in the service and had been in Hawaii for several months, she still hadn't figured out certain things.

"The Navy never has drills on a Friday morning, nor do they do them in the dark," Jo replied, her tone perturbed. "Plus, *that* is a civilian alarm, which means the city is sounding the sirens rather than the military."

"Is that..." Patricia started to ask.

"That's very, *very* bad," Jo said, shrugging her nightgown over her head as she quickly strode to her wardrobe. Turning, she saw Patricia turning to avert her eyes.

"I'd suggest you go get dressed as well," Jo said evenly, trying not to rattle Patricia. "Dress in something you'd wear to harvest back home."

"Is that really necessary?" Patricia asked.

No, I just want you out of my room, Jo nearly snapped, then caught herself.

"Wish I could reassure you, Patricia, but I think this is not a drill," Jo responded, putting on her brassiere. She grabbed a thick, denim shirt and work overalls. Turning back to the door, she saw Patricia still standing there in shock.

"Well, you can stand there until some Jap soldier shows up, or you can do what I said," Jo snapped, causing Patricia to recoil, then start to flush in the gibbous moonlight streaming through Jo's window.

"Sorry, I don't mean to be short, but those sirens can mean only one thing: We are under or about to be under attack," Jo said. "Now, I know you prefer mythology to world events, but the only people who can reach us out here are the Japanese. Given that there are a significant number of Japanese on the island, there could be a Fifth Column already committing sabotage or paratroopers landing. Either way, I want to get *as far away from Pearl Harbor as possible.*"

"Shouldn't we hear gunfire if the Japanese are invading?" Patricia asked, her voice somewhat skeptical.

"Should, unless they got the drop on us," Jo replied, her tone impatient. "Or we may have captured some of them early or seen them as they are a little ways out to sea. Tell ya what—if I'm right, you can ask the Jap raping you."

Patricia glared at her.

"There's no need to be melodramatic, Jo," Patricia replied sarcastically. Jo shrugged as she began putting on her boots. Patricia, waiting for an answer, realized she wasn't going to get one. Shaking her head, the Alabaman headed back towards her room.

I don't know if she's getting dressed or not, but I'm leaving in about ten minutes, Jo thought. She went to the footlocker at the foot of her bed and popped it open. Pulling out the rack of clothes to reveal a false bottom, Jo reached in and pulled out the .38 caliber revolver and box of ammunition. As she started to load the gun, she realized her hands were shaking.

The door opened again behind her, and Jo immediately revaluated her roommate. Patricia stood before her in a set of coveralls, and was cradling a pump shotgun. The taller woman had a bandolier of shells around her shoulder, and there was a large revolver in a shoulder holster under her left arm.

"Where in the Hell did you get those?!" Jo asked, shocked.

"Why don't you ask the Jap you're convinced is going to rape me?" Patricia asked harshly.

Lord save me from the Cobb family, Jo thought. *Their tempers are going to be the death of me.*

"Okay, I'm sorry, but you were being annoying," Jo replied, going into her closet and grabbing a canvas sea bag. Unlike the usual issue model, Jo had sewn two straps onto the front of the sack.

"Come with me to the kitchen, we've got to take some food," Jo said, turning to find Patricia standing with her hand to her mouth.

"Oh my God, my brothers!" Patricia said.

"Your brothers will be fine," Jo said gently. "We've got to get the Hell out of here. Just out of curiosity, can you actually shoot those guns?"

Patricia gave a snort of derision.

"I'm from the South, with four brothers and a very protective father," Patricia drawled. "I demanded to be taught to shoot at age five."

Jo looked at the pistol.

"That thing is as large as your forearm," she observed.

"It's a Webley," Patricia replied simply. "Kicks like a mule, but it makes one hell of a hole in whatever you shoot."

"That works for me," Jo said as they reached the kitchen. Patricia started to reach for the light, and Jo stopped her.

"Let's not attract any more attention than we need to," Jo said. "Just grab cans."

PEARL HARBOR
0400 LOCAL (0900 EASTERN)

WELL I GUESS WE KNOW HOW MUCH EVERYONE LISTENED TO ADMIRAL Jensen's new directives on readiness, Captain Greenman thought angrily.

"Just how many of the damn escorts *are* ready to sail?!" Admiral Jensen was roaring.

"Sir, we will have four to eight cruisers and twelve destroyers ready to sail within two hours," the nervous looking captain from the Operations cell reported. Greenman, looking at Admiral Jensen's face, could tell that the answer was *far* from satisfactory.

You're talking to a man who joined the fleet when flogging was a recent memory, captain, Greenman thought, feeling sorry for the sandy blonde officer. *Don't let some other idiot's inability to perform be the reason you're stuck on some oil barge next week.*

"Captain Loftman, I want *you* to *personally* make a note of all ships that are not ready to sail within *two* hours as I directed less than forty-eight hours ago," Jensen seethed. "You let every single captain in this fleet know I don't want to hear any more bullshit about how they were preparing for Saturday inspections or gave too many of their crews liberty. I sent out a war warning, and any vessel who is not prepared to sail when these battleships cast off will have a new captain when we return."

The ominous threat caused a brief work stoppage in the *Arizona*'s flag plot.

"Yes, sir," Captain Loftman replied.

"You may also inform the squadron and division commanders they may expect letters of reprimand as well when we return," Jensen continued in the same menacing tone. "I will **not** be lied to by my officers."

Well actually you probably will, Greenman thought, then shook his head with a smile. *I just don't see it happening nearly as often as it might have before.*

"Something funny, Captain Greenman?" Vice Admiral Bowles asked, his tone acidic. The PACFLT Chief of Staff was looking around the flag plot at the officers bustling to and fro.

Oh shit, Greenman thought, gripping the documents in his hands much tighter.

"No, sir," Greenman replied. He felt almost every officer in the room turn to look at him.

"Well how about you brief the intelligence situation and maybe we can all share in your joke?" Bowles said, his voice making it clear that he was not asking a question.

"Yes sir," Greenman replied, his voice rasping as his mouth went dry. He moved to a map of the Pacific that was hanging from the starboard bulkhead. He searched for a map pointer.

"Not so funny when you're the rabbit, is it?" Admiral Jensen observed uncharitably. "Don't worry about a damn pointer, I think we're all familiar with our theater. Tell me where the Jap fleet is."

"Yes, sir," Greenman said, fighting to keep his voice level. "The last report we received from Washington was confident that the Japanese fleet, minus the battleships *Fuso* and *Yamashiro*, departed the Sea of Japan four days ago headed south and east…"

"South *and* east?!" Admiral Jensen asked. "Thanks, that's helpful Captain. Are you sure some of them weren't heading north as well?"

"My apologies, sir," Greenman said, feeling sweat starting to form in his armpits. "Washington believes the carriers are headed to the Marshalls with two of the *Kongo* class as their escorts, while the Main Body is heading south to strike the Dutch East Indies and Philippines."

"What is Washington basing this on?" Admiral Jensen asked.

"Sir, ONI didn't see fit to tell us what the source of this information was," Captain Greenman replied, speaking of the Office of Naval Intelligence. As soon as the words left his mouth, he regretted the statement.

"Did it ever occur to you to ask?" Admiral Jensen snapped, his nostrils flaring.

"Yes, sir," Captain Greenman replied. With a start, he realized he was unconsciously coming to a position of attention and stopped himself.

I will not let this bastard intimidate me, he thought fiercely.

"Rather than make Admiral Jensen keep asking you questions, cut to the chase: Who told you no?" Vice Admiral Bowles snapped.

Greenman turned to look at the Chief of Staff.

"Sir, I was told the head of ONI himself," Greenman said evenly.

"Well this would have been nice to know before *the war starts*," Admiral Jensen roared. "Think maybe I might have had a word with Admiral King about ONI's lack of support?"

"No, sir," Greenman said.

"I mean, I might want to know the reliability of a source before I make my dispositions based upon it," CINCPACFLT continued, his tone mocking. "If it came from some Chink laundry man whose cousin told him some Jap ships passed him while out fishing, I'm going to be suspicious. On the other hand, if it was a freighter captain bound for Vladivostok, that's a whole different matter."

"Sir, I..." Greenman began.

"Nevermind, Captain Greenman," Bowles snapped before he finished. "Let's make the rather presumptuous assumption that ONI knows what in the Hell they're talking about and we don't have six Jap carriers rounding Diamond Head when the sun comes up."

"Sir, I would certainly hope they're sighted before then," Greenman replied, his tone hot.

Shit, he thought, seeing Jensen's face briefly register shock then switch back to even more intense anger. Before the senior officer could immolate him, he was saved by Captain Loftman.

"Sir, message from Admiral Pye," Loftman said.

"We will revisit this, Captain Greenman," Jensen snapped, then turned to Loftman. "What is it?"

"*California* will be ready to move in twenty more minutes, *Colorado*, *Pennsylvania*, *Nevada* thirty, and the rest of the battleforce within the hour. Destroyer Divisions One and Two are the only ones prepared to sortie at full strength with the battleline, the remainder of the vessels will be straggling to catch up."

"Understood," Admiral Jensen snapped, then turned to Bowles. "I am serious, Admiral Bowles. Every single one of them, relieved as soon as we return. I don't care if you have to brevet promote or transfer captains from the staff to make it happen, and I give even less of a damn how much BuPers screams about it."

"Yes, sir," Bowles replied.

"Admiral Fletcher?" Jensen asked, looking once more at the chart.

"*Lexington* and *Saratoga* are currently moving up the channel," Captain Loftman replied. Jensen turned and looked at him, the shock plain on his face.

"What?!" CINCPACFLT asked.

"Sir, apparently Admiral Fletcher ordered all of his ships to be on one hours notice, not two," Captain Loftman replied. "Given that he threatened to see to it that any vessel that was not ready would have its entire wardroom shoved over the side while they were in dry dock, he seems to have gotten better results than the rest of the fleet."

Looks like Fletcher is taking this a whole lot more seriously than everyone else has, Greenman thought.

"Fletcher is a good man," Jensen observed. "Hopefully *Hornet* will get here soon so I can have at least four of my five carriers."

"Sir, as per your order Admiral Fitch began maintaining radio silence once he was two hundred miles out of San Diego," Captain Loftman replied. "Best guess based on the plan he sent us is that the *Hornet* is four hundred and fifty miles away."

"Halsey?" Jensen asked.

"Sir, Vice Admiral Halsey confirmed receipt of the war warning," Loftman replied, looking at his notes. "He respectfully asks what your orders are given the directive from Secretary Knox."

"Fucking Limeys," Bowles spat. "I still can't believe they got the *Lexington*'s aircraft."

Well the President had to figure out some way around that restriction on Lend Lease, Greenman thought, this time keeping his face impassive. *If Congress didn't intend for the restrictions to already include already produced aircraft, they should have said so.* Greenman was politically agnostic, but even he had to admit that the incoming Congress' restrictions on aiding the Commonwealth were somewhat self-defeating. The fact that the *Lexington*'s air wing was now flying obsolescent aircraft so that the Commonwealth's carriers could field at least three air groups that didn't include *biplanes* was an unfortunate byproduct.

Should still be more than enough to beat anything that the Japs have, Greenman thought. *Even the **Zero** that no one knows anything about, other than that crazy Army general over in China.*

"Well once the damn Brits figure out how to use them, that will give us another carrier," Jensen replied. "I was informed by Admiral Kimmel that the *Wasp* may be heading our way soon once the two Brit carriers in the Atlantic work up with the new planes as well. I'll take two carriers for the price of one being slightly behind for another month."

Bowles' expression communicated what he thought about Jensen's calculus.

"So, Greenman, what are the carriers going to do once they get to the Marshalls?" Jensen asked, turning back to the intelligence officer. "How about you give me your opinion this time, rather than just regurgitating what some idiot in Washington thinks?"

"Sir, the enemy carriers are likely in the Marshalls to support a strike on Wake," Greenman replied evenly. "Once that is done, your opposite number will probably keep them in the Marshalls in anticipation of this fleet's attack."

Vice Admiral Jensen smiled thinly.

"I suppose that is one drawback of having the same warplan for twenty years, isn't it?" the man observed. "At least we're not those poor bastards in the Philippines. Can you believe they were talking about us sending two battleships out there when the *New Mexico*'s returned from the Atlantic?"

"I'm sure Vice Admiral Hart would have appreciated the help, sir," Greenman allowed. "He's about to have a lot on his plate."

"Better him than me," Jensen replied with a shake of his head. "Maybe he can do me a favor and pick off a couple of their battleships before he dies."

Well that's certainly a charitable way to look at things, Greenman thought angrily.

CINCPACFLT looked at the clock.

"Vice Admiral Bowles, send the signal to all vessels that we will complete assembly at Point Falcon no later than 0800. Please inform our friends over at Schofield Barracks of our plan, and that we would appreciate it if they would start their searches in a timely manner," Jensen ordered.

"Aye aye, sir," Bowles said.

"This staff will conduct a briefing for all squadron and division commanders in here at 0900," Jensen said. He looked pointedly at Captain Greenman.

"It would behoove *you* to have a better idea of what the Hell is going on," Jensen snapped. "You ask ONI some questions, come back and tell Vice Admiral Bowles who told you no. Is that clear?"

"Yes, sir," Captain Greenman replied stiffly.

"Good," Jensen replied. "I'd hate to have to make you swim back here."

The man's tone made it clear that the quip was not an offhand joke.

I don't intend to be working on my breaststroke anytime soon, Greenman thought angrily.

7
WAR

War! That mad game the world so loves to play.

— **JONATHAN SWIFT**

OPANA RADAR STATION
0630 LOCAL (1140 EASTERN)
27 MARCH 1943

"CORPORAL, I HAVE A BLIP!" Private First Class David Jessup intoned breathlessly. Barely eighteen years old, Pfc. Jessup's freckles and short brown hair made him look like an escaped extra from *Our Gang* more than an Army private.

Corporal Joseph Lockard exhaled wearily. Slender, brown haired, handsome, and just a few months past twenty years of age, Lockard was the NCOIC of the Opana Radar Station.

The worst part about training the newbies is that they get excited about everything, Lockard. As one of the first soldiers trained on the use of radar in Hawaii, Lockard knew the rush that came from finally getting a contact after several hours spent gazing into the green screens. Almost eighteen months of service had taught him that the initial rush of excitement was usually better tempered with a heavy dose of caution.

All of us being out here on alert for two hours probably hasn't helped matters any, Lockard thought.

"Make that two blips," Jessup said excitedly.

Well now that is somewhat more uncommon, Lockard thought. *But not completely unheard of.* After a couple of civilian aircraft had completely vanished, instructors taking pilots out for navigational training had started flying in pairs if they were going on a particularly long flight.

Pays to have someone who can at least tell the authorities where to start looking, Lockard thought grimly.

"Today would be the day some idiots decide to go out on a pleasure flight," he muttered. "Stupid tour guides probably don't even realize there's a war on."

"Should we call headquarters, corporal?" Jessup asked.

"For two planes? Who do you think we are, the Navy?" Lockard asked derisively. "HQ's already gone back to Condition Yellow from Red. I doubt General Short will change his mind based on two blips, and I don't intend to explain to a three star why we got everyone spun up again. Let me see what you've got."

Coming over to the screen, Lockard took a long look.

"Okay, of your two contacts, one is heading north at roughly two hundred knots," Lockard said. "I don't think the Japanese have a seaplane base at Barber's point, do you?"

"No Corporal," Jessup said sheepishly.

"Now that other aircraft winging south is a bit odd...wait, now it's turning further west and out to sea," Lockard said.

The corporal looked at his watch, then did some quick math.

"Probably that search plane we were told launched before dawn," Lockard said finally. "Keep an eye on it, but I don't think one plane is going to do that much damage."

"Roger, Corporal Lockard," Jessup replied, his voice dejected.

THE THREE-MAN CREW OF *TONE*'S NO. 6 SCOUT HAD NO IDEA HOW close Death had come to joining them on their flight. Even if they had, it was doubtful they would have cared. The three men were dedicated, and they also knew that they were running low on time. The *Kido Butai*'s first strike was already airborne, and they had roughly another hour to find the American fleet before they had to turn back. Continuing their southwesterly course, all three men continued to strain for some sign of smoke as the sun cracked the eastern horizon.

U.S.S. SARATOGA
0640 LOCAL (1140 EASTERN)

IT WAS A BEAUTIFUL DAWN, THE SKY SHOT THROUGH WITH BEAUTIFUL colors. Standing on the carrier *Saratoga*'s deck next to his fighter, Peter Byrnes had a moment to enjoy the sight as the carrier began coming around into the wind.

"You going to keep looking at the sights or get in your bird, Byrnes?!" Lieutenant Commander Donald A. Lovelace, VF-3's executive officer and his section leader, shouted. Shaking himself out of it, Peter climbed up on the *Wildcat*'s wing and into the cockpit. Quickly strapping in with the help of his grinning crew chief, Peter quickly checked over his switches and chute.

Hopefully I won't need this, Peter thought. *Indeed, it'd be nice if I was back in time to make my date with Patricia.* While he'd been torn between Patricia and Jo with which one he wanted to ask out, getting Sam and David's tacit blessing the night before while at the latter's house had made up his mind.

I'm sure she'll understand if I'm a bit delayed, however, Peter thought, running up his engine. He'd been slightly surprised that the *Saratoga* was launching her first combat air patrol so late, but rumor had it that Admiral Fletcher had wanted to stagger the fighters so that he could maintain a constant, strong patrol.

Fool's errand for everyone involved, methinks, Peter thought. *We're a long way from Tokyo. At least I get to fly.* Fletcher, much to the scout pilots' chagrin, had opted to rely on land based reconnaissance in order to maximize his striking power. With the exception of the four SBD's spotted aft for anti-submarine searches, neither the dive bombers or torpedo pilots would get to fly that day.

"Let's go, let's go, let's go," Peter muttered, as the first VF-3's fighters lifted off the *Saratoga*'s deck. Peter watched as the tubby plane jerkily climbed, its pilot cranking up the *Wildcat*'s gear by hand. Quicker than usual, the next two *Wildcats* launched, leaving him in the slot to take off down the teak deck. As the launch officer dropped to his knees and pointed forward, Peter shoved the throttle to the firewall and accelerated down the deck. As he floated off the end of the *Saratoga*'s bow, he reached down and began furiously cranking his own wheels up.

This is the worst part of the flight, Peter thought as he gave the bar the requisite number of turns plus an extra to make sure the gear was truly locked. *Mess it up and not only do you get a nice bruise on your leg, but there's a decent chance you'll end up in the drink.*

Putting the fighter into a gentle port bank, Peter took a chance to look around. Ten miles away, he could see the battleline steaming ahead with the *Arizona* followed by her sister ship, *Pennsylvania*, then the *Nevada*, *Oklahoma*, *Tennessee*, *California*, *Maryland*, *West Virginia*, and *Colorado*. Combined together, these ships were the most powerful battleline in existence in the world, bar none.

It would be nice if the Japanese did come this way, Peter thought with a smile. *Maybe end the war in a day with those guns and our carriers*. Looking further to the south as he came around, he could see the *Lexington* and *Yorktown* roughly fifteen miles away from the *Saratoga* and each other. The two vessels were coming into the wind to launch their anti-submarine aircraft, their CAP of fourteen F4F *Wildcats* already airborne.

Even with three carriers, we can't keep this large a CAP airborne for long, Peter thought. *Be nice if the Army boys would give us some help here soon.*

Kido Butai Strike Force
0645 Local (1145 Eastern)

IT IS A GLORIOUS DAWN, ISORO THOUGHT AS HE LOOKED AROUND HIM with a sense of awe. Below him, the fighter squadrons of the *Kaga*, *Hiryu*, and *Soryu* were stretched back in a massive V of vees, each individual *chutai* maintaining perfect formation as they weaved protectively over their charges.

Ninety-six **Zeroes**, Isoro thought with pride. *They cleared the air over Chungking with less than twenty back in '41*. At an altitude only slightly below that of the fighters were the one hundred and eight dive-bombers of the 1st and 3rd Carrier Divisions. Despite the loss of two of their number, one to ditching and another due to engine failure on the flight deck, enough dive-bombers remained to easily suppress the anti-aircraft fire of the American fleet. Lastly, forty-five torpedo bombers, each armed with a long, cigar-shaped aerial torpedo underneath their fuselage, constituted the main effort of the *Kido Butai*'s first strike .

Turning back forward, Isoro felt an ever greater sense of strength as he looked over the rest of *Akagi*'s fighter squadron.

Hopefully we can also seize control of the air with our nine **Shiden**, Isoro thought. Once the position of the enemy fleet was received, it was the mission of the *Akagi*'s fighters to fly ahead and engage the enemy CAP. The fighters from the other three carriers would then arrive with the remainder of the strike with an altitude advantage over any scrambling Americans, in addition to being well-placed to engage any Army fighters attempting to interfere from Hawaii.

We are lucky that Admiral Yamaguchi now commands us, Isoro thought to himself. *I doubt Admiral Nagumo would have been as daring. He also would have doubted our ability to seriously damage the battleships at sea.* Allegedly Admiral Nagumo, having just returned from Germany on 1 March, had publicly decried Yamaguchi's plan as far too dangerous. The rumor had allegedly led to several of the torpedo pilots pasting a photo of the *Kido Butai*'s commander to their forward windshields so that he could see the destruction they were going to wreak first hand.

I can understand their annoyance, but perchance Commander Fuchida having his crew chief paint the admiral's visage on the front of his torpedo was a bit much, Isoro thought. *We are samurai, and such an insult is beneath us.* Looking at his watch, Isoro narrowed his eyes in worry.

The scout plane needs to hurry up and do its job, he thought. *I am ready to make an acquaintance with my American friends.*

Apparently Lieutenant Commander Itaya had the same thought. With a waggle of his wings, the *Akagi*'s fighter leader began to climb and accelerate. Isoro advanced his own throttle to follow.

U.S.S. ARIZONA
0700 LOCAL (1200 EASTERN)

"SIR, *ATLANTA* REPORTS A RADAR CONTACT, RANGE FORTY THOUSAND yards, altitude approximately eight thousand feet," the talker at the back of *Arizona*'s flag bridge stated.

Captain Greenman whipped his head around from where he had been reaching for a glass of water. At the front of the bridge, Admiral Jensen turned towards the talker whose report had cut him off mid-sentence while talking to the staff. That a petty officer would dare to interrupt him was beyond his comprehension.

"I assume that the *Atlanta* has reported this to the *Lexington*, correct?" Jensen inquired icily, his tone indicating that the man had better know the answer to his question.

"Yes, sir," the petty officer replied.

See if he tells you anything else, you arrogant bastard, Greenman thought disgustedly.

"Then do not interrupt me again, understood?" Jensen replied, steel in his voice.

"Yes, sir," the petty officer replied.

"STARBOARD!"

The single shouted word from the pilot of *Tone* No. 6 brought the observer's eyes to the right side of the aircraft. Straining his eyes towards the horizon, the Japanese lieutenant saw the smoke. Bringing up his binoculars, he quickly fixed on the ends of the smoke trails. Like small water bugs on a massive puddle, the ships causing the smudges quickly sprang into view even as the pilot began a shallow turn to bring the vessels closer. Swinging from right to left, the observer quickly classified the ships by size.

"Eight battleships! This is the entire fleet!" the observer shouted. He put the binoculars down and got ready to jot down his contact report. As he grabbed his pencil, the world suddenly tilted to the left.

"Fighters to starboard!" both the pilot and the rear gunner sang out simultaneously. Looking back in the direction of the enemy fleet, the observer could see the four small dots in the sky. As the observer watched, the aircraft began to get larger.

We are all dead, the man thought grimly. With its two floats underneath and the single machine gun in the rear gunner's cockpit, there was no chance of either outrunning or outfighting the enemy fighters. With their nearest help over an hour away, there was nothing that they could do if they were unable to evade. Quickly, the man began typing out what would probably be his last transmission.

SCARLET TWO
0710 LOCAL (1210 EASTERN)

"BOGEY, ELEVEN O'CLOCK LOW!" PETER BARKED, SEEING THE GLINT of cockpit glass far below the *Wildcat*.

Lovelace should have trusted the vector, he thought to himself. The *Lexington*'s fighter direction officer (FDO) was notorious for giving bad altitude readings. All three carriers' fighter pilots had simply started adding five to ten thousand feet to any headings the man gave them.

"Got it," Lieutenant Commander Lovelace replied evenly. "Byrnes, let's go see who in the hell this is."

"Roger," Peter replied, bunting his nose forward to follow his leader down. Both men shoved their throttles forward to pick up speed as they finished a broad turn that brought them over and behind the olive green bogey.

I hope this isn't some dumb sports plane out on a lark, Byrnes thought to himself. He wasn't sure if the civilian authorities had grounded all aircraft given Germany and Japan's declaration of war. Even if they had, Peter knew how Hawaii's civilian populace worked.

If this is some pilot taking his kids out so they can see what the fleet looks like, I hope they take his license away, Peter thought. *It's one thing to do that during peacetime, but there's a war on.*

As they closed, the outline of the aircraft became clearer. The twin pontoon floats underneath obviously identified it as a floatplane. While uncommon, Peter knew that there were at least two or three amphibians that regularly flew tour groups from Oahu. As the two *Wildcats* closed from behind, the float plane pilot put his nose down and started to dive towards the water.

Well, you wanted to get a look at the Navy, Peter thought. *Now you're about to get to see a very close one...*

The burst of machine gun fire could not have surprised them more if it had been a lightning bolt from heaven. Stunned, neither Peter nor Lieutenant Commander Lovelace took evasive action as the gunner quickly corrected his aim and fired again. The long ribbon of tracers intersected with Lovelace's cockpit, smashing through the canopy glass from the front quarter and taking the top off the man's head. With horrible fascination, Peter watched as the other *Wildcat* porpoised upward, then suddenly twisted and fell off to starboard in a tightening spiral.

Holy fuck! Peter thought, his mind in a haze.

"Scarlet Two, break!"

The shouted radio call brought a Pavlovian reaction from Peter that saved his life. Still in shock, Byrnes watched as bullets seemed to zip by his aircraft, the sound of bullets striking the fuselage and wings as he turned acting like a cold bucket of water to the face. Reaching down, he pulled the charging handled for the F4F-3's four .50-caliber machine guns, diving down then bringing his nose back up in a short zoom climb as he tracked the turning floatplane. Rolling the fighter, he dived down from the port side in an almost full deflection shot as he fired a snap burst.

The crew of *Tone No. 6* never had a chance, the four streams of half-inch bullets chewing through aluminum, men, fuel, and control surfaces with ridiculous ease. With a bright puff of orange, the Aichi burst into flames and smoke. Letting off of the trigger, Byrnes watched as a man stood up out of the inferno, jumping over the mortally wounded airplane's side towards the Pacific below. Following the plane down with his eyes, Byrnes watched as the Aichi exploded well above the water. The lone crewman continued to plummet, hitting the unforgiving Pacific with a small splash.

Hope you rot in Hell, you bastards, Peter thought fiercely.

"Scarlet One, Scarlet One, this is Scarlet Base. Report current status!" a frantic voice asked. After a moment, Peter realized it was the *Saratoga*'s radioman.

"Scarlet Base, Scarlet Base, this is Scarlet Two," Peter intoned angrily into the microphone. "Scarlet One is down, no chute."

There was dead silence at the other end of the radio as the import of what he had said sank in. Looking down at his hands, Byrnes realized that both of them were uncontrollably shaking.

"Sweet Jesus," he muttered. "Guess I might be late for that date after all."

U.S.S. ARIZONA
0720 LOCAL (1220 EASTERN)

ABOARD THE *ARIZONA*, CHAOS WAS ENSUING.

"I want more fighters launched immediately," Admiral Jensen roared. "I also want a message sent to General Short inquiring as to why my fighters are having to defend my fleet when we are still within the Army's area of responsibility?!"

Captain Greenman felt as if he'd had ashes poured into his mouth as he watched the Pacific Fleet's staff dashing to carry out CINCPACFLT's orders. It did not take long for the moment he dreaded to come.

"Captain Greenman, how do you explain this?!" Admiral Jensen asked archly, the tone of his voice clearly indicating the explanation had better be a good one.

Ever since the crazy message had been relayed from the *Saratoga*, Greenman had been trying to figure out a possible explanation himself.

"Sir, there are three possibilities, and I will cover them from most to least likely," he began calmly. "First, there is the possibility that

Japanese fifth columnists have obtained control of an aircraft and flown out to determine the location of our fleet. Since we will have to wait until *Sara*'s fighters land to get a full description of the aircraft, if this is the case we will have to wait a few hours to investigate it."

"Captain," Jensen said icily, "I hope your next two alternatives make more sense than the shit you just pulled out of your ass and handed to me."

Greenman felt his pulse begin to race. In his mind, that was a viable option and not the least likely by any means. Reports from Europe had indicated that the Germans had made extensive use of Fifth Columnists in their rampage through Western Europe. The Japanese were far more underhanded and shifty than the Germans, which meant that it was entirely plausible that they had secreted an aircraft, machine gun, and pilot onto Oahu.

There was a pregnant pause, the air full of Jensen's suppressed anger and Greenman's obvious fear.

"Continue, Captain," Vice Admiral Bowles snapped. Looking over at him, Greenman felt faint.

"The second alternative, sir, is that the Japanese have detached a force of a seaplane carrier and one or two cruisers to keep an eye on our fleet," Greenman continued. "These ships would have set up a base somewhere within range and launched aircraft to try and determine when we sortied. Such a base would require a sheltered inlet far from observers..."

The look on Jensen's face made Greenman stop dead in his tracks. It was obvious that the Admiral had heard enough on the second theory. Gathering his thoughts, he prepared to go into his final theory when Jensen raised his hand.

"Admiral Bowles, I want you to personally see to Captain Greenman's transfer to another post, preferably the worst, ass-backward post in the entire Navy," Jensen said, his voice resembling what Greenman imagined Jehovah's had sounded like in the Old Testament.

Oh God, I am ruined, he thought.

"Captain Greenman, I am sure the Honolulu zoo has baboons that can do better intelligence analysis than you performed. I want you out of my sight, *now!*" Jensen thundered. Greenman turned to grab his cap.

"What part of *now* are you not understanding, Captain?!" Vice Admiral Bowles asked. "You can go without a damn cover; you're not fit to wear one anyway!"

Greenman turned and looked at the man.

"Sir, you can go to Hell," he snapped. Before he could say anything else, Captain Loftman was handing him his hat.

"Captain Loftman, stop helping that idiot!" Admiral Jensen barked. "Inform Vice Admiral Fletcher I want an immediate air search launched, and the Army informed that there is a Japanese submarine somewhere in the area that is likely surfaced waiting for a seaplane to return. Fifth column my ass!"

Greenman was stepping out of the compartment when he realized that Vice Admiral Bowles was right behind him.

"How *dare* you tell me to go to Hell, Captain?!" the senior officer roared. "So help me God, you're going to be in Alaska commanding a barge moving Eskimo shit by the time I'm done with you."

Bowles was obviously not expecting Greenman to laugh at his comment.

You have no idea how absurd you look right now, Greenman thought, then mentally got a hold of himself.

"Sir, if my third theory is right, there won't be any of you left alive to write those orders," Greenman snapped.

Bowles drew back in shock, then laughed in the other man's face. It was a short, sharp bark, similar to the one given by a schoolyard bully when he is promised that his favorite victim will get even some day. It said, in no uncertain terms, that the last thing the laugher was worried about was the threatened event coming to pass.

"What was that theory, Captain Greenman?" Bowles asked with a laugh. "Japan making an alliance with Mars and little green men arriving in space ships to kills us all? Let me run downstairs and see if we can raise Flash Gordon on the radio to see if he can save us," Bowles snapped, the disdain in his voice clear.

There are none so blind as those who will not see, Greenman realized. He brought himself to the position of attention.

"Sir, I do not recall my third theory," Greenman sneered. "I will proceed to the bridge and inform Captain Van Valkenburgh that your orders are for me to return via floatplane to Pearl Harbor immediately."

"You smug bastard," Bowles snapped, the veins in his neck becoming visible. "You're lucky that I don't have you put overboard. That seems like a fair solution to your idiocy. Make it happen. I do not expect to see you when we return to Pearl Harbor, understood Captain?"

"Yes, sir, completely," Greenman responded. Bowles favored the man with one more glare, and then turned around to return to the chart room. With a start, Captain Greenman realized that the Marine Gunnery Sergeant had moved beside him from his post guarding the ladder leading up to Flag Country.

"Sir, may I speak freely?" the tall, fit Marine asked as soon as Bowles was out of earshot. Greenman turned towards the man, the surprise evident on his face.

"Certainly, Gunny," Captain Greenman replied.

"With all due respect, sir, you should've knocked him out," the Gunnery Sergeant said. " We Marines occasionally get struck with temporary blindness."

Greenman looked at the blonde haired man in shock. Before he could recover, the Gunnery Sergeant executed a sharp about face and returned to his post.

He's right, I should've. Not like I could get in any more trouble, Greenman thought a few moments later as he descended to the *Arizona*'s bridge.

OPANA RADAR STATION
0730 LOCAL (1230 EASTERN)

"HOT DAMN. I'VE GOT SEVERAL BLIPS, BEARING OH TWO ZERO!" Private Jessup shouted, his voice cracking embarrassingly on the last syllable.

A sinking feeling in his stomach, Corporal Lockard rushed over to the screen.

First our relief gets a flat tire, now the equipment goes on the fritz? Lockard thought. *Good ol' Murphy is outdoing himself to...oh my God.*

If the screen was malfunctioning, it was a type of malfunction Lockard had never seen before.

"Don't think that's a bunch of folks out for a joyride, Corporal," Jessup observed quietly. Lockard could tell the man was not being snide, as the enormity of the moment was registering with him as well.

The Japs are here, Lockard thought. Snapping himself out of it, he grabbed the handset that connected him to the plotting room at Fort Shafter. Spinning the handle like a man possessed, Lockard waited patiently for someone, anyone to pick up on the far side. Five long minutes later, he heard a voice on the other end.

"This is Opana Station," Lockard said rapidly. "We have multiple plots, bearing oh two zero, speed approximately two hundred and twenty knots, altitude unknown."

UNBEKNOWNST TO LOCKARD, THERE WAS PANDEMONIUM ON THE other end. The report of the downed reconnaissance aircraft had managed to make its long, tortuous transition down the Army chain-of-command to the plotting room at Fort Shafter.

"Opana, stand-by, we are handling a situation right now," the young private responded, a captain shouting instructions in his other ear. The young soldier quickly switched the lines, silently wishing he had never come to work that day.

ON LOCKARD'S END, THE FRUSTRATION NEARLY MADE HIM THROW the handset across the room. Turning back to the radar screen, he was about to open his mouth when suddenly the radar screen and lights flickered once, twice, then went completely out.

"Dammit!" Jessup shouted. He and Lockard locked eyes with one another. Both of them had forgotten that the alert had required them to start the generator that powered all of their systems two hours early. Lockard had intended to refill the generator when their relief had arrived, but the pair of men being fifteen minutes late meant that the radar had died at precisely the worst possible time.

"Jessup, you take this phone and you tell the bastard on the other end you've got important information," Lockard said. "I'm going to go out and restart the generator."

As he ducked out the door, he heard Jessup begin talking into the headset.

"This is Opana! We have lost power, but we had a shitload of blips before the screen..."

WAVING OVER THE DUTY CAPTAIN, PFC. DARNELL LOOKED DOWN with shaking hands at Opana station's last report.

"Sir, Opana just reported a shitload of bogeys," Darnell said excitedly, running a hand nervously over his buzz shaven head.

"How about you give me an actual report, private?" Captain Charles Wray asked. A reservist, Graham was already unhappy at having been stuck with "The Shaft," as his squadron's pilots called duty in the plotting station. As Darnell corrected himself, Wray looked at the two NCOICs conferring with each other on the other side of the map table. Suddenly what the private was saying registered.

"Wait, did you say Opana thinks they have several dozen blips heading towards Oahu?!" Wray asked.

"Yes, sir," Darnell replied, his exasperation showing.

Wray looked at the man unblinking for several seconds until he regained his bearings.

"Sergeant Ash, sound general alert, enemy aircraft inbound!" Wray shouted.

MINUTES LATER, ARMY PILOTS RUSHED TOWARDS THEIR AIRCRAFT across Oahu. It would be at least ten minutes before they were able to get into the air in any appreciable strength, another five minutes before they were formed up and at a decent altitude. Unfortunately, it would be later, in the midst of recriminations and accusations, that Captain Wray's error in repeating the vector to the NCOs present with him in the plotting room would be discovered. As over thirty P-38 and P-40 interceptors thundered off to the north*west*, the Japanese strike force passed to the north*east* of Honolulu toward *Tone No. 6*'s last reported position.

U.S.S. NAUTILUS
0745 LOCAL (1235 EASTERN)

FIRST HAD COME THE PLANES, AT LEAST TWO HUNDRED OF THEM, their collective engines loud in darkness. The instant he had heard the aircraft, Lt. Commander Freeman had ordered a crash dive, taking the *Nautilus* down to one hundred feet for thirty long minutes as they waited for bombs to begin falling. When no explosions had been forthcoming and a periscope search had revealed nothing but the brightening sky, Lt. Commander Freeman had brought the submarine back to the surface. Ordering radio silence, the *Nautilus*'s master had immediately ordered full speed and begun to head north on the surface. Now, low on the horizon, was smoke, and a great deal of it. In that instant, Nick realized that his commander was a brilliant man. Taking his eyes from the binoculars for a moment, Nick looked at his superior.

"How did you know they would come south, sir?" he asked.

"Carriers always want to make the range shorter," Lt. Commander Freeman said. "Those planes were bound for somewhere, my guess being Pearl Harbor."

"Sir, shouldn't we warn the fleet?" Nick asked.

Freeman looked at him with a slight smile.

"The Army has radar stations, patrols, and observers to detect strikes—they won't catch us by surprise, not unless something horrible happens," Jason said. Turning back to the horizon, he gave a feral smile.

"These bastards coming south, on the other hand, aren't going to know that we are here unless we tell them," Freeman continued. "I'm willing to bet, judging from those smoke trails, that they sail close enough for a shot. After that, I'll make a damn contact report."

This man is either crazy or the most intelligent officer I've ever met, Nick thought, his eyes wide.

"All right gentlemen, I have those ships sailing at twenty knots almost directly at us," Freeman observed. "Anyone else seeing something different, now is the time to tell me I have buck fever."

There was silence on the *Nautilus*'s bridge.

"Very well then," Freeman said, stepping to the voice tube. "All hands, rig for dive. Lookouts coming below!"

Like a well-oiled machine, the bridge crew moved down the conning tower's hatch, Nick then Freeman being the last two. As the hatch clanged close, Nick could already feel the submarine starting to sink and hear the sound of air rushing out of the ballast tanks, eliminating the submarine's buoyancy reserve.

I really hope that's not the last time I see the sun, Nick thought morbidly.

"All stations rigged for dive, taking her down, sir," Lieutenant Harold Banes reported from his perch behind the planesman. The *Nautilus*'s executive officer was slated for promotion within the next six months, with a boat of his own likely within the next year. A tough officer, with pale blonde hair, Banes was four inches taller than Nick at five pounds less weight.

Every time I see the XO I want to lock him in a restaurant for four months, Nick thought.

"Take her to seventy-five feet, stop all engines, rig for silent running. Once we're there, sound tell me what you hear," Freeman barked. Barely skipping a beat, he turned to Nick.

"What's my fish status, Cobb?" Lt. Commander Freeman asked. Nick saw Ensign Workman, junior officer of the boat and his assistant torpedo officer, flash him six fingers than four.

"Sir, all twelve tubes are loaded," Nick replied.

"Ensign Workman and I checked the weapons ourselves," Senior Chief Petty Officer reported from the back of the compartment. Pound was the current Chief of the Boat, the most powerful enlisted man aboard the *Nautilus*. Standing all of 5' 5" and skinny as a pipe cleaner, Pound often commented he had the voice of an elephant in the body of a field mouse. Like Lt. Commander Freeman, Pound was revered by all of the men aboard the *Nautilus*.

Thank God he's here, Nick thought appreciatively. *He's been in submarines since the Great War.*

"Sir, contact, high-speed screws, bearing two eight oh," the sound operator said.

The old man was right, Nick thought. Freeman nodded in acknowledgement and then turned to the gathered officers and chief.

"Figure at least four carriers based on how loud those planes were," Freeman said. "They'll probably have at least six tin cans, possibly a couple of cruisers, maybe even one of those fast *Kongo*s."

Nick swallowed as he thought of just how many ships that meant.

"Gentlemen, I'm not planning on being greedy," Freeman continued. "We'll shoot at one ship, two if another blunders in front of the stern tubes. I assume contact warheads on the fish?"

"Yes, sir," Nick and Ensign Workman said simultaneously.

Was there any other acceptable choice? Nick thought wryly, far more successful in hiding his smile than Workman. Lt. Commander Freeman's disdain for magnetic exploders was well-known to his officers. A simple man, Freeman thought relying on a magnetic warhead to work perfectly after being jostled during loading and possibly sitting in a tube for hours on end was the height of stupidity. Nick was inclined to agree with that assessment.

Don't really care if the folks at the Bureau of Ordnance swear it will break a ship's back, Nick thought. *Too many things that can go very, very wrong, whereas hitting a ship in the side with a metal pin has worked for decades.*

"Very good," Freeman said. "Six shots bow, four stern, so we have something in reserve, then we head down to take our licks. Questions?"

There was dead silence in the control room.

"All right, let's go do our jobs," Freeman said grimly.

Scarlet Two
0815 Local (1315 Eastern)

"All Scarlet fighters, all Scarlet fighters, this is Scarlet base," Peter's headphones crackled. "Multiple bogeys, bearing oh three oh relative. Come to course oh seven zero, angels one zero, gate."

Peter snapped back to paying attention to flying with a start, the replaying mental images of Lieutenant Commander Lovelace's cockpit shattering being forced from his mind. As odd man out from his division, he had taken up a position two thousand feet higher and upsun, weaving to cover the rear of the others. It was not a preferred position, being in direct violation of Lieutenant Commander Thach's principles of teamwork and mutual support, but it was better than forming a three-plane section that would unbalance the formation.

"Roger Scarlet, intercepting bogeys," Lieutenant Noel Gayler, Scarlet Three, acknowledged. Peter skidded the fighter to take a glance into the sun. It was still clear, no sight of enemy aircraft anywhere. Coming back onto course, Peter listened to the *Saratoga*'s other two divisions acknowledge the orders from their carrier.

"Scarlet Two go ahead and come back down here," Gayler started to say. "I'm not sure I like dangling you up there in the..."

"Scarlet Eight, Scarlet Eight, would you care to join the rest of your flight?" another voice interrupted.

Peter started to key his throat mike to ask for Scarlet Three to finish his sentence, but was jammed out of the frequency by the *Sara*'s controller ordering everyone to clear the fighter control net.

That could be a problem, Peter said, starting to bank and descend as Gayler and directed. With all of *Sara*'s fighters on one frequency, things were going to be quite chaotic once contact was made.

We need better radios, he thought to himself. There had been rumors about such radios being in the works, but that was right up there with some gull-winged wonder fighter that was allegedly being developed to replace the *Wildcat*. Personally, Peter would believe both of them when he flew either.

"Two, did you copy my last transmission?" his headphones crackled. Just as he keyed the mike, the *Lexington*'s controller came onto the net, trying to talk them into contact with the multiple bogeys.

Someone get this annoying bastard off of the radio, Peter thought.

. . .

"Enemy fighters! Twelve o'clock low!" someone called out over the radio.

Alerted, Isoro strained to see the enemy fighters.

"All *chutai*, attack!" Lieutenant Commander Itaya barked. Like a well oiled machine, the three-man flights broke from the squadron formation, descending like hawks upon rabbits. His nose down, Isoro finally spotted their short, tubby targets.

The unfortunate recipients of Itaya's attack were the first two divisions of VF-2, the *Lexington*'s fighter squadron. As with all combat organizations, leadership determined a great deal of a unit's effectiveness. In the case of VF-2, the commanding officer was a careerist who was better suited for an administrative job rather than leading men into combat. While VF-2 now had the highest maintenance, gunnery, and efficiency ratings in the fleet, its pilots knew very little about what it took to survive in the air. Thus, as the twelve F4Fs struggled for altitude, their communications frequency jammed with the directions of *Lexington*'s talkative FDO, none of them thought to look above and behind them.

As he dived, Isoro waggled his wings, signaling his wingmen to choose their own targets. The *Shiden* were outnumbered, but with the advantage of altitude and surprise, their numbers should prove more than sufficient to shatter the American formation. He watched as Lt. Cdr. Itaya opened fire, the 20mm tracers heading towards the lead American fighter.

It was only as the diving *Shiden* opened up that Yellow Two, the squadron commander's wingman, saw the diving fighters out of the corner of his eye. The man never had a chance to give a warning, dying moments after Itaya's burst shattered Yellow One's cockpit. In that first, violent dive the nine *Akagi* fighters shot down or critically damaged five of the *Lexington* Grummans before zoom climbing back up to altitude.

Isoro snap rolled his fighter over onto its back, cursing his luck as he whipped his head around to find another *Wildcat*. His target had reflexively jerked in response to the American leader exploding, meaning Isoro's burst had barely clipped the fighter's wings. Forewarned, the Americans were now going to be far tougher targets. His vision reddening as he finished his loop, he spotted a lone *Wildcat* turning to try and rejoin his section leader. With a kick of the rudder and movement of the stick, Isoro rolled the *Shiden* to cut off the American's turn, his speed advantage bringing the hapless Grumman into range.

As per usual when Isoro was about to engage a target, time seemed to slow. The American pilot, either warned or somehow sensing danger, turned to look at Isoro. Squeezing his trigger, Isoro felt the *Shiden* shake as his four cannon fired. Time suddenly sped up again as he watched pieces flying off the Grumman's wings and fuselage, culminating with the entire tail section separating. Kicking his rudder and pulling up, Isoro clawed for altitude again, doing a quick check of his tail.

"More enemy fighters approaching! We are attacking!" came the garbled shout from the second *chutai* leader.

Looking around, Isoro suddenly realized that the man was right and there were many, many more Americans approaching from their same altitude and below. Signaling to his wingmen, he advanced the throttle and began climbing for height, wanting to gain an advantage before the Americans got within range. Fighting against superior numbers was nothing new to the Japanese pilots, and there were reinforcements on the way.

U.S.S. Arizona
0820 Local (1320 Eastern)

"WOULD SOMEONE LIKE TO EXPLAIN TO ME WHERE IN THE HELL THE Army is?!" Admiral Jensen roared.

When they had received word that there were numerous aircraft inbound, CINCPACFLT and his staff had moved from the flag plot to the *Arizona*'s flag bridge. Now, as he looked out the window at the numerous falling smoke trails and listened to the panicked reports coming over the FDO net, Admiral Jensen felt a slight sense of concern.

"Order the battleline to flank speed, bring us around to course two seven zero true," Jensen ordered. "Maybe if we sail back towards Oahu the Army will actually do its damn job!"

I am going to have that bastard Greenman shot, Jensen thought, feeling the *Arizona*'s deck starting to throb beneath his feet.

"Sir, we have contacted headquarters. The duty officer reports the Army interceptors headed the wrong way," Vice Admiral Bowles reported. "They are sending their reserve aircraft our direction, and they should be overhead within thirty minutes."

"If we have thirty minutes," Jensen growled in return.

IN THE SKIES ABOVE THE TASK FORCE, THINGS WERE BEGINNING TO go poorly for the *Akagi*'s fighters. The first loss to the Americans had come from the second *chutai*, which had foolishly attacked six of *Saratoga*'s reinforcements in a head on run. In a simple test of skill, the *Shiden*'s superior speed and firepower were neutralized, with one fighter falling to Lieutenant Commander Thach, VF-3's squadron commander, and the second to Lieutenant Edward "Butch" O'Hare.

The seven remaining *Shiden* suddenly found themselves heavily outnumbered as eight of *Yorktown*'s fighters arrived on the scene. A prudent choice for Itaya would have been to lead his surviving fighters away from the furball. Unfortunately, the easy success of the initial dive and the *Akagi* squadron leaders inherent aggressiveness led him to reengage on terms that favored the Americans. In a swift, brutal series of exchanges, two more *Shiden*s fell in exchange for three *Wildcat*s. Itaya, easily cutting in behind Thach's turn, never saw Thach's wingman before the latter sawed off the lead *Shiden*'s port wing.

. . .

Isoro shoved his throttle to the firewall and pulled up, hoping his wingmen followed him. Kicking his rudder to avoid a Grumman trying to shoot at him, out of the corner of his eye he watched Lieutenant Commander Itaya's fighter whirl wildly out of control.

It is time to leave, he thought, fear making his breath come in short huffs. Checking for his wingmen, he noted with some slight satisfaction that Watanabe and Yoshida were both still with him.

We tried to do our job, but there were simply too many of them, Isoro thought angrily. *Where is the rest of the first wave?!* Turning, he looked around to clear his tail. With a sense of relief, he realized that none of the Americans were chasing his retreating *chutai*. Looking to port, he saw two more *Shiden*s closing up to reform. Returning to look forward, he saw that his question had just been answered, as first a few, then dozens of dots appeared to his north. Looking like a swarm of angry bees, the first wave's escorts began to separate from their charges and head towards Isoro's approaching fighters.

I sincerely hope they don't mistake us for enemy aircraft, Isoro thought with an impending sense of doom. He was about to key his radio when he heard the Commander Fuchida acknowledge the *Akagi* fighters and begin to give orders to the strike group. As the escorts thundered past, Isoro turned to look at his fuel gauges and checked over his fighter. As he watched the torpedo bombers begin their turns to move ahead of the American battleships and the dive bombers split into their separate *chutai*s, Isoro put his fighter into a gentle bank.

We can stay for a few more minutes of combat, he thought. *Let us see how the Americans deal with being outnumbered.*

ACTS OF WAR

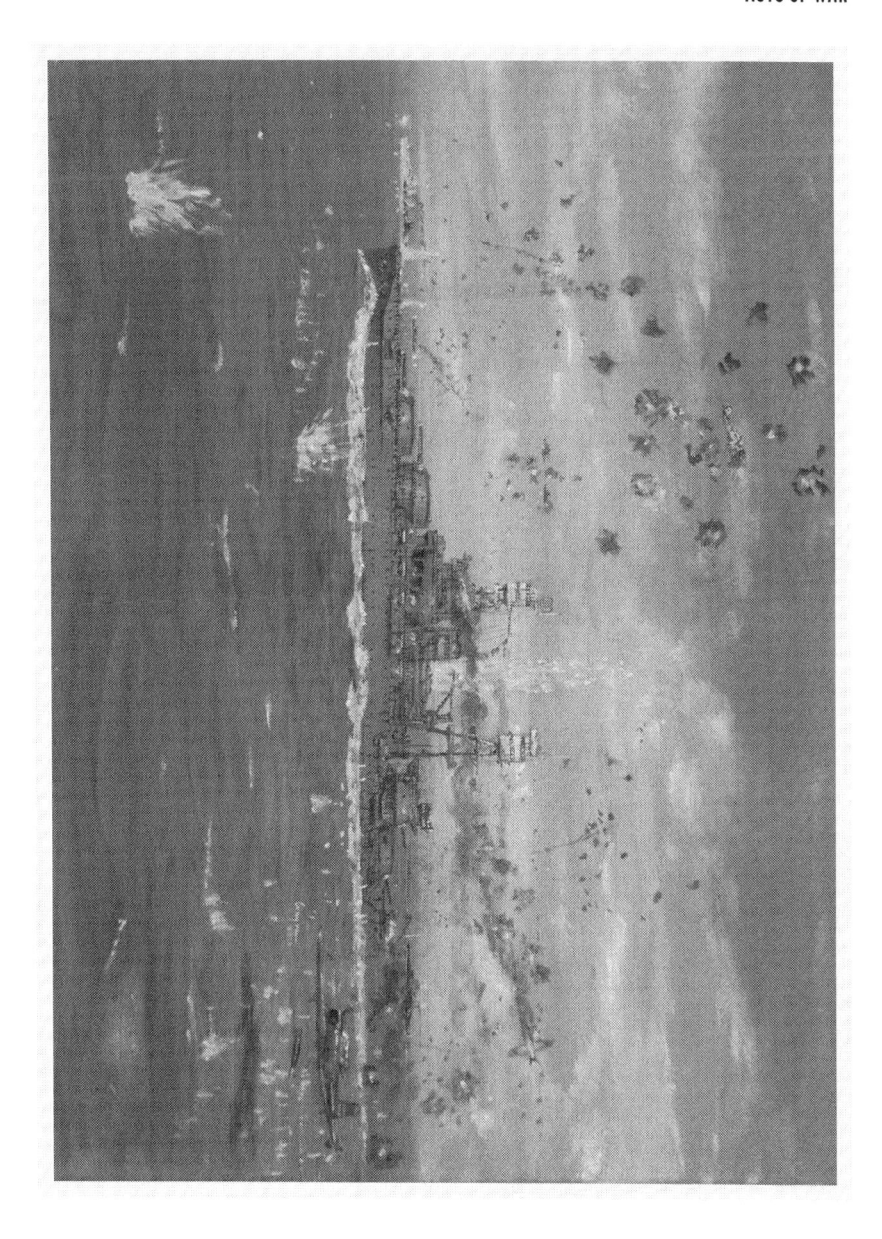

8

GÖTTERDÄMERUNG

Despite the claims of air enthusiasts, no battleship has yet been sunk by bombs

— **ARMY-NAVY GAME PROGRAM, NOVEMBER 29, 1941.**

KIDO BUTAI
0835 LOCAL (1335 EASTERN)
26 MARCH 1943

"SIR, Commander Fuchida reports contact with the enemy fleet. There are three carriers present," Captain Kaku reported out of breath, having just run up from the radio room to *Akagi*'s open bridge. To Rear Admiral Kusaka's obvious annoyance, the junior officer handed Vice Admiral Yamaguchi the position report directly.

We do not have time to get hung up on protocol, Kusaka-san, Yamaguchi thought as he took the message. After a brief perusal and glance at the map, he made his decision.

"Order Fuchida to strike the battleships as planned," Yamaguchi said.

Kusaka and Kaku looked at him in shock.

"It is too late to change the plan," Yamaguchi snapped. "Order the second wave to divert to the carriers. Turn the fleet south, we may have to launch a third strike after all."

"Sir, but there are three carriers," Kusaka said. "Combined with the enemy's land based aircraft, they may overwhelm our CAP!"

Admiral Yamaguchi clenched his fists at his side, fighting down the urge to physically beat the man before him.

*He would not question Nagumo in such a manner, and I will **not** allow him to question me this way*, Yamaguchi thought.

"Admiral Kusaka, you have your orders! Carry them out or confine yourself to your cabin!"

Akagi's master, Captain Hasegawa, locked eyes with Admiral Yamaguchi over Kusaka's shoulder. A strict disciplinarian, Hasegawa did not suffer fools gladly nor accept the questioning of orders. With his one glance, Admiral Yamaguchi saw that if Kusaka continued to argue Hasegawa would quickly and brutally end the discussion by hauling the man below.

Kusaka had decent survival instincts if not the best control of his tongue. Realizing he had overstepped his bounds, he bowed apologetically.

"Sir, I will carry out your orders," Kusaka stated solemnly. Executing a sharp about-face, he turned and exited from the *Akagi*'s bridge.

The tension of the moment broken, Yamaguchi turned back towards the bow of the carrier. Behind him, he could hear the Captain Hasegawa barking the orders to bring the *Akagi* about.

SCARLET TWO
0840 LOCAL (1340 EASTERN)

"TALLYHO! MULTIPLE BANDITS, TWELVE O'CLOCK HIGH!" SCARLET Three sang out, sighting the massive wing of dive bombers heading for the Pacific Fleet.

Shoving his throttle forward, Byrnes cast a worried glance at his fuel gauge. The *Wildcat* was not exactly the longest-legged of aircraft, and he had spent far too much of the last hour at full throttle. As the CAP strained for altitude, Peter saw a large number of the dots break off and begin accelerating towards him. Utilizing their altitude advantage, the *Zero*es began closing rapidly in a shallow dive.

"Holy shit!" someone shouted over the fighter net. As warnings went, it left much to be desired, and as last words went it was embarrassingly common. Peter was one of three pilots in the entire American force to see a sky full of charging Japanese aircraft, and as such he was at least able to roll his fighter and attempt to dive out of the way.

ISORO HAD USED A RUSE THAT HAD WORKED TO GOOD EFFECT against the Chinese and their mercenary pilots. Knowing that the enemy would be fixated on the closing bombers, he had swung his force of *Akagi* fighters wide and to port of the bombers direction of advance. Moving at full throttle, he had swiftly opened the range to roughly four or five miles then moved back in. Followed by several *chutai* of *Kaga* and *Soryu* fighters who had quickly realized what he was up to, Isoro had managed to obtain the drop on the less experienced American pilots.

Only two services in the entire world had regularly practiced deflection shooting during the pre-war period. One had been the United States Navy / Marine Corps, who had managed to turn the action into an art form. The other, ironically, had been the Imperial Japanese Navy, the USN's most likely opponent. Coming in high and from the side, the training plus experience of the old China hands in the *Akagi* and *Kaga* contingents made surprise attack particularly deadly.

Isoro, at the lead of the charge, chose the leading enemy fighter as his target. Opening fire at just under two hundred yards, he watched his burst slam into the center of the *Wildcat*'s fuselage. In a mixed blessing, the storm of cannon fire killed the commander of VF-5 before his half-empty fuel tanks turned the *Wildcat* into a flying crematorium. Isoro, having learned his lesson from the first engagement, immediately pulled up into a zoom climb as his shattered prey fell away engulfed in flames.

ISORO'S KILL WAS DUPLICATED BY FOUR OTHER IJN PILOTS, VF-5 being the unfortunate victims as the lead squadron. Only the innate toughness of the *Wildcat* and *Zeroes*' weaker armament saved the Americans from suffering far worse casualties, as five more *Wildcat* pilots found themselves piloting damaged mounts. Mistaking the Americans' evasive dives for death spirals, the IJN pilots believed that they had managed to destroy all ten, rather than just five, of VF-5s advancing CAP.

As the remaining CAP fighters turned towards Isoro's sudden bounce, they suddenly found themselves beset on all sides by the remaining first wave escorts. Attacking by squadrons, the *Zeroes* gave the Americans little chance. Fighting and dying bravely, the Americans took five *Zeroes* with them in exchange for all but three of the remaining CAP fighters. These remaining fighters, Peter among them, dived away in bewildered shock.

Roaring past the scene of the CAP's demise, the dive bombers from the carriers began choosing their targets.

Standing on the stern of the *Arizona*, binoculars to his eyes, Captain Greenman began to speak softly.

"Yea, though I walk through the Valley of Death," he whispered, thinking back to his days as a young choir boy at a Catholic cathedral in Chicago. The intelligence officer had lost a great deal of his faith since joining the Navy, to the point where his wife had begun to chastise him for it in front of the children.

They're probably enjoying a nice spring day in Chicago...

"Sir, we're not going to be able to take off!" the *Arizona*'s aviation officer shouted from the seaplane's cockpit. "We need to get this plane over the side!"

Before Greenman could respond, the Pacific Fleet's outer screen opened fire.

. . .

DESPITE ADMIRAL JENSEN'S BEST EFFORTS, THERE HAD NOT BEEN enough time to train for every occurrence. One of the drills that had fallen by the wayside in lieu of increased time conducting surface gunnery had been anti-aircraft defense of the entire battleline. Based on Captain Greenman's estimates and existing USN doctrine, Admiral Jensen had believed that the odds of a massed attack on the entire Pacific Fleet were extremely low. Furthermore, the Royal Navy's experience had indicated that sustained, rapid anti-aircraft fire with heavy weapons was a sufficient deterrent to torpedo attack and a passable defense against dive bombers. Unfortunately, as Admiral Jensen and his subordinates were about to find out, the *Kido Butai*'s first wave was several orders of magnitude more lethal than a couple dozen of Italian torpedo bombers or *Staffel* of German *Stukas*.

In a matter moments, the American fleet was bedlam, as every gun within range opened fire on the approaching dive bombers. Utilizing timed fuses that required slow, manual loading for their heavy five-inch guns, the majority of the screen was poorly equipped to do anything but put a barrage of steel in front of the approaching dive bombers. Even with radar on several ships, the shifting range and three-dimensional shift required as the battleline turned away made engaging targets guesswork for many of the older ships. As evidenced by their bursts being off in range and height, many of the anti-aircraft officers guessed wrong.

All of this changed as the AA cruiser *Atlanta*, tucked in close to the battleline's starboard side, erupted like a sea-going volcano. With her massive battery of sixteen five-inch guns firing under advanced radar control and each of her shells equipped with proximity, rather than timed, fuses, there was little guesswork involved in her actions. As Greenman watched, the cruiser's guns beginning to immediately take effect, with two of the unfortunately named *Suisei* bombers resembling their namesakes as they fell out of the Japanese formation. There were several cheers before *Arizona*'s own guns began to belatedly fire, the eight single 5-inchers barking as Greenman felt the deck heel under his feet.

Nothing can survive that storm, Greenman thought.

. . .

THE INTELLIGENCE OFFICER WAS SOMEWHAT RIGHT. EXPLODING IN bright flashes or bursting into flames from hits to their unprotected fuel tanks, sixteen of the approaching dive bombers did not make it to their push over points. A further six were forced to jettison their bombs, the pilots frantically trying to hold their aircraft together. But in the awful equation of warfare, there were simply too many bombers for the limited number of guns to stop.

Leading the surviving dive bombers was *Akagi*'s squadron commander, Lieutenant Takehiko Chihaya. Immediately realizing the deadly execution that the *Atlanta* was wreaking on the strike group, he pushed over from twelve thousand feet and led his seven surviving bombers down towards the small light cruiser. One of *Kaga*'s *chutai*, their squadron leader dead, followed Chihaya in his attack, one of their number exploding from a 1.1-inch shell just after bunting over.

The nine remaining bombers followed each other with dive brakes extended, the *Atlanta* swelling before them. Her maneuver options limited, the anti-aircraft cruiser threw over her helm at the last moment in an attempt to evade the attack. Chihaya, his bomber the focal point of most small arms fire, missed close to starboard with his pair of 500-lb. bombs. Not a total loss, the two explosions sprang open the cruiser's seams and killed several of her exposed crew.

Even as the *Atlanta* was shuddering from the two near misses, the next two *Suisei* succeeded where their squadron leader had failed. Chihaya's wingman would have also missed if not for the cruiser's mainmast. As the first of the two 500-lb. bombs exploded to port, the second semi-armor piercing weapon, the bomb exploded as it hit the jutting structure, nearly slicing it in two. The explosion's fragments knifed through the *Atlanta*'s gunnery director, killing everyone in that structure, as well as scything down many of the 1.1-inch anti-aircraft crews. Below, the radar screen immediately went black as the *Atlanta* was blinded.

The startled and shaken cruiser's captain did not even realize his ship's predicament before the third *Suisei*'s payload arrived amidships. The first bomb, armed with a semi armor-piercing fuse, passed diagonally all the way down to the forward engine room before exploding. The second hit further aft and to starboard, destroying the light cruiser's No. 2 boiler room in a gout of steam that cooked the occupants at their post. The combined blast whipped the AA cruiser like a rat in a terrier's grasp, depriving her of power and opening her port side and bottom to the sea. Like a man savagely stabbed in the heart shortly after being punched in the head, the cruiser suddenly staggered and began losing speed.

The stagger indirectly saved the vessel's life, the sudden motion throwing off the next three bombers in a flurry of near misses. Correcting on the fly, only the last dive bomber managed to correctly aim its weapons. Both bombs hit far astern, with one exploding atop the cruiser's No. 7 turret and the second passing down through the stern and detonating on its way out of the ship. Ablaze, with steam and smoke pouring from her midsection, the *Atlanta* heeled violently to port towards the battleships she was screening.

The *Atlanta*'s ordeal was mirrored by the majority of the screen. Of the four destroyers damaged by the IJN onslaught, the destroyers *Cassin* and *Downes* were the only two to be sunk. In the case of the *Cassin*, two hits were enough to break the destroyer's back, leaving her to shudder to a stop and begin settling on an even keel. As for the *Downes* the result was not as pristine, but no less fatal, as a pair of bombs ignited her bunkerage while simultaneously knocking out her powerplant. Adrift and afire, the destroyer would last until nightfall before her depth charges exploded.

The cruisers screening the Pacific Fleet's BBs suffered a relatively higher loss. The *Pensacola* was the most fortunate, her uncannily accurate AA fire netting two of the nine dive bombers attacking her while damaging a third. This resulted in her collecting a single bomb hit abaft that necessitated the abandonment of one fire room and caused some minor flooding. While slowing her, the *Pensacola* still had more than enough speed to maintain her position with the battleline even without the engine room. She would be the luckiest of the six cruisers present. Astern of *Pensacola*, the *Northampton* and *Minneapolis* suffered four hits apiece, while the light cruisers *Helena* and *Honolulu* were struck by three bombs, and the unfortunate *Raleigh* by five.

By far the oldest of all the vessels, the *Raleigh* was nowhere near strong enough to absorb five hits. Seemingly in an instant, the elderly cruiser burst into flames from stem to stern. *Helena* and *Northampton*, while not as vulnerable as the *Raleigh*, were also set ablaze as their hits found aviation stowage for their seaplanes. The *Minneapolis* and *Honolulu*, although not set ablaze, were both subject to severe flooding that their crews began the struggle to control. In a matter of moments, the sextuplet of defenders, as well as their anti-aircraft defenses, were removed from the Japanese torpedo bombers' paths.

That any of the screen survived given the dive bombers' stunning accuracy was owed primarily to the presence of friction. Rather than following Fuchida's orders, the leader of *Kaga*'s final chutai, determined to get a hit on a battleship, pressed on past the escort vessels. Disoriented by the heavy AA fire, the sudden loss of their squadron leader to a five-inch shell during the approach, and another *chutai* leader to a 1.1-inch shell that had missed its intended target, seven *Soryu Val* bombers followed the *Kaga* leader down on *Arizona*.

HEARING THE MACHINE GUNS OPENING FIRE BEHIND HIM, Greenman turned to see the string of *Vals* coming down from the *Arizona*'s bow. Unlike the sleeker *Suisei*'s, the fixed-gear *Vals* were armed with only a single bomb. As Greenman watched, the lead bomber stooped down like a hawk with extended talons, its dive brakes fixed underneath the wing. As the *Arizona*'s machine guns began to find the range, the Japanese pilot released his weapon and started to pull up. Feeling strangely detached, Greenman watched as the black orb descended towards him. As time dilated, he had time to realize that the fact the bomb wasn't changing shape meant it was basically heading right towards him. As men screamed and ducked behind him, Captain Greenman had time for a final defiant thought.

I hope I see you in Hell, Admiral.

The bomb actually missed him by three feet astern. A high explosive type, it detonated on contact with the *Arizona*'s deck. The resulting explosion annihilated Greenman, the seaplane crew, and the ten sailors attempting to rig the craft for jettisoning over the side. The *Kingfisher* itself burst into flames as hot fragments first sliced open its full fuel tanks then ignited the pool of aviation fuel.

. . .

On the flag bridge, Admiral Jensen turned to Vice Admiral Bowles as the *Arizona* shuddered from the hit.

"How bad are we hit?!" he shouted. Bowles, unable to hear him, stepped forward to ask CINCPACFLT to repeat himself in the din. His face red with frustration, Jensen opened his mouth to shout again…

The grizzled Marine gun captain in charge of the *Arizona*'s forward .50-caliber mount had hunted quail his entire life. Unlike most of his fellows, he switched from firing at the lead *Val* about halfway through that aircraft's dive. Having missed with his initial burst, he held down the Browning's butterfly triggers as he corrected his aim on the second bomber into the chute. The hapless *Soryu* pilot that was his target had just enough time to see sparks fly off his canopy, then had the whole world go black as his skull was shattered by the large .50-caliber bullets. Pilotless, the *Val* continued its last dive. One of the bridge lookouts had just enough time to scream a warning before the aircraft, its crew, and its payload slammed into the *Arizona*'s bridge just above the starboard wing.

Detonating instantly, the *Val*'s payload instantaneously killed or wounded every man on the bridge and half of those on the flag bridge. Admiral Jensen, having dived to the deck in the last moment, had a fragment lay open his back like a meat cleaver. Vice Admiral Bowles, having dived the other way, was miraculously only nicked by a splinter the size of a large coffee mug. Unfortunately for both men, as well as every other conscious casualty on the bridge, the *Val*'s misting fuel was simultaneously ignited and propelled by the explosion. As a preview of what many of the two men's subordinates had prayed they would suffer for eternity, both Bowles and Jensen died hearing their own screams and smelling the flesh cooked off their bodies.

. . .

ACTS OF WAR

THE NEXT *SORYU VAL* IN LINE, TAKING DAMAGE FROM SEVERAL weapons, released his bomb while simultaneously pulling desperately back on the stick. As a result, the missile hit flat to the *Arizona*'s deck, causing the bomb to break apart as it impacted abreast the No. 2 turret. An unfortunate sailor was the only impediment to the weapon's casing and contents before they hurtled harmlessly over the side. The remaining dive bombers, thrown off by the ferocity of the fire and shock at watching the lead aircraft crash into the bridge, missed close aboard the burning, turning battlewagon.

Seemingly as suddenly as it had begun, the dive-bombing attack was over. The danger, however, was not. All eyes in the rear of the battleline focused on the AA cruiser *Atlanta* as the vessel, obviously slowing, continued her slow turn towards the battleship *California*. Desperately sounding her siren, the smaller vessel seemed to be screaming like a desperate maiden being dragged to a sacrifice as she hurtled towards the larger vessel. The battleship, already beginning her own turn to port to follow the *Arizona*, put her helm harder over. This forced every vessel astern of her to cut their corner similarly, the *West Virginia* and *Colorado* having to ring up all astern. In normal circumstances, this would have had little effect. Unfortunately, the circumstances weren't normal. Even as crews throughout the fleet were dealing with the effects of the dive-bombing attack, sharp-eyed lookouts spotted the torpedo bombers on the final mile of their run.

The forty-five *Kate*s, long cigar-shaped torpedoes underneath their fuselages, had begun their attack as the dive bombers started to hit the screen. The torpedo bombers had split, twenty-four to port, twenty-one to starboard of the American battleships. Erroneously believing her to be the flagship, four *chutai* had initially concentrated on the *California*. However, as that vessel threw her helm hard over and was lost in the smoke behind the burning *Atlanta*, the *Kate*s to starboard were forced to shift their aim to *West Virginia* and *Colorado*.

Due to the dive bombers ferocity, all eyes had been on the diving, wheeling aircraft. By the time the American ships began belatedly shifting their fire, it was almost far too late. If not for the fact that the *Kate*s had bore in to almost minimum range, there would have been hardly any time to engage the attacking planes before they dropped.

Even with the shift, only two of the highly vulnerable torpedo bombers were destroyed before releasing their payloads and initiating climbing turns either away or over their intended prey.

Believing that his task was to destroy as many battleships as he could rather than just damaging some of them, Fuchida had instructed his pilots the night before that they would only attack the front and rear of the expected American column. Thus, only the *Pennsylvania, Arizona, Maryland, West Virginia,* and *Colorado* had weapons launched at them. In the case of the former two vessels, no evasive action was taken, the *Arizona*'s executive officer realizing too late that the bridge was a mass of flames while the *Pennsylvania* was following her flagship. In the case of the last three, evasive action was either too late or ineffective due to the low speed necessitated by the *California*'s emergency turn.

Arizona had been targeted by a *chutai* from the *Hiryu*, led by Lieutenant Joichi Tomonaga, and two *chutai* from *Kaga* making the short run from starboard. The long months of training in the Kurile Islands paid off for all three groups. Tomonaga's drop was textbook, all three bombers releasing as one. The six bombers from the *Kaga* were a bit more ragged, their fish staggered in entering the water. As a result, despite disparate numbers, the *Arizona* received two blows from starboard and three to port.

Had the weapons not been equipped with the *Sandaburo* warheads, the *Arizona*'s torpedo protection system would have limited the damage to moderate rather than devastating. With the warheads, however, the four combined weapons that struck aft of the ship's main mast knocked out her power, ignited a bunkerage fire, and most tellingly, partially severed one of her screws. Spinning wildly, the *Arizona*'s prop shaft began ripping a massive hole in the vessel's stern like an auger wielded by a crazed child. Feeling the vibration and aware of what was happening, the battleship's executive officer ordered all stop. Even as he did so, reports reached him of the final weapon having hit forward and ruptured the battleship's aviation fuel stowage.

. . .

THE *PENNSYLVANIA* RECEIVED HER BLOWS AT THE SAME TIME AS HER sister ship. Six Japanese torpedoes, two starboard, four to port, found the battlewagon's flank. Two of these ignited her bunkerage, the flames immediately complicating damage control efforts even as the ship lost half her power. The next two hit far astern, severing the battleship's rudder and destroying her steering room. The last two, launched by separate *chutai*, detonated just ahead of the forward magazine, sending hot fragments lancing into the black powder bags used to propel the vessel's seaplanes. Unlike the main magazines, the catapult powder magazine was not well equipped to flood and required the manual opening of the necessary valves. As the powder began to conflagrate, the magazine's crew chief began to race for the valves to flood the space. As fast as the man was, the flames were faster. With a roar, first the half-ton of black powder, then the *Pennsylvania*'s forward magazines exploded before thousands of horrified eyes.

Even as the *Pennsylvania* was exploding, the *Maryland* was being struck. Somewhat obscured in smoke that affected the IJN pilot's accuracy, the vessel suffered only two hits, both forward on either side. Far more fortunate than the *Pennsylvania*, the hits were sufficiently spread out that the TPS kept fragments out of the forward magazine spaces. Still, heavily damaged and with flooding starting to take hold, the *Maryland* hove out of the battleline and began to slow.

The *Colorado* was not so fortunate as her sister. Having managed to conduct more of a turn, the namesake of her class took all four of the torpedoes within the last two hundred feet of her hull on the starboard side. Her TPS perforated, the "Buckin' Bronco" shuddered like her namesake, then began rolling sickeningly towards the four massive wounds. Losing power, with water pouring into her side, the *Colorado* shuddered and began to slow. Feeling the ship's sickening slope, the vessel's damage control officer began turning the necessary valves to counterflood even as the order came down from the bridge. As more water poured into the opened spaces, it began to slosh from starboard to port with the battleship's residual motion. Gaining momentum, the hundreds, then thousands of tons of water began to batter at watertight doors, seals, and bulkheads with steady momentum.

For *West Virginia*, the damage was nearly as severe as that handed out to *Colorado*, as three torpedoes, two portside and one starboard, hit her abaft. With the extensive damage, thankfully at least on opposite sides, the battleship's crew was at least given a chance to begin damage control measures even as the ship lost ability to steer. Due to the stringent measures and stern discipline of her master, Captain Bennion, every man aboard the *Wee Vee* knew their task and immediately set to fighting to save their ship. However, even as the vessel began counterflooding, it was apparent she was *in extremis*.

ABOARD THE *ARIZONA*, FRAGMENTS FROM THE *PENNSYLVANIA*'S FIERY demise swept across the vessel's stern. Men who had begun coming onto deck to escape the torrents of seawater pouring in below were crushed or slashed by the storm of metal from their sister ship's demise. The steel remnants of turrets, armor, and all the metal that went into making a fighting also cut down the men starting to deal with the bridge fires while simultaneously igniting new ones. In a matter of moments, the *Arizona* was beset by over two dozen fires topside, with precious few experienced men to fight them.

Exacerbating matters, the torpedo strikes forward had ruptured the battleship's aviation fuel storage. Runnels of gasoline, passing through the gaps in hatches caused by the torqueing of the vessel's hull due to the torpedo hits or along the wiring strung to maintain her electrical system, began to congregate in several of the vessel's forward compartments. As these found natural pathways from deck to deck, the vapor from the evaporating gasoline began to fill spaces.

CIRCLING TWELVE MILES AWAY WITH FOUR *ZEROE*S IN ATTENDANCE, Commander Fuchida watched through binoculars as the black smoke cloud began to clear over the *Pennsylvania*'s grave. Turning, he saw that the *Colorado* was clearly finished, with the *Arizona* and *West Virginia* severely damaged. Despite being down by the bow, it was clear that the *Maryland* would likely survive. His heart pounding in his chest at the success they had achieved, the *Kido Butai*'s strike leader brought his glasses up and searched the horizon. With a start, he saw two unmistakable silhouette's, their flat shape indicating their type if not their class. Cursing quietly, he began signaling back to *Akagi*:

SECOND STRIKE MUST EXPEDITE. CARRIERS MOVING AWAY. RECOMMEND THIRD STRIKE.

AKAGI
0900 LOCAL (1300 EASTERN)

"SIR, WITH ALL DUE RESPECT, WE *CANNOT* RISK A THIRD STRIKE!" Rear Admiral Kusaka said, his voice desperate. "I know we have won a great victory with an opportunity to do even more, but the enemy will surely be looking for us now."

Below him, the *Akagi*'s deck crew labored to switch armament on the *chutai* of *Kate* aircraft that had just landed from anti-submarine patrol. Having launched almost every flyable airframe on his flight decks and all his reconnaissance aircraft, Yamaguchi did not have aircraft readily available to keep a constant anti-submarine patrol operating until *Tone* and *Chikuma*'s aircraft returned.

Perhaps Kusaka is correct and I am relying far too much on luck, Yamaguchi thought. *As the Americans say, Dame Fortune is a fickle woman.* As he looked down on the flight deck, he saw something that made him realize he might not be the only one relying far too much on the fair lady's good graces.

"Captain Hasegawa, a word with you please?" he said calmly, motioning for *Akagi*'s captain to come and join him.

"Yes, sir," Hasegawa said, coming over from the other side of the bridge. Yamaguchi saw Kusaka's eyes tracking the man like the main gun battery of a battleship. *I will have to watch those two. Hasegawa may not realize the enemy he has made, and he is far too good of a man to suffer from the hand of a fool.*

Leaning in so that his hand was not visible to the rest of the bridge crew, Yamaguchi pointed down to where the deck crews had neatly stacked several high-explosive bombs that had originally been destined for the second strike.

"I think that those weapons can find a far more secure home than our flight deck, don't you?" Yamaguchi asked. "I would hate to have the glorious victory we are currently experiencing reversed by a damaged aircraft splashing into those."

Hasegawa, his face tight with embarrassment, nodded.

"I will see to it personally," he stated. Giving a short bow, he exited the aircraft carrier's bridge.

Yamaguchi turned to where the crew was still readying the *Kate*.

A submarine would be most unfortunate at this time, he thought to himself.

"Sir, so that we may plan, what is the primary target for the third strike?" Admiral Kusaka asked, appearing next to him at the window. Below them, Hasegawa exploded out of the island like a miniature typhoon, administering a vicious physical beating to the unwitting deck officer in charge seemingly without breaking stride. From his perch on the bridge, Yamaguchi would not have bet on the man making it out of the infirmary for at least two weeks.

Discipline is not something to be taken lightly, he thought bemusedly to himself. *Hasegawa does his job well.*

"We will reattack the battleships," Yamaguchi stated. "The new warheads have worked, and we have a chance to cripple most of the American fleet."

"Helmsman, port thirty degrees," the *Akagi*'s officer of the deck barked.

"Aye aye, sir," the helmsman responded. Yamaguchi, looking out the bridge window, watched as the carrier's bow slowly came around to their left. The *Kido Butai* was steaming in a near continuous box along a southeast to northwest line as they waited for the first wave to return. Rather than run the risk of collision, Yamaguchi had directed that the force would make purposefully shallow turns at each end of their evolution.

. . .

Two hundred feet below the carriers, the *Nautilus* moved forward like a sleek, silent metal sea monster.

"That's twice, sir," Nick intoned, the sound of the *Kido Butai* thundering over audible even without headphones. "Total time was roughly one hour."

Lt. Commander Freeman nodded, his face set with a smile. The first time the *Kido Butai* had closed into range, the *Nautilus* had been horribly positioned to have a shot on any of the various vessels. Now, with their latest turn and the *Nautilus*'s slow, steady creeping forward, the next time the ships came back the submarine should be well placed to shoot at *something*.

Six of the bastards, Nick thought, fighting to contain his excitement. *Plus two battleships and cruisers to boot.*

"Okay gentlemen, we're only going to get one shot at this in an hour," Lt. Commander Freeman said. "This is what we're going to do."

As the *Nautilus*' commander quickly outlined his plan of attack, Nick remembered something a Naval Academy professor had drummed into the future officers.

*Never, **ever** be predictable*, he thought. *It will get you killed. We're about to teach some Japanese that little lesson in spades.*

Opana Radar Station
0910 Local (1410 Eastern)

"Sir, multiple contacts, altitude unknown, bearing oh two zero, speed one eight zero knots," Private First Class Justin Carlson intoned, adjusting his scope without having to take his eyes off of it. "Estimate that this raid totals approximately one hundred aircraft."

Opana Radar Station had suddenly had its numbers augmented in light of the debacle earlier that morning. As news began to trickle in of an awful fight off the coast of Oahu with explosions and smoke visible from the beaches, General Short had belatedly realized that the Navy was truly needing help. With that realization, as well as the information that the first radar-controlled intercept attempted by Fort Shafter had been about as well executed as Casey Jones's train trip,

Short had directed that a field grade officer be immediately sent to Opana.

Like all idiotic orders issued by a higher headquarters without further clarification, this one had been followed in letter only. Sitting behind young PFC Carlson and Corporal George Elliott was a large, overweight quartermaster lieutenant colonel who knew as much about radar as he did about leading a bayonet charge. Fortunately for the second attempt at radar interception, Lieutenant Colonel Edsel Daugherty realized that he was the village idiot.

"What do you need me to tell Fort Shafter, Corporal?" he asked Elliott, reaching for the sound powered phone.

"That they need to launch interceptors on this bearing, at least twenty thousand feet altitude, sir," Corporal George Elliott stated, handing the man a piece of paper. A deep, dark anger burned within Elliott's gut. Unlike everyone at Fort Shafter, to include his own self, Elliott did not blame Corporal Lockard for the failure of the initial intercept. He blamed the stupid captain who even now was back with his pursuit squadron getting ready to launch against this second raid. The man had shit the bed, and judging from reports that were being relayed from Pacific Fleet headquarters by the Army's liaison officer, the young captain's error had led to many, many deaths.

I hope some Japanese fighter rips you to shreds, Captain Graham, he thought to himself.

"Sir, I have additional contacts heading in the other direction, well spread out," Carlson intoned. Elliott, for probably the fiftieth time in the last month, was glad that they had inherited Donald Carlson. The man had been formerly assigned to the Washington, D.C. area. Unfortunately, he was far from an excellent soldier, his generally slovenly appearance and carefree attitude making him a great deal of enemies.

Hell, unless he's in front of a scope, the man is useless, Elliott thought. *In front of one, however, he's better than even Lockard and me.*

"What was that bearing again, Carlson?" Elliott asked, realizing something. As the young PFC repeated it, Elliott wrote it down and strode to the map, doing some quick calculations in his head. Double-checking himself against the map, he turned to face Lieutenant Colonel Daugherty.

The man was already on the phone, Elliott's original scratch paper in his hand. Moving quickly, Elliott wrote down another note, along with some coordinates.

"This is Lieutenant Colonel Daugherty. Get me General Short immediately. I don't give a damn if he's in a meeting, tell him that I have a young man here who just might be able to tell him where the enemy is!" Daugherty shouted, his jowls jiggling. He paused, listening to what was being said on the other end of the phone, his face getting redder.

"Then give me your name, you idiot, so I can make sure you get shot for being an incompetent moron!" A few minutes passed, then Daugherty's face broke out in a slight smile.

General Short, sir, I have a young man who wishes to speak with you," Daugherty said. "He thinks he knows where the enemy carriers are."

There was a pause.

"No sir, I have no idea, but I'm sure he can explain it."

As he took the phone, Elliott realized why Daugherty had made the rank of lieutenant colonel.

FAR OUT TO SEA, TWO GROUPS OF WARRIORS PASSED ONE ANOTHER, firing recognition flares as they approached. One group moved in a tight, ordered formation. The other, however, was strung out, with several aircraft showing obvious signs of damage. Even as the two groups approached one another, a *Val* finally gave up the ghost, its engine dying. The crew, realizing they were far from rescue, rode the dive bomber into the water rather risking capture.

As he watched the approaching formation, Isoro felt a great weariness run through his body like he had just run a great race. His *chutai* had somehow survived intact, the only damage being some bullet damage to the rear of his own fighter. The shots had come in from almost full deflection, passing through his tail and out the other side of his control surfaces.

"Bastards," he muttered. Looking as the flights of *Zero*es passed his fighter he gave a tired wave. *Hope you enjoy the decks we cleared for you,* he smiled. The Americans had to be out of fighters, as the dive bombers and torpedo bombers of the first wave had been able to attack without any hindrance other than anti-aircraft fire. If several of the *Zero*es had not attempted to strafe the destroyers in the outer screen, the losses would have been even fewer.

Boredom is dangerous to a fighter pilot, Isoro thought, shaking his head and scanning the skies. *But I doubt the Americans will be able to launch even ten fighters to oppose the second wave.*

U.S.S. YORKTOWN
0930 LOCAL (1430 EASTERN)

ISORO WOULD NOT HAVE BEEN FAR OFF. LOW ON FUEL, HIS *WILDCAT* leaking fuel from its peppered fuselage, himself leaking fluid from shell fragments in his chest and arm, Peter had headed for the first carrier deck he saw. That the *Yorktown*'s escorts had nearly blown him out of the sky just rounded out the day he was having.

Now, as he watched Scarlet Two being pushed over the side of the *Yorktown* while a corpsman worked to patch his wounds, he hoped that the man was not about to tell him he wasn't able to fly. The bird in question was currently being brought up from the hangar deck, where it had been quickly brought down from the hangar deck roof storage.

Looking around, Byrnes realized that there were only five more fighters spotted on the *Yorktown*'s deck. The carrier was pounding south, headed in the opposite direction from that of the enemy's approach. Astern of *Yorktown* to starboard was *Saratoga*. To that vessel's starboard side was her sister, the *Lexington*. The three vessel's escorts had fallen into an impromptu screen, the expectation being that each carrier would turn to maneuver independently if enemy aircraft were detected.

Everyone is going to think Fletcher is yellow because we're heading south, Peter thought, gasping as the corpsman finished stitching his chest. *There's no point in staying near the battleships.* The columns of smoke still visible over the horizon were a mute testimony to the Japanese being in Hawaiian waters in obvious force.

At least they're getting ready to fly off the torpeckers and dive bombers once we get what fighters we can back airborne, Peter thought, hearing the sound of engines revving on the *Yorktown*'s hangar deck. *No use having the chickens in the nest when we don't even know where the Japanese are, and I'd imagine Ford Island is actually **closer** to the enemy.*

As he looked to starboard, Peter saw the *San Diego*, the *Atlanta*'s sister ship, suddenly start blinkering furiously.

That can't be good, he thought. *That can't be good at all.* A moment later, the *Yorktown*'s loudspeaker confirmed his fears.

"Pilots, man your planes," came the tinny report from the island. "Enemy aircraft inbound. I say again, enemy aircraft inbound."

"That's the best I can do, sir," the corpsman said, adding some final bandages. "I truly don't think you should be flying."

Finishing his cigarette, Peter chuckled. The sky seemed frighteningly blue, the pain from his wounds felt especially sharp, and no cigarette had ever tasted so strongly in his life. He was *alive*...and he hated every moment of it. Far better men than himself were dead, of that he had no doubt. Men with wives, children, mothers, and fathers. Men who would have gone on to do great things for the Navy and the nation, for mankind. Men who he had sat down to breakfast with just that morning, talking of the idiocy of the alert and of sailing out of Pearl Harbor in the dark of night when it was obvious the Japanese fleet was nowhere near the Hawaiian Islands. As he looked back over the vessel's stern towards *Saratoga*, he thought of his brethren, his squadronmates, and thought of how little time anyone was guaranteed.

Well, Patricia, I hope you find some man who deserves you, he thought disgustedly. *I don't think I'm coming back from this one.*

"I probably shouldn't," Peter replied, his voice distant. Reaching inside of his pocket, he pulled out his wallet. Taking out twenty dollars, he handed it to the corpsman.

"Take this. Where I'm going it doesn't spend all that well," Peter said resignedly. With that, he went to mount up on the spotted fighter.

9
RESTITUTIONS

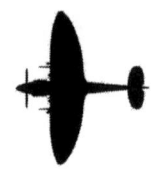

To be defeated is pardonable; to be surprised—NEVER!

— **NAPOLEON BONAPARTE**

OPANA RADAR STATION
0955 LOCAL (1455 EASTERN)
26 MARCH 1943

"SIR, contact should be right about now," Corporal Elliott intoned. *Let's see how much better this one goes*, he thought.

THE ARMY AIR CORPS COUNTERATTACK CONSISTED OF ALL THE fighters that could be launched across Oahu. Cobbled together, the fighters had been assembled just south of Oahu, then sent south to sea along the Japanese strike's course. In an ironic twist of fate that the British had learned during the Second Battle of Britain, such a massive wing was actually counterproductive in terms of conducting an ambush. Whereas a handful of squadrons may have been able to gain superior position and surprised the IJN's escort or dived through it to the bombers, it was impossible to hide the fifty-six fighters moving like a cloud of hornets towards the Japanese second strike.

Seeing the approaching enemy aircraft, the *Shokaku*'s fighter commander waggled his wings to lead forty of his fellows towards the Americans. The resultant engagement was like a clash of medieval knights, over a hundred aircraft hurtling at each other with speeds near six hundred miles per hour. Neither side wanted for malicious intent or effort, machine guns and cannon spitting out tracers at rapidly swelling aircraft. For the Americans, it was a harsh awakening to the skill and expertise that the IJN possessed. On the other hand, the Japanese became quickly cognizant of the fact they were facing far tougher and more heavily armed opponents than poorly-trained Chinese or indifferently led Soviets. More brutally, for eleven pilots it was a basics physics lesson reminding them that two objects could not occupy the same space at the same time, as five *Zero*es and six pursuits caromed out of the sky.

Once more, the inherent toughness of American aircraft made the encounter a lesson that several defenders survived to remember. Although three P-40s and four P-38s were shot down in the initial clash, another five pilots turned smoking, leaking, and battered machines back towards Oahu. The Japanese casualties were far worse, the equation of massed machine gun fire plus unarmored, exposed gasoline tanks yielding eight blazing *Zero*es. Two more *Zero*es were damaged, in one case badly enough for the fighter to begin losing height with a severely wounded pilot at the controls. The remainder of the escort, although shocked by the incredible volume of fire that they had flown through, whipped their maneuverable fighters into tight turns to regain position to protect their charges. The Americans, determined to get through to the bombers, used their momentary advantage in relative speed to continue closing with the fixed-wing *Val*s, sleek *Suisei*'s, and torpedo carrying *Kate*s they saw before them.

What the unfortunate Americans did *not* see were the eighteen *Shiden*s that had moved up sun rather than make the initial head on run. For several of the *Lightning* and *Warhawk* pilots it was a fatal oversight, as the *Shokaku*, *Zuikaku*, and *Hiryu* fighters fell upon their prey like tigers to their meat. Scattering like quail as four of their

JAMES YOUNG

number were destroyed outright and another two damaged, the Army pursuits swiftly forgot about attempting to intercept the second wave. In the swirling, turning dogfight that followed, three more *Zeroes* and two *Shiden* fell in exchange for five *Lightnings* and three *Warhawks*. Unprepared for the Japanese fighters' maneuverability, and shocked as over half their squadron leaders were killed, first a few, then several more, and finally the majority of the surviving American fighters dived away back towards Oahu.

For their part, the *Shiden* pilots turned and began to head for home even as several of their *Zero* counterparts turned to try and regain coverage on the advancing dive and torpedo bombers. Once more, at heavy cost, the Japanese escorts had achieved their purpose. Despite losing over one-third of their total number, they had managed to protect the majority of their charges. While a diminished strike, the second punch from the Japanese carriers was still a fearsome one with nothing between it and the American fleet.

Pearl Harbor Hospital
1015 Local (1515 Eastern)

"You think you two adventurers can stay out of trouble if I leave you alone for ten minutes?" Nancy Hertling asked with a twinkle in her eye.

"Yes Aunt Nancy," Jo said wearily.

I am so embarrassed, she thought.

"Try not to shoot anyone," Nancy replied with a smile, walking out the door in her nurse's uniform.

"Well, that escape plan lasted all of twenty minutes," Patricia noted from where she sat, cleaning the giant Webley.

I'm still shocked Nancy managed to talk the guards into letting us keep our weapons, Jo thought. *Almost as shocked that Patricia looks more bored than scared now.*

"You know, I wasn't expecting to run into Aunt Nancy and Uncle K heading out of town, okay?" Jo replied. "They had a point though—we were safer riding onto post with them than running off into the hinterlands where other crazies might have been headed."

*I'm going to let the **other** in that sentence slide*, Jo thought. *I'll chalk it up to both of us being tired from those planes waking us up this morning.* The roar of Army fighters had startled them both out of their borrowed hospital beds twice.

"Do you think Peter's okay?" Patricia asked, causing Jo to start and look at her.

Hmm... Jo thought.

"Well, either you think your brothers are capable of taking care of themselves or you like Lieutenant Byrnes more than you let on," Jo observed with a smile.

Patricia looked up, her eyes wide in shock, then narrowing.

"Maybe I just know he's out with the fleet..." Patricia started.

"You mean like Nick?" Jo shot back with a chuckle.

Patricia growled in frustration.

"Fine, I like him, okay?" she replied to Jo's amusement.

"I think Peter's fine," Jo said. "Actually I think all of your brothers are fine. As Uncle K said this morning, the Japanese are probably on the other side of..."

The distant roar of an aircraft engine made Jo stop midsentence. There were several shouts from outside the ward they were sitting in, with several medical personnel rushing by the door. Jo and Patricia both swung to their feet, the latter holstering her pistol before they stepped outside to the window where several doctors and nurses were gathered looking into the sky. Rather than gazing where the collective group was peering, Jo watched as the heavy cruiser *Chester* went sailing by Ford Island at a high rate of speed.

She's going a little fast for the channel, Jo thought worriedly. The *Chester* was the sister ship to her father's *Houston*, and the sight made her stomach suddenly clench in worry. Following everyone else's eyes, the growing dots made her suffer fear of a different sort.

What if those are Japanese? she thought. Apparently she was not the only person with that thought, as several sirens began to wail. Below her second-floor window, she watched as two soldiers jumped into the sandbagged position beneath her. The first soldier in charged the weapon while the second man grabbed the belt of bullets, ensuring a good, clean feed into the weapon. With their tin pot hats, short sleeve khakis, and youthful faces the soldiers made her think of little boys playing war.

As she looked back up, however, she realized that the men were not playing by any means. Finally succumbing to damage suffered during the clash with the Japanese escort, one of the returning fighters began streaming smoke. Realizing that his fighter was uncontrollable, the pilot attempted to turn away from Hickam Field and Pearl Harbor. Watching the plane drunkenly point its nose to the south, Jo suddenly felt nausea. Unable to take her eyes away, she watched as the fighter began to lose altitude.

Oh my God, she thought frantically. *Oh my God.*

As if defying her prayers, the fighter suddenly exploded in a ball of fire and smoke. The fireball arced down towards the groves of pineapple trees below, its pilot dead at the controls. Jo watched as Patricia, shocked, swept her hand up to her mouth, her eyes wide. Below her, one of the soldiers began cursing, ripping his helmet off in disgust. Unbidden, her thoughts turned to the Cobbs.

Please Lord, let them be okay, she thought, desperately hoping she was having a nightmare yet knowing that things were all too real.

"Is that it?" Patricia asked quietly, counting the returning dots as they came into view. Numbly, both women thought back to the formation they had watched arrowing so powerfully out to sea. These bedraggled survivors, arriving in dribs and drabs, seemed to be some sick practical joke.

"That can't be it," Patricia continued, her voice strained as she reflexively touched her pistol.

We are lost, Jo thought, looking back towards her pistol on the dresser behind her. *Maybe we shouldn't have come in with Nancy, as I'm suddenly not sure if we're going to own this place in the morning after all.*

EWA NAVAL AIR STATION
1025 LOCAL (1525 EASTERN)

Captains Samuel and David Cobb were both patient men. Having a precocious younger sister and two high-spirited younger brothers had that effect on most people.

All thoughts of weddings were far from the two men's minds now as they sat fuming in the cockpits of their two F4F-3s. VMF-14 had been sitting on the tarmac now for almost five hours, fully armed and ready to roll. Initially, the pilots had believed this to be yet another drill, nothing to be really concerned about. That thought had been dispelled when a badly damaged *Wildcat* had come in fast and hot to slam down on the tarmac. The injured pilot had quickly hopped out of his smoking fighter and ran for his life, barely making it fifty yards before the plane had exploded. Rushing over with the crash crews, Sam and Eric had gotten on the scene just as the pilot, eyes wide and voice panicked, had finished explaining what had happened.

Whilst one man could have been explained away as a coward or perhaps exaggeration, the arrival of two more damaged fighters, both *Wildcat*s from separate squadrons, confirmed the man's words almost beyond the shadow of a doubt. The Japanese were in the Hawaiian Islands in force. Moreover, they had roughly handled the fleet's fighter squadrons and possibly the fleet itself.

Yet still we sit here and wait, Sam thought disgustedly. *I'm not saying Major Bowden is yellow, but he's definitely starting to resemble a ripening banana, no matter what headquarters keeps telling him.*

"Here comes Major Bowden!" David said suddenly from up in his cockpit. Sam turned and looked, seeing their squadron commander walking purposefully towards the flightline.

"He doesn't look happy," Sam said, raising his hand to his eyes to shade them. "As a matter of fact, he looks downright pissed off."

"Yep, that he does," David replied. As they watched, Bowden pointed directly at them, then waved them over with his right hand. In his left he was carrying an object that looked like a small bag. Sam waited for David to hop down beside him, then started running over towards the man down the flight line. Whereas the action would normally have brought forth the catcalls and comments of their fellow pilots, today there was dead silence.

"Sir?" Sam asked after rendering the proper courtesies. Bowden returned their salute, his face still red with anger.

"Gentlemen, by order of Pacific Fleet Headquarters, we are *still* forbidden to take off without the express order of Admiral Jensen, CINCPAC. I just spent the last hour talking to some idiotic Lieutenant Commander duty officer who fails to appreciate that there is a war on, and judging from the reports we have received the Fleet could use some help. How are you gentlemen on your ship recognition?" Bowden asked, as the squadron executive officer, Captain David Wharram, came up behind them.

The two brothers looked at each other, then back to Bowden.

"Fair, sir," both of them replied in unison. Bowden took a moment to gather his thoughts, having expected two separate answers.

"I think you're both full of shit, but you've also got the most hours of anyone here except for myself and the flight leaders. More importantly, I know you've both trapped on carriers in the last year, whereas most of us have not. I'm not about to take off the entire squadron against the orders of the duty officer, but I am going to take steps to get those orders changed," Bowden said rapidly, his tempo increasing with his obvious agitation. Thrusting out his left hand towards Sam, he continued.

"Inside this bag is a message for Rear Admiral Fletcher, asking him if he needs us to serve as replacement fighters," Bowden said. "Then asking him if he will not only overrule that son-of-a-bitch at headquarters, but see that the individual in question is cashiered from the service as soon as possible."

Sam and David looked at each other, then at Bowden with a slight smile. Bowden did not return it. If anything, his face grew darker.

"I am not joking, gentlemen, I really have asked for that asshole's relief," Bowden snapped.

Okay, I'm sorry, you're not yellow, Sam thought, seeing just how angry Bowden was. *Indeed, you look positively murderous.*

"If you can, you are to land aboard the carriers and deliver this message to Admiral Fletcher personally . If you are unable to land aboard the carriers, you are to drop this message bag onto the nearest vessel you see in good shape. Do your best not to get shot down. That is all," Bowden said as Sam took the bag.

The two men looked at each other, then back at Bowden.

"Sir, which direction are our friendly carriers," Sam asked.

Bowden started at the question, as if suddenly remember something. He reached into his pocket and pulled out a piece of paper.

"This is the bearing to Point Falcon," Bowden said apologetically. "The pilots advise flying low, as apparently our Japanese friends have us outnumbered."

Taking the sheet of paper, Sam noticed the blood staining the top of it. Along with everything else that had happened that morning, it brought home the seriousness of what was happening to him.

"Well, sir, let's hope that things aren't as bad as they were a few hours ago," Sam replied. "The Japanese have to go home eventually."

WILDCAT F-19
1030 LOCAL (1540 EASTERN)

THINGS WEREN'T NEARLY AS BAD AS THEY HAD BEEN THAT MORNING for the American Navy fighters. Indeed, with each man present being a survivor in some way or another, things were far better. Thanks to radar and the bloody clash with the Army fighters, the twenty *Wildcat*s actually managed to get the drop on their opposite numbers.

Let's see how you like being bounced, you assholes! Peter thought with exultation, the *Val* in front of him swelling in his gunsight. Squeezing the trigger was almost orgasmic with regards to the carthartic release, as the rushing Japanese dive bomber flew directly into the F4F-4's six .50-caliber streams. One moment the fixed-wing aircraft was huge in Peter's gunsight. The next its fuel tanks and bomb converted it into a dirty orangeish brown crematorium that Peter unwittingly flew through. Fighting the urge to throw up his hands to protect his face, Peter felt the *Wildcat* shudder as debris slammed off his fuselage.

Who's next?! he thought, face darkened in a snarl. *Who's fucking next?!* Wrenching the stick over, he brought the *Wildcat* around to line up on a second, lower *chutai* of *Vals*. For a brief moment he realized that the bright lights at the edge of his vision were tracers as the tail gunners tried to draw a bead on him, but then nothing mattered but him and his target. Again the *Wildcat* shuddered, the four streams of fire shattering his target's rear canopy in a gout of blood and glass. Pulling the stick back into his stomach, vision darkening, Peter walked his short burst back through the dive bomber's tail control surfaces. Watching the rudder fly off the airframe, Peter had a brief moment of exultation before rolling down and away.

Like Norse berserkers amongst their enemies, the USN fighters had laid waste all about them as they attacked into the Japanese formation. Two *Vals* and three *Kates* in addition to Peter's two kills were arcing down towards the ocean. Another dive bomber and torpedo bomber struggled on with battle damage or wounded crewmen. In return, four *Wildcats* had been knocked out of action, two of them permanently, by the bombers' massed tail gunner fire. As he leveled off below the *Vals* but above the *Kates*, Peter took one moment to make sure his wingman was still with him, then lined up on the descending torpedo bombers.

Shit they are fast, he thought, feeling the *Wildcat* shake as he only slowly gained on the Japanese torpedo bombers. Aiming for a *chutai* leader near the rear of the formation, Peter was far more aware of the *Kate*'s tail gunners firing than he had been of the *Val*'s. A sound like hailstones hitting a barn roof told him that at least one of the gunners had struck his fighter, but he ignored it as he finally got within range and squeezed the trigger.

Dammit! Peter thought as his fighter slewed to the side, the impromptu maneuver telling him one of his four guns was jammed. The hosed burst still managed to kill the *Kate*'s rear gunner and start a stream of fuel going backward as Peter skidded away. Out of the corner of his eye he saw another pair of *Vals* falling out of the sky wrapped in flames. As he worked the charging handle in a desperate attempt to clear his guns, Peter realized that the fight was starting to reach the edge of *Lexington*'s screen.

I don't want to get shot down by my own...

Peter never had time to finish the thought, as a flicker of gray and muzzle flashes in his rearview mirror was his only warning that *Zeroe*s had joined the fight. Even as Peter started to throw his stick over, twenty-millimeter shells began tearing apart his fighter. Only the fact the *Wildcat* had been modified with boiler plate behind the seat kept his death from being instantaneous, as the cockpit became alive with hot engine oil, shell fragments, and canopy glass. Falling off on one wing, the *Wildcat* fell downwards trailing a dark streamer of smoke. Reaching up to pull the canopy back, Peter cursed as twisted metal sliced through his gloves and into his hand.

Gotta get out, he thought. Wrenching the shattered canopy backward, he felt the rush of air increase. The Pacific seemed to be rushing up towards him as he rolled the fighter onto its back, quickly unclasped his seat straps, and lunged out of the cockpit. The pain of his stitches ripping seemed to be a signal to every other wound to make itself felt, and Peter belatedly realized he was shot through this right arm and leg, with severe burns on his left leg from the engine oil. Ignoring the agony, he wrenched his D-ring to open up his chute, and immediately discovered to his all consuming discomfort that he'd improperly aligned his groin straps. As the white hot agony shot through is testicles, he opened his mouth to scream and slammed hard into the Pacific.

The saltwater did nothing to ease Peter's pain, but it strangely provided clarity as he quickly struggled back to the surface. Fighting his way free of his chute, the pilot quickly swam away from it in a rush of adrenaline and fear. Belatedly realizing he heard no onrushing engines or other indications that someone might strafe him, Peter stopped and began trying to inflate his Mae West. To his relief, the device still worked. As Peter finished blowing up his life jacket, he suddenly felt light headed.

Dear God, don't tell me I came this far to bleed to death, he thought.

The shark strike was sudden and violent. One moment Peter was lightly treading water, the next there was a terrible rending of flesh and sinew as a tiger shark seized the young officer's left leg. Attempting to scream, Peter's cry ended in a gurgle as the shark began moving forward and downward. Shaking, the twelve foot fish finally rent the leg from Peter's torso, causing him to bob upward like some macabre top. Peter screamed briefly before the sudden, massive loss of blood sent him into shock. He never felt the second shark, a smaller tiger, bite into his left arm.

•

Peter and his fellow officers' sacrifice had not been in vain. Shocked at the ferocity of the American's fighter defense, with several *chutai* and squadron leaders dead or limping back towards the *Kido Butai*, the second strike was nowhere near as coordinated as the first. In addition, the *Lexington*, *Saratoga*, and *Yorktown* had swiftly diverged their courses, gaining separation between their battle groups. Finally, whereas the Pacific Fleet's battleships would be fortunate to reach twenty-one knots on a good day, the carriers and their escorts were already passing thirty knots as the Japanese finally acquired them. The extra speed greatly increased the time it took for the Japanese aircraft to reach attack position. Erupting in smoke and flame, with the destroyers beginning to belch smoke from generators as well as their funnels, the carrier task forces presented a far more difficult target for the attackers.

Even before reaching their pushover point, *Val*s began to disappear in explosions from 5-inch shells. Resolutely pressing on, the dive bombers were then subjected to the densest automatic weapons array in the Pacific Fleet. While professionals and combat veterans, none of the dive bomber pilots had ever been faced with fire so thick. Without prior coordination, desperate to get through the hurricane of fire, and cognizant that their bombs would easily pierce the teak wood decks, the *Val*s and *Suisei*s ignored the screen and concentrated solely on the *Lexington* and *Saratoga*. It was a tribute to the pilots' bravery that thirty dive-bombers made it to the pushover point without a single aircraft breaking off and fleeing. It was a mark of their skill that of those thirty men, in the face of ferocious anti-aircraft fire, six made successful drops. Through pure luck, only three more of the dive bombers were swatted down on their way out of the carrier escorts' maelstrom.

Constructed from the hull of a battlecruiser, the *Lexington* had been the United States Navy's second flattop. Handled skillfully by her master, she managed to avoid all but two of the deadly missiles dropped by the Japanese dive bombers. The first bomb hit near the bow, piercing the through the flight deck near the forward elevator and passing into the hangar spaces below. Despite having flown off half her strike aircraft to Oahu, the Lady Lex had not had time to complete launching the entire air group. Even worse, in the rush to get the first bunch of aircraft off, the hangar crew had not completely secured an auxiliary fuel cart. Whereas normally the small 500-lb. bomb would have merely bent the elevator shaft and caused minor damage, the resultant secondary explosion caused a large gout of flame to burst upwards from *Lexington*'s flight deck followed by dense black smoke.

The second weapon dropped on the old Lady Lex hit in the middle of the vessel's long flight deck. Continuing on through the bottom of the hangar deck, the missile exploded inside one of the ship's galleys that was also serving as an aid station. The execution among the gathered corpsmen was awful, the blast and fragmentation killing a dozen and injuring twenty-five more. However, other than starting another fire, the hit did not severely damage the *Lexington*'s structure or affect the ship's ability to function. Heavily ablaze forward, but with her propulsion plan intact, the *Lexington* continued her evasive course as torpedo bombers began boring in from either bow.

The *Saratoga*'s ordeal was far worse than her elder sister's. Not as ably handled by her captain and the target of the sole *Suisei* squadron present, *Sara* suffered five hits down her length. The first bomb came in at an angle through the aft lift, passing down the elevator well to the deck underneath the hangar deck and continuing on to explode in a paint locker. Splashing about, the oil based paint immediately burst into an intense conflagration. The next weapon, hitting almost simultaneously, pierced the top of turret No. 1., and on the starboard 8" gun's breech. In an instant, the entire turret's crew and many of the men standing in the catwalks lining the carrier's flight deck were killed or horribly wounded. Moments later, the ammunition within the turret began burning and exploding, causing further casualties and causing smoke to pour back over the vessel's island, temporarily blinding the bridge crew.

Bomb hits three and four caught the carrier as she answered her helm to starboard. Slashing at an angle into the vessel's side, the two weapons exploded one deck above the No. 1 engine room. The detonations forced hot fragments of varying size through the roof of the compartment, starting a large fire and knocking most of the engineers off their feet. Even worse, the shock from the impacts caused the carrier's turboelectric engines to fail. The final bomb, a large armor-piercing weapon, was dropped just as the *Suisei* carrying it lost its wing. The strange physics that were imparted were the only reason the weapon hit, but also caused it to angle strangely as it passed through the *Saratoga*'s hull. As a result, it caused a great deal of additional fragmentary damage before finally exploding in the heart of the carrier's steering room. On the large carrier's bridge, the helmsman's eyes grew large as the man attempted to throw the ship's helm over and received no response. Choking and gasping in the smoke, his voice drowned out in the din of gunfire and the roar of flames from the No. 1 turret, the helmsman unsuccessfully attempted to get his captain's attention.

As the dive bombers pulled up from their dives, the *Kates* completed their final runs on the two carriers. In addition to facing the same typhoon of automatic weapons fire the dive bombers had, the *Kates* had the added benefit of the three heavy and four light cruisers of the screens also firing their full broadsides at the approaching bombers in order to raise water columns in their path. With far longer runs than the dive bombers, faster targets, and the disconcerting effect of water erupting in their faces, the *Kates* were both not as successful as their dive bombing brethren, yet triumphant beyond their wildest expectations.

The *Saratoga*, her helm still unresponsive and locked into a tight turn, absorbed four hits to starboard. The first weapon, running deep, failed to function. Its sole accomplishment was to scare the forward fireroom crew almost to death with a sound like a bell clapper. The men present barely had enough time to void bowels or empty bladders before soiled undergarments and their good fortune became almost academic. Impacting in almost perfect formation, the first torpedo a few moments before its two sisters, the three weapons destroyed the carrier's elevator shaft, started a massive fire in her bunkerage, and most overwhelmingly, exploded her torpedo magazine.

The blast was a massive thing, the bright orange fireball spewing from the *Saratoga*'s flight deck like a roiling, living mass. The dirty smoke formed a brief, distinctive mushroom cloud that towered over the deck before being dispersed by the carrier's forward momentum. It was a testimony to the *Sara*'s robust construction that the vessel did not instantly break in half and sink. Instead, her entire aft end afire, secondary explosions erupting from her stern, and the Pacific rushing into her ruined aft end, the carrier coasted a stop and began settling by the stern.

The *Lexington* was going through her own suffering even as the *Saratoga*'s magazine detonated. Handled more ably than the *Saratoga*, the Lady Lex was still a large, long target. Two torpedoes on her port side opened her engineering spaces. A third hit forward caused cracks in the aviation gasoline stowage. Even as brave, doomed men in the fire rooms attempted to secure the boilers and escape, the *Lexington* was struck on her starboard quarter by a final weapon that destroyed her pumping room. Ablaze forward, with water pressure falling precipitously throughout her fire mains, the *Lexington* staggered forward barely under steerage way.

In moments the attack was over. Steaming undisturbed, the *Yorktown* turned away from her wounded brethren and prepared to steam into the wind so she could accept the USN's surviving fighters. Shaken, those members of her crew topside looked back towards the blazing *Saratoga* and *Lexington*. For years, these two vessels had symbolized the strength of American naval aviation. Now, like twin ill omens for American's chances, they lay broken and wounded. Moreover, with the *Saratoga*'s seemingly imminent demise and the *Lexington*'s future very much in doubt, *Yorktown* was the only American carrier remaining with the Pacific Fleet's main body. As such, she was a priority target for her foes. At the barked orders of her task force commander, *Yorktown* turned south, gathering what escorts she could around her. With only twelve fighters left to guard her precious flight deck, there was nothing more that she could do in the area.

For the Japanese, the cost had been steep. Scattered, the strike group began to straggle north to their rendezvous point.

Semper Flight
1045 Local (1545 Eastern)

Trying to simultaneously fly and look at the ships ten miles away, Sam Cobb once more cursed everyone above his squadron commander.

*That fucking duty officer needs to be **shot**, not cashiered*, Sam thought disgustedly. *Or someone on the staff below needs to be.* Internally, his guts were churning, left hand trembling on the stick as he tried to continue holding the binoculars. He could see the listing *Colorado*, blazing *Arizona*, and settling *West Virginia*. Three destroyers and what appeared to be a light cruiser were in attendance to the three battleships, but with a sick feeling in his stomach Sam had a feeling things were not going well. As if to reinforce his horror, the *Colorado* suddenly jerked in the water and began to roll towards starboard. Before Sam's terrified eyes, the 33,000-ton ship accelerated like a carnival ride, her mast smashing into the mass of black dots surrounding her with a visible splash.

*Holy shit, that's...*he had time to begin thinking before David interrupted his thoughts.

"Bogeys, three o'clock low!" his twin reported tersely. Turning, Sam saw the four forms low on the water. The aircraft were four *Kate*s, the survivors from a pair of *Zuikaku* and *Shokaku chutais*. Realizing information would be at a premium, the senior officer of the group had diverted to take a look at the burning American battleships on his way back to the carrier.

Well hello you bastards, Sam thought as he gazed at the four olive green aircraft with bright red circles. Kicking his rudder and putting the stick over, Sam brought the *Wildcat* around and shoved the throttle forward. His pulse quickening and mouth suddenly dry, he took a deep breath to steady himself as he closed on the now fleeing group of bombers. Charging his guns, he activated his throat mike.

"I've got the leader, you get the second section," he ordered David.

"On it," his brother replied. For a brief moment, Sam felt the weight of every hour of classroom instruction, flight training, and gunnery practice that had brought him to this point. Kicking his rudder to bring him in from high on the starboard side, he lined up on his target.

WITH TWELVE PAIRS OF EYES WITHIN THE GROUP OF FOUR BOMBERS it should have been impossible for the two *Wildcat*s to gain surprise. Unfortunately for the *Kate* crews, all their eyes were on the waters where the glistening red bottom was slowly disappearing or the *Arizona* and *West Virginia*'s continued struggles against the sea, turbulent waters where the *Colorado* had just disappeared and debris was still shooting violently up to the surface. As such, the only warning that the four *Kate*s received was the startled yelp of the rearmost plane's tail gunner when he looked up upon hearing the growing sound of aircraft engines.

SAM SQUEEZED THE TRIGGER AS THE *KATE* REACHED THE EDGE OF HIS gunsight. Having underestimated the torpedo bomber's speed and his own closure rate, he fired too late for his streams of fire to have a chance to converge. Rather than an airframe rending buzzsaw, his two second burst was a hailstorm that put impacts all over the target. Still, while not spectacular, the burst more than did its job. Caught just as he was beginning to shout instructions to the plane's observer, the *Kate's* pilot was slain almost instantaneously by two bullets smashing his right arm and evacuating his chest cavity. Whether the plane would have survived the partially severed rudder cables, fuel leak, or damaged engine became academic as the mortally wounded man slumped forward. Nose down, the *Kate* became the last roller coaster the other two men would ever ride as it hurtled into the Pacific.

Swinging his head around, Sam watched the cloud of debris and fireball that had been David's target arcing downwards. His brother was pulling up and turning towards him, and Sam made a quick check of David's tail knowing that the other Marine was doing the same for him. When neither one of them saw anything, they turned back towards the two *Kates*, the Japanese bombers running away and descending to right above the water to force the Americans to make shallow attacks rather than the preferred diving slash.

"I've got first run," David grunted as the two brothers completed their turn and accelerated after the running Japanese aircraft.

"Got you covered," Sam said, pulling up and astern of David's fighter as they circled wide of the two Japanese bombers.

Both *Kate* pilots sideslipped, attempting to keep the Americans in the cone of fire from their tail gunners. David pushed his nose over into a slight dive, choosing the left-hand *Kate* to engage. Once in range, the Marine opened fire, followed moments later by the tail gunners of the two bombers. The initial burst was behind the target, but Sam watched as his brother corrected as he swung in behind the bombers.

Watch those gunners, you idiot, Sam thought worriedly. He need not have been concerned, his brother only firing a quick two second burst before snap rolling away. The burst of fire smashed into the *Kate*'s rear, the huge .50-caliber bullets scything through the rear gunner's arms and knocking a portion off the tail stabilizer.

"Gunners are a little friskier than I thought," David muttered. "I'm all right though."

"Going in," Sam replied. "Starboard torpedo bomber." With that, he put his own nose down and, making a curving turn, came in from full deflection. The *Kate's* gunner still managed to turn his machine gun towards Sam, but the combination of the *Wildcat*'s angle and the wind from the *Kate*'s passage pushing against the bullets caused the man's burst to go mostly wide. Sam, in turn, put his three second burst through the *Kate*'s forward fuselage, cockpit, and wingroot. The starboard wing fluttered off, sending the *Kate* into a quick spin to the side. Before the pilot had chance to realize his bomber was missing a wing and he himself had two ruined legs, the *Kate* was smashing into the Pacific in a plume of spray.

Sam ended his run to see David slipping onto the last bomber's tail. Noting the lack of return fire and ruined rear cockpit, David closed to point blank range before squeezing the trigger. The end was blissfully quick, the four streams cutting through the pilot and observer prior to setting the fuselage on fire. Streaming smoke, the torpedo bomber nosed into the water and cartwheeled tail over nose before resting with its belly towards the sky. David pulled up over the wreckage, rejoining with his brother.

Sam realized his breath was coming in rapid gasps, his pulse racing.

We just killed those men, Sam thought. Between the *Colorado*'s death and their four kills, war was suddenly very, very real to Sam.

"Goddamnit," he muttered, suffering a chill despite his cockpit being hot as hell from the sun. *My brothers are out there. Tootsie's back at Pearl. These bastards could be invading us*! Suddenly, it was extremely important that he and his brother find what was left of the American fleet, if only to convince themselves that the situation was not as bad as they thought.

U.S.S. NAUTILUS
1050 LOCAL (1550 EASTERN)

NICK WOULD HAVE BEEN TOUCHED THAT HIS BROTHER HAD THOUGHT of him. Especially since he was most definitely in harms way. *Nautilus*, after much careful maneuvering, had found herself in position to strike.

"Sir, first escort has passed over us!" the sound man reported.

The tension in the control room went up another notch, every man realizing what Jason's next command was going to be.

"Periscope depth! Up periscope!" Jason barked. "All ahead one third!"

The *Nautilus*'s began coming up on an even keel from her current depth of one hundred feet, the planesmen working in smooth concert at their station. Crouching down, Lt. Commander Freeman grabbed the handles of the periscope as it came up above waist height. He did not need to give any more orders, the crew knowing exactly what he had planned.

"Tubes one through six flooded and ready in all respects!" Ensign Workman intoned from his station. From where he sat at the torpedo data computer (TDC), Nick prepared to begin entering the range and bearing of enemy ships. An analog device, the TDC did most of the math necessary to tell *Nautilus* where she had to aim her torpedoes in order to get a hit.

"Periscope depth, sir," Lieutenant Banes barked.

Lt. Commander Freeman was already aware of that fact, the scope coming up through the Pacific depths. Nick felt his palms go sweaty as he watched the *Nautilus*'s captain hurriedly lower the magnification.

"Target one, angle on the bow starboard twenty-five degrees, heading oh nine oh, speed twenty-six knots, range one thousand yards!" he barked. There was an audible intake of breath, everyone amazed that they were so close to the enemy. Nick, ignoring the fear that tried to grip him, entered the data into the TDC as Chief Pound began updating the *Nautilus*'s manual plot.

"Match bearings...mark!" Freeman barked, ordering the last entry to made into the TDC.

"Bearings set!" Nick shouted back.

"Torpedoes one through six set!" Workman reported.

"Fire one!" Freeman shouted.

There was the hiss of compressed air as *Nautilus* expelled her first war shot barely thirty seconds after her periscope had passed through the waves. The vessel jumped as the twenty-foot-long torpedo exited the bow tube, lightening the bow before the planesmen corrected it.

"Fire two!"

Once more the process was repeated.

"Fire three! Fire four! Second target!" Freeman shouted, spinning the scope. "Twin carrier!"

Nick could tell the *Nautilus*'s commander was fighting to keep his voice calm.

Even if they kill us after this, these shots are a submarine commander's dream, Nick thought, fighting to control his own elation.

"Target two, angle on the bow one nine zero, heading oh eight five, same speed, range twelve hundred yards! Match bearing!" Freeman barked.

Time was not on their side. Their first shots had almost certainly been sighted in the clear Pacific, and the ships would already be beginning to take evasive action.

"Bearings set!" Workman replied, his voice several octaves higher.

"Fire tubes nine through twelve!"

The *Nautilus* jumped three more times, the planesmen correcting again to keep the vessel from broaching. Lt. Commander Freeman started to turn the periscope again, then suddenly stopped.

"Take her deep! Rig for depth charging, all ahead flank!" Freeman shouted, his voice full of obvious terror. The crew sprang into action, Freeman slapping the periscope handles upwards as the device slipped back in its runners.

"Jap tin can, two thousand yards and closing," *Nautilus*'s master said resignedly.

We are dead, Nick thought as he gripped the TDC to keep from falling forward as the *Nautilus* dived. *Still, we got our licks in.*

ADMIRAL YAMAGUCHI WAS WATCHING THE APPROACH OF THE *Akagi*'s final *Shiden*.

"I need to speak with that *chutai* leader as soon as he lands," Yamaguchi said. "If we are going to launch a third strike, I want to know what went...*What in the hell is that destroyer doing?*"

The last exclamation was in response to the destroyer *Akigumo* heeling out of line from behind the *Zuikaku*, smoke pouring from her stack. Yamaguchi brought up his binoculars as his signals officer began relaying his question. As he watched, he saw the *Zuikaku* and *Shokaku* also suddenly start to turn, both of them heeling hard away from each other.

Submarine, Yamaguchi had time to realize, nausea starting to turn his stomach just as *Nautilus*'s torpedoes arrived.

WITH THE RANGE AS SHORT AS IT WAS, THERE WAS ALMOST NO chance that *Nautilus* should miss. Unfortunately, the Bureau of Ordnance, in one of those decisions that made perfect sense in peacetime, had only tested a handful of torpedoes with live warheads in the previous decade. If they had tested live torpedoes, they would have realized that the weapons' contact exploders had a terrible habit of bending on impact, rather than striking back into the warhead as designed.

Nautilus's first bow torpedo, hitting directly opposite the *Zuikaku's* first fireroom, suffered such a malfunction, hitting with a *thud!* Each and every man in the compartment had a few shaken seconds to realize that they had just narrowly escaped Death's scythe before the second fireroom crew caught the Grim Reaper's back swing. Exploding with a roar, the second torpedo immediately snuffed out half of the carrier's propulsion and knocked most of the vessel's crew off their feet.

The third torpedo hit the Japanese carrier forward, the shock effect causing the *Zuikaku's* flight deck to leap forward in a jostling of deck hands, just landed aircraft, and fuel bowser. The mixture of hot engines, rent fuel tanks, and live ordnance had predictable effects, the fireball visible from the *Akagi's* flag bridge. Less visible, but far more ominous for the large carrier, was the locking of the forward elevator in the down position and disruption of the hangar fire sprinklers.

Lt. Commander Freeman had misjudged the *Zuikaku's* speed by a couple of knots. As a result, the final torpedo almost missed the carrier. Almost, in this case, was potentially worse than a full on hit, the torpedo impacting on the carrier's port shaft. The resultant blast ripped the prop off, the still-turning blade whipping to the side and ripping a huge portion from the rudder before descending into the depths. Listing, afire on her deck and from damage belowdecks, the *Zuikaku* continued her lazy turn and began coming to a stop. As the shocked members of the *Kido Butai* watched, the recently returned aircraft on deck continued to explode in an ominious pyrotechnic display.

Like her sister, *Shokaku* benefited from the Bureau of Ordnance's miserliness. The first torpedo to find her slammed into her hull abreast the forward bomb magazine. Rather than detonating in what would have been a spectacular, and fatal blow, the dud weapon broke apart on impact. It was followed by a second dud that hit abreast the aviation gas storage, then a third that would have deprived the carrier of all power.

The third torpedo from *Nautilus*'s stern tubes finally functioned as designed, staving in the side of the *Shokaku*'s steering room. In an instant, the *Shokaku* lost the ability to correct her turn, continuing on to port towards the battleship *Kirishima*. Reacting quickly, the latter vessel's master put the battleship's own helm hard over, the two vessels passing within one hundred yards of one another. Barking orders, the carrier's captain brought his vessel to a slow stop even as signal flags were run up to inform the rest of the *Kido Butai* of the ship's predicament.

Akigumo, her captain beside himself from rage, charged down on the *Nautilus*'s position even as the spray from the torpedo strikes was still settling. The second-youngest tin can in the Imperial Japanese Navy, the destroyer was one of the best equipped vessels to deal with a submarine threat. Accelerating quickly, the vessel passed over the *Nautilus*'s position and, at the signal from her gunnery officer, began rolling depth charges from her stern. Nicknamed "ash cans" due to their shape, the weapons were set for a close pattern that was intended to shatter the American submarines' hull.

As the vessel continued on, the assistant gunnery officer at the stern watched the swell behind the *Akigumo* for explosions. Belatedly, the man realized that the depth charge crew had forgotten to arm the weapons for a shallow setting in order to catch the rapidly diving American submarine.

"Splashes, sir," the *Nautilus*' soundman said from his board. Nick, moving quickly, snatched the phones off the man's head.

"I think you'll want to be able to hear in the morning, Seaman Jenkins," he said in way of explanation. "That's probably going to be a little loud."

In reality, I don't need a blow by blow of my own death, Nick had time to think.

Click! Click! Click! Click!

The sound of the depth charge fuses arming was clearly audible to every man within the submarine. For a brief, frozen moment of time, the men in the control room all winced in anticipation.

BOOM! BOOM! BOOM! BOOM!

The *Nautilus* jumped violently both vertically and sideways. Nick watched the XO pitched off his feet, as a string of charges exploded seemingly all around them. In reality, the error in depth setting for the charges had been the worst thing that could have happened to *Nautilus*, the intended setting having been far too shallow. The world jumped violently, seemingly blurring with the violence of the submarine's motion. The roar was primordial, like some huge sea monster had the *Nautilus* in its jaws and was shaking it like a bone. Paint chips descended like snow from the bulkheads and ceiling, adding to the surreal effect.

Then just as suddenly as it had begun, the attack was over. Nick saw that the XO was having difficulty in picking himself back up and reached down to help him.

OVERHEAD, THE *AKIGUMO*'S ASSISTANT GUNNERY OFFICER WAS charging towards the petty officer in charge of fuze settings. Before the startled man could react, the angry lieutenant kicked him hard in the groin, then shoved the doubled over man overboard. Screaming at his crew, the man ensured the settings were corrected for the *Akigumo*'s second pass as the destroyer came back around. Astern, the mistaken petty officer burst to the surface, fighting to keep his head out of the water in the *Akigumo*'s wake. Five hundred yards behind him, the destroyer *Yugumo* began charging in on the *Nautilus*'s position.

"ANOTHER DESTROYER," CHIEF POUND OBSERVED, THE SOUND OF high speed screws audible in the hull.

Click! BOOM! *Click!* BOOM! *Click!* BOOM! *Click!* BOOM! *Click!* BOOM!

The second string of charges caused far more damage than the first one. The control room was suddenly plunged into darkness as every light bulb shattered. Nick felt himself tossed though the air, slamming into the plot table where he held on for dear life, the wind knocked out of him. Across the room in a shower of sparks and arcing electricity, the "Christmas Tree" indicator exploded. Dimly, Nick heard the sounds of several men screaming and water beginning to spray in the boat.

"Damage report!" Lt. Commander Freeman shouted, still holding onto the periscope. His voice instantaneously stopped the panic that was threatening to run rampant through the control room.

"Someone plug these damn leaks!" Chief Pound roared in the darkness. "Start acting like you're a submarine crew and not a bunch of schoolboys!" Instantly reacting to the voice of Chief Robert Pound, the crew jumped to their jobs.

"Sir, we've got no response from the rudder or the stern planes!" a voice stated tremulously.

"Flooding in the engine room!" came a cry from astern.

Well destroyer captain number two appears to know his shit, Nick thought angrily. His opinion seemed to be spot on as the damage reports continued to come in. The second string of depth charges had physically bent the submarine's hull just aft of the crew's mess. The *Nautilus*'s stern had similarly been bent, the port propeller shaft banging against the hull before the engineering crew had stopped it. In addition, the blasts had been so violent that multiple leaks had developed and were now rapidly flooding the stern of the boat, making the diving crew fight to keep her on an even keel.

"Lieutenant Cobb, what's the plot?" Lt. Commander Freeman asked, turning to look at Nick, who in turn looked at the sonar operator. Jenkins put the headphones back over his ears.

"Sir, the situation is too confused," Jenkins said. "I've got screws all over the place and the sound head sounds like it received damage."

"Understood. We'll stay down here for another hour, then we'll see where we stand," Freeman announced to the control room. Rubbing his arms, Nick could already feel the submarine starting to get chilly inside from the loss of power.

"Sir, I'm not sure if we can stay ahead of the flooding," Chief Pound stated quietly. "We may need to start the pumps here shortly."

"If we start the pumps, those Japs will be all over us," Freeman said.

"We'll take our chances for a little bit longer. Don't worry, she won't sink underneath us."

The *Yugumo*, captained by Commander Shigeo Semba, was the *Nautilus*'s second assailant and *Akigumo*'s sister ship. Signaling her companion, Semba inquired as to whether or not the destroyer had regained contact with the American submarine after their two depth charge runs. When the *Akigumo* responded in the negative, the *Yugumo* began pinging for the American vessel on her own. Between the two vessels, the body of the unfortunate petty officer floated, his insides crushed from the underwater explosions.

Aboard the *Akagi*, Yamaguchi watched the vessels astern through his glasses and quietly felt himself getting ready to explode.

"Why did we not detect the American submarine when we passed over it?" he asked his assembled staff. The men looked back at him impassively, none of them having a good answer to the question. There was a strained silence, broken by Admiral Kusaka.

"Sir, it is likely that the destroyers were focused on their plane guard duties," Kusaka replied, his face impassive and voice even.

I know what you're thinking, Yamaguchi thought, having the urge to assault the man.

"Sir, is it still your intention to launch a third strike?" Kusaka asked in that same flat voice.

Clenching his fists, Yamaguchi looked back astern at the two heavily damaged carriers. In moments, his aggressiveness and hubris had been terribly punished.

The most important part of gambling is knowing when to quit, he thought. Now, with *Zuikaku* clearly in danger of sinking, and *Shokaku* desperately trying to rig some sort of steering with her engines, most people would have agreed that it was far past time to leave. His nation had just begun a war with a nation more than ten times larger than it in population, resources, and industrial strength. While he had been willing to trade *Soryu* and *Hiryu* for success prior to the December '41 crisis, *Shokaku* and *Zuikaku* were a far different matter.

Every vessel we lose, every plane that is destroyed, and every pilot killed in effect gives the Americans double their number, he thought, recalling Admiral Yamamoto's final orders to him. *If the aviators are to be believed, I am looking at a great victory being converted to a narrow defeat.*

"Sir?" Rear Admiral Kusaka inquired, his voice somewhat less restrained. Yamaguchi turned to the man, meeting his eyes.

Damn you, I want nothing more than to tell you that we will indeed strike again, Yamaguchi thought. *But even more so with two flight decks out of order, we will barely be able to land the aircraft we have airborne unless the second strike took far heavier losses.*

"Order the *Tone*, *Akigumo*, and *Yugumo* to stand by the *Shokaku*. Order the *Abukuma* to assist the *Zuikaku*. If the *Zuikaku* does not regain power within two hours, she is to be scuttled and *Abukuma* will also aid the *Shokaku*."

Yamaguchi turned back to look over the rest of the *Kido Butai*.

"All other vessels are to come about and follow us. Move this vessel to our second Point Option. Inform *Tone* to signal all returning aircraft that approach of our new position. All carriers are to cease re-arming their aircraft for a third strike," Yamaguchi said stolidly.

Taking a deep breath, he looked over the staff. Many of the officers, Captain Genda among them, looked positively despondent.

"We have gained a great victory today, men," Yamaguchi said. "It is time to keep it from becoming a Pyrrhic one."

10
CULMINATIONS

A hero is no braver than an ordinary man, but he is brave five minutes longer

— **RALPH WALDO EMERSON**

U.S.S. Hornet
1115 Local (1615 Eastern)
26 March 1943

HORNET, much like a hive of her namesakes, was abuzz with activity. The news of the attack on the Battleline had reached the carrier a bare thirty minutes after the refueling had been complete. The task force commander, Rear Admiral Aubrey Fitch, had immediately directed anti-aircraft formation to be assumed and a full CAP to be scrambled.

"Still no report from the Battleline," Lieutenant Commander Couch observed in VB-8's ready room.

That's a bad sign, Eric Cobb thought from where he watched several of his squadron mates engaged in an intense acey deucey tournament. *Either Admiral Jensen is too busy or he's forgotten he's got a carrier floating around out here in the North Pacific.*

The sounds of aircraft being moved around the hangar deck were clear in the ready room. Eric felt as if his skin was crawling from nervousness as he attempted to remain impassive.

"Lieutenant Cobb," Lieutenant Commander Couch said from the front of the ready room. "A word, please."

What did I do now? Eric thought to himself. The two men stepped out onto the catwalk just outside the ready room.

"Admiral Fitch's staff fucked up and forgot that we may want to launch a search," Couch said with disgust. "I want you to lead it."

What? Eric thought, looking at his commander in shock.

"There's a method to my madness, Lieutenant," Couch replied. "Despite my protests, Commander Ring has stated none of the torpeckers will fly any of the sectors, and that I am to make sure I use experienced officers in conjunction with nuggets. Your name was specifically mentioned."

Of course it was, Eric thought. *Hornet*'s CAG had made it quite clear that he was not impressed with getting a high profile addition to his air group. The man had seemed further upset that Eric had studiously avoided screwing up.

"If you fly the first mission, odds are you'll dodge the anti-submarine patrols," Couch continued. "If you find something, I want you to concentrate on getting a contact report off, then hit the first flight deck you see."

"Who do you want me to have as my wingman, sir?" Eric asked.

"You'll take Read," Couch replied. "They're arming your birds on the flight deck as we speak. Rear Admiral Fitch was not impressed with the staff or Commander Ring, so you two need to hurry."

"Aye aye, sir," Eric said. Couch turned and went back into the ready room, with Eric right behind him.

"Ensign Read, we've been asked to go on a date with some geishas," Eric said nonchalantly. "Hopefully we get stood up, but grab our gunners and let's go."

Read, a fresh-faced teenager from Missouri, looked up at Eric as if the latter had just suggested they go get a full back tattoo of President Roosevelt's face put on. While not the most inexperienced man in the squadron, that was only because he had precisely one more hour than the most inexperienced man, Ensign Kelly. Tall and dark-haired, Read's voice had a slight accent that betrayed his Missouri boot heel roots.

"Aye aye, sir," Read replied.

FIVE MINUTES LATER, BOTH MEN STOOD ON THE *HORNET*'S FLIGHT deck. Eric watched as the flight crew finished climbing all over the aircraft, the wooden surface beneath him vibrating with the sensation of engines being run up for final checks. As their gunners walked past them, Read started to walk. Snaking his hand out, Eric grabbed the young ensign's Mae West.

"Easy killer, not yet," Eric said. "Just because there are Japs about doesn't mean we change our routine. Pilots go on last."

Read looked sheepish for a moment, but nodded. Eric looked back out at the aircraft to see his tail gunner, Radioman First Class Willie Brown, doing a visual check of his twin machine guns. Brown was a Pacific Fleet regular, having last been aboard the U.S.S. *Enterprise* before *Hornet*. Rumor had it that Brown's critique of one of Air Group Six's senior dive bomber pilots was the reason he had been "shuffled" to the Pacific Fleet enlisted replacement pool. The man in question had allegedly put his *Dauntless*, quieter gunner, and himself into the water off Bremerton not three days later making the same mistake Brown had warned him about.

I wonder if it's true that he said he "wasn't very sorry for the officer, but sure did feel bad for that gunner's wife?" Eric thought. *Or "painting rocks beats feeding fishes?"*

Shaking his head, Eric saw that it was time for Read and him to get to their planes. Checking that he had all the necessary maps and codes one last time, Eric strode out to the *Dauntless*.

"I hope you don't have to use those, Brown," Eric said, climbing up on the wing after doing a quick walkaround and checking the 500-lb. bomb slung underneath the SBD's belly.

Brown gave him an appraising look.

"Sir, I get the feeling I won't have to work as hard to keep you alive as my last pilot," Brown replied with a smile.

"Well I'll do my damndest not to give you free swimming lessons," Eric said. "My last gunner said the water was a bit cold."

Brown gave him a respectful nod as the airplane crew chuckled. Eric found himself glad that he had an older, steadier hand with him this mission. Working quickly, two men from the squadron's ground crew helped him strap in. Making sure the straps were tight, Eric took the clipboard from the plane's crew chief and signed for the aircraft.

I wish I had Rawles, but I don't blame the man for taking Secretary Knox's offer, Eric thought. *Unfortunately some of us really didn't have that option.*

"Good luck, sir," the man said, taking the clipboard back.

Is good luck finding the enemy or not? Eric thought, nodding his thanks.

The launch of the sixteen *Dauntless*es that comprised *Hornet*'s search was part ballet, part circus act. As a plane was prepared to launch, it was placed under the control of a plane director. This sailor, usually a petty officer signaled directions to the pilot, who did not have a clear view forward due to the plane resting back on its wheels and the length of the nose. This plane director, once he got the aircraft to a certain point on the flight deck, handed it off to another of his compatriots and went back to directing aircraft from the congested area on the vessel's stern. The second plane director, once he had the pilot's attention, checked to make sure the flaps and other control surfaces were in proper position for takeoff, then guided the aircraft forward to its launch position. Once present, the pilot made eye contact with the launch officer, who gave him the signal to conduct the final checks of the aircraft, most importantly his engine. Once these were complete, the pilot gave the launch officer the signal he was ready. With that, and giving the aircraft one more once over, the flight officer waved his checkered flag, directing the pilot to immediately launch.

Sitting and hoping that the airplane doesn't have something go wrong with it is the hardest part of all this, Eric thought grimly. *I'm pretty sure getting chummed by my own carrier will make for a rather tragic end.*

Eighth in line, Eric did not have long to wait before he was being signaled forward to take his spot in preparation for takeoff. As the seventh *Dauntless* waddled its way into the sky, Eric pulled up to where the launch officer was waiting for his aircraft. Following the man's signals, Eric checked all of his control surfaces then advanced the throttle. Satisfied everything was working, he gave the launch officer his thumbs up. Without further ado, the officer waved his checkered flag towards the end of the flight deck.

As Eric lifted his foot off the brakes, the *Dauntless* seemed to leap forward. As with every launch so far that day, his went without a hitch. Pulling back gently on the stick after retracting his gear, he began a turn to starboard and started to climb. Once he reached ten thousand feet, he kept his aircraft level and waited for Read to catch up with him. Five minutes after his wheels had left the *Hornet*'s deck, Eric collected his wingman and turned to begin the search into their sector.

"This oughta be a quiet flight," he muttered to himself.

"Beats the alternative, sir," Brown replied, continuing to scan the skies around their aircraft.

"True," Eric replied. "I think I've had enough excitement for this war already."

U.S.S. YORKTOWN
1125 LOCAL (1625 EASTERN)

BOTH SAM AND DAVID FELT VERY, VERY WEAK IN THE KNEES AS THEY stood aboard *Yorktown*'s wooden deck. Partially the weakness was delayed shock from having just taken part in the destruction of four aircraft while being shot at themselves. Mostly, however, it was looking at the vessels gathered around the *Yorktown* and realizing they comprised the majority of what had once been the United States Pacific Fleet. The smoke from *Lexington* and *Saratoga*, the latter having just succumbed to her terrible wounds, was still visible on the northern horizon.

I can't believe how bad this has been, Sam thought, his stomach queasy. *Depending on how many fighters made it back to Oahu, the fighter squadrons suffered something like thirty percent losses.*

Yorktown, her protective cloak of escorts gathered around her, continued to steam to the south at twenty-five knots, having accelerated after it was clear the sixteen fighters aboard were all that she was going to recover at the present time. The carrier had recovered five more *Wildcats*, but the wrecks had quickly been shoved over the side. While twenty more *Wildcats*, VMF-14's among them, were inbound and another eight were overhead, it was pretty clear that the day had not been a good one for the USN's fighter pilots.

"Did you ever hear any word about Peter?" David asked somberly.

"Plane boss said that a Lieutenant Byrnes took off in one of their spare fighters when the the second wave was inbound," Sam replied. "Said he gave some deckhand a $20 bill and didn't expect to come back."

David swallowed heavily and looked away for a second.

"What happens now, you think?" David asked once he'd regained his composure, watching the smoke from the burning *Saratoga* recede on the horizon. "Do you think those bastards are going to invade?"

Sam thought for a moment, chewing on his bottom lip.

"No, they won't. This is a raid," Sam stated unequivocally. "There's still too much of our Navy left, not to mention soldiers on the islands, to make seizing Hawaii worthwhile."

"How can you be so sure?" David asked, his tone clear that he was wanting Sam to explain rather than challenging his twin.

"The Japs did this same thing right before the war they fought with Russia at the start of the century, and for the same reason—if they'd had caught our fleet in harbor, they could've sunk the whole lot at the moorings," Sam said.

"Seems like they did a pretty good job of catching it at sea," David observed disgustedly.

"Not enough, though," Sam said. "We saw, what, five battlewagons still in one piece? Even if they shot up the Army boys like some of Admiral Fletcher's staff claimed, they've got to have fighters left, and plenty of those big bombers of theirs."

"For all the good they've done today," David replied bitterly.

"Just like we didn't know how bad things were out here, we don't know what the Army boys are up to north of here," Sam observed. "Either way, the Japanese couldn't have known they'd do this well, and you don't send a whole bunch of transports across the Pacific unless you're damn sure that you're going to win."

David looked at his brother, surprised at the calm conviction with which he spoke.

"So what happens now?" he asked, curious to see what else Sam was going to come up with.

"Now, if they're smart, they cut and run," Sam said. "This was a big raid, but it had to have cost them. It doesn't seem like they hit the Army bases at all, and while those guys can't find their asses with both hands and a map most of the time, today might be their lucky day." Sam paused for a second to take a long pull of the canteen some sailor had given him after landing.

"You ever seen a good poker player at work? You know, like Captain O'Shea in VMB-21?" Sam continued. "Ever wonder why he always seems to make lots of money? Because when he takes a big pot, he leaves right away. If that Jap admiral has a lick of sense, he'll do the same."

"All hands, all hands, incoming *friendly* aircraft. I say again, incoming *friendly* aircraft," the *Yorktown*'s loudspeaker uttered. "Any man who opens fire will be shot on orders of the captain."

Sam and David looked at each other, then began scanning the sky.

"Well I'm pretty sure Major Bowden will appreciate *that* story when he lands aboard," David observed wryly.

U.S.S. *NAUTILUS*
1235 LOCAL (1735 EASTERN)

ABOARD THE *NAUTILUS*, THE CONTROL ROOM RECEIVED THE FIRST good news of the day.

"We've just stopped the last leak," Lieutenant Banes reported as he returned from astern, his face weary. "However, I think the aft batteries compartment is starting to flood."

Nick paled at that news. While it was doubtful that the *Nautilus* would ever be repaired, at least it was appearing more likely that they wouldn't have to surface and fight it out with superior enemy forces. When contacted by seawater, submarine batteries underwent a chemical reaction whose usual byproduct was chlorine aerosol.

Who knew I'd join the submarine force and still end up possibly dying from being gassed? Nick thought.

"At least the bastards stopped depth-charging us," Freeman observed grimly.

Still don't know why or how that happened, Nick thought. The Japanese assaults, while not as accurate as their initial salvo, had still served to keep the crew from affecting proper repairs. Now, as the XO had noted, they were managing to actually gain on the intake of water into their vessel. The submarine had already taken on enough excess weight that keeping her level was difficult, which meant that some air might have to be pumped into the ballast tanks. While noisy, an almost guaranteed to reveal their position, it was far better than the other option of not being able to surface.

"Sir, we might be able to stay down here until nightfall," Chief Pound quietly muttered. "Provided those bastards don't lay into us again."

Lt. Commander Freeman looked up at the control room's ceiling, squinting as if he was trying to see through the intervening three hundred feet of water.

"I just hope that they have more problems up there than we do down here," Freeman noted. "Although I don't think we hurt either one of those carriers as badly as we should have, there's a chance they're still sitting up there and we'll have to fight their escorts."

"We're not going to be able to maneuver with the hull bent like it is," Chief Pound replied. "I'm not sure either one of the deck guns will work."

"I'm hoping that won't matter, Chief," Freeman said. "If it comes to deck guns versus our remaining fish, we're dead anyway. We can't win versus a tramp steamer right now, much less two destroyers."

Chief grunted his agreement. Nodding to the other officers, he headed back aft to oversee the damage control efforts of the crew.

W<small>HETHER THROUGH DUMB LUCK OR FAST COURIER TO</small> N<small>EPTUNE</small>, Freeman's prayers were in the process of being partially answered. While she was still ablaze below, *Zuikaku*'s crew had managed to put out the flight deck fire. More importantly, the crew managed to gain power back to the starboard propeller shafts, allowing the vessel to creep forward at eight knots. With her rudder severely damaged and missing one shaft, the carrier wallowed into and out of turns, but she could still move forward, which meant she had gained a reprieve from being scuttled. As *Tone* drew alongside to aid her in firefighting, the *Zuikaku*'s executive officer began ordering the jettisoning of damaged aircraft over the flight deck's side. Those aircraft that had been saved from the earlier inferno remained gathered on the stern, the hangar deck too much of a shambles for them to be struck below at that time.

Aboard the *Shokaku*, conditions were far better. Gradually building steam and power, *Shokaku*'s engineer estimated that her top speed would be twenty knots while steering with her engines. This speed would allow her to get some lightly loaded *Zeroes* off of her deck to establish a combat air patrol of the two crippled carriers. While it would be another fifteen to thirty minutes before the carrier would be able to carry out the launch operations, her situation was greatly improved from lying dead in the water without the ability to steer.

Having given up attacking the American submarine after losing contact, the *Akigumo* and *Yugumo* continued to circle warily, their crews very alert after the failure of the screen that morning. *Abukuma* continued to circle on the opposite side of the carriers, her lookouts also watchful for the tell-tale feather of an American submarine periscope. Not one eye looked skyward. Aboard the *Tone*, the heavy cruiser's radar set sat motionless as her captain attempted to maneuver alongside the damaged *Zuikaku*.

For only the second time that morning, someone in the Navy had gotten something right. The assignment of search sectors aboard the *Hornet*, more through dumb luck and the *Nautilus*'s intervention with a torpedo spread, had almost succeeded in its intent of putting the *Hornet*'s most experienced dive bomber pilots in sectors most likely to discover the Japanese fleet. Given the large combat air patrol that Admiral Yamaguchi belatedly directed over the *Kido Butai*'s four undamaged carriers, it was a sign of Fortune's shifting allegiances that the two *Hornet* dive bombers found the crippled *Zuikaku* and *Shokaku*. In the lead SBD Lieutenant Aaron Carson, USNA '32, had sighted the burning column of smoke from *Zuikaku* from forty miles away. Closing through scattered clouds, Carson had made sure of the position, then signaled his wingman, Lieutenant (j.g.) Vincent Larson, to climb higher with hand and arm signals. Now, circling wide to the north to avoid having the carrier's smoke blown into their path and also take advantage of scattered clouds starting to move into the area, Carson was satisfied he'd done his best to assure their success. The two dive bombers had maintained radio silence during their long, tense climb, neither pilot wanting to give any warning of their approach.

"Nuckowski, start transmitting," Carson barked into his oxygen mask as they entered the scattered clouds. Far below them and about three miles to their front, he counted the Japanese vessels once more. "Two carriers, with escorts, the last position I gave you right before we started circling."

"Roger sir," ARM$_2$ Nuckowski replied, and immediately began hammering out a contact report in Morse code. Across from them, Lt. (j.g.) Larson's gunner began following suit. The process took only a few moments, after which both gunners unshipped their twin .30-caliber machine guns and stood ready to repel any fighters. Exactly as Carson had planned it, the two dive bombers began their dive upsun from the burning *Zuikaku*. As he began to build up speed, Carson pressed his eye against the telescopic sight piercing the front of his windshield. Looking through it, the *Zuikaku* immediately became larger, the singed red ball at the forward part of her flight deck providing a convenient aim point. Extending his dive brakes, Carson settled down into his dive and listened as Nuckowski began calling off the readings from the altimeter.

As Carson passed eight thousand feet, lookouts aboard the *Abukuma* finally spotted the two dive bombers. By then, it was far, far too late for anyone to prevent the attack. The few desultory rounds that were fired by the light cruiser and the *Zuikaku* herself did not even register with either pilot before they released. On a stationary, basically undefended target attacked by two experienced dive-bomber pilots, the results were almost foregone. Carson's weapon missed his point of aim by a mere ten feet, slamming through the planking weakened by the earlier flight deck fire and into the hangar deck. The weapon landed amongst the damage repair parties attempting to put out the last of the hangar deck fires started by *Nautilus*'s torpedoes, killing over half their number. Larson's aim was thrown off by his reacting to the explosion of Carson's bomb. As a result, the weapon carried towards the carrier's stern and straight into the aircraft gathered there. While their tanks had never been refilled after the first strike, there was more than enough fuel to ignite a strong blaze on the *Zuikaku*'s flight deck.

Both SBDs pulled out of their dives, Carson and Larson retracting their dive brakes. Carson, having noted the *Akigumo* astern of their target, had started an immediate turn to port during his dive. This added just enough deflection that the startled destroyer's gunners missed him during egress. Unfortunately Larson, his blood pumping from the exhilaration of scoring a hit, decided to take on the *Akigumo* with his twin fixed guns on his way out. It was a decision as foolhardy as it was brave. While the two streams of .50-caliber bullets killed the destroyer's captain and helmsman, the zero deflection shot Larson provided made it all too easy for the destroyer's 25mm gunners to knock out the SBD's engine. Realizing he was now an impromptu glider pilot, Larson managed to keep the dive bomber level and slammed into the ocean a half mile from the destroyer. Moving like greased lightning, he and his gunner scrambled into their life raft. Ten minutes later, they became the Imperial Japanese Navy's first American prisoners of war, as the just strafed *Akigumo* picked both men up. Five minutes of *Bushido*-fueled hospitality and a decapitation later, *Hornet*'s general direction and proximity were conveyed to an alarmed Vice Admiral Tamaguchi.

AKAGI
1245 LOCAL (1655 EASTERN)

"WHERE IS THE *HORNET*?" YAMAGUCHI ASKED.

"The surviving American aviator is still being interrogated. He is steadfastly refusing to reveal the *Hornet*'s location despite the *Akigumo*'s best efforts," Kusaka paused, seeing his commander's mind racing.

*Is **Hornet** alone?* Yamaguchi thought to himself. If she was, he was being presented with another great opportunity. However, the refugees from *Shokaku* and *Zuikaku* had reduced his number of operable flight decks to three, *Kaga* having taken on so many aircraft that she could strike no more below. Still, with three to one odds and the advantage of surprise, it would be well worth the risk.

*On the other hand, if **Enterprise** steams with her, the odds are much worse.*

"Sir, Rear Admiral Hara wants to know if you want to scuttle the *Zuikaku*?" Kusaka asked.

Yamaguchi nearly nodded in the affirmative, then stopped himself.

"No. Order the *Akigumo* to remain near the *Zuikaku*. The *Shokaku* is to begin proceeding for the Home Islands with the remainder of the group. If the *Zuikaku* puts out her fires and recovers power by nightfall, she is to proceed under the escort of the *Akigumo*. If she does not, the *Akigumo* is to scuttle her and rejoin the group with the *Shokaku*."

From the dumbstruck expression on Kusaka's face, Yamaguchi could see that he did not grasp the reason for his orders. Looking at the rest of the staff, he saw that a few bright lights, most notably Commander Fuchida and Captain Genda, understood the reasoning with crystal clarity.

I will have to replace several members of this staff once we return to Japan. They do not think well on their feet, Yamaguchi thought. *In this kind of warfare that is incredibly dangerous.*

"*Hornet* will surely launch her strike at the last reported location for the *Zuikaku*. The smoke from the *Zuikaku* will draw the enemy aircraft like moths to a flame," Yamaguchi explained patiently. He could see more members of the staff starting to catch on.

"If the strike is launched at maximum range, the enemy will not have time to search for the *Shokaku*. If it is not, they will still have to split their force to make sure the *Zuikaku* sinks while continuing to search for the *Shokaku*, Yamguchi continued to explain. "This reduced force will give the *Shokaku*'s fighters a better chance at defending their vessel."

"But what if the fighters are not successful?" Kusaka asked. "Will we not have sacrificed both carriers for nothing?"

"Do you truly believe the *Shokaku*, in her damaged state, will be able to outrun the *Hornet*, nevermind the strike group?" Yamaguchi asked, his tone annoyed. "If they are successful, we will have risked nothing more than what is already on the board. If they are unsuccessful, the *Shokaku* may still survive the damage and make it home. In either circumstance, we will have a chance to sink the *Hornet*."

*Of course, if there are two carriers, then the **Shokaku** is definitely doomed,* Rear Admiral Yamaguchi thought. *I need more information!*

"It does not say if *Tone* has launched her own reconnaissance aircraft in an effort to find the *Hornet*," Yamaguchi said. "If she has not done so, direct her to do so immediately."

The staff hurried to do Yamaguchi's bidding. Signal flags quickly fluttered into the air, directing the *Kido Butai* to come around to an easterly heading. In the hangar decks of the three operational carriers, men began the backbreaking operations required to launch another strike.

U.S.S. HORNET
1330 LOCAL (1830 EASTERN)

THE *HORNET*'S FLIGHT DECK WAS A CLOSELY ORCHESTRATED CHAOS AS she began to launch her Sunday punch. Circling above the carrier, Eric took a moment to wipe his brow. With plenty of fuel in his tanks and it being quite obvious that he was not going to be flying on this strike, it was time to sit back and wait for the carrier's deck to become clear.

Not sure it was the brightest idea to immediately recall all scouts that had not made contact, Eric thought. *But his logic was sound.* Rear Admiral Fitch, listening to his staff, had determined the best course of action was to launch the strongest strike possible at Carson's contact. That had necessitated assuming some risk in the form of landing the anti-submarine patrol to add to the *Hornet*'s punch. Fitch had then directed that the returning scouts would be landed, immediately refueled, and launched to replace the anti-submarine aircraft. Confronted with two carriers, it was Fitch's intent to bag both.

Shouldn't someone be asking why one of those carriers was ablaze when Carson found them? Eric mused. Brown had decoded Carson's repeated contact and action report, as well as the fact that his wingman had gone down.

Seems like scouts always get it, Eric thought grimly. *Maybe that's why the new air group reorganization just lumps all the SBDs into one squadron.* It had taken some getting used to at first, but Eric could now see the utility of just having every plane type in one unit.

Guess I'm going to miss out on that strike after all, he thought angrily, watching as *Hornet* came into the wind.

"Makes you wish we were going with them, doesn't it?" Brown asked from the backseat. Eric pondered his answer for a moment.

"Not in particular," he replied. "I'm not in a hurry to get my head blown off," Eric responded.

Brown laughed into the intercom.

"Don't let Commander Ring here you say that, sir," Brown said. "He's been chomping at the bit for this day his whole life it seems."

"I get a feeling this war is going to be long enough for plenty of people to get more chances at killing me," Eric observed. "I don't see any reason to give them extra."

"Sorta the way I look at it," Brown responded. "I don't doubt my own ability, or to tell the truth, yours."

Eric smiled at his gunner's blunt assessment.

Okay, most officers would not let that go, he thought briefly as Brown continued.

"Problem is, I'm sure there's some arrogant, competent yellow bastard who will be able to shoot just as well as I can," Brown said, his voice surprisingly jovial. "Problem is, he'll be on a ship with something besides these twin peashooters and that means Mrs. Brown is going to get a letter about her son while I'm finding out if my pastor was right about Hell."

"That's the last of the dive bombers," Eric noted, putting the aircraft into a turn. "Time for the torpedo bombers to hurry up or the *Wildcat* pilots will all be swimming home." The contact report, at one hundred seventy-five miles, was just barely within the F4Fs' combat radius. As a result, only six of the tubby fighters were accompanying the strike. A very small escort, it was the most that the Captain Mitscher was willing to risk.

"Hey, what's that over to starboard?" Brown asked. Eric turned his head from where the first *Avenger* was rolling down the *Hornet*'s flight deck. Bringing up his binoculars he focused on the distant speck. As it jumped into his vision, he realized in an instant it didn't look like anything the United States flew.

"Looks like we're not the only people who have seen our friend," Brown stated. "*Wildcat*s are going after him from seven o'clock."

Eric turned to look just in time to see the *Wildcat*s descending as they passed behind the *Dauntless*'s rear towards the enemy.

"Sucks to be that bastard," Eric said.

"Yeah, but who's he talked to already?" Brown replied.

THE COMBAT WAS QUICK AND ONE-SIDED. THE FIRST *WILDCAT* missed its target, thrown off by a sudden last second maneuver by the agile aircraft. The second *Wildcat*, however, did not miss. With a bright smear of reddish orange against the sky, the float plane was gone...but not before it had indeed made a contact report.

IJNS AKAGI
1405 LOCAL (1905 EASTERN)

YAMAGUCHI WATCHED THE LAST OF THE *KIDO BUTAI*'S STRIKE recede into the distance. The report for *Tone*'s scout had been quickly relayed to Commander Fuchida, the transmission being repeated four times so that Fuchida would not be required to respond and give away his strike's existence.

The *Kido Butai* had launched more than enough aircraft to finish one carrier. Thirty-six fighters, forty-five dive bombers, and twenty-one *Kates* had left the three operational flight decks on their way towards the *Hornet*. Ten of the remaining fighters currently orbited overhead in response to the *Tone* scout's final report that the *Hornet* was launching. Another nine fighters were currently winging their way towards the *Zuikaku* and *Shokaku*.

We lost so many aircraft on the second strike, Yamaguchi thought. When adding in those aircraft damaged beyond easy repair aboard the carriers, the current strike that had left the *Kido Butai*'s decks was a maximum effort. While the reports strongly indicated that both the *Lexington* and *Saratoga* were sinking, the destruction of an air group's worth of aircraft and their crews had been a stiff price to pay.

"Sir, *Tone* reports four-engined aircraft in sight," Rear Admiral Kusaka reported, handing him the note.

That is another unpleasant surprise! Yamaguchi thought.

"Inform the *Tone* that additional help is on the way and her priority is to defend the *Shokaku*," Yamaguchi barked.

THE SECOND MESSAGE WAS HARDLY NEEDED. INDEED, EVEN AS IT WAS received, the heavy cruiser was gaining headway from the *Zuikaku's* side, elevating her 8-inch guns to engage the big four-engined bombers with the IJN's special anti-aircraft. Warned by *Tone*'s now operating radar, the *Shokaku*'s eight aircraft CAP had reached the big Boeing's altitude. Awed by the B-17s' size, the eight *Zeroes* bore in on the lead section of bombers in an attempt to save their ship.

For their part, the B-17s were led by the commander of the 18th Bombardment Wing, Colonel Michael Dekeyzer. Launched on the Opana radar station's reciprocal bearing, the aircraft had been hastily armed with a mixture of whatever weapons were on hand, including everything from 500-lb. general purpose bombs to three aircraft which carried six 2,000-lb. experimental bombs intended for use against fortifications. That the eighteen B-17s were the only shore-based attack aircraft capable of reaching the carriers was a sad testimony on the Hawaiian Air Force's preparedness and equipment.

Forming up into a long column, the Japanese fighters began their assault on the six three-plane vics. To respond to this attack, each B-17 carried up to ten machine guns, with the majority pointing towards the rear quadrant. Not realizing the potent firepower they were about to face, the *Zeroes* began their approach from this direction, finding themselves barely able to overhaul the B-17s in their climbing turns. Through dumb luck the B-17 gunners all opened fire more or less simultaneously. The resultant volume of tracers startled the *Zeroes*, while the immense size of the Boeings threw off the pilots' range estimates. As a result, the *Shokaku*'s CAP only managed to damage the rearmost bomber, causing it to drift backward with two engines ablaze. In turn, the gunners turned one *Zero* into a flaming comet and severely damaged two more.

The five surviving *Zeroes* quickly reassessed their course of action. Two of them, having watched their second *chutai* leader of the day be immolated, turned after the cripple. The remaining *chutai* grimly attempted to close with the remaining seventeen bombers once more, but were kept at a distance by the focused machine gun fire. Breaking off, the pilots decided to try one more pass, this time from ahead. Reaching maximum range, the two wingmen lobbed some rounds from their 20mm guns at the big Boeings then broke off lest they enter the storm of .50-caliber bullets again. The *chutai* leader, braver or more foolhardy than his wingmen, refused to break off. His fire cleared the flight deck of one B-17, but the *chutai* leader paid for his perfidy upon trying to pass through the bombers. Locked into a crossfire by several top turret gunners, the *Zero* amazingly did not burn as it cartwheeled downward with a thoroughly dead pilot.

The CAP was broken just as it was time for the anti-aircraft gunners to begin. Almost as one, the entire *ad hoc* task force began firing. The Boeing's high altitude saved them from the majority of the anti-aircraft fire, but two of the *Tone*'s 8-inch fragmentation shells burst directly below the leader of the last vic. In a bright flash and thunderous roar, the B-17 disappeared as hot steel. The bomber's remnants slammed back into its two wingmen, the B-17s staggering in the air but continuing on their runs. Fourteen thousand feet underneath the large bombers, the helmsman of every vessel that had steerageway began their evasive maneuvers. In the case of the *Shokaku*, a barked command from her captain brought her bow around into an unwieldy circle as the B-17s attacked by vics.

It was only as his own bomber was about to release that Colonel Dekeyzer realized he had failed to direct the actions of the sixteen remaining bombers. His vic was pointed directly at the stationary *Zuikaku*, the easiest target on the ocean below. With a muttered curse he reached for the radio as his own aircraft released its ordnance over the Japanese carrier. The colonel might as well saved his breath, as by the time he got the command transmitted every B-17 had released its bombload.

The crew of the *Zuikaku* could only watch and cower as over sixty bombs fell 12,000 feet down towards them. Some men instinctively attempted to run for cover as the weapons fell. Others, especially those few dive bomber and torpedo pilots who had had the misfortune to recover aboard before the *Nautilus*'s attack, threw themselves on the deck. Finally, desperately, some men dived overboard in the horrible moments that death floated down towards them.

Every single man who chose the last act died in the water, as the *Zuikaku* was missed by over fifty bombs. Three hundred feet below the carrier, the combined explosions of these near misses severely shook the *Nautilus*, leading several men to conclude the vessel was under depth charge attack once more. Simultaneous with the dozen or more of these weapons that were close enough to smash in her hull plating, knocked her turbines and boilers off of their mountings, and annihilate the crew that had jumped in the water, the *Zuikaku* received eight bomb hits in the space of twenty seconds.

The first five hits were 500-lb. general purpose or semi-armor piercing that served to complete the destruction of the *Zuikaku*'s wooden flight deck. As horrible as the physical destruction and human carnage wrought by these bombs were, they were relatively minor in light of the three hits interspersed within their impacts. Two of these hits were from 1,000lb. armor-piercing bombs, while the last was a 2,000-lb. anti-fortification weapon. All three found avgas storage or magazines as they cut through the carrier's hull. To those on the vessels around her and the aircraft above, it seemed as if a volcano erupted from the *Zuikaku*'s hull from amidst the forest of the near-misses' water columns.

Aboard the *Tone*, the commander of the Fifth Carrier Division, Rear Admiral Chuichi Hara, had had more than enough. After a quick exchange of signals with the *Shokaku*, the carrier and heavy cruiser turned towards the northwest and Japan, continuing at the *Shokaku*'s top speed of twenty knots. The captain of the *Akigumo*, looking back at the flotsam and debris that had once been one of the two best carriers in the Japanese Navy, inquired if she should pick up survivors. Hara's response was a short and direct negative. The answer, while seemingly inhumane, was the correct one in the mind of the *Akigumo*'s captain. Smoke pouring from her stacks, the destroyer began accelerating from the spreading circle of burning oil, debris, and pitifully few shouting men that were all that remained of the once proud *Zuikaku*.

IJNS A<small>KAGI</small>
1435 L<small>OCAL</small> (1935 E<small>ASTERN</small>)

"S<small>IR, THE</small> Z<small>UIKAKU HAS BEEN SUNK BY</small> B<small>OEINGS</small>," RA<small>DM</small>. K<small>USAKA</small> said solemnly. "The *Tone* and her group are moving northeast at best speed."

Yamaguchi fought the urge to scream.

"Were there any survivors?" the *Kido Butai*'s commander asked once he trusted his voice again.

"Rear Admiral Hara did not feel the limited number of survivors justified the risk of additional vessels," Kusaka replied.

Yamaguchi thought for a moment, then nodded. RAdm. Hara was at the scene, which meant that he had obviously seen something that had prompted him to believe there were few, if any, men to pull out of the Pacific. While such a decision might seem coldhearted to a sentimentalist, in the hard arithmetic of naval warfare, the lives of under a hundred men did not justify risking those of thousands. Especially when those thousands were aboard one of the six, no *five* fleet carriers in the IJN.

"Any sighting of the American carrier's strike?" Yamaguchi asked.

"No, not yet, sir," Kusaka returned.

Yamaguchi looked at his watch and did the mental calculations in his mind. If the *Hornet* had received a report from her two dive bombers, she should have launched immediately. It was what he would have done. Motioning for Kusaka and Captain Kaku to join him, Yamaguchi moved towards the map of their area.

Even without the Zuikaku as bait, it is unlikely that the Americans would have enough aircraft to strike at us, Yamaguchi thought. *I have done all I can, it is in the pilots' hands now.*

U.S.S. NAUTILUS
1500 CENTRAL (2000 EASTERN)

"CHIEF, TIME TO TAKE HER UP," LT. COMMANDER FREEMAN SAID, his voice hoarse from the bad air.

Nautilus's fight for survival had been almost won when the B-17s had dropped their bombs on the *Zuikaku*. The numerous detonations had shaken loose some of the shoring that the crew had managed to plug leaks in the submarine's hull with. Unfortunately, one of these leaks had begun to empty into the aft battery room, with the expected results for the air supply.

Here's to hoping Lt. Commander Freeman was right about there being nothing over our heads, Nick thought worriedly. Coupled with the sounds of *Zuikaku*'s demise, the high-speed screws exiting the area were indicative *something* had gone wrong aboard one of their targets.

Too bad it appears we didn't get the other bastard, Nick thought angrily. *Still, as fast as those screws moved off, something spooked those enemy ships bad enough we became an afterthought.*

"I couldn't agree more, sir," Chief Pound responded as the control room crew immediately began preparing to surface.

"Blow negative," Lt. Commander Freeman ordered. "Ten degrees up angle."

"Ten degrees up angle, aye aye," the planesman responded, making the necessary adjustments.

Lt. Commander Freeman was turning to give another order when the submarine suddenly lurched then twisted sideways, listing ten degrees to starboard. Loose items and unwary crew went with the roll, slamming into metal bulkheads.

"What in the hell?!" Jason asked.

"Sir, it would appear that we have damaged dive planes," Chief responded laconically. Despite the tilt, the submarine continued to rise. Always a slow vessel to surface, with the extra water aboard *Nautilus* did not set any speed records on this occasion. Four long minutes after giving the order, Lt. Commander Freeman was finally able to lead the way out of the conning tower.

Holy shit, Nick thought, the odor of burning fuel the first thing that hit his nostrils as he followed Lt. Commander Freeman up into the air. Gagging, he managed to take in a breath. Once he had control of his breathing, he felt his stomach drop out at horrible scene before him. An oil slick at least a quarter mile in radius lay to *Nautilus*'s starboard, portions of it still afire. Intermingled amongst the oil was the sundry parts and instruments that made up a man of war. Most horribly, however, was what remained of *Zuikaku*'s complement. Not fifty yards away and upwind of the submarine, shapes that were clearly recognizable as human burned in their lifejackets.

"Holy fuck," Ensign Workman said. With that, he turned and lost his stomach over the side of the conning tower. Nick grabbed the young officer's belt to keep him from leaning too far over.

"Raft astern!" one of the lookouts croaked out, then lost his lunch over the side as well. Nick turned from where he had a hold of Workman's belt. Approximately one hundred yards behind the *Nautilus*, a flat piece of wood roughly ten feet by eight feet floated in the muck. Looking closer, Nick could see six men sharing the piece of debris. Covered in oil, the men looked strangely pathetic; their white eyes showing out like those of an actor wearing blackface.

"Sorry about that, sir," Workman gasped. "The smell got to me."

Lt. Commander Freeman looked at the young officer.

"Ensign Workman, the only reason I didn't lose it is that I'm the captain," Freeman replied. Walking to the voice tube, he swallowed heavily once more.

"We have potential prisoners topside. Have a party form on the stern," *Nautilus*'s captain gasped out.

"Aircraft to starboard!" a lookout shouted.

"Shit!" Nick muttered as he turned to look towards starboard. Seeing the group of forty aircraft approaching from the northeast, Nick realized that they were all dead.

"Get those damn machine guns up here!" Lt. Commander Freeman shouted down the hatch.

No way we'll get armed in time, Nick thought. *No fucking way. God help us if this was their carrier that just blew up.* As he studied the approaching forms, Nick suddenly felt the weight of the world slip from his shoulders.

"They're friendly!" he shouted, recognizing the squat shape of the *Dauntlesses* and *Wildcats*.

"Break out the flag," Jason ordered, wiping his mouth. "Let's make sure the recognition is mutual."

The order was quickly relayed below. A few moments later the Stars and Stripes were handed up the conning tower. One of the lookouts quickly shimmied up one of the broken periscopes and attached the flag.

The submarine had obviously been sighted by the group of aircraft, as two of them broke off and began to approach. The rest of the group began a gentle circle at long range, the formation stepped up into the sun. Nick studied the approaching aircraft carefully, trying to figure out what ship they were from.

"I *really* don't like the way those two are approaching," Workman muttered. The two aircraft had descended to roughly five hundred feet three miles away and were now turning towards the submarine in line abreast.

"Steady gentlemen," Lt. Commander Freeman warned, seeing the two sailors tensing at their machine guns. "If there's going to be friendly fire, we're not going to start it."

The two aircraft were accelerating and descending in what was definitely starting to resemble a strafing run. Nick could hear the sound of the racing engines as the two bombers started to gain speed. Feeling the urge to dive behind cover, he looked over at Lt.

Commander Freeman.

"Come on you guys, tell me you're not going to be stupid," the *Nautilus*'s captain said resignedly, his hands clasped behind his back.

It was over in moments. Screaming low towards the *Nautilus*, the *Avengers* began pulling up one hundred yards short of the submarine. A small black object flew from the rear cockpit of each bomber, one overshooting the submarine, the other landing on her forward deck. Nick and the two crewmen ducked as the bombers hurtled over, waggling their wings as they pulled up to rejoin their fellows. Freeman didn't even flinch, looking at the small message bag lying next to the ruin that was the forward deck gun. After the bag was retrieved and brought to him, Lt. Commander Freeman quickly barked for a signal lamp and handed the message to Nick. The younger officer looked down at the message.

GLAD TO SEE THE SILENT SERVICE ADMIRING ITS HANDIWORK. SIGHTING REPORT STATED THERE WERE TWO CARRIERS AND OTHER VESSELS. ASSUME YOU HAVE SUNK ONE, LOOKING FOR OTHER.—COMMANDER RING, CHAG.

"It would appear that our yellow friends are about to meet their opposite numbers," Jason remarked with a grin. Turning to the sailor who had just brought up a portable signaling lamp, he began composing his message. Nodding, the sailor quickly sent the *Nautilus*'s reply:

APPARENTLY CARRIER ALLERGIC TO FISH. SISTER SHIP, SHOKAKU CLASS, LAST HEARD HEADING WEST ABOUT THIRTY MINUTES AGO. BELIEVE SHE MAY HAVE SAME ALLERGY. GOOD HUNTING—LCDR FREEMAN, CO U.S.S. NAUTILUS.

. . .

THE LEAD *AVENGER* WAGGLED ITS WINGS AFTER THE SECOND sending of the message. Climbing up towards its fellows, the big torpedo bomber led the way off to the northwest.

"I hope they get that bastard," Workman seethed. Freeman nodded as the bridge crew watched the two dive bombers fly off.

Is Eric up there? Nick wondered, his mouth suddenly dry. The thought of his brother flying off into danger scared him more than the past three hours had. The Japanese had already nearly killed him. He doubted that the Cobb family luck would hold up through another serious test.

"Swimmers, port bow!" one of the lookouts shouted. All hands turned to look, seeing the men that the lookout was speaking of. There was a group of about twenty, all of them linked together around a portion of *Zuikaku*'s flight deck.

"We'll aid them after we get that other group," Freeman barked, gesturing towards the first six survivors they had sighted. "Boarding party forward!"

The crew of the *Nautilus* sprung to carry out the orders of their commander. Motivated by the ancient law of the sea, Lt. Commander Freeman was preparing to help the survivors in any way that he could. In five minutes, Chief Pound had several men standing on the submarine's bow armed with pistols, a trio of Tommy guns, and a couple of boathooks. With a crisp order from Freeman, the *Nautilus* began moving forward toward the raft.

Seeing the submarine edging towards them, the six men began frantically kicking and beating the water, trying to drive their raft away from the vessel.

"Stupid bastards must think we're going to hurt them," Workman muttered.

"No, I don't think that's it at all," Freeman said quietly, his face growing hard. The *Nautilus*'s commander turned towards the sailor manning one of the anti-aircraft machine guns.

"Stand ready," Freeman ordered crisply.

Nick turned to look at his captain in horror, misunderstanding his order. As a result he missed one of the Japanese survivors, a pilot, pulling out his pistol. He did hear the shot, however, and turned just in time to see one of the sailors at the bow crumple with a bullet in his abdomen.

There may have been a more stupid action that the man could have performed, but what he had done was dumb enough. Lt. Commander Freeman never had a chance to give the order, every man with a weapon and clear line of fire unleashing on the survivors. For a full half minute the *Nautilus*'s deck was a cacophony of small arms fire as the six men were slaughtered.

"Cease fire! Cease fire!" Chief Pound shouted, finally reaching over and striking one of the Tommy gunners before he the man could finish reloading. The sailor jumped in surprise, dropping the drum magazine over the side with a curse.

Nick looked at the chewed and torn remnants of the wooden flight deck, watching as one of the men who had been actually aboard the wood slipped down into the water leaving a stream of blood. Suddenly, uncontrollably, he felt his breakfast coming up. Leaning over the edge of the conning tower, he was violently sick. Embarrassed, he wiped the back of his mouth as he stood back erect. Looking back towards the bow, Nick saw Chief Pound replicating his action, the grizzled old sailor wiping his mouth with the back of his hand.

"Sir, the other one!" one of the anti-aircraft gunners shouted, shortly before a bullet whined off the conning tower. The horrific scene was repeated with the larger raft, and a stunned silence hung over the *Nautilus* as the last Japanese sailor slipped beneath the waves.

"What in the Hell is the matter with these people?" Ensign Workman asked plaintively.

"Death before dishonor," Nick replied. All the men on the bridge turned towards him.

"What did you say, Lieutenant Cobb?" Freeman asked.

"Sir, the Japanese believe in death before dishonor," Nick explained. "They call it *Bushido*."

"Bullshit is more what it seems like, sir," Workman said angrily.

"Either way, we're getting out of this debris field. All head slow," Lt. Commander Freeman said. With a horrible groan and shudder, the *Nautilus* began edging forward at a stately five knots.

U.S.S. Hornet
1510 Local (1835 Eastern)

"GODDAMNIT!" Eric shouted, punching instrument panel as the *Dauntless's* engine refused to turn over for the third time.

"Sir, we've got to put her aside and pump out the fuel tanks!" the plane handler standing on his wing said.

Eric could not believe it. The Wright Cyclone had been running like a dream when he'd set down on the deck. Now the bitch was refusing to start despite the best efforts of himself and the plane chief. With the third failed attempt, the air officer had decreed that the aircraft was a "strike," and would have to be sent below in order to clear the flight deck for other aircraft. The plane's tanks would be pumped clear of fuel to avoid it becoming a torch should the *Hornet* be attacked.

Eric fought the urge to let loose with even more curse words. In almost three years of flying he had *never* had an aircraft crap out on him. Now, on the first day of the war, on something as mundane as *anti-submarine* patrol, his freakin' engine had apparently packed up for the day. Nodding at the crew chief's words, he quickly unstrapped himself and began getting out of the dive bomber.

For a split second he looked to his right at Ensign Read's aircraft, now being moved forward to spot. It would be completely within his bounds if he bumped Read out of the plane. Fighting the temptation, he shook his head against the plan.

Read needs some more flight hours, Eric thought charitably. *It's going to be a long war.* Walking towards the *Dauntless*, he noted Read was studiously avoiding turning back to meet his gaze.

Doesn't mean I can't mess with him some, Eric thought with an mischievous smile. As Eric walked towards the *Dauntless,* he saw Read take a quick glance into the rearview mirror then quickly look down at his instruments. Read's gunner, on the other hand, began resignedly unstrapping himself from the aircraft. Eric quickly waved him back down into his seat. Running the last few feet, he jumped up on the dive bomber's wing and tapped Read on the shoulder. The ensign turned around, his face impassive as he started to unbuckle. Eric placed his left hand on the man's shoulder then extended his right.

"Good luck, Read," Eric shouted. "Make sure it's enemy before you drop a bomb on it...my brother's a submariner."

Read looked up at him in surprise, then smiled as he realized what Eric was saying.

"Yes, sir!" he replied, shaking Eric's hand. Eric hopped back off of the dive bomber's wing and headed for the island, getting ready to head back to VB-8's ready room. Brown was waiting for him at the doorway, his chute already off his back.

"Didn't you think I was going to take the plane from him?" Eric asked, raising an eyebrow.

"No, sir, actually I didn't. He needs the practice," Brown replied.

Eric's reply was cut off by the intercom suddenly blaring General Quarters. The two men looked at each other, then up towards the sky. Far above the carrier they could see a division of four fighters streaking off towards the southwest, gaining altitude. Behind them, Read's *Dauntless* began its takeoff run, hurtling down the deck and into the sky. Even before it was airborne, the plane handlers were maneuvering two more *Wildcats* into position for a hurried launch.

Looking around at the vessels on the screen starting to open the distance and begin elevating their guns, both men felt terribly exposed.

"Well, it would probably be a good idea to get the hell off the deck," Eric muttered.

The *Hornet* had been outfitted with the latest air search radar prior to her departure for the Pacific. As a result, her fighters had ten minutes more to gain altitude than their comrades flying from the *Yorktown, Lexington,* and *Saratoga* that morning. While hardly a tremendous boon for the *Wildcats*, it was enough to give them a three thousand foot altitude advantage as they began engaging their opposite Japanese numbers. *Hornet*'s fighter direction officer (FDO), Lieutenant Al Fleming, had been able to talk with some of his British counterparts during his training. One of the men had been a pilot in the First Battle of Britain and a direction officer in the Second. The one lesson that the man had imparted to Fleming was the absolute criticality of fighters being able to attack *en masse*.

As a result, Fleming took a portion of the extra ten minutes gained by the *Hornet*'s radar to gather all but four of those fighters currently airborne on Combat Air Patrol. As the enemy strike passed a point forty miles from the *Hornet*'s deck, he released these fighters to attack the approaching formation. Unwittingly, the Japanese pilots played directly into Fleming's hands. The *Zero* and *Shiden* pilots, believing that the majority of their foes would be still climbing from the deck of their carrier, had just begun to accelerate forward and below their charges when the *Hornet*'s CAP began streaming down from ahead and above.

CURSING EVEN AS ANOTHER *CHUTAI* LEADER CALLED OUT HIS sighting of the incoming American fighters, Isoro pulled back hard on his stick. The stubby American fighters were already hurtling over his fighter as they dived, their sights fixed on the accompanying dive bombers. Even as the *Shiden*'s superior power meant that he and the *Akagi*'s fighter squadron reacted quicker than the *Zero*es, Isoro could tell there was no way they could stop the *Wildcats*' initial charge.

FOR THE SECOND TIME THAT DAY, THE DIVE BOMBERS SUFFERED THE unbridled onslaught of American fighters. In a ball of fire and flame *Akagi*'s squadron leader, Lt. Chihaya, was killed by the initial bursts of .50-caliber machine guns. His two wingmen joined him a moment later, as the entire initial rush concentrated on the front of the formation. Revenge was taken on one VF-8 *Wildcat*, the pilot collecting a tail gunner's bullet to the head through the top of his canopy.

ISORO WAS ALREADY SEEKING TARGETS AS HE FINISHED HIS HALF loop, the Grummans that had attacked the dive bombers circling around for another pass. Putting his fighter into a roll, Isoro cut inside a section's turn, bringing his nose around to try and gain lead. Realizing that Isoro was going to gain sufficient lead, the American attempted to reverse his course. It was a panicked maneuver, and it only made the *Wildcat*'s imminent destruction that much quicker. Missing with his first burst, Isoro corrected and watched the Grumman's port wing and tailplane fly off under the four cannons. Isoro immediately pulled up as soon as the enemy fighter was finished, relieved to see Watanabe finishing off his victim's wingman.

Turning back towards the dive bombers, Isoro was just in time to watch another four *Wildcats* attacking from the opposite side of the formation. In a beautiful display of deflection gunnery the lead *Wildcats* each claimed a dive bomber. Cursing in frustration, Isoro went at once for the leader.

That will be your last…

The only warning Isoro received that his *chutai* was itself under fire was Yoshida's *Shiden* exploding in a ball of flame. Rolling, Isoro and his sole remaining wingman avoided a similar fate as two *Wildcats* hurtled past them, diving for the Pacific below. Isoro put his nose down to follow after checking for any other enemy aircraft. Frustratingly, he found himself unable to close the range as the Americans dived through eight thousand feet back towards their carrier. As black puffs of smoke began to appear around him, Isoro cursed in frustration and pulled up.

I am not flying into anti-aircraft fire for two kills, he thought. Searching around him, he watched as the dive and torpedo bombers hurtled past, their formations showing obvious gaps as a result of the American bounce.

THE SIXTEEN FIGHTERS OF VF-8 HAD ACQUITTED THEMSELVES WELL while suffering heavy losses. In exchange for eight of their number, the *Wildcats* had destroyed five dive bombers and four fighters. On the debit side, however, was the fact that they had not managed to completely disrupt the *Kido Butai* strike. With over four times their number of Japanese fighters seeking to kill them, the *Wildcats* were all forced to disengage as Isoro's assailant had. The defensive CAP broken, the *Hornet*'s final defense was up to her screen.

Unlike the escorts from the morning's battles, the *Hornet*'s three cruisers and five destroyers had worked as a team for several months. With not a single vessel over one year of age, CV-8 was surrounded by the best anti-aircraft defenses the USN had to offer. Astern of the carrier, the anti-aircraft cruiser *San Diego* swung out her five-inch guns, while the light cruisers *Denver* and *Montpelier* shifted to the *Hornet*'s starboard side. The destroyers *Fletcher, Radford, Mervine, Quick*,and *Doyle* remained in their diamond formation, their guns also swinging out towards the approaching dive bombers.

The death of Lt. Chihaya was critical to the prosecution of the dive bombing attack. With Commander Fuchida coordinating the torpedo bombers, discipline broke down amongst the disorganized *chutai*. The predations of the screen's gunfire only exacerbated this problem, the two of the five dive bombers destroyed or severely damaged prior to pushover being *chutai* leaders. The tightly disciplined Japanese attack method, while devastating in its effects, did not endure the loss of key leaders very well. Whereas the *Kido Butai* had launched a tremendous hammer blow, the shaft guiding the hammerhead's fall began to splinter over the carrier.

Twenty bombers dived on the *Hornet* in one long undulating column. Seeing the bombers coming, Captain Mitscher ordered the carrier's helm far over into a tight port turn. Below the island, the gunners on the carrier's flight deck edge enjoyed the best aiming in the entire task group, each bomber coming down a seemingly straight line right at them. In the VB-8 ready room, Eric listened with a tight grip on his seat as the carrier's five inchers, 1.1-inch, then 20mm cannon all swelled to a growing crescendo. As the vessel heeled over ever more in her turn, Eric attempted to set a good example for the other two pilots in the room by continuing to read the western paperback someone had left from earlier.

Through a combination of pilot fatigue, *Hornet*'s evasiveness, and the dense anti-aircraft fire put up by her screening vessels, the first nine dive bombers missed. The following three bombers managed to place their bombs alongside the wildly maneuvering carrier, causing her plates to open and let in the Pacific. It would be the next two bombers that actually damaged the wildly turning carrier. Orphaned when his own carrier was damaged, a *Zuikaku chutai* leader kicked his rudder to follow the rapidly maneuvering *Hornet*, determined to get a hit. Pulling out barely four hundred feet above the Pacific, the Japanese lieutenant had just enough time to look in his rearview mirror before a 20mm shell decapitated him.

The dead man's 250-kg armor piercing bomb slammed through the *Hornet*'s elevator, the hangar deck, and finally exploded amongst the forward damage control party. In addition to causing twenty-five casualties in the confined space, the bomb destroyed several compartments' watertight integrity and started a fire. The carrier whipped with the blast, throwing standing men to their knees or to the deck.

Following the example of his leader, the next *Val* also released at barely one thousand feet, the pilot pulling back on the stick to clear the carrier. The man's bomb impacted the carrier seventy feet aft of his leader's, likewise punching down to the third deck and starting a serious fire amidships. Unlike his leader, the *Val* pilot managed to escape the attentions of the gunners as he attempted to recover his aircraft. The remaining six bombers all placed their bombs close aboard, staving in portions of the carrier's side and causing casualties amongst her anti-aircraft gunners. In exchange, the guns of the carrier and her escort would damage two more of the enemy aircraft and kill the rear gunner of a third as the dive bombers moved off.

The bombers that did not go after the *Hornet* had split their attentions amongst the cruisers. Mistaking the long, multi-turreted *Denver* for a battleship, seven of the *Suisei's* dived on the light cruiser. With most of her gunners contributing to the storm of fire above the *Hornet*, the light cruiser's defense was in the hands of her captain. It would not be enough, as four semi-armor piercing bombs found her. The first weapon shrugged aside the armor of her No.1 turret and continued on to explode in the handling room. Amidst the chaos of shells exploding in secondary explosions, a brave lieutenant managed to give the order to flood the magazines before being killed by fragments, thus saving the ship from a massive explosion. Even as the man was sacrificing himself, the cruiser's other hits halved her speed, destroyed her sick bay, and started a serious fire in her hangar.

The *Montpelier*'s gunners, less devoted to saving the *Hornet*, put up a storm of anti-aircraft fire that caused all but one of her assailants to miss, albeit several close enough aboard to cause leaks and kill crew topside. The last bomber, a *Val*, managed to knock out two of the cruiser's secondary turrets and necessitate the flooding of a magazine. With smoke streaming behind her, the light cruiser continued to keep up with the *Hornet* as the carrier steamed at full speed.

Anxious to get out of the fire being thrown up the by American task groups, several of the bombers attacked the destroyers among the outer screen. Fast, nimble targets, the five DDs all managed to evade the bombs hurled at them with expert ship handling. Unfortunately, while not nearly as permanent as hits were, these maneuvers had the effect of placing the destroyers out of position as the *Kates* closed the range.

The synchronization of attacks between the dive bombers and the torpedo bombers was not nearly as smooth as it had been that morning. Part of this was due to the *Hornet's* higher speed, while part was due to the efforts of the last fighters to launch from the *Hornet*. Three of these late *Wildcats* managed to launch an attack on Commander Fuchida's group as the twelve *Kates* were approaching their assault position. Doing no damage, the attack still served to disrupt the attackers' flow to their drop points. As a result, the U.S. gunners had two brief minutes to depress their guns, take aim, and begin firing at the *Kates*.

Fuchida's group had swung to the port of the *Hornet*, while a mixed bag of nine *Kates* led by Lieutenant Tomonaga approached from starboard. As the *Kates* hurtled for their drop point, the entire task force began concentrating their fire on them. Zipping in between the massive geysers of water from the *Denver* and *Montpelier*'s quick firing main battery, then pressing on through the storm of tracer fire reaching for them, the *Kates* unsuccessfully attempted to defy the law of averages. First one from Fuchida's group, then two more from Tomonaga's burst into flames, crashing just inside the destroyers of the outer screen.

The losses caused even the strong Japanese morale to crack. Several of the bombers released their loads early, adrenaline and fear once

JAMES YOUNG

more convincing several of the pilots that the that the *Denver* and *Montpelier* were battleships. In the case of the former, no one saw the torpedoes until it was far too late. One of the deadly missiles passed close astern, the wake being lost in the froth from the cruiser's own props. The second missile stopped half of those same props a few moments later, slamming into the *Denver*'s starboard engine room. The blast knocked many of the cruiser's crew to their knees or to the deck as it extinguished half of the black gang's lives. Feeling the vibrations and the drop in speed, the cruiser's captain immediately ordered "all stop" in order to avoid worsening the damage. The *Montpelier*, once more leading a charmed life, avoided all six of the tin fish headed for her.

Captain Mitscher, his cragged face calm even in the face of the terrible din, had quickly realized the greater danger came from port. Waiting until almost the last moment before the *Kate*s had to release, he calmly ordered the *Hornet*'s helm kept over to port in order to give Fuchida's eleven remaining *Kate*'s a narrower target. As the carrier finished what was the tightest circle she'd ever made, her crew watched as several tin fish headed for her side.

BELOW MITSCHER, IN THE READY ROOM, ERIC FOUND HIMSELF understanding the terrifying aspect of being aboard a ship under air attack. While there had been a short respite, the continued cacophony of gunfire told him that the *Hornet* was still under attack.

Torpedo bombers, he thought grimly. Looking at his companions, he calmly put the book down, slipped out of his seat, and lay flat on the deck. The two other men, in a scramble of chairs that was almost comical, quickly mirrored his actions.

FUCHIDA'S MEN WERE NOT TO BE DENIED. DROPPING THEIR ELEVEN weapons at almost suicidally close range, the *Kate*s broke away to the bow and stern of the *Hornet*. Another of their number was blotted from the sky by a 5-inch shell from the carrier as they withdrew, but it was too little too late. As they watched the wakes approach the port edge of the flight deck, both Mitscher and Fitch realized that they had done all they could. Grabbing onto something nearby, both men braced for impact as the first torpedo found the carrier's bow, exploding just forward of the avgas magazine. In a fluke of fate, the explosion failed to cause a massive secondary explosion or fire as water quickly rushed into the space the weapon opened. The second tin fish hit further aft, just behind the aft 5-inch magazine. The explosion snapped the two port shafts and opened the magazine and hull to the sea.

The *Hornet*'s crew did not even have time to react to the two explosions before two more torpedoes arrived from starboard. *Hornet*, the eighth carrier to be bought for the United States Navy, had been based on the *Yorktown*, the sixth carrier. While this had allowed the Navy to produce the vessel more rapidly than a new design, it also meant the USN had to accept the *Yorktowns'* shortcomings. Chief among these were the carriers' adjacent boiler and engine rooms. It was at either end of these compartments that both torpedoes hit with massive plumes of water that reached almost over the carrier's stack and island. The carrier's lights flashed once, then went dark as the vessel's power was knocked out. As the water from the torpedo plumes rained back onto the carrier's deck, her crew could feel the vessel starting to slow. It was a mixed blessing to have been hit by the equal number of torpedoes to port and starboard, as the vessel started to rapidly settle on an even keel instead of threatening to capsize.

The egress was only slightly less difficult for the *Kate*s than their ingress had been, as the *San Diego* was wholly undamaged. Several of the fleeing aircraft were damaged, but only one more fell to the guns of the American task force. With the remaining *Hornet* fighters either engaged or forced off by the circling escort, the strike group suffered no more losses as the aircraft began to form back up.

WATCHING FROM TWELVE MILES AWAY, ENSIGN READ FELT HIS heart in his throat. The *Hornet* was clearly seriously hurt, as was the *Denver*. The Japanese strike had been very effective, despite the anti-aircraft fire that continued to darken the sky above the task group.

"I counted at least three torpedo hits, sir," his gunner, A1RC Van Dort, intoned.

"There were four," Charles replied grimly. While he had only limited knowledge of torpedo bombing, it didn't take a genius to figure out four hits did not bode well for their ship. Even from their distance and in such a short time after the attack, the *Hornet* was noticeably lower in the water.

"The old girl doesn't look so good," Van Dort said quietly, giving voice to Charles' own fears.

Both men should have been paying closer attention to their immediate surroundings. While it was a very human tendency to be concerned about the ship that was their home, like most inclinations the concern was potentially fatal in a combat zone. In the end, that potential was only realized in one case. Van Dort had just enough time to register motion out of the corner of his eye before a burst of machine gun fire extinguished his life. Charles did not realize his aircraft was under attack before the tail end of the same burst as well as two cannon shells shattered the cockpit canopy, sent fragments into his left arm, and shards of the instrument panel into his chest and face.

The follow on burst struck with even greater violence, the dive bomber getting hit with six more cannon shells in addition to more machine gun fire. The *Dauntless*'s structural integrity was the only thing that kept Ensign Read alive. Hard hit, its engine out, the dive bomber literally fell out of the sky from ten thousand feet. Its assailant, a *Soryu* Zero, continued on to the rendezvous point, its pilot convinced that no aircraft could recover from that much damage.

Stunned and bleeding, Charles managed to regain enough of his senses to attempt pulling out at two thousand feet. His controls unresponsive, Charles was only able to bring the SBD's nose above the horizon and hit the Pacific with some degree of a glide rather than a plunge. Still, the impact was hard enough to throw Read against his shoulder straps, bounce his head off the bombsight, and hurl Van Dort's corpse halfway out of its seat. Dazed, Read had enough presence of mind to begin unstrapping himself and stand up.

"Van Dort!" he shouted, spitting out blood at the end of his call. When he heard no response, he turned around and nearly passed out from dizziness. Gripping the canopy's edge to steady himself, what he saw sprawled across the rear half of the canopy was barely recognizable as a human being, much less the young man whom had flown off the deck with him a few minutes before. While an adolescence full of hunting deer and other game in rural Missouri had made Charles intimately familiar with the effects bullets had on flesh, seeing these effects on a human left him in mental shock for a few moments.

The lurching of the dive bomber as it began to slide into the depths brought him out of it. Moving quickly and trying not to think about the carcass that had formerly been his gunner, Charles worked to free the *Dauntless*'s life raft from its berth in between the two cockpits. He was successful just as the aircraft's wings slipped under, knocking him into the water. Grasping the raft tightly, he watched as the Pacific swallowed the rest of the SBD in seconds, the tail disappearing with an audible gulping sound.

Reaching underneath the bundled raft, Charles found the D-ring connected to the automatic inflation device. Giving the ring a sharp pull, Charles was gratified when the CO_2 cartridge worked as planned. Suddenly exhausted, he barely managed to pull himself up and into the raft, gasping with pain. Lying on his back, looking up into the blue sky, he could see several Japanese aircraft circling high overhead and approximately ten miles to his south.

Just my luck, I get the anti-submarine sector that lay right across the course to their assembly point. Coughing, he spat out some blood into the raft. Looking at the red patch, he felt himself starting to drift into unconsciousness.

Hope that...doesn't make...sharks jump in the raft, Read thought stupidly, then passed out.

IJNS Shokaku
1510 Local (2010 Eastern)

Simultaneously with *Hornet*'s receipt of her wounds, Air Group Eight found themselves approaching the damaged *Shokaku*.

Nautilus had been slightly off in her direction guess. The captain of the *Shokaku*, wanting to shorten the distance between himself and Japan as much as possible, had come around to a very sharp northwest heading. Only the sharp eyes of one of the dive bomber pilots, coupled with the heavy smoke being produced by the fast running vessels allowed Commander Ring and his pilots to bring themselves into attack position, coming in from the carrier's port side.

Ring quickly ordered the *Wildcat*s to descend with the torpedo bombers, leaving the dive bombers to fend for themselves. It was a decision motivated based on Ring's estimation on which force was likely to do the most damage to the wounded Japanese carrier, especially given that she had already taken at least one hit from a submarine. Unfortunately it took away the *Wildcats*' biggest advantage over the *Zero*es that swarmed in like bees protecting their hive. In moments, the half dozen Grummans found themselves fighting for their own lives, leaving twelve more IJN fighters to continue their assault on the *Dauntless*es and *Avenger*s. With two of their number shot down, the remaining F4Fs dove away out of the battle.

The Japanese fighters' initial assault culled two *Avenger*s from the VT-8 in exchange for moderate damage to one fighter. Lieutenant Commander Waldron and Commander Ring closed up the formation as the Japanese pilots returned for their second run. Slashing from port, the *Shokaku*'s squadron leader flew into a stream of .50-caliber fire. With a dead man at its controls, the *Zero* slammed directly into Waldron's *Avenger*, both aircraft disappearing in a ball of fire. Doggedly, the VT-8 *Avenger*s continued to press on, the *Zero*es breaking away as the torpedo bombers reached the limit of anti-aircraft range from the *Shokaku* and her escorts.

Several miles above, the *Zero*es that had dispatched the *Wildcat*s joined their remaining fellows in attacking VB-8's dense formation. Like their American counterparts, the *Zero* pilots did not hesitate to attack into the face of superior numbers. Unlike the *Wildcats* over *Hornet*, the *Zero*es did not have self-sealing tanks or an altitude advantage. Whereas the tail gunners of the *Val*s and *Kate*s would have to get very lucky to inflict fatal damage on *Wildcat*s with their 7.7mm machine guns, each and every one of the fifty-two .30-caliber machine guns firing from the *Dauntless*es were capable of putting down a *Zero* with a tracer round to the fuel tanks. Even worse, in the case of one of Kaneko's wingmen, recovering anywhere in the front of the SBDs exposed the light fighters to twin .50-caliber machine guns. In exchange for killing Lieutenant Commander Couch and shooting down or crippling four more SBDs, the high cover *Zeroe*s lost three of their number.

The American attack, through sheer dumb luck, was close enough in timing to split the fire from *Shokaku*'s screen. Without an anti-aircraft cruiser or true fire control radar, the IJN's barrage relied primarily on range guesstimation. Although damaging several of the approaching bombers, the IJN's shooting was mainly pyrotechnically impressive versus actually effective. For the torpedo bombers, this was cold comfort, as the initial storm of anti-aircraft fire plus the final assault of the *Zeroe*s killed Commander Ring, his tail gunner managing to flame one last IJN fighter before the fighter torpedo bomber crashed into the Pacific.

Suddenly, a young ensign named George Gay found himself at the head of the VT-8 formation as they reached their drop point. Coolly, realizing that he was going to get only one chance, Gay maneuvered his throttles and stick to press in close to the massive Japanese carrier. Releasing his torpedo, Gay very quickly found himself hurtling by the *Shokaku*'s bow, his bow and belly gunners firing as their aircraft passed down the carrier's side. The remainder of VT-8 followed his example, dropping at insanely close range then strafing on their way out.

Far above, as Gay and his comrades were releasing their torpedoes, VB-8 was pushing over into their seventy-degree dives. Shaken by the death of their commander and Kaneko's suicidal ramming, their net jammed by the frantic calls of the dying torpedo bomber pilots, VB-8's attack was cursed by the squadron's relative inexperience. Of the twenty-one dive bombers that reached the pushover point, three were destroyed before they could release their ordnance. Of the eighteen remaining dive bombers, twelve dived for *Shokaku*, while the other six altered their dives to attack the *Tone*.

The heavy cruiser was limited in her evasive maneuvers by the need to stick by the damaged *Shokaku*'s side. Even so, the six dive bombers attacking her only managed one hit, a 1,000lb. bomb that hit her astern. Coming down almost vertically, the bomb smashed into the cruiser's hull and penetrated down to the aviation gasoline storage tank. For a brief, poignant moment, the men stationed on her stern looked at the round hole, their bodies clenched expecting the inevitable blast and secondary explosion. When neither followed, there was a moment of disbelief, followed by relief, then as senior NCOs and officers administered on the spot physical admonishment, a rapid return to their grim determination in repulsing the attack.

Aboard the *Shokaku*, it seemed as if the sky was an endless stream of American dive bombers for two long minutes. In the end, the twelve *Dauntless*'s managed to put four bombs, three 1,000lb. and a solitary 500-pounder, into the long wooden flight deck. The 500lb. bomb exploded on contact with the structure, blowing a 15-foot wide hole in the wooden timbers. The three 1,000lb. armor-piercing bombs, on the other hand, easily pierced the wooden planking, the hits marching from the bow to the stern.

The first pierced the flight deck and detonated in the crew's quarters forward, starting a moderate fire in a bedding and a rag locker. The damage control crews in the area had just started to move towards the fire when the second bomb found the ready ammunition for the carrier's forward 5-inch guns. The resultant secondary convinced several of the departing American pilots that the carrier had suffered a massive ammunition explosion and was surely done for. While not quite that serious, the bomb did serve to start a white-hot fire forward and kill the majority of the forward gun crews on the starboard side. The final bomb exploded aft in the hangar deck, destroying four aircraft and killing or wounding sixty men, including twenty aircrew that had been impressed into aiding the carrier's damage control efforts. Amazingly, the hot fragments only served to start a minor fire that was quickly brought under control by the damage control crews in the region.

Picking himself up from the deck of his bridge, the *Shokaku*'s captain had just enough time to watch the wake of a single torpedo disappear under the lip of his flight deck. Cursing, he braced himself for another explosion. Like the crew of the *Tone*, he was pleasantly surprised by the lack of detonation, as yet more brave men were failed by the Bureau of Ordnance. The carrier, burning heavily, straightened from her turn to port and resumed their course.

Angry, seeing the nearest flight deck issuing smoke, the *Zeroe*s attempted to intercept some of the outbound strike aircraft. In two instances, the Japanese fighters were able to send *Dauntlesse*s into the Pacific. However, in true man bites dog fashion, one of the *Dauntlesse*s managed to bring its twin forward guns to bear and add one more destroyed aircraft to the horrible toll taken on the *Kido Butai*'s air strength.

Then, once more, the skies were clear of enemy aircraft. *Hornet*'s strike had been decimated in order to place four bombs onto the *Shokaku*. Seeing the carrier's flight deck holed and issuing smoke, those *Zeroe*s with over half their fuel remaining requested the last known location of the other four carriers. Of the four fighters that chose this route, only two would find friendly decks.

The other two fighters, as well as their pilots, would never been seen again by human eyes. Facing the pitiless swells of the Pacific, one of the men would end his own life with his pistol while staring at the picture of his wife and child. The second man would go mad from the heat and believe himself in Tokyo Bay, only a hundred yards from shore. With the actual distance to the shores of Tokyo Bay being several thousands times that, he would drown far from home.

Hornet
1535 Local (2035 Eastern)

Really wish we'd paid more attention during the damage control drills, Eric thought as he stood on the *Hornet*'s slanting deck. *Oh wait, our CAG decided that we should all remain in our ready rooms during most of them.*

"You men! Come with me!" a lieutenant commander shouted from forward of the island. "We need to push some planes over the side!"

Seeing several ensigns and gunners hesitating, Eric stopped.

"Come on unless you want to be swimming!" he shouted. The junior officers started moving forward, moving faster as Eric began giving them the "hurry up" gesture. Eric was pleased to see that Brown did the same for several of the gunners, if with far more profanity and a literal kick in the pants in one case. As they descended back to the hangar deck, Eric saw the lieutenant commander starting to divide men into groups of ten for different tasks. Moving forward, Eric nearly fell and realized that the *Hornet* was starting to slant slightly towards port.

That's not good, he thought. *We're also a lot closer to the ocean than we should be.* Crabwalking, Eric and the airmen were directed to a spare *Avenger* that had crashed down from the hangar deck's roof. Grabbing a wing edge, Eric listened as one of the usual plane handlers gave hurried instructions on the best way to move the heavy torpedo bomber. Wisely, the gathered men worked with, not against, the *Hornet's* slant. As he pushed, Eric detected the faint aroma of avgas wafting back from the carrier's bow.

I should not be smelling avgas, Eric thought.

"I hope we give those yellow bastards as much hell as they're giving us," a sailor grunting beside Eric muttered.

"I think that is definitely..." Eric began.

The explosion was completely unexpected and horrible in its effect. Two separate crews, one for emptying fuel tanks and one for disarming aircraft, had been working on the *Hornet's* hangar deck in anticipation of the incoming Japanese strike. The crew emptying fuel tanks had been complete in their tasks and had proceeded to their normal stations. The crew disarming aircraft, however, had been delayed by a belt of .30-caliber ammunition jammed in an SBD's twin tail guns. They had been completing their task when the second Japanese bomb had permanently ended their efforts, leaving behind a 500-lb. depth charge surrounded by flames. The high explosives shredded the depth charge's light case, leveling the thirty men attempting to put out the fires in *Hornet's* flight deck. The fragments and blast hurled down the hangar deck, scything into the men moving the *Avenger*.

Eric came back to consciousness with a left shoulder blade that felt like it was afire, pinned on his stomach to the deck beneath him. There was a moment of silence, the crackle of flames forward audible as he lay on the cold steel. The slaughterhouse smell of spilled insides and the sight of a pair of brown shoes drumming frantically before going still added to the surrealness of the scene. Then the screaming, shouting, and sound of running feet started. Reaching behind him, every move agony, Eric felt something wet and gelatinous in the small of his back.

Oh God, he thought, then passed out.

Several dozen feet above Eric, the burst of fire from the *Hornet*'s forward flight deck, followed shortly by a larger, more severe explosion from deep within the carrier's hull was enough for Admiral Fitch and Captain Mitscher.

"Marc, let's get the boys off," Admiral Fitch said resignedly. "She's a loss."

Captain Mitscher nodded, his lined cheeks streaked with tears as he turned to his XO.

"Give the command abandon ship," he rasped. "Ask the screen to stand by to scuttle."

An hour later, the captain and his admiral both slid down lines off the carrier's stern. As a boat from the *Montepelier* plucked both men from the water, the *Fletcher* lined up on the carrier's damaged port side. Setting her torpedoes for a deep run, the destroyer fired a full spread of five tin fish. To the gathered bystanders' shock and anger, only two of the five weapons functioned in the gathering dusk. Despite settling somewhat faster, the *Hornet* gave no indications that the two blows were fatal. Realizing that there were no guarantees the destroyers would not need their torpedoes before his force reached Pearl Harbor, Admiral Fitch directed the *Montpelier* to sink the hulk with her broadsides. Firing rapidly at five thousand yards, the light cruiser reached her tenth salvo before causing an internal bulkhead to rupture. With the roar of rushing water, the *Hornet* rolled onto her beam ends and slipped beneath the waves.

. . .

Despite being struck in the Battle of Hawaii's final act, the *Hornet* was not the last vessel to succumb to the Pacific. The *Arizona*, her fires out of control due to a stray spark igniting the ruptured avgas storage, had been scuttled as night fell in order to avoid serving as a beacon for possible Japanese night bombers. Even later than her, the hard fighting *West Virginia* suddenly and dramatically gave up the ghost while under tow from the fleet tug *Navajo*. So rapid was the battleship's demise that in the darkness the tug's crew had no time to realize their charge had gone under. In a final, terrifying postscript to the Battle of Hawaii, the 1200-ton *Navajo* was dragged backward and partially underwater before her tow lines snapped. Shaken, the tug's captain brought his vessel about to pull survivors from the still churning waters over the larger vessel's grave.

11
DETRITUS

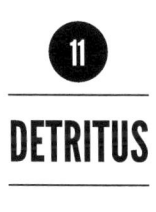

Errors and defeats are more obviously illustrative of principles than successes are...Defeat cries aloud for explanation; whereas success, like charity, covers a multitude of sins.

— **MAHAN: NAVAL STRATEGY, 1911**

Pensacola Naval Air Station
0510 Eastern Time (0010 Hawaii)
27 March 1943

THE POUNDING on his door roused Adam from his deep slumber. Cursing soundly, he got up from the bed he had just collapsed into two hours before. After sitting at alert the entire day waiting for non-existent German aircraft to start appearing in the Florida skies, he had spent the entire evening doing the necessary paperwork to transition from a peacetime to wartime squadron.

The smartest thing Lieutenant Colonel King did was immediately ground all squadrons, Adam thought. *Last thing we wanted to have happen was a Battle of Barking Creek between us and the Army.* He grabbed the .45 pistol he kept in the nightstand and headed towards the door.

"Who the Hell is making that bloody racket?" Connor asked in a whisper as Adam stepped into the main hallway. With a smile, Adam noted that the Commonwealth officer had also armed himself immediately after awakening.

Probably the duty officer sent to tell me to round up my pilots, Adam thought.

"Wait a damn minute!" Adam shouted, buttoning his uniform jacket.

Errand boys get to wait while I get presentable, Adam thought. *If there's one thing that helps one's subordinates keep their shit together, it's seeing the old man with **his** shit together.*

"I hope Jerry's not blood invading," Connor observed, stepping into the main hallway while buttoning up his own jacket. Stopping, both men looked at each other and nearly burst into laughter.

"Squadron Leader Michaelson would be proud," Connor said, speaking of their former commander.

"Well, he'd be proud if he wasn't probably dead," Adam replied with gallows humor. "But he was right about a proper uniform saying a lot about a man's self-discipline, I guess."

The pounding continued, this time even more angry. Adam grabbed the door and swung it open against the chain, .45 ready to shoot through the space.

"What in the...oh, hello Chaplain, sir," Adam said, his voice showing his surprise at Lt. Colonel King and Chaplain (MAJ) Stephen Grimes standing together on his doorstep. The latter officer was a tall, blonde haired, blue eyed man who had looked more like a dockworker than a man of God.

"Contrary to what you probably believe, Colonel Gatling is not looking to kill you with his bare hands," King observed drily, looking down at the .45. "As a matter of fact, the task you now have before you will be suitable punishment for releasing your squadron on two day pass without informing me beforehand."

Adam mentally winced at the man's tone.

When King says "more suitable punishment," why does my mind have a vision of a governor selling a convicted killer to cannibals so he can save on Old Sparky's electric bill? Adam thought.

"Thankfully for you, Major Haynes, I refuse to be one of those panic mongers that feels the Germans have either the naval assets or the desire to reach all of the way across the Atlantic and attack Pensacola," Lieutenant Colonel King continued. The man was about ot continue when he was interrupted by the chaplain.

"Sir, there are travel arrangements Captain Bowles must make," Major Grimes intoned quietly.

"Bowles?! What the fuck? He couldn't get help from Daddy so he turned to a higher power?!" Adam exploded, turning to the chaplain.

"'Daddy', or as we professional Marines prefer when referring to flag officers, 'Vice Admiral Bowles,'" King began, his tone firm, "will not need the chaplain's intercession to speak with a higher power, Major. The man was killed in action in Hawaii this morning."

"Hawaii?!" Adam asked, truly stunned.

"The Japanese have attacked the Pacific Fleet," Lieutenant Colonel King replied. "No official word on how bad the damage overall is, but from what Rear Admiral Whitaker has been told by Washington we are out at least the *Arizona*."

"Shit," Adam said. "Sir, how do we know about Vice Admiral Bowles' death already?"

"Because apparently Admiral Jensen, Commander In Chief, Pacific Fleet, was on the flag bridge with his entire staff when some Japanese dive bomber tried to fly through one of the portholes," King replied evenly.

Adam mentally winced. He certainly didn't agree with political animals, but no one deserved to die burning to a crisp after being doused with avgas. He heard Connor's intake of breath and realized his friend was seeing the same image, except with first-hand knowledge of the sight, sound, and smell.

"Let me guess my punishment, sir—I get to find Captain Bowles and break the news to him as his commanding officer?" Adam asked, letting an expression of displeasure come across his face.

King favored Adam with a slight smile that did not reach his eyes.

"Yes, Major Haynes, that's correct," Lieutenant Colonel King said. "You will take the chaplain and you will find Captain Bowles in the next twenty-four hours."

"Roger, sir," Adam said. "Captain Bowles is at his quarters or the officer's club because I took away his pass privileges since I restricted him to post over the next three days."

"What?!" King asked, just barely keeping his voice down.

"Bastard wants to be a squadron commander, he can do what his squadron commander is doing over the next three days, which is figuring out how to get ready for war," Adam replied flatly. "I needed policies typed up and mimeographed, I figured he could do the dirty work until his nose goes down far enough for an oxygen mask to fit it."

"Yes, we'll just pretend that he "walked into a door" as someone was opening it, not got his ass kicked by his squadron commander like the scuttlebutt says," Lieutenant Colonel King said, clearly unimpressed. Looking at his watch, King turned to Chaplain Grimes.

"I trust that you'll keep Major Haynes from killing his subordinate, chaplain?" King said.

"Yes, sir," Chaplain Grimes replied.

"Then I'll leave you to it," King said. All three officers came to attention and saluted King, who returned the gesture then headed back to his car. The young lance corporal driving started up the vehicle then got out to open his wing commander's door.

"Well, guess we're going for a drive," Adam said. "Bowles lives on the other side of Pensacola.

"That's fine with me," Chaplain Grimes replied. "Provided you both put away your pistols."

FORTY-FIVE MINUTES LATER THE THREE OFFICERS FOUND THEMSELVES standing in front of a single-story, white ranch home. The house was dark, but Bowles's vehicle was parked out in front. Killing the engine and the headlights, Adam hopped out and waited for the chaplain to make his way around the vehicle.

This is something I didn't expect to be doing as a squadron commander, Adam thought.

"Probably best if I wait by the car," Connor said quietly.

"Yes, that might be a good idea," Major Grimes said apologetically. The Commonwealth officer leaned back against the sedan's side, and

Adam fought the urge not to smile as he realized the man had a hidden pistol underneath his uniform jacket. Turning around and squaring his shoulders, Adam marched up towards the door, Grimes having to move quickly to keep up despite being much taller. Just as Adam started to reach up to use the knocker, he distinctly heard a female voice shouting something incoherent from the far corner of the house.

Shit, Adam thought. *Bowles has company, and from the sounds of it she's enjoying herself.*

"What's going on?" Major Grimes asked, looking at Adam.

"Uh, nothing Chaplain," Adam replied, quickly knocking loud enough to wake the dead. Bowles' neighbors obviously owned a dog, as the animal started howling at the top of its lungs. The timeless chorus of man's best friend was taken up by several other animals, leading to lights beginning to snap on in several houses.

Well, if the Germans were going to bomb Pensacola tonight, some navigator is thanking me for lighting up his target, Adam thought, embarrassed. There was a rustle on the other side of the door, followed by a shape moving in front of the windows.

"What do you want?!" Bowles inquired angrily from the other side of the door.

"Captain Bowles, this is Major Haynes," Adam said flatly. "Open the door, please."

There was a few moments' pause, then the sound of a key turning in the lock on the other side. The door opened to reveal Bowles standing in an undershirt and a pair of shorts.

"Well, if it's not the international flying team of losers, sir," Bowles slurred, whiskey rolling off his breath like a morning fog. The splint on his nose was slightly askew as he regarded Adam and Major Grimes. "I recognize Melting Wax back by the car, but I haven't met the third member of your group. Is he one of the Frenchmen you flew with? Or was it Polacks?"

Adam had to resist the urge to give Bowles a straight right to the jaw to help sober him up. Fortunately, Major Grimes had been around many arrogant young officers in his short tenure at Pensacola.

"Good evening, Captain Bowles," Grimes said.

Bowles's façade crumbled like castle walls confronted by modern battleship guns. He backed up from Grimes as if the chaplain was the Ghost of Christmas Past, stumbling over his dress shoes and falling on his back.

"Oh God, no," he shouted, knowing in an instant why the chaplain was standing there. "No!" he continued to shriek.

Adam heard the sound of footfalls coming up the sidewalk as the same time as naked feet came rushing from the back of Bowles house. Moments later, Adam, Connor and Grimes found themselves looking at a tall, curvy, and attractive blonde in a hastily fastened robe. The woman looked down at Bowles, then up at the three of them. Realizing with a start that she had not fully fastened her robe, the woman cinched the belt tighter.

The boy at least has good taste, Adam thought, hearing Grimes' sharp intake of breath. *Although Chaplain Grimes is probably about to lose his shit.*

"Mrs. Burke, what in the hell are you doing here?!" the chaplain shouted angrily. Adam's head whipped to the chaplain, then back to the woman.

"Burke?! As in Captain Todd Burke?" he asked darkly, then turned back to where Bowles was sitting on the ground, rocking himself with his head in his hands. The woman gave out a strangled cry, then turned and rushed back into the bedroom.

I could strangle you, you son-of-a-bitch, Adam thought, flexing his hands.

"He just found out his father died, mate," Connor said quietly, reading Adam's body language. "You can strangle him later."

I wish I was back to the days of simply flying for survival, Adam thought darkly. *This delivering bad news, figuring out how to deal with one officer screwing another officer's wife, and policy letter shit is for the birds.*

"Come lad, no need to carry on like this," Connor said amiably. "What would you mother think if she saw you carrying on like this?"

Bowles recovered enough to gain his feet, then turned to look at the three officers, tears filling his eyes.

"My mother. Oh God, has anyone told her?" Bowles sobbed.

"No son, you are one of the first to know. The Pacific Fleet hasn't informed any of the wives in San Diego yet," Grimes responded, barely able to maintain his role as a sympathetic counselor in the face of obvious adultery. Adam could see the man's facial muscles struggling, with his knuckles white on the Bible.

You know, do chaplains go to Hell if they kill a sinner with God's word? he wondered idly as Bowles managed to gain control of himself.

"How?" he asked, looking at the chaplain. "He was in Hawaii, not out in the Philippines."

"The Japanese caught the fleet just outside of harbor. Your father was killed instantly aboard the *Arizona*," Adam lied smoothly, meeting the chaplain's eyes.

Yes, it would serve him right to tell him his Dad likely died screaming like a banshee, Adam thought. *But payback for finding him diddling another man's wife can wait until he returns from San Diego.*

"Captain Bowles I will return back here at 0900 to take you onto post for you to have orders cut," Adam said. "Have your bags packed for your stay in San Diego when I return."

"T-thank you, sir," Bowles responded, his voice despondent.

Stepping back, Adam motioned for Connor and Grimes to move back towards the car, then shut Bowles front door. Several neighbors were looking at him quizzically, but a hard glare sent the handful of curious individuals back inside their houses. Grimes looked as if he wanted to say something about Adam's actions, but a small shake of the head from Connor convinced Grimes to hold his counsel until they were back in the vehicle.

"He's in no condition to drive Mrs. Burke back to post, Major Haynes," Major Grimes intoned as soon as the doors were closed. Adam started the car and shifted it into gear.

"I realize that, Chaplain," Adam said, his face set in a snarl. "Personally, I'm hoping he gives her the car to drive home, goes back in the back room, and blows his brains out. Failing that, I will give Mrs. Burke a ride back to post, and she can explain to her husband where she was."

Grimes was taken aback by the vehemence of Adam's response. Turning to Connor, he could see the same look of disgust on the British officer's face.

"What do you intend to do about this situation once Captain Bowles returns?" Grimes asked, changing tack.

Adam shrugged as they pulled off from the house.

"I don't know. This is definitely outside of my area of expertise," Adam said, exasperated. "I've never had to deal with something like this before."

"Yes, generally we and the Poles were a little bit too busy trying to kill Germans to screw our mates' wives," Connor remarked, barely keeping an edge on his own temper.

"Might I make a suggestion?" Grimes asked.

"Certainly, chaplain," Adam replied.

"Do not sit on this in an attempt to save your squadron, Major Haynes," Grimes said, his tone righteous. "As terrible as this is, it must be brought out into the open and dealt with. Otherwise, once word gets out, as it surely will, your men will assume you are another in a long list of politically-minded officers attempting to protect Captain Bowles's career."

"What is there left to protect? His Daddy's dead," Adam responded. "From what I've seen, he's not going to get very far on merit alone."

"The son of a dead war hero, killed in action in the first battle of the war? Whose death, I am sure, will take on a tragic circumstance since it is so early in the conflict," Grimes said mockingly. "Trust me on this, Major Haynes, Captain Bowles has far more political power now than you realize. If you do not bring this to light now, before he has time to be lionized in the press and by the Marine Corps, you will not have a chance to punish him later."

Adam thought about what the chaplain was saying, then realized the man was probably right.

"Thank you, chaplain," he said. "Hopefully, this will be the last time I need your help."

Grimes chuckled at that one.

"We're at war, Major Haynes," the former pastor said. "If this is the last time you'll need my help, it will be because one of us is dead."

U.S.S. Houston
Surabaya, Dutch East Indies

0530 Local (1530 Eastern)
28 March (27 March Eastern)

Jacob stood at the back of the *Houston*'s flag plot, listening as rain and wind lashed the heavy cruiser's side.

War's been on for over a day now and here we sit, still in harbor because of rain, Jacob thought. *Well at least it has screwed up the Japanese time table too. At least, as far as we are concerned. Those poor bastards in the Philippines probably feel differently.*

"Yesterday, the submarine *Sailfish* sighted a large enemy surface group entering Cam Ranh Bay," Rear Admiral William Glassford stated, scanning the gathered officers. A tall man with dark hair, lined face, and piercing eyes, Glassford was Vice Admiral Hart's tactical commander at sea and an aggressive one at that. "The commander estimated the force consisted of four enemy cruisers and six destroyers. It is my belief that this force will attempt to interfere with our reinforcement of Borneo."

Or alternatively, they'll be landing at the same time the Australians try to, Jacob thought. Glassford paused, again looking over each captain as if searching for signs of obvious cowardice.

"It is my intent to seek and destroy this force whether this front passes today or not," Glassford said. "We will be operating under the limit of friendly air cover from Jesselton and Brunei. Fighter direction will be handled by the *Australia*."

There was a slight shift as Glassford's words sank in, the nervousness in the room ramping up a notch.

"If we meet the enemy in daylight, we will seek a range of fifteen thousand yards," Glassford said, gesturing for his aides to start handing out mimeographed fighting instructions. "Destroyers will screen against their opposite numbers, then be released for torpedo attack against enemy cripples. Cruisers will operate in line ahead and engage their opposite number."

"What is our plan if there are battleships?" Captain Gordon of the *Exeter* asked.

Run like Hell, Jacob thought. *Your ship just got out of dry dock, you idiot, are you trying to go back?*

"Commander Marshall," Glassford asked, turning to his intelligence officer, "what is the maximum speed of the *Kongo*-class."

"Twenty-eight knots, sir," Marshall replied, deadpan.

"The slowest ships we have here are our four-pipers at twenty-nine knots," Glassford replied simply. "If we see enemy battleships, we will make smoke and break contact. Admiral Phillips will then bring up the *Prince of Wales* and *Revenge* from Australia and we will have another go at our friends with our big brothers as back up."

The officers chuckled tightly at Glassford's joke.

Of course, that plan only works if no one's damaged, Jacob observed mentally. *If the **Kongo**s show up after someone's gotten themselves crippled, we'll be wishing the **Prince of Wales** was a little closer.* Jacob could not fault Admiral Phillips for wanting to be cautious in light of recent events.

"What is our plan in case of air attack?" Captain Fitzpatrick, new master of the H.M.A.S. *Australia*, asked.

"All vessels will maneuver independently and fight off their attackers," Glassford replied.

Standing to the rear of Admiral Glassford, Jacob saw several of the British lower ranking officers exchange glances.

It's our doctrine, Jacob thought to himself, feeling the sweat from the already sweltering tropical heat trickle down his back. *American commander, we fight American doctrine.* In absence of heavy ships for whom they were providing a screen, the official navy doctrine was for cruisers and destroyers to use their superior maneuverability to evade enemy attacks. Given the differing maneuvering circles of the vessels and the confined waters they would be operating in, separating and fighting it out made sense.

It's not like the Pacific Fleet staying together seems to have made much of a difference, Jacob thought bitterly. *They even had carriers.*

Glassford was about to respond to the glances when *Houston*'s watch officer, Lieutenant (j.g.) Merriweather came in the door with a message flimsy. For a brief moment the young officer paused, not wanting to interrupt the briefing until Captain Wallace waved him over to his seat near the compartment's aft bulkhead. The OOD walked over and handed the flimsy to Captain Wallace and waited patiently at parade rest, feeling the eyes of the room on him. *Houston*'s master took one look at the message then handed it to Admiral Glassford.

As pale as the old man just got, somehow I doubt that's news the Japanese have said "just kidding," Jacob thought.

Glassford read the message once, his fingers whitening on the paper. Face set in a thin line, the flag officer turned to the captains.

"Gentlemen, I regret to inform you that the Port of Darwin is currently being attacked by carrier and four-engined aircraft," Glassford said. "There is no word yet on losses, but this force will sortie within the next thirty minutes. Good luck to you all and Godspeed." The group came to attention and saluted Glassford, which he returned.

Jacob was already passing through the hatch by the time all of this happened, the Lt. (j.g.) Merriweather in tow. He began giving orders as soon as both of the men were in the passageway.

"Sound General Quarters immediately," Jacob ordered calmly, knowing things were about to get rather interesting. "Where is the harbor pilot?"

"I have sent someone ashore to get him, sir," Merriweather responded. "I have already passed the word for the ship to begin going to General Quarters but did not want to interfere with the briefing with the ship not being in imminent danger."

"Good man. The captain will be on the bridge shortly, probably with Rear Admiral Glassford right behind him. Make sure you render the proper respects and are aware of the readiness of each of the departments. I am heading back to Battle Two," Jacob stated.

"Aye aye, sir," Merriweather responded. Jacob headed out onto the main deck then back towards Battle Two, checking on the *Houston*'s anti-aircraft guns as he went.

Jacob had just stepped into Battle-2 when air raid sirens began sounding all around the harbor.

There's no way the Japanese should be able to bomb in this storm, but stranger things have happened, Jacob thought.

"Status report," Jacob barked as he stepped into Battle Two.

"Sir, we've got steam and can start moving as soon as you want us too," Lieutenant Connor reported. "All boilers are lit, the watch is all present, we're ready to sail as soon as the captain gives the order."

Jacob nodded, his face creasing with the first smile of the day. Seeing this, the sailors standing in Battle Two with him all breathed a sigh of relief. It was not a good day when the first thing that happened was the XO went ballistic because someone failed to do their job.

"Sir, the pilot is aboard," one of the talkers stated, relaying the message from the bridge.

"Thank you," Jacob replied.

Houston was as ready as a man-of-war could be. Now it remained to see what the next few hours brought.

Pearl Harbor, Hawaii
1630 Local (2130 Eastern)
27 March

With over forty Navy and Army fighters circling overhead, the *Yorktown* eased her way into Pearl Harbor's carrier berth #1. Sparing a moment to look down at her wooden deck, Sam could see that the ship's crew appeared to be at general quarters, guns manned just in case. Around the harbor, the carrier's escort was also tying up to their quays.

Even with all these fighters, not sure we'd be able to stop another attack like the last one, Sam thought. *At least those Army jerks managed to fight to something resembling a draw. Looks like even our* **Wildcats** *are outclassed by the new Japanese fighter.* "Ramshackle copies of Western designs my ass." Sam nearly clenched his fists thinking about the idiots in intelligence that spread that rumor.

"All right gentlemen, tighten it up," Major Bowden's voice came over the radio. Sam snapped back to reality, bringing his flight back around to orient on that of the squadron commander's.

Okay, Sam, need to stop getting distracted, he thought to himself. *Be a shame to score two kills on day one of the war then run into someone on day two. At least all four of our kills got confirmed.*

"All aircraft over Pearl Harbor, all aircraft over Pearl Harbor, this is

Octagon Base," Sam's radio crackled. "Unidentified aircraft inbound bearing three zero zero, altitude twenty angels, range one hundred fifty miles from Oracle Station. All Army aircraft, move to intercept."

What kind of radar direction is that?!, Sam thought to himself. Then, after a moment, he thought about how bad life had to be for the controllers below. There were aircraft from three different services, five different wings or groups, and eight different squadrons flying over the *Yorktown*. Giving an order to a "Red Flight" would probably lead to total chaos.

"Look sharp, Marines, we're next in the batting order," Bowden barked over the net. The plan, worked out hurriedly between the staffs of Vice Admiral Pye, now the acting Commander-In-Chief, Pacific Fleet, and General Short, was for Army aircraft to make any initial interceptions. These interceptions would be followed by those of the Marines and Navy fighters.

"All Army aircraft, all Army aircraft, belay the last order. Incoming aircraft are friendly, I repeat, friendly aircraft," the controller corrected.

I wonder who in the hell that could be, Sam thought to himself. *Enterprise?!*

OVER AN HOUR LATER, AS THE APPROACHING AIRCRAFT BEGAN making their initial contact with the fields that would be receiving them; Sam realized he had been correct in his assumption...and that Vice Admiral Halsey had brought friends.

"Okay Green and Red flights, time to go home," Bowden's voice came over the radio. "Blue and Yellow flights are on station."

"Roger Red One," Sam replied. "Do you want Green Flight to recover at Hickam, over?" Sam asked.

"Green One, this is Red One," Bowden said. "Negative, meet me on the ground."

I don't know why he sounds perturbed, Sam thought to himself. *He briefed Hickam as a possible secondary field, and Ewa is kind of crowded at the moment.* Looking over at David, he saw his twin brother raise his hand and shake a finger at him.

Laugh it up, knucklehead, Sam thought. *You know he'll just make you Green Flight leader if he relieves me, right?*

The short flight back to Ewa was made in silence. As Red Flight was the first one to land, Sam kept Green at ten thousand feet for top cover. Once the runway was clear, he led the flight down, not wanting to keep Bowden waiting. As he shut down his aircraft and shoved back his canopy, he noticed Bowden still at his aircraft conferring with two men. With a start, he realized one of the men was MAG-21's executive officer, Lieutenant Colonel John McKenna. The other man had his back to Sam, but was wearing Navy whites and looked strangely familiar.

"What gives?" David asked, coming up to stand beside his brother. Seeing both Cobbs were done shutting down, Bowden motioned for both men to come over.

That's unusual, Sam thought. *Major Bowden usually likes to keep squadron business in the squadron, not out in the open for everyone to see.* As they walked closer, Sam suddenly recognized the officer in question and had to restrain himself from throwing his arms around Nick. Pausing, he saluted Bowden and McKenna, both men returning the gesture with sly grins.

"What in the Hell are you doing here?" Sam asked his younger brother.

Screw military bearing, Sam thought, grabbing his brother in a bear hug before he had a chance to answer.

"Good to see you two, sir," his brother said. "You're hurting my ribs."

"We'll leave you three to get caught up, then you come find us at Flight Ops," Major Bowden said.

"That's all three of you come find us, gentlemen," McKenna added.

"Yes, sir," Sam said. All three Cobb brothers saluted Bowden and McKenna as the two men walked off.

"Lieutenant Colonel McKenna was very helpful in finding you guys," Nick said after a moment.

"His son's on Wake," Sam replied quietly. "Now, again, what in the hell are you doing here? Shouldn't you still be at sea with *Nautilus*?"

Nick winced.

"*Nautilus* is gone," he began, then gave his brothers a quick run down of how the war's first day had gone for *him*. Sam and David looked at him in awe, their eyes wide in shock as he told them of the attack on the *Zuikaku* and *Shokaku*.

"We had just started to try and come back in when the port engine seized up," Nick finished. "We made an S.O.S. call back to Pearl for a tow. They sent the *Tautog* and *Narwhal* to give us what aid they could. Division commander takes one look at *Nautilus* and ordered us to scuttle her, he wasn't risking two more subs to save a wreck."

Sam could hear the pain in Nick's voice.

"So, to answer your original question, everything but this spare pair of whites is currently sitting in a 'wreck' at the bottom of the Pacific," Nick finished grimly. "I'm here because the division commander immediately requested a *Catalina* to fly back Commander Freeman and myself to speak with Rear Admiral Graham about our weapons' failures. Which is fine, as even with bum torpedoes we still got at least one, maybe two of those bastards."

"I thought the Army boys were trying to claim a carrier?" Sam asked.

"Yeah, ask them what condition they found her in," Nick replied derisively.

"We better go join Major Bowden," David interrupted, pointing towards the hangar where Bowden and McKenna were waiting outside Operations.

"Have you guys heard from Eric?" Nick asked worriedly. "I understand *Enterprise* and *Victorious* just arrived in range, but haven't heard anything about *Hornet* after seeing her air group."

As if on cue, the door to Operations opened to reveal a familiar form joining Bowden and McKenna.

That can't be good, Sam thought, both David and he starting to slow. Nick had enough time to look at them puzzledly before the third officer spoke.

"Gentlemen, we really have to stop meeting like this," Chaplain McHenry stated, his tone indicating he was only slightly joking. "I am glad to see you as well, Lieutenant (j.g.) Cobb, as my next stop was

Rear Admiral Graham's office to find you before Major Bowden and Lieutenant Colonel McKenna informed me you were here.

"What's happened, sir?" Sam asked evenly, even as he felt his palms start to sweat.

"Again, your brother Eric is alive," McHenry started out. "He's been wounded."

"Shit," David cursed angrily, then gained control of himself.

"It would appear that your family has plenty of heroes in it," Bowden said, his voice flat. "Unfortunately, it would appear that you are all also here in Hawaii or close by."

McKenna looked from the squadron commander to the Cobbs.

"Whole family?" McKenna asked, eyes narrowing.

"Sir, our sister is here in the islands as well," Sam replied. "She is rooming with an officer's daughter in Honolulu."

McKenna's eyes narrowed further.

"So if the Jap fleet comes back with transports, there's a chance all of you will be caught on this island together?" McKenna asked incredulously.

"Yes, sir," Sam and David answered simultaneously.

"Okay, that's it," McKenna snapped. "I am giving you two a direct order. You will decide immediately which one of you is going to do the speaking, effective immediately. What does your sister do here in the islands?"

"Sir, Patricia works in the public library," Sam replied.

"Sir, some people do not have a problem with entire families being potentially in harms way," Bowden said. "I have a good friend who serves on the *Juneau*, and he says that they have five brothers on board."

"I think that's the dumbest thing I've ever heard," McKenna snapped. "In light of Lieutenant (j.g.) Cobb's near miss aboard his submarine, Lieutenant Cobb's wounding,you're your encounter with four enemy aircraft, I think it's time we give your mother some relief. You're both grounded, effective immediately."

"Sir, Captain Cobb is..." Bowden started.

"I'll send you replacements, Major Bowden," McKenna said, waving away the protest. "As soon as it can be facilitated, I'll also send orders for you to send these two back to the mainland."

Both Sam and Eric's faces fell in shock, a look mirrored by Major Bowden.

"In light of your change of status, you gentlemen have three days pass. Use this time to find your sister and get your affairs in order," McKenna continued. "I don't care what in the hell other people do, I'm not going to be responsible for your mother going to a looney bin."

"Sir, my wife..." David began.

"Will be evacuated at the earliest opportunity with the rest of the dependents," McKenna said. "I've already got the G-1 making up the list. I strongly suggest you gentlemen get your sister on it as well."

Nick, Sam, and David all looked at each other.

"Sir, with all due respect, that's not a good way to keep my mother's sanity or my brothers safe," Nick said quietly.

"Lieutenant (j.g.) Cobb, that's none of my business," McKenna said simply. "If she wants to stay here, good luck to her. I don't imagine the Army or Navy's going to march anyone out of here at bayonet point."

Looking at his watch, Lieutenant Colonel McKenna turned to Major Bowden.

"I'm going to need you to be at headquarters in two hours, Major Bowden," McKenna said. "The old man should be back from Fleet Headquarters around then. I suspect we are going to be going to visit Wake."

"Yes, sir," Bowden said.

"Until then, carry on," McKenna replied. The group came to attention, Bowden saluting and receiving the courtesy in return. As McKenna got into the wing car, Major Bowden turned back towards the two men.

"I think he's being too sentimental," Bowden snapped. "But orders are orders."

"Sir, what's happened with Wake?" Sam asked.

"The Japanese tried to invade yesterday afternoon," Bowden replied. "Wake's fight went a lot better than ours did, but casualties were still heavy. Lieutenant Colonel McKenna's son was listed among the wounded, and his wife's extremely distraught."

Well now I understand the comment about our mother, Sam thought.

"You need to go find your sister," Bowden continued. "Then you need to go find your brother. Scuttlebutt is that the *Denver* will be in later today due to torpedo damage with *Hornet*'s survivors."

"Someone's talking too much, sir," Nick said, his voice incredulous. Bowden looked left and right, then back at the three Cobbs.

"Scuttlebutt, in this case, is Mrs. Bowden," Major Bowden observed, drawing a slight smile from Sam and David as Nick colored. "I think she feels she can trust me, seeing as how she sleeps next to me every night."

"Understood, sir," Nick replied sheepishly. "My apologies."

"No apologies needed," Bowden replied. "If I didn't have an inside source someone would be talking way too much indeed. You three get going—I think you need to get to your sister sooner rather than later."

Honolulu
1700 Local (2200 Eastern)

I'm going to lose it, Patricia thought, desperately trying to focus on *Rifleman Dodd* as Jo wandered around the living room dusting. *We've been under martial law since dawn, I have no idea where my brothers or Peter are, and she's dusting that mantle **again**.*

"You could help, you know," Jo snapped out of the blue, facing away from her.

Patricia closed her book with exaggerated calmness.

"If you haven't been able to get the dust off the last thirty times you dusted it, I don't see where an extra pair of hands can help," Patricia replied, her voice overly polite.

Jo whirled towards her.

"Damn you all to hell," she shrieked. "Some of us didn't just come out here to find ourselves a husband! Some of us actually have family that could be getting shot at!"

Patricia found herself resisting the urge to throw the novel at her.

Find a husband! I'll show you find a husband! Patricia thought, clenching her hands together so tightly she was certain she drew blood. She gave Jo a small smile.

"At least I've got a snowball's chance in finding a husband," Patricia said, the coolness and exact pronunciation of her words making them cut all the deeper. "Of course, if you weren't always trying to make yourself out to be so manly, you might have better luck. Or maybe you just need to throw yourself at someone besides every...single...one...of...my...brothers."

Jo visibly staggered back.

"What?! Why you..." Jo started to say, tears forming in her eyes.

"How *dare* you tell me I don't understand family?" Patricia asked, her voice almost a hiss. "Or do you just forget men that you do everything short of shake your undergarments at to get their attention?"

"This coming from a woman who is so scared of her body she can't even figure out when a man is interested," Jo shot back.

"Well I'm sorry I haven't put a vacancy sign over my navel," Patricia replied. "I hear the going rates are kind of steep though. Or is that only when your father finds out?"

"Get out of my house," Jo snapped, her voice flat.

Just pulling out all the stops, aren't you? Patricia thought, her vision beginning to get red tinged.

"Go to Hell," the youngest Cobb snapped, her face pallid with rage. "I paid rent on the first, and it's not *your* house," Patricia said. "My God, Jo, what is the matter with you?!"

"You oblivious little twit," Jo seethed. "Didn't you see Uncle Keith?"

"W-what?" Patricia asked.

"Didn't you think it was a little odd that Aunt Nancy didn't say goodbye to us?" Jo snapped.

Okay, so now I see what's getting to you, Patricia thought.

"I assumed she was busy, Jo," Patricia said, forcing her voice to be calm as she stood. She noticed Jo gripped the feather duster tighter, but continued to move closer. To the other woman's obvious surprise, Patricia put her arms around her. It was if someone had blown out the center of a dam in front of a rain swollen reservoir. Grabbing the taller woman like a drowning man clinging to a life preserver, Jo began sobbing into her chest.

Oh hell, Patricia thought.

"Oh God, I'm sorry, Jo," Patricia said.

"I-I-I barely recognized him," Jo gasped in between sobs. "But when Aunt Nancy ran towards the stretcher when they were escorting us out, I knew it had to be him."

"What happened to the *Northampton* doesn't mean the same thing is happening to *Houston*," Patricia said. "I'm sure your father is fine."

"I'm sorry I forgot about the boys," Jo said quietly, still shaking. "It just shook me is all."

"I really don't think you're mannish," Patricia said, causing Jo to laugh.

"Patricia, I'm about as far from mannish as a girl can get," Jo said. "Frumpy, maybe, but this gal knows she has curves."

"So does this mean you're not kicking me out?" Patricia asked.

"Oh no, I fully expect you to have your stuff packed and on the porch by morning," Jo replied, laughing. "I'll pay you back your three days rent as soon as I can get to the bank."

"I can't tell if you're joking…"

The knock on the door startled them both. The two of them broke the embrace and dabbed at their eyes with handkerchiefs. The knock came again, louder and more insistent.

"I've got it," Patricia said.

"No, better let me," Jo replied. "Contrary to what you assumed, my name *is* actually on the deed."

I get the feeling we're okay…but nothing I said will be forgotten, Patricia thought.

I really shouldn't have started that fight, Jo thought, stepping up to the door. *Yeah, I don't **think** she meant half of what she said, but every word in anger has at least a grain of truth.* Looking through the peephole, Jo was startled to see a Navy lieutenant in dress whites accompanied by two seamen in khaki. Both sailors were armed with rifles, the weapons slung over their shoulders.

What in the seven hells is this? Jo thought, opening the door with weak knees.

"Ma'am, are you Miss Josephine Morton?" the sandy brown haired officer asked in a upper Midwest accent, his face showing concern at Jo's appearance. Jo's mouth worked once, and she had to swallow to get enough spit to move her tongue.

"Y-yes," she stammered, meeting the man's green eyes.

"Ma'am, I am Lieutenant Molnar from the *Northampton*," the officer said. "I am currently the acting executive officer."

"I already know about Commander Hertling," Jo said heavily, drawing a puzzled look from Lieutenant Molnar.

"Ma'am, we're not here about Commander Hertling," Lieutenant Molnar said quietly. "We have Mrs. Hertling in the car. When you say you know about him, what do you mean?"

Oh God, Jo thought.

"If Nancy is here, I don't think I know as much as I think," Jo said, her voice so soft that Molnar could barely hear her.

"Ma'am, I regret to tell you that Commander Hertling expired from his wounds at 1400 today," Molnar said. "Nurse Hertling was sedated at that time."

That's not a good sign, Jo thought.

"On the advice of the doctor who was attending Commander Hertling, I asked Mrs. Hertling if there was someplace I could take her so that she would not be alone," Molnar stated. "I know your father and understand this may not be the best time for you to receive visitors..."

"Mrs. Hertling is always welcome in my home, lieutenant," Jo snapped, then caught herself. "I'm sorry, it's a stressful time. I'll come out with you to the car."

The next five minutes were the longest in Jo's short life. Nancy was barely responsive to her when she opened the back door, a coat drawn about her body despite the fact that the temperature was quite warm. As they walked back to the house, Lieutenant Molnar and the seamen grabbed Nancy's luggage. When they reached the house, Jo went to take Nancy's coat and immediately saw why the woman had been wearing it: the front of her nurse's gown was covered with blood and other liquids.

"Miss Morton, thank you for your help. I hope that your father makes it back all right." Lieutenant Molnar said quickly at the door. Looking past Jo to where Nancy stood staring vacantly out the doorway, Molnar moved to make eye contact.

"Mrs. Hertling, Commander Hertling was a great officer. He will be missed."

Nancy nodded numbly. Lieutenant Molnar, at a loss, signaled his escort to move back towards the car. Jo closed the door, then turned back to Nancy.

"Aunt Nancy, let's get you cleaned..."

"They tell me he simply slipped away," Nancy said, her voice with a faraway tone. "I know that's a lie. I heard him screaming."

"Aunt Nancy, let's not think about that right now," Jo said, taking Nancy's arm. Nancy turned and looked at her.

"Jo, he didn't even recognize me when I talked to him," Nancy said. "He kept asking for Ann."

Ann was his first wife, Jo thought, nausea twisting and turning sinuously in her stomach.

"Ten years of following him from base to base, spending months without him at home, and he can't even get the right name on his deathbed," Nancy said, the last part coming out as a sob.

Looking on as Jo tried to comfort Nancy, Patricia felt helpless.

*I will never, **never** marry a man in the Navy*, she thought to herself.

There was another knock on the door. Patricia moved past Jo to the peephole, then suddenly let out a squeal of joy.

What in the hell, you stupid... Jo thought, turning to give Patricia a piece of her mind until the door opened. Patricia flew through the door and threw herself at Sam, hugging her brother so hard he almost fell over. She then let him go and grabbed David, then Nick, the whole time weeping.

There's only three of them, Jo thought, seeing the pained look that briefly crossed Sam's face. David, for his part, paled at Nancy's state, giving Jo an inquisitive look.

Later, she mouthed, moving Nancy towards the bathroom.

"You stay with your friends," Nancy said measuredly. "I'm not going to swallow a bottle of pills or slit my wrists."

"Hello Tootsie," Sam was saying. Patricia stopped dead in her happiness.

"What is it, Sam?" she asked, her mood turning on a dime.

"Eric..." David started to say.

"No," Patricia breathed, staggering backward before Sam grabbed her.

"He's wounded, Tootsie," Sam said in a rush, steadying his sister.

"H-h-how bad?" Patricia asked.

"We don't know," Sam and David said simultaneously, and even Jo knew that was a bad sign.

"You're lying," Patricia snarled, looking at both of them.

"Patricia," Sam said, and Jo startled at his voice.

That's a Sam Cobb setting I've never heard, Jo thought. *I'm all right with never hearing it again.*

Patricia stopped dead, looking up at her brother.

"Sorry Sam," she replied, then started. "Do you guys have any word on Peter?"

Sam and David looked at each other, and Jo felt as if she wanted to throw up.

"He's missing," Sam said. "We were on the *Yorktown* after he took off and asked around, but the last anyone saw of him was he got bounced by three of those bast...Japanese."

If Sam's cussing in front of his sister like that, he knows more than he's letting on, Jo thought. Fortunately for the Cobb twin, his sister was too staggered to catch his statement.

"I...I see," Patricia said. "Excuse me."

With that, Patricia ran past Jo towards the back of the house. Ducking into her room, Patricia slammed the door before she started sobbing.

"You okay?" David asked Jo.

"I'm sitting here with the blood of a man I considered my uncle all over the front of my dress and a young man I was fond of is dead, David," Jo replied, her voice seeming as if it was coming from outside of her body. "I am about as far from okay as you can get."

"We are leaving Hawaii," Sam said in a rush.

Jo looked at him, aghast.

"Well fuck you too, Sam Cobb," she snapped, seeing all three brothers look at her like she'd just grown a second head.

"I'm sorry," Sam said apologetically, holding up his hands. "I didn't..."

"Didn't what, Sam?" Jo asked. "Think that would piss me off even more? For God's sake, you big oaf, even your own sister accused me of waving my panties at you. Did you think that maybe *now* was not the best time to tell me this news?"

David and Nick were looking at Sam, their expressions basically saying, *"She's got a point, dumbass."*

"Get out," Jo snapped. "All three of you."

"What?" Nick asked. "What did I do?"

"Be born from the same mother as that dumbass," Jo snapped. "Is your entire family hard of hearing? Why do I have to keep repeating that phrase?"

"But why?" David asked.

"Because I've got to console your sister and help my Aunt Nancy get my Uncle Keith's blood out of her hair," Jo barked, her speech so rapid the brothers had a hard time following her. "Because your brother isn't attracted to me and now he's leaving. Because I feel like the sun rose in the west yesterday and nothing's come back to normal. Because I don't want to see any of your faces for a couple of days *and this is my damn house.*"

Sam gave her a look, and she felt like she'd kicked a puppy. He started to open his mouth when David stopped him.

"We're on pass to get our things together," David said evenly. "Let us know if you change your mind. Good evening."

With that, the three Cobbs walked out the door.

Ten minutes later, when she was getting the last of the dried blood out of Nancy's hair, their tears commingling in the pink water, Jo cast her eyes out the window at the dusk sky.

Dad, wherever you are, I hope that you're safe, she thought. *Lord, I pray that you keep him that way.*

Pearl Harbor
0400 Local (0900 Eastern)
29 March

Pain was the first sensation that shot through Eric's mind. Distant pain, but pain nonetheless. He opened his eyes to find himself lying on his stomach. Moving his tongue, he realized his mouth felt like cotton. Moving his toes, he suddenly realized that he could feel his legs again.

Thank you, God, he thought, moving to roll over. He realized with a start that he could not moved, a strap being cinched across his lower back.

"What in the hell?!" he muttered. With a start that told him exactly where is wounds were, Eric also realized that he did not hear the dull throbbing of a ship's engine.

Where in the hell am I? he thought, fighting down the urge to panic. He turned to look beside him and saw a man completely swathed in bandages.

Hospital bed, he thought.

"Aw, you're awake," a voice he did not recognize came from behind his head.

"Damn Bob, looks like you've lost your bet!" the mummy in his field of view said.

"Nurse! Nurse! Lt. Cobb is awake!" he heard the voice of Charles Read from somewhere behind him. A moment later the young ensign's footfalls approached his bed.

"Read, what in the Hell is going on with me?" he rasped out, attempting to put all the force he could into his question.

"Sir, you were injured in the back," Charles replied, coming into view. The ensign's left arm was in a sling, and there were obvious bandages underneath his uniform shirt. The shirt itself was two sizes too large, indicating it was borrowed.

Looking into the ensign's face, Eric immediately detected a change. He was not able to put a finger onto it before Charles spoke again.

"The *Denver*'s doctor patched you up," Charles said, and Eric realized the man was no longer the bright-eyed ensign who had taken off from the *Hornet*'s deck. "The docs here cleaned up some of his work when you got here and they kept you sedated most of last night."

"What happened to you?" Eric rasped out.

A shadow crossed over Read's face.

"My sector had those little yellow bastards' rendezvous point in it. I got bounced by some fighters," Read replied matter-of-factly. "Van Dort..."

Read swallowed hard, shaking his head.

"Van Dort and I and I were too busy watching the *Hornet* get hit and weren't paying attention," the officer continued, his voice near tears. "He didn't make it."

"Glad to see you're awake, Lieutenant Cobb," a woman's voice said. A voluptuous brunette who looked like she was just barely tall enough to be a nurse walked into his field of view. "I'm Beverly Bowden, the ward nurse here. I've heard so much about you."

Eric raised an eyebrow and was about to speak before Nurse Bowden laughed.

"The look on your face is priceless, Lieutenant," she said, almost purring. "My husband is VMF-14's squadron commander."

"Sam and David," Eric said, smiling as Nurse Bowden took a cup of water from an orderly. Holding it up to his lips, she let him drink half of it then set it down on the table next to his bed.

"I think the doctors are going to try and sit you up later," Nurse Bowden said. "They wanted to make sure the stitches and such were going to hold. You broke your shoulder blade and got quite a few fragments in your legs."

"What about my back wound?" Eric asked, puzzled.

"That wasn't a back wound, you idiot," the mummied man said. "You put your hand in some ensign's brain."

Eric was startled at that, then suddenly remembered the two ensigns who had been standing next to him.

"Petty Officer Rourke, I will have the orderly sedate you even further," Nurse Bowden snapped. The mummy looked like he wanted to argue, then thought better of it.

"I'll be back later, Lieutenant Cobb," Nurse Bowden said, satisfied she had deterred mummy from saying anything else.

"Please excuse me for not getting up when you leave," Eric said wryly.

"That's okay, I understand chivalry is dead inside this ward," Nurse Bowden said with a slight smile. Eric watched the nurse as she continued to journey down the ward. She stopped and joked with a sailor who had obviously lost a leg, getting the man to break out in laughter before she left.

"Yeah, it is definitely too bad she is married," Charles observed. He turned back to Eric.

"Where's *Hornet*?" Eric asked.

"Bottom of the Pacific," the mummy man said with a snort, then gasped in pain.

"It's bad," Ensign Read said quietly. "*Hornet*, *Sara*, and *Lexington* are all gone. Lady Lex looked like she was going to make it, but an I-boat got her and the *Salt Lake City* both."

"Holy shit!" Eric said, then immediately looked to see if any nurses were present.

"Pretty sure there's been worse language than that in this hospital lately," Charles continued. "They got the *Arizona*, *Pennsylvania*, *Colorado*, and *West Virginia* too. Killed Admiral Jensen, Vice Admiral Bowles, Rear Admiral Kidd, and *Maryland* took a couple of fish, a bunch of the cruisers got smacked around, and the destroyers didn't go unscathed either."

Eric was stunned. Their father had taken them to see the *Colorado* once when all of the boys were far younger. It was this trip that had almost guaranteed every one of the boys being in the Navy in some capacity. The vessel had seemed so large, so solid then that he had trouble imagining her being gone.

"What in the Hell were our fighters doing?" Eric asked.

"Getting the shit shot out of them," Charles replied. "Seems like the Japs can make some fighters after all, and those fuckers can shoot too. I can testify to that first hand."

"Still, there were three carriers plus Army's fighters," Eric said.

"Sorry sir, that didn't seem to matter a hill of beans," Charles replied. "The torpedo and dive bomber squadrons are untouched, though, so it's not a total loss."

"We do *anything* to them?" Eric asked.

"The *Nautilus* put holes in a couple carriers, the Army claims it sunk one," Read replied.

"What happened to the *Nautilus*?" Eric asked, his tone worried.

"She was sunk," Charles said. "That's the word."

*Nick...*Eric thought, his eyes stinging.

"*Hornet*'s strike put at least two, probably three bombs into another carrier, and the torpedo guys swear they got at least two hits," the junior officer continued.

"I bet Lieutenant Commander Couch is pissed that there were only three hits," Eric said, shaking his head.

Charles took a deep breath.

"Lieutenant Commander Couch is dead. So are Commander Ring and Lieutenant Commander Waldron," Charles replied, his voice starting to have some emotion come back into it. "Lieutenant Commander Mitchell is still upstairs in the burn ward. He'll probably never fly again."

There was a strained silence for a few moments as Eric let what his wingman was saying sink in. *Hornet*'s air group had been decapitated in less than twenty-four hours.

I guess carrier fights are far worse than all the theorists thought they'd be, Eric thought. *No one's going to be able to say any of our officers were scared to lead from the front of the formation.*

"But, you'll be pleased to know, Radioman Brown survived the explosion on the hangar deck with minimal injuries," Charles said. "He's gone back into the Battle Fleet gunner pool, much to his disgust. He said to get better soon, there can't be that many intelligent pilots left."

Eric cracked a smile at the last comment.

"Somehow I don't have problems seeing Brown saying exactly that," Eric said. "Probably with lots of other pilots in earshot."

Charles was prevented from answering by a commotion in the hallway.

"Uh, sir, she can't go in there! It's against regulations!" someone shouted.

"Then you and your regulations can try to stop her," a gruff, familiar voice bellowed. "When you lay a hand on her, I will take your arm, your regulations, and anything else loosely attached *then feed them to you*."

The argument moved into the hospital ward as the doors opened.

"Whoa, look at *that* skirt," Charles breathed. "I can see why those two captains don't want the orderly touching her."

Eric grimaced at Charles' comment.

"Did you say two captains, Ensign Read?" Eric asked, closing his eyes and smiling.

"Yeah, but don't worry about them. You've got the wartime wound working for you," Charles said.

"Whatever you do, do *not* look at the woman like you just talked about her," Eric said.

"You know, you could have told us that you were going to be on a morphine binge when you arrived in Hawaii," Sam said, stopping at the foot of Eric's bed. "Of course, you never were that considerate of a person, you little knucklehead."

"Yes, because if you were, you would've saved some of the morphine for us!" David quipped.

"Nevermind scaring your poor little sister to death," Nick said, then after a moment's pause, "Sir."

Turning to look at Patricia, pain shooting through his shoulder, Eric raised an eyebrow. She was standing with her hands clasped in front of her brown dress, hair held up off her face by a bright flower.

"Tootsie, you have anything to add?" he rasped.

To Eric's surprise, Patricia completely lost her composure at his comment.

"Oh God, Eric," she sobbed, bending down to hug her brother, but not knowing where to begin.

"Miss Cobb, as long as you don't touch the bandage, it shouldn't hurt," Beverly said, appearing behind Sam. She turned to the biggest of the Cobb children as Patricia embraced her brother's back and stroked his hair.

"Next time you ask me to do you a favor, don't threaten to hurt one of my orderlies," Beverly said. "I've still got to work here, and there won't always be some huge oaf around that could probably bend one of them in half."

"Nancy Hertling's been staying with Patricia and Jo Morton since Commander Hertling passed," Sam said apologetically. "It's made her a little distraught, so I wanted to make sure she had a chance to see Eric. I didn't think it was too much to ask for her to come into the ward."

Nurse Bowden rolled her eyes.

"Five minutes, Captain Cobb, five minutes," she said.

"Thank you, Beverly," Sam said sincerely.

CHARLES WAS COMPLETELY MORTIFIED AS HE WATCHED THE COBB family reunited. *Oh my God,* he thought. *I called his sister a "skirt".* Feeling his cheeks burn as he continued to look at Patricia, he tried to figure out how to make things right.

It was at this point that he realized Patricia's other three brothers were in turn looking at him. Nick simply had one eyebrow raised and an amused smirk on his face. The two twins, on the other hand, looked like they were about to kick Charles' ass, broken arm and all.

Oh God, I'm going to die, Charles thought.

"Ensign, I don't believe we've met," the one on the left stated icily. The unspoken, *"So there's no reason you should be looking at our sister"* hung clearly in the air. The smaller of the two, he still appeared to have a twenty to thirty pound weight advantage on Charles.

"Uh, hello," Charles stammered.

"Is that how they talk to superior officers where you're from?!" Sam nearly bellowed, stopping all traffic in the ward. The same orderly he had threatened to abuse earlier poked his head around the door, a stern look on his face. Help, however, came from an unexpected quarter.

"Knock it off!" Eric snapped from his bed. "He's my wingman!"

Nick piped up from behind his two brothers.

"So why isn't he in a damn bed like you are?"

That was enough for Charles. Turning to look at the younger man, he was about to snap off a retort when Patricia suddenly stood up.

"If you gentlemen will excuse me," she said briskly, her tone indicating that there was no question in her words. She spared a withering look for her four brothers.

"Where are you going?" Nick asked, rising from the chair he had been sitting in.

"I've listened to you all squabble for twenty-one years," Patricia said, her voice dripping with disdain. "I've never thought it more inappropriate, nor do I find it comforting that even after having lived out here with all of you for four months I'm still just a damn kid in your eyes."

"You're not a kid in our..." Sam started.

Patricia stopped what she was doing, then took a deep breath.

"I will tell you this for the umpteenth time: *Women*, my dear ignorant brother, *enjoy* being looked at," she said slowly, as if talking with a dimwitted child. "The ensign, while not exactly discreet, was *looking* at me. He was not, as that gentlemen with the two broken legs in the corner is, *leering* at me."

"I'm sorry, I didn't mean to..." Charles started to say.

"Please, ensign, just stay out of this," Patricia stated. "It's a fight that's been going on for my whole life, and it's only gotten worse since I went through puberty."

"Oh crap," Eric muttered from the pillow. "Here we go..."

"As I was saying," Patricia continued, ignoring her brother. "Judging from the ensign's blushing cheeks, he probably said something about my appearance to Eric. Since he is still breathing, it was probably not too vulgar."

"Patricia," David started to interrupt.

"Will someone please let me finish a thought?" Patricia sighed, exasperated. There was a chuckle from several of the surrounding beds. "When *you* first saw Sadie, you probably had a good long stare. Not because you loved her, but because she is a beautiful woman. Probably even said something lecherous, knowing you."

"Wait, uh..." David began to reply.

"She's got you there, David," Sam replied lowly.

"So, pardon me if I don't want to be around while you attempt to brace this poor ensign for doing the same thing."

"Charles. His name is Charles," Eric groaned from the bed.

"And everyone here not currently wearing a bandage or with a permanent bed is now going to leave this ward," Beverly stated flatly, having come back up behind Sam and David. All of the Cobbs except Eric turned to look at her.

"Told you what would happen if you caused too much of a ruckus," she said, low enough for only the Cobbs' to hear. "Old Harry there went and bent Commander Wills' ear. I barely managed to keep you all from getting thrown in the hack."

Nurse Bowden does not seem to be happy, Charles thought.

"I don't think you guys will be coming back as a group anytime soon," Beverly continued, her voice harsh.

"Dammit," Nick muttered. He was immediately cuffed by Sam.

"Watch your mouth in front of the ladies, Nick," Sam said. Charles initially thought he was kidding until he saw the man's eyes.

"So, I would suggest all of you officers move out," Beverly said, making shooing motions. "I managed to get your little sister some additional time, but then again, she didn't threaten to kill Harry with his regulations."

Charles watched the play of emotions over everyone's face.

"Take care, Eric," Nick stated, realizing when it was time to exit an area. "Try not to eat the hospital out of house and home." For the first time, Charles saw that the other officer was clearly upset by his brother's wounds.

"We'll be back," Sam and David both said in unison. Charles looked askance at the two of them.

"Yes, they always do that," Patricia said wearily, pulling up a chair on the other side of Eric.

Patting their brother on his uninjured shoulder, both twins headed for the door. Sam favored the orderly with a scowl as he walked by, making the man take a couple of steps back.

Beverly watched them go, sighing and shaking her head.

"Sam does have a bit too much temper for his own good," she said, turning back to Patricia. She reached into her pocket and pulled out a slip of paper.

"What I didn't tell them was that I got a pass for you," she said. "Just show this to the guard at the front gate of the base, then to the nurse at the admittance desk. If anyone gives you any trouble, tell them to talk to me."

Patricia's shock was plainly visible. Looking at her askance again, Charles saw her face flush a little bit. It made her look even more beautiful.

"Ensign Read," Eric said from the bed, startling him.

"Yes, sir," Charles responded, looking down at him.

"This *woman* is my sister, Patricia. Patricia, this is Ensign Read."

Patricia stuck her hand out. Charles took it gently, then was surprised by the strength of her grip.

"Hello," Patricia said, smiling. *She has pretty eyes*, Charles thought. A shadow passed over Patricia's face, and he saw the eyes suddenly go cold.

Well you sure don't learn quickly, do you? Patricia thought, angry at herself. It wasn't that Ensign Read wasn't a handsome man, his eyes seeming to be dark brown pools that she could get lost in. It was the fact that Nancy Hertling had only just fallen to sleep after awakening from a screaming nightmare not four hours before.

Nurse Bowden moved the paper, regaining Patricia's attention.

"Oh, thank you," Patricia said, releasing Charles's hand. Beverly gave her a knowing smile, then moved off.

Having regained her senses, Patricia mentally shook herself.

Yes, he's attractive, she thought to herself. *He's also in the military, and there is no way that I am going to allow myself to fall for him.*

What in the hell? Charles asked, seeing the look Patricia gave him before turning to her brother.

"Is there anything that you need me to bring you?" Patricia asked Eric, her voice going soft.

"I guess my comic book collection would be too much to ask for?" Eric retorted, reaching out to pat his sister's leg.

"I think after having you yell at me for losing some of them that I learned my lesson about that," Patricia replied softly. "Plus I'm not sure I'm welcome back at Mom and Dad's house anytime soon. Although I understand Joyce might have helped me out some with that."

Eric laughed bitterly.

"Well here I am in a hospital bed," Eric replied. "She might have had a point about my luck."

"Nevermind her," Patricia said with a shrug. "I'm just glad you're okay, and she can enjoy a nice, long life as a spinster as far as I'm concerned."

"Has anyone told Mom and Dad that I'm hurt?" Eric could suddenly see his parents getting the telegram and starting to worry.

"I think I'm lucky to know," Patricia replied. "But we sent them a letter knowing we were all relatively fine." *Physically, anyway*, she thought.

"I'm not relatively fine," Eric said, his voice rising.

"So I fibbed a little bit and Nick forged your handwriting," Patricia said. She heard Ensign Read laugh. "Sam said you weren't likely to die and it was only a little white lie. She'll be worried enough soon, even with Sam and David going back to the mainland."

"What?!" Eric asked.

"We can talk about that later," Patricia said. "I'm not walking back to my house, and I don't want Sam and David causing a scene."

"Fine," Eric said. Patricia stood, and she noted that Ensign Read stood with her.

A gentleman, she thought, then kicked herself. *I need to get a grip.*

"Ensign Read," she said coolly, nodding.

"It was a pleasure to meet you, Miss Cobb," Charles replied.

"Likewise, Ensign," Patricia found herself saying with a smile. With that, she turned to leave the ward.

IJNS Akagi
North Pacific
0650 Local (1350 Eastern)
30 March (29 March)

"LIEUTENANT HONDA!"

Commander Fuchida's shout shook Isoro out of his reverie. He turned and came to attention as the *Akagi*'s CAG approached him. To Isoro's surprise, he saw Captain Genda right behind Fuchida as they approached him at the *Akagi*'s stern.

"Sir," Isoro said, bowing formally.

"Beautiful morning," Fuchida said, as they stood and looked at the sun low on the eastern horizon. "Unfortunately it looks as if we will have stormy weather ahead."

Isoro nodded, the sky one of the reddest he had ever seen.

It is as if the gods are weeping blood at what we have unleashed, he thought. Even with several *Zuikaku* orphans, the *Akagi*'s pilot accommodations were noticeably empty. *Regardless of the cost, we have proven that the Americans are very beatable.*

"When we return to Japan, your squadron will be detached from *Akagi*," Fuchida said. "You will be sent to the south."

Isoro nodded again.

This assignment does not please me, he thought inwardly.

"Sir, who will be commanding the squadron?" Isoro asked.

"We do not know yet," Fuchida answered. "You will likely meet your new commander when you reach Formosa."

"Your squadron will be held in reserve until we attack the Indies," Captain Genda said. "The fighting in the Philippines is heavy, but the Americans lost many of their bombers on the first day."

"Sir, how did we accomplish this?" Isoro asked, incredulous. "The Philippines are several hours behind Hawaii!"

"Our forces trailed them back to their base then attacked when they landed," Genda replied. "Our losses were not as bad as we expected, but were still quite heavy."

This seems to be a recurring theme, Isoro thought. Fuchida spoke as if he had read Isoro's mind.

"Congratulations on your kills," Fuchida said. "Your squadron did an excellent job during both strikes."

"Thank you, sir," Isoro said, bowing again. "If I may ask, how long will my squadron be at Kure before we leave?"

"Three days," Fuchida replied. "Do you have someone you wish to see?"

"No sir," Honda replied. *At least, not that I'm going to admit to.*

"The poor man probably wants to eat something that did not come from a can," Genda said with a laugh. "Do not worry, you will have a chance to enjoy your status as a member of the *Kido Butai*. They are already telling tales about us to everyone who will listen."

I hope this is not a long war, Yamaguchi thought, looking over the casualty forms. *We cannot continue at this rate.*

"Sir, I have informed Combined Fleet Headquarters that we lack the aircraft to aid at Wake," Rear Admiral Kusaka stated stiffly, standing before his desk at parade rest.

A decision you heartily disagree with, Yamaguchi observed silently. He dipped his pen into the inkwell at his desk and made a notation on the casualty report form.

*It would appear that the **Suisei**, while it holds many improvements over the Aichi, is horrifically vulnerable to heavy anti-aircraft fire.*

"Permission to speak freely, sir?" Kusaka asked.

"Denied," Yamaguchi said coolly, causing the other man to stiffen.

I'm going to let you stand there for awhile, Yamaguchi thought uncharitably. He continued to make notations as he read, continuing for thirty pages as Rear Admiral Kusaka grew noticeably angrier.

"Do you know the reason why I did not divert this force to strike Wake Island, Rear Admiral Kusaka?" Yamaguchi asked, then continued before Kusaka could respond. "Because I see no reason to lose even one more airplane seizing a simple atoll in the middle of the Pacific."

"But sir..." Kusaka started to respond.

"I was not finished," Yamaguchi snapped, causing the other admiral to shut up. He finished writing a short note for the front piece of the *Kido Butai*'s after action report.

Production of the Sandaburo warheads must be increased at once, Yamaguchi thought. *It is critical to the war's success.*

"If we capture Wake, as I think we will after Vice Admiral Inoue realizes how many forces he already has, the Americans will likely attempt to take it back," Yamaguchi said. "When this happens, we will need every pilot we have to strike them one more heavy blow. It is the only way we will succeed."

Kusaka looked as if he would like to say something, but Yamaguchi stood from behind his desk. Reaching to his right, he pulled out a simple courier's portfolio.

"Also included in this packet are your transfer orders, I thought I would give you an early start on your movement to Vice Admiral Inoue's staff," Yamaguchi said. "Since you are so fixated with Wake, it is perhaps a move for the best."

He keeps a straight face despite the fact I have just basically relieved him, Yamaguchi thought, looking at Kusaka. *No matter, he will soon not be my problem.*

"I have instructed Captain Genda to make a *Suisei* ready for your departure," Yamaguchi said. "May you have good fortune."

Kusaka took the courier's bag, stepped back two steps, and bowed. Yamaguchi gave the man a short nod in return, and then watched as the junior flag officer exited his day cabin. Turning, he went back to the map of the Pacific that was hung on the bulkhead. Exhaling heavily, he regarded the Dutch East Indies.

Our entire war effort comes down to those islands, he thought. *I wish the* **Kido Butai** *could fully participate*. Shaking his head, he returned to his desk and sat down, placing his feet up and tipping his cap down over his eyes. *But, for now, we have done our part, and we must rest.*

Less than two minutes after he sat down, Vice Admiral Tamon Yamaguchi, victor of the Battle of Hawaii, slept for the first time in weeks.

ACTS OF WAR DRAMATIS PERSONAE

U.S.S. NAUTILUS

Lieutenant (j.g.) Nicholas "Nick" Elrod Cobb

Lieutenant Commander Jason Freeman

Ensign Larry Workman

Lieutenant Commander Harold Banes

Chief Robert Pound

U.S.S. HOUSTON

Commander Jacob Thoreau Morton

Chief Petty Officer Roberts

Seaman Third Class Teague

ACTS OF WAR DRAMATIS PERSONAE

Captain Sean Wallace

Lieutenant Adam Connor

Lieutenant Commander David Sloan

VMF-21

Major Adam Jefferson Haynes

Captain Scott Walters

Captain Keith Seidel

Captain William Kennedy

Captain Jacob Bowles

Captain David West

Captain Todd Burke

Wing Commander Connor O'Rourke

VB-8

Lieutenant Eric Melville Cobb

Ensign Charles Read

Radioman First Class Willie Brown

VMF-14

Captains Samuel and David Cobb

Major Max Bowden

PEARL HARBOR AND OAHU

Admiral Hank Jensen

Rear Admiral Daniel Graham

Vice Admiral Jacob Bowles

Patricia Ann Cobb

Josephine Marie Morton

Joanna "Sadie" Cobb

Nurse Beverly Bowden

Lieutenant Colonel John McKenna.

Commander Keith Hertling

Nurse Nancy Hertling

ALABAMA

Alma Cobb nee Lee

Samuel Cobb

Elma Cotner

Theodore Cotner

Joyce Cotner

ACTS OF WAR DRAMATIS PERSONAE

Beauregard Forrest Cotner

AFTERWORD TO ACTS OF WAR

I would like to take this opportunity to thank a few people for their help with this novel. As always, my wife Anita has been her usual supportive self. It is not easy, nor exactly fun, being an author's spouse. Writing, by and large, is a solitary activity, and at least in my case, very streak oriented. Doing little things like, oh, making sure I eat and occasionally come out of the room to interact with humans is not always properly rewarded by the proper amount of gratitude. However, no matter how much I may get annoyed, I am grateful that I am married to a wonderful woman who has always been willing to help me get things done. Even when I grumble about being forced to go to sleep when I have "just one more paragraph," I know that I drafted about as well as any man in ye olde wife lottery. Love you honey, and here's to many more "Hey, I have an idea..." discussions in the future.

Second, I'd like to thank other individuals who have lent me beta reading support and lent me help with this manuscript. Kat Mitchell, despite her protestations, two major moves, and occasional bout of absentmindedness has done another great job correcting my grammar. My sister, Catherine Cole, put her editorial skills to use when she could between her numerous other commitments. Author Alma Boykin has provided a willing ear and eye to scan over things and

AFTERWORD TO ACTS OF WAR

sometimes save me from myself in earlier iterations. Mary Cantrell provided professional editing service on short notice despite me being delayed thanks to an onset of Murphy. Finally Patricia Hildebrand, in addition to introducing me to Mary, is responsible for inspiring a version change via stating, "I've watched lots of World War II documentaries, and I can't tell where this deviates from what actually occurred." Well, 150 pages later, I hope that the Point of Deviation from our actual timeline was much clearer.

Lastly, as always, thank you for purchasing this book. Please tell your family and friends about it, and if you liked it give it a rating on Amazon. Merchandise associated with it is available on Redbubble, CafePress, and and Etsy. Finally, you can find me at my blog, where I also talk about air warfare, sea battles, and science fiction.

ABOUT JAMES YOUNG

James Young is a science fiction and alternative history author and editor hailing from Missouri. Leaving small town life, James obtained a bachelor's in military history from the United States Military Academy then went on to spend six years as an armor and staff officer in Korea, the Pacific Northwest, and Germany.

After serving his commitment to the Republic, James returned to the Midwest to obtain his Masters and Doctorate in U.S. History from Kansas State. License for evil, er, Ph.D. in hand, Dr. Young now spends his spare time torturing characters, editing alternative history anthologies with far more famous authors like S.M. Stirling and David Weber (check out the Phases of Mars series), and admiring his wife's (Anita C. Young) award-winning artwork.

Website: https://vergassy.com/
Newsletter: http://eepurl.com/b9r8Xn

        facebook.com/ColfaxDen
        x.com/youngblai
        amazon.com/James-Young

ALSO BY JAMES YOUNG

USURPER'S WAR SERIES

Acts of War
Collisions of the Damned
Against the Tide Imperial

USURPER'S WAR COLLECTION

On Seas So Crimson

PHASES OF MARS ANTHOLOGY SERIES

(Editor and Contributor)
Those in Peril
To Slip the Surly Bonds
Trouble in the Wind

NOVELLAS

Pandora's Memories
A Midwinter's Ski
Ride of the Late Rain

VERGASSY UNIVERSE

An Unproven Concept
Aries' Red Sky

NONFICTION

Barren SEAD

Made in the USA
Columbia, SC
05 June 2025